ANNABELLE ARCHER'S HOLIDAY COLLECTION

A WEDDING PLANNER COZY MYSTERY COLLECTION:
BOOKS 11, 15 & 17

LAURA DURHAM

BROADMOOR BOOKS

PREFACE

Thanks so much for reading this collection of Annabelle archer holiday books. Included in the collection are two novellas and a novel—books 11, 15, and 17. If you haven't read any of the series, I suggest you start with book 1, *Better Off Wed*, so you can enjoy the relationships between the characters develop, but each book is a complete story and there shouldn't be any spoilers regarding previous mysteries.

The holiday books are always a little lighter and cozier than the other mysteries in the series, and I hope they fill you with holiday cheer and warm fuzzies! Wishing you the happiest of holidays!

Laura Durham

MARRY AND BRIGHT

AN ANNABELLE ARCHER WEDDING PLANNER
HOLIDAY NOVELLA #11

For my father,
with love and thanks for his support

CHAPTER 1

"Are you sure this isn't too much?" I asked as I draped a string of white Christmas lights over the top of my living room window.

Kate looked up from where she stood at my wooden dining room table unpacking a box of ivory pillar candles. "Of course it isn't too much, Annabelle. You know what they say, nothing succeeds like excess."

I looked around my apartment, usually the picture of simplicity and less-is-more decor, and wondered if we hadn't taken the concept too far. Glass cylinder vases filled with colorful glass ball ornaments sat in the middle of the coffee table, dining table, and the counter dividing my kitchen and living room. Large paper stars that resembled snowflakes hung from the ceiling at various points so that anyone over five feet tall had to duck and weave to make it across the room, and a red berry wreath hung over the flat screen TV on one wall. A candle that smelled like gingerbread cookies burned in the kitchen, reminding me that I'd only had a bottled Frappuccino and granola bar for breakfast.

"Did Oscar Wilde say that?" I asked, stepping down from the stool.

Kate flipped her blond bob off her face. "I always thought Richard came up with that one. It sounds like him." She held up two pillar candles. "Speaking of too much, remind me again why you have boxes of battery-operated pillar candles."

"From the Hunter wedding," I said. "Remember how they wanted to buy the candles instead of renting them from the florist, but they didn't have anywhere to store ten boxes of candles so they asked me to hang on to them?"

Kate's mouth dropped open. "That wedding was three years ago."

"I know," I said, joining her at the table and flicking the underneath switch on a chunky candle. "That's why I'm conscripting them into service for the holidays. My office is reaching maximum wedding leftovers capacity."

As the owner of the Washington, DC wedding planning company Wedding Belles, I'd inherited everything from pillar candles to leftover cocktail napkins to extra Jordan almonds from nearly seven years' worth of couples. My home office down the hall was filled with boxes of items waiting to be picked up by brides and grooms although most, I knew, never would be. Once the wedding was over, the desire for pastel candies and anything wrapped up in tulle seemed to be abandoned as quickly as the pre-wedding diets.

"I think after three years, the candles are yours," my assistant said. "What other goodies do you have tucked away in the office? I might be in need of some holiday gifts."

I eyed her. "Does this mean I'm getting a pillar candle from you this year?"

"Don't be silly." She arranged candles between the glass cylinders of ornaments that ran down the counter dividing my living room and kitchen. "I was talking about gifts to give the men I'm dating."

"How many gifts are we talking?" Kate's dating life was active, to say the least. "I doubt most men would be thrilled with the kinds of things left over from weddings, unless one of them is dying for a 'Gillian and Ted' wine opener."

"Not many. I was actually looking for something small to give as a token to the men I'm breaking up with, but I wouldn't mind a 'Gillian and Ted' wine opener."

"You're breaking up right before Christmas?" I asked. "And you need consolation prizes?"

"Now you're making me sound heartless." She rested a hand on her hip-hugger jeans. "I've decided to turn over a new leaf and start the year by dating intentionally, which means I need to clear out the men who aren't long-term prospects."

"Dating intentionally? I thought you made it a policy to avoid any relationship longer than the average life span of a goldfish." I placed two candles on the bookshelf by my front door and arranged the small bowl that held my keys between them. "What does 'dating intentionally' even mean? It sounds a little new-agey for you."

"Your relationship with Reese has inspired me," she said. "I admire how you two took it slow, and neither of you lost yourself when you moved in together. Most women vanish once they get a serious boyfriend, but you've still made time for me and for Richard and the rest of the friends you had before Reese came along."

"Thanks," I said, "but it's not like I had a choice. You work for me, so I couldn't exactly stop seeing you, and if I'd ghosted Richard, he would have made a voodoo doll with long auburn hair and used it as a pincushion."

"He wouldn't hex *you*. I wouldn't put it past him to have a voodoo doll that's tall, dark, and hunky like your boyfriend though." Kate smirked at me. "Come to think of it, I wouldn't mind a doll like that."

Even though I'd only moved in with my cop boyfriend, Mike Reese, a couple of months ago, I'd made a concerted effort to spend time with my friends so my best friend, Richard Gerard, wouldn't have any reason to feel left out.

"Speaking of the city's most dramatic caterer, why isn't Richard here helping us decorate your apartment?" Kate asked. "I would have thought he'd relish this since you've never really done much to your place aside from hanging up a sad fake-pine wreath."

"Well, part of the reason I'm going all out for the holidays is to bring us all together," I said. "I thought we should have a party for our crew here to celebrate another successful year."

"And to celebrate surviving another year."

I knew Kate meant the run-ins we'd had with kidnappers, jewel thieves, and murderers while planning weddings for the city's most famous and infamous. "You make it sound like we plan weddings in a war zone."

She shrugged. "There have been days. . ." She flopped onto my yellow twill couch. "So what does a crew party have to do with Richard not being here?"

"If we're having a party, we need a tree, right?" I pointed to a corner I'd cleared out next to one of the tall windows where a tree stand stood at the ready. "Richard and Reese are out getting the Christmas tree."

Kate nearly dropped the candle she was holding. "Are you telling me you sent your boyfriend and best friend out on a team-building exercise? I hope they don't kill each other in the process."

"I made sure Reese didn't take his gun." I liked to think he would never shoot an unarmed man, but after a few hours of Richard nitpicking Fraser firs, I couldn't guarantee it.

"Assuming both Richard and Reese return from this expedition in one piece, a holiday party sounds like fun." Kate rubbed her hands together. "We should do a secret Santa gift exchange. That way we don't go bankrupt buying everyone presents."

"Or so everyone doesn't get identical 'Gillian and Ted' wine openers from you."

"Exactly." She winked at me. "Although you might get a wine opener *and* a candle."

I put a hand to my heart. "I'm touched."

"Will this shindig be before or after the Douglas wedding?"

"Before," I said. "We might not be alive after another Debbie and Darla event, even if it is the son's wedding this time."

Debbie and Darla were a mother-daughter duo we'd first worked with when we'd planned Darla's very WASPy wedding to Turner Grant the Third. The women had rarely been sober for any of our meetings with them, and Darla's wedding had been a bourbon-soaked extravaganza. Even though the son's bride-to-be did not consider mint juleps to be the breath of life like the family she was marrying into did, any party with Debbie and Darla was bound to be eventful.

"Coming through." The door to my apartment flew open, and Richard strode into the room with both arms waving. "Make way, people. Make way."

The tip of a tree poked through the doorway, and then Reese lurched into view, covered almost entirely by the prickly green branches of the pine tree he held with both arms. "Don't worry. I've got it."

Richard pushed the couch over an inch. "Right through here, Detective."

I rushed over and grabbed the sagging trunk of the tree as Reese struggled to keep it from falling to the floor. Bits of pine needles adorned his chocolate-brown hair, and he tried to blow both an errant curl and a branch off his forehead.

"Did you carry this up the entire staircase by yourself?" I asked.

"Don't be ridiculous." Richard touched a hand to his dark hair, still perfectly spiked up. "I navigated and opened all the doors."

"That's true," Reese said. "If it hadn't been for Richard, I never would have known which way to turn at each of the landings."

Richard sniffed. "Well, not all of us dress like lumberjacks. I couldn't afford to get pine sap on my Armani pants."

Kate eyed Reese's jeans, untucked blue flannel shirt, and brown lace-up boots. "Too bad. The lumberjack look is a good look."

Reese and I got the tree across the room and lowered it into the stand. I stood back and admired the full tree that nearly reached the ceiling. I wrapped my arms around my boyfriend as he wiped both sweat and pine needles off his face. "It's perfect."

"Of course it's perfect," Richard said. "It's not too skinny. It's not too fat. It doesn't have any gaps. It doesn't lean to one side. Trust me, we made sure this was the best tree out there."

Reese let out a long breath. "He's right about that. Richard insisted we go to seven different lots before we found this one."

Kate put a hand over her mouth, I presumed to stifle a laugh. "Seven? That must have taken hours."

"Yep." Reese kissed my forehead. "Four to be exact."

"Why don't I get you both a drink?" I suggested, giving Reese a final squeeze and heading for the kitchen.

Richard sank down on the couch next to Kate. "That would be divine. Picking out trees is exhausting."

I opened my refrigerator and looked in the door for where Reese kept the microbrew beers he enjoyed. I picked out two bottles. Richard wasn't usually a fan of beer, but I didn't happen to have a bottle of wine. As I closed the door, I felt an arm reach around me.

"I couldn't wait," Reese said, taking one of the beers from me and enveloping me in a hug. "This was the only thing that kept me from killing Richard for the past four hours."

"The thought of a cold beer?" I turned around and leaned into him, feeling the hard muscles of his chest.

"No, the thought of you. And knowing how unhappy you'd be with me if I came back without your best friend."

I looked up at him. "I'm sorry Richard was so . . . well, so Richard, but thank you for going with him. It means a lot to me, and I think he's really warming up to you."

He twisted off the cap of his beer bottle and took a swig. "Yay me."

"I should probably get this to Richard," I said, holding up the other bottle. "Even if he barely broke a sweat."

As I took a step toward the living room, Reese pulled me back and kissed me. His lips were soft, and I could taste a hint of pale ale as he deepened the kiss. He grinned when he let go and left me blinking up at him. "That's another thing that kept me from becoming homicidal."

I tried to regain my composure as I walked back into the living room and handed Richard a beer.

He looked perplexed. "What is this?"

"Reese's favorite," I said. "He thought you'd appreciate it."

Richard couldn't stop himself from smiling. "Did he now?" He nodded at Reese as the detective came back in and sat down on the overstuffed chair. "Well, never let it be said that Richard Gerard is not up for a little adventure."

"So what do you think of Annabelle's apartment so far?" Kate asked, sweeping an arm wide. "Can you believe all of this was done with leftovers from past weddings?"

"Yes, I can," Richard said as he glanced around the room. "As a matter of fact, just seeing all these things is giving me wedding day flashbacks."

Kate gave him a dismissive wave. "No one else will know, and I think it shows just how creative and clever wedding planners can be."

Richard took a long draw from his beer and grimaced as he swallowed it. He set the bottle on my coffee table and stood. "It's been delightful, but I'd better retrieve my dog from your nutty neighbor before she decides to give him a perm."

"Hermes would look adorable with curly hair," Kate said.

"He would look like a poodle." Richard walked to the door and picked up his crossbody man bag from where he'd left it on the floor. "Yorkies do not have curly hair."

"If Leatrice asks, I'm not here," I said. As fond as I was of my downstairs neighbor, I was not as fond of her habit of popping in unannounced when Reese and I were trying to have some alone time, or when Kate and I were trying to work, or when I was trying to enjoy a few moments of quiet.

"Consider it done." Richard opened the door and paused with his hand on the knob.

Buster and Mack, our favorite florists and good friends, stood in the doorway. The two burly men each topped six feet and three hundred pounds and both sported goatees—one dark red and the other brown. They had bald heads and tattoos that were mostly covered by the black leather pants, vests, and jackets they wore. A "Road Riders for Jesus" patch emblazoned the front of their vests, as well as one that said "Ride Hard Die Saved."

My eyes dropped to the squirming bundle in Mack's arms that wore a pink-and-blue-striped cap and was wrapped in a pink blanket.

"Is that a . . ." Kate began.

"Baby?" I finished for her when I finally found my voice.

Richard turned around, his eyes wide. "Does anyone else feel like one of these things just doesn't belong?"

"We didn't know where else to come," Buster said, his deep voice cracking. "You've got to help us."

CHAPTER 2

"Why do you have a baby?" I said as the two men came inside.

"Is there something you want to tell us?" Richard asked, taking a step back from the now-whimpering infant. Richard was not a fan of anything as unpredictable and messy as a baby.

Mack jiggled the tiny baby, and she quieted. Sleeping in the crook of his beefy arm must have been like being nestled in a warm cocoon. He looked down at her, his face pinched. "Someone left her on our doorstep."

Kate scooted over and patted the cushion next to her for Mack to sit. "At Lush? Why would someone leave a baby outside a floral shop?"

"Not Lush," Buster said. "At the Born Again Biker Church."

"Oh." Kate nodded. "That makes more sense."

Richard cocked an eyebrow. "Does it?"

Buster and Mack were part of a Christian motorcycle gang, and even though I'd never been inside, I knew their church was in a nondescript building in the warehouse district of Northeast DC where there was plenty of parking for Harleys, and no one lived nearby to care about the sound of revving motors on a Sunday morning. Their gang consisted of bikers like them with piercings, tattoos, and questionable pasts. Many were former members of what they called 1 percent gangs, the violent criminal organizations like the Hell's Angels and Bandidos, who had seen the error of their ways and now tried to help other lost souls.

Mack sat down on the sofa, and the springs groaned under his weight. "We were cleaning up after our service. Buster and I are serving as ushers this month. Nearly everyone else had cleared out, and we were locking up when we saw her."

"You didn't see anyone close to the building when you found her?" Reese asked. "Sometimes people who leave babies stick around to make sure they're found."

Buster shook his head. "No, but to tell you the truth, we were so startled we could have missed seeing someone."

"I can imagine." I walked behind Mack and leaned over his shoulder to get a better look at the sleeping child. I wasn't an expert on babies, but this one looked to be only a few weeks old. Her tiny face was round and plump, and she had a wisp of light-brown hair peeking out below her knit cap. One pink fist was in her mouth, and she appeared to be sucking on it.

Buster swung a pale-green quilted diaper bag down from his shoulder and let it flop to the floor. "She came with this and a note." He dug a piece of paper out of the side pocket of the bag and handed it to Reese.

I joined Reese as he went to the dining room table holding the note by the top corner and two fingers. He put the crumpled sheet of lined notebook paper on the flat surface and we both leaned over it.

"Read it out loud," Kate said.

"I'm sorry." I read from the paper. "Please take care of her. I can't. I only want what is best for Merry, and it isn't me."

"That's so sad." Kate put a hand to her mouth. "She even has a name."

"Merry," I said. "As in Merry Christmas."

"That's a little on the nose, wouldn't you say?" Richard asked. "A baby found in December named Merry. Are we sure there isn't a hidden camera somewhere?"

The baby began crying, and Mack started humming—a sound like a throaty rumble that reminded me of his Harley starting up. "You're okay now, little Merry."

Richard cleared his throat. "This is all very sad, but what are you going to do? It's not like you two can take care of her."

"For once, I agree with Richard," Reese said, looking up from examining the note. "We need to call social services."

Mack looked up, his face stormy. "No. I was a foster kid, and I wouldn't wish that on anyone, especially not a sweet little baby."

I didn't know much about either member of my go-to floral team's past, aside from the fact that they'd been designers in New York before coming to DC. Looking at the determined expression on Mack's face, I knew now they'd had experiences I might never understand.

Buster nodded. "Someone left her with us for a reason."

I wondered what kind of person would leave a baby on the threshold of a biker church since DC had safe haven laws that allowed parents to drop off a baby at any hospital anonymously. Either someone desperate who couldn't get to a hospital, didn't know the law, or had a connection to the church.

Mack rocked the baby back and forth, his face softening as he gazed down at her. "That's why we came to you. Whoever left this baby was in a bad place. We need to find them and help them."

"You want us to help you find out who abandoned the baby?" I looked back at the note on the table. "And this note is all we have to go on?"

"You found Kate when she was missing," Buster said. "And you've tracked down more than one killer."

I noticed Reese folding his arms across his chest. "Technically the police discovered the perpetrators. We only helped out."

"A habit I'm trying to break her of," Reese said. "You really should turn this matter over to the police. Our department has more resources than any civilian could access."

Buster and Mack were silent.

Kate stood up. "I think we all need something to drink." She looped her arm through mine and pulled me toward the kitchen. "I know I do."

Once we'd ducked into the kitchen, I opened the refrigerator door. "A few more mircrobrews and a few Diet Dr Peppers. Oh, and one last bottled Mocha Frappuccino."

Kate peered over my shoulder. "I can tell Richard hasn't been here for a while. He always kept you stocked up with bubbly and wine." She motioned to the beers. "Let's bring those. We need to lower the temperature in the room a bit."

"Buster and Mack don't drink," I said.

She made a face. "I've got to tell you, that's the only thing about them that makes me wary."

I grabbed two bottles by the neck and gave her a look. "Really? *That's* what makes you wary?"

She reached around me and took two cans of soda from the door. "Well, that and the fact that they don't curse. How they can work with brides and not want to drop the F-bomb every ten minutes is beyond me."

I lowered my voice in case they could hear me through the open space above the dividing counter between the rooms. "What do you think about this baby thing?"

"Pretty grateful no one dropped a baby on my doorstep, I can tell you that much."

I looked at Kate in her low-slung jeans and crop sweater. Kate embraced being single with a vigor usually reserved for religious zealots, and I had a hard time imagining her settling down, much less wanting to be a mother.

Kate nudged the refrigerator door closed with her hip. "That being said, they are our friends and they asked for our help. If the holidays aren't the time for helping out friends in need, I don't know when is."

I followed her back into the living room feeling properly chagrined for hesitating about helping Buster and Mack. Kate was right. Our friends were trying to do a good thing. Helping them find who left the baby was the least we could do.

Kate handed Buster and Mack each a can of Diet Dr Pepper and took one of the beer bottles from me, twisting off the cap and taking a sip. "So has Reese agreed to help us yet?"

My boyfriend shook his head. "No way am I getting roped into another one of your crazy plans."

Kate took her place on the couch again, tucking her legs up under her. "Crazy seems like a strong word."

"I don't blame you, Detective," Richard said, nodding his head at Reese. "This isn't a case of trying to find a killer before they find us or trying to find Kate before the kidnapper eliminates her. If someone left a baby for a bunch of bikers to find, they aren't winning any parent-of-the-year contests. This child is better off being put into the system so a good home can be found for her."

Mack sucked in air and Buster growled. Richard moved closer to Reese.

"I think both sides make good points," I said. "Since Buster and Mack found the child, I think we should at least attempt to do what they're asking. If we can't find the person who left the baby after a week, maybe they can consider letting her be put up for adoption."

A look passed between the two men and both gave curt nods.

"That seems fair," Buster said.

"So do you have room at your place for a baby?" Kate asked.

"We already put out a call to our biker brotherhood." Mack shifted the baby to his other arm. "Slim and Big Beard are bringing us a bassinet and some secondhand baby clothes tonight."

"What about car seats and swings and changing tables?" Kate took a swig from her beer. "Wait a second. Do they make infant car seats for Harleys?"

Mack laughed. "We're using one of the floral vans instead of our bikes, and she was dropped off in a baby car seat you hook in to the seat belts."

"If you want, I can take a look at it to make sure it's hooked in properly," Reese said. "The police check infant car seats for parents all the time."

Buster let out a breath. "Would you? It took us forever to get it in, and I'm not sure it's right."

"No problem. Where's your van?"

Mack glanced at my wall clock. "We can't do it now. We have to go to the final meeting with Debbie and Darla and the bride-to-be."

Kate looked at me, her eyes bugged out. "I totally forgot about that meeting. We're supposed to be at Lush in ten minutes."

"I lost track of time," I admitted. "This day has flown by."

Kate set her beer on the coffee table and stood up. "We'd better run if we want to beat the client there." She stared down at the sleeping baby. "What are you going to do with her?"

Mack looked at Reese and Richard. "Is there any way one of you could watch her? It would only be for a few minutes. We'll rush right back."

"She'll probably sleep the whole time," Buster added.

Richard staggered back a few steps, his palm pressed to his chest. "You must be out of your mind. I do not do babies."

Mack stood up and walked toward Reese, who also took a step back. "We don't have anyone else to ask."

For once in my life, I felt lucky to have a meeting with a bride.

Richard began to head toward the door, and Reese caught him by the sleeve. "Don't even think about leaving me alone with this."

"What?" Richard spluttered. "If you think I . . ."

"Oh, I do think you're going to stay right here." Reese grinned showing lots of teeth. "I'd hate to think of what might happen to you if you don't. APBs on all your catering trucks, speed cameras installed on every corner of your neighborhood, a certain BMW convertible booted every single morning."

Richard gasped. "You wouldn't."

Reese looked at the baby then back at Richard. "Try me."

Richard mumbled something about police brutality before shrugging off his jacket and hanging it over the back of a dining room chair. "It appears I'll be staying."

Mack transferred the baby into Reese's arms and touched her cheek gently. "Thank you, Detective."

Richard cleared his throat.

"Thank you, too, Richard," I said, scooping up my purse and backing out the door with Kate. "We'll be back before you know it."

Buster and Mack reluctantly walked out into the hallway, glancing back at the two men and the baby.

Reese winked at me as he swayed Merry back and forth. "Don't worry. Uncle Reese and Auntie Richard have this under control."

The last thing I saw before pulling the door closed was Richard's face as he shot daggers at my grinning boyfriend. "Auntie Richard indeed!"

CHAPTER 3

"So how can we make this the quickest floral meeting in history?" Kate asked as we followed Buster and Mack into their chic Georgetown shop.

I breathed in a combination of fresh flowers and dark roast coffee, and my eyes went from the galvanized metal buckets of roses and hydrangea stacked on shelves along one wall to the shiny-chrome cappuccino maker dominating a high metal table at the back of the shop. "Hope the clients are a no-show?"

"We do not want that." Buster's boots echoed off the cement floor as he strode to the back of the space and fired up the high-end coffee machine. "I'm already cutting it close with any changes to the floral order. They do know this isn't a meeting to rethink the look, don't they?"

"I explained it to Darla." I hopped up onto a stool around a high top table. "I can't guarantee she was sober when I told her though."

"I can bet she wasn't," Kate said.

I looked out the glass front of the store and could see shoppers and tourists walking by. No sign of our clients. Then again, we had made it across Georgetown in record time. I reached into my black Longchamp bag and pulled out the file for the Douglas wedding, setting it in front of me and flipping to the latest version of the floral proposal. "You'll send me a new proposal after today, right?"

Mack produced a box of cookies from a cabinet and began arranging them on a plate. "If there are changes."

"So that's a yes," Kate said, taking the seat next to me.

I turned to the back of the proposal, took a pen out of my bag, and clicked it. "If we're going to figure out who left that baby, I need to get more details."

Mack joined us and put the cookies in the middle of the table. "Ask us anything."

"Are those chocolate chip?" Kate asked, eyeing the oversized cookies. "You're not trying to sneak a raisin by me, are you?"

Mack winked at her. "Never. Those are made with real butter, real sugar, and lots of real chocolate."

The steamer nozzle hissed behind us as Buster put the finishing touches on four cappuccinos before carrying them over to us on a sleek metal tray. "There isn't much to tell aside from what we told you earlier. We searched the diaper bag, but the only thing in it of any interest was the note."

Kate took her cappuccino, putting her nose close to the surface and inhaling deeply. "Between the cookies and the gourmet coffee, I may never leave."

I tapped my pen on the table and let my own cup cool in front of me. "I'm assuming none of your members or church attendees were pregnant before today."

"Most of the people who come to the Born Again Biker Church are men, though we do get some wives and lady bikers. None of them have been pregnant that I've noticed," Mack said.

"Nope," Buster backed him up. "And even of the guys with girlfriends, I can't think of a one who's mentioned a pregnancy. Of course, we'll ask everyone."

I made a note that the church didn't have any expectant mothers. "So that's a bit of a dead end. What about homeless women? Any of those hang around the church?"

Mack leaned forward on his elbows and steepled his hands in

front of his face. "Northeast DC has its share of homeless people, but not too many women, and none of them in our neighborhood young enough to have a baby."

Strike two. I made a note on my paper.

"What else is in that area?" Kate asked, taking a sip of her coffee. "Maybe the person was there for another reason and saw the church."

"Good thinking," I said, motioning to her to wipe the trace of foam off her upper lip. "What other businesses are near the church?"

"Aside from the Atlas Performing Arts Center not too far away, we've had a real influx of trendy restaurants lately," Buster said, taking a large gulp of his cappuccino. "We have a Bullfrog Bagels, Toki Underground, and even a dumpling shop and cocktail bar that stays open until two a.m."

Kate's eyes lit up. "I need to check out the H Street Corridor again. First Union Market takes off and now this."

"I'm surprised you aren't up on it," I said. "Considering how much you go out."

She sighed. "I've had a string of politicos lately who don't want to leave Capitol Hill. See? This is exactly what I was talking about earlier. It's time for me to clean house and shake things up a bit. Date some men who like adventure."

"I thought you wanted to turn over a new leaf and stop dating so many men."

"That was before I found out about the dumpling and cocktail bar," she said.

I shook my head as I turned my attention back to my list. "So theoretically anyone going to those places could have seen your church and gotten the idea to drop off the baby."

Buster rubbed a hand over his dark-brown goatee. "Since our church isn't usually open at night, I would think it would be someone who sees the neighborhood in the daylight."

"So maybe an employee instead of a patron," I said then shook my head. "That's still an awful lot of people to consider."

"And no idea where to start," Kate said.

"I still think Annabelle was right earlier." Mack shifted on his stool, and both his leather pants and the stool legs groaned. "It has to be someone with a connection to our church or someone in it. They had to feel like it was a safe place to leave the baby. The note wasn't written by someone who didn't care what happened to Merry."

I agreed with him. The person who had written that sad note had thought they were doing the best for their child.

A bell above the door rang as it was flung open, and Darla and Debbie bustled inside along with a blast of cold air and a willowy woman with long white-blond hair.

"So sorry we're late," Darla said, walking in front of the two younger women. "We were having a late lunch at that new Peruvian Gastrobar."

Debbie, almost an exact replica of her mother from the brown bobs held back with Burberry headbands to the red Tory Burch shoes, winked at us. "We're on a pisco sour kick."

I braced myself for the possibility they would want to change the entire theme of the wedding around their new favorite cocktail. With Debbie and Darla, anything was possible.

"Hi, Caroline," I said to the woman I assumed was the bride-to-be. "How was your flight from Los Angeles?"

"It was fine," she said, rubbing her arms briskly. "I just didn't think it would be so cold."

Darla laughed. "California girls have such thin blood."

I knew the bride was a California girl, but it seemed odd that she didn't think DC would be cold in December. To be fair, I only knew her through the emails we'd exchanged, and most of her replies to my questions had been efficiently brief.

In addition to the almost blindingly blond hair, Caroline seemed as opposite from her future in-laws as you could be. She wore black from head to toe, and her only makeup seemed to be dark eyeliner and red lipstick. If I didn't know better, I would have called her style goth glam.

How had we missed this? Since Daniel Douglas and his fiancee lived on the other side of the country, we'd done all the planning with

Debbie and Darla. I felt a flutter of panic as I realized that nothing about the wedding we'd planned reflected the bride in front of me.

Darla threw an arm around Caroline. "She's tickled about all the wonderful ideas we've come up with, aren't you honey?"

Caroline gave me a smile that didn't meet her heavily lined eyes. "Tickled."

Oh boy.

"Let me get you all some cappuccinos so you can warm up." Buster hurried to his coffee station. "It's gotten bitterly cold out there."

Caroline pulled her coat tighter around her neck as she took a seat next to me at the high table. "This is why I hate winter."

Kate shot me a look, and I knew she was thinking the same thing. Why on earth was this woman having a December wedding?

It took Debbie two tries to make it onto one of the metal barstools, and Kate had to grab her arm to keep her from tipping over to the other side. Darla leaned against the table, and I got a whiff of expensive perfume and booze. Knowing Darla, she could be wearing the pisco sours as well as drinking them. I wouldn't put it past her to dab top shelf liquor onto her wrists and behind her ears after a spritz of Chanel.

Mack pulled out his copy of the last floral proposal as I flipped mine back over. "Did you have any particular changes in mind, or should we just review the quantities?"

"I wanted to change the bridal bouquet," Caroline said before Darla or Debbie could open their mouths.

"That's a great place to start," Mack said, finding the description of the bouquet on the first page of the proposal. "What part did you want to tweak?"

The bride folded her hands on the table. "I'd like to take out the ivy and berries."

Buster set three steaming hot cappuccinos on the table, and Darla gave the coffees a sad look. "You don't have anything to make these Irish, do you?"

I leaned back and shook my head so that Buster could see me but Debbie and Darla could not.

Buster patted Darla's hand. "I'm so sorry."

Mack glanced down at the proposal and blinked a few times. "You don't like ivy and berries?"

Caroline shuddered. "Too Christmasy."

"But the entire theme of the wedding is holiday inspired," Buster said as he took the seat next to Mack.

Caroline made a face. "I know. I should have looked over things sooner, but work has been insane. I'd really rather the wedding not have anything to do with the holidays."

Darla sucked in her breath. "Does that mean you don't want the Dickens-style carolers for cocktail hour?"

"You're joking, right?" the bride asked.

Darla's cheeks reddened, but I put my hand over hers before she could reply. "It's not the end of the world to cancel the carolers. We can keep it classic with a string quartet."

"I'd rather play some acid jazz from my iPod playlist," Caroline said.

Debbie almost slipped off the stool. "Acid jazz?"

"No problem," I said. "Just send me that playlist, and I'll find a jazz group that can play it."

Mack scribbled in the proposal. "So if we remove the ivy and berries, the bouquets are just roses and mini callas."

"But not the roses and not the white mini callas," Caroline said. "Can you get the ones that are dark purple?"

Mack didn't look up. "Just dark purple mini callas?"

"Caroline, honey," Darla said, taking a sip of her nonalcoholic cappuccino and cringing. "You can't have your girls walking down the aisle with black flowers."

"They're not black," Caroline said. "They're dark purple."

"To-may-to, to-mah-to," Darla said to me in a stage whisper.

"I have no doubt Buster and Mack will come up with something stunning," I said, partly to appease the bride and partly to quiet the mother of the groom. Even though Darla was technically my client and was writing all the checks, I couldn't in good conscience let the bride be steamrolled into a wedding she hated. "Why don't we compromise and have the ceremony feature the dark callas and keep the more seasonal floral designs we've already planned for the reception?"

"I was hoping to have succulents instead of flowers in the middle of the tables," Caroline said.

Nothing said love like a bunch of cactus, I thought as I noticed Darla pale.

"Succulents?" Buster asked. "Why didn't you say succulents in the first place? We've been on such a succulent kick lately."

Mack bobbed his head up and down. "It's true."

"Instead of cactus centerpieces, what about a baby succulent at the top of every guests' place?" I said to Caroline. "Do you like that idea?"

"That could work," Caroline said.

Kate leaned close to Darla. "You know tequila comes from a succulent."

Darla's eyes widened. "You don't say? Maybe we should add a tequila bar to the wedding."

"I think we're good with two gin-and-tonic stations as well as two main bars already," I said. I did not want a rehash of the wedding we'd done where we'd had a tequila fountain instead of a champagne fountain and guests had had to be carried out.

"If you say so," Debbie said. "But I do love a good margarita."

I felt my phone buzz and slipped it out of my pants pocket without looking down. "So are we all set for changes then?"

All three women nodded as they stood and gathered their things, but Caroline pulled me close as her future mother-in-law and sister-in-law teetered off ahead. "I'm telling you now, if I see so much as one holly berry or scrap of velvet ribbon at my wedding, I will walk out."

I opened my mouth to respond, but she released my arm and strode off, the only one of the three who looked like she wasn't about to topple over.

"She's not what I expected," Kate said once the bride was on the sidewalk.

"You didn't expect a blond version of the Grinch?" Buster asked.

Mack threw his pen on the table. "I'm going to have to do an entirely new floral order and have it rushed. The only good thing is no one else will be buying up all the cacti in December."

I looked down at my phone display. "This isn't good."

"I think disaster is the word you're looking for," Buster said.

"What?" Kate asked, noticing my expression and looking over my shoulder.

"It's from Richard," I said, reading from the screen, "SOS. Bring diapers."

Kate put an hand on my shoulder. "I think you may need to move, Annabelle."

CHAPTER 4

"We came as quickly as we could," I said as I pushed open the door to my apartment, a plastic grocery bag filled with diapers swinging from my wrist. "After a quick stop for supplies."

Buster and Mack hurried past me holding their own grocery bags, but stopped a few feet inside to take in the scene in my apartment.

"It's worse than we imagined," Kate whispered, coming up behind me.

I wasn't sure if it was worse, but it was definitely stranger.

Reese stood in the middle of the living room wearing nothing but his jeans, holding the baby—no longer wrapped in a blanket—to his chest. My downstairs neighbor Leatrice was perched on the edge of the couch strumming a ukulele and humming what sounded like the theme to *Hawaii Five-O*. Her sweater had a giant reindeer face and a light-up red nose blinking off and on, which went well with the antler headband holding back her jet-black, flipped-up hair.

I could see Richard's head through the opening between my living room and kitchen and could tell he stood at the stove. What on earth was he cooking at a time like this? It smelled like he was curdling cream.

Reese's shoulders relaxed when he saw us. "You're back."

Buster and Mack clustered around Reese as they inspected the sleeping baby. She had on nothing but a tiny diaper and was splayed across Reese's chest as he swayed from side to side.

I dropped my bag of disposable diapers on the floor. "Is everything okay? Richard's text sounded panicked."

Reese raised one eyebrow. "Well it would, wouldn't it? It is Richard after all."

"What's going on?" I asked, taking off my coat as I realized my heater was going full blast. "Why are you half naked?"

"Leave the man alone," Kate said as she looked my boyfriend up and down, smiling and nodding. "He clearly had a reason for embracing his inner caveman, and I, for one, think we should encourage it."

I elbowed her, and she yelped.

Leatrice stopped strumming her ukulele and popped up. "Skin-to-skin contact calms the baby. We tried a lot of other things before this finally worked."

"A lot," Reese said, his left eye twitching as he spoke.

"When did you get here?" I asked Leatrice. "I thought you were babysitting Hermes."

"I was, but Richard texted me to come up and help." She looked around the floor. "Hermes is here somewhere." She cupped a hand over her mouth. "He might be pouting. He's a little jealous of the baby."

The baby whimpered, and Leatrice quickly strummed a chord. "She doesn't like it when I stop." She sat back down on the couch and resumed her slow, plodding version of *Hawaii Five-O*, the chords only slightly connected to the melody.

"I didn't know she played the ukulele," Kate said.

I rubbed my temples. "I don't think she does."

"In here," Richard called out in a loud whisper from the kitchen and waved a wooden spoon.

"I'll be right back," I told Reese as I headed to my kitchen.

Richard stood at the stove wearing a Santa apron—a gift from Leatrice I thought I'd hidden well in the back of a drawer—and stirring something in a copper double boiler, while Hermes was curled in the corner with his back to him. The Yorkie's tiny black-and-brown ears were tilted back, so he could listen to what was going on even if he was pretending to ignore it.

I put a hand over my nose. "Is this really the time to be cooking? And what in heaven's name is that? It smells like curdled milk."

Richard put a hand on his hip. "I'll have you know I'm heating up formula."

"In a double boiler? I didn't even know I had a double boiler."

Richard narrowed his eyes at me. "I gave it to you two Christmases ago." He waved a hand at the shiny pot with two handles. "It's top-of-the-line copper and an excellent heat conductor."

"That doesn't explain why you're warming up formula in it," I said, stepping closer and getting a stronger whiff of the strange smell. "I thought you were supposed to put the bottle in a pan of boiling water."

Richard glanced at the double boiler, then looked at me, then looked back at the bubbling formula. "Well how was I supposed to know that? I've never taken care of a baby before. All I know is that your boyfriend asked me to warm up the formula."

I leaned over the simmering contents and noticed a skin forming on top. "How long have you been boiling it?"

"About fifteen minutes. It has to be sterilized, darling," Richard said, giving me an exasperated look.

"The bottles need to be sterilized, Richard. Not the formula itself." I put a hand over my mouth to keep from laughing.

Richard stared down at the bubbling formula. "Oh. I take it we can't give this to the little crying machine?"

I put a hand on his arm. "Probably not."

"Well, that's just great." Richard threw his spoon on the stovetop, and drops of formula splattered onto the counter. "Not only did I spend the last hour listening to a wailing child and a crazy old woman singing television theme songs, but my dog isn't speaking to me and my dish is ruined."

I squeezed his arm. "I think it's very sweet you tried to make her formula."

Richard crossed his arms and turned away. I couldn't help noticing how similar he and Hermes looked as they both faced the wall and pouted.

"If it makes you feel better," I said, "I think Buster and Mack will be taking Merry with them."

Richard twisted around, his mouth turning up at the corners. "They will? Are they all leaving now?" He pushed past me. "Well, I'd better say goodbye to the little angel."

I bent down. "Come on Hermes. I know you're listening to every word I say, and I'm pretty sure you understand me." His head turned toward me ever so slightly. "The baby is leaving."

He jumped up, gave a small yip, and scampered past me, his jeweled collar jingling as he ran.

I followed Richard and Hermes back into the living room and tried not to gape or scream. Not only was Reese shirtless, so were Buster and Mack.

"What happened?" I asked Kate, sidling up to her. "I was only in the kitchen for a few minutes."

"I can't really say." Kate looked shell-shocked. "It all happened so fast."

I'd never seen the biker florists without several layers of leather, and I'd never imagined them being so hairy, especially since neither had a hair on their heads. "I don't suppose those are sweaters?"

Kate shook her head with her lips pressed together. "I'm afraid not."

The men appeared to be taking turns holding the baby to their skin as Leatrice played the theme to *The Love Boat* and sang the words in a high-pitched, off-key warble. I noticed that Reese had stepped away and reached for his blue flannel shirt.

He walked over to me as he slipped it on and began buttoning it. "I hope your meeting went well." I caught the subtext loud and clear. I owed him big time.

"It did," I said. "I mean, the bride changed the entire wedding and threatened to walk out if it is even remotely holiday themed, but aside from that it was great."

He gave me a confused look.

"Thank you again for everything today." I slipped a hand inside his shirt and around his waist. "And thank you for not killing Richard several times over."

He kissed the top of my head and pulled me close. "You're very welcome. It might be one of my greatest achievements to date."

I swatted at him. "Was he that bad?"

"I'll give him credit for trying, but he's really never been within fifty feet of a baby, has he?" Reese laughed. "Once we convinced him you could not swaddle a baby like you fold a pocket square and sent him to the kitchen, things were much smoother."

"Did I hear my name?" Richard joined us, his black leather body bag slung across his chest and Hermes sitting happily inside, his eyes barely peeking above the flap.

"I was just saying how you and I were partners in crime today," Reese said, thumping Richard on the back and sending him forward a few feet.

Richard steadied himself and straightened his shoulders. "I always say it's about teamwork."

I'd never heard Richard say anything close to that, but I chose not to point it out.

"Well, I'd better hit the road," Kate said, glancing at the clock on my wall. "I have a hot date tonight, and I'm going to try to get him to take me somewhere near the H Street Corridor."

"Any particular reason?" Reese asked. Until the past few years, Northeast DC wasn't someplace you actively sought out for great restaurants.

"We were brainstorming people who might have had a reason to leave their baby at the Born Again Biker Church, and we thought that maybe it was someone who worked at one of the new restaurants in the area."

Richard rolled his eyes. "Don't tell me you're getting mixed up in another investigation."

"Yes," Reese said looking down at me. "Please don't tell me."

"This is hardly an investigation," I said. "It's not like there's a crime or a victim or any danger involved."

"All those are debatable," Reese muttered.

Kate hiked her black-and-white-striped Kate Spade purse over her shoulder. "Compared to all the murder investigations we've poked our noses into, this is a cakewalk."

I shot her a look. "Thanks."

"Give me one good reason for trying to track down the person who abandoned this baby," Richard said.

I shrugged. "If you're fine with babysitting, we won't bother."

Richard's face went slack. "What do you mean?"

I cast a glance behind me at the two burly, shirtless men cooing at the baby. "If you think they're going to give up this child, then you haven't been paying attention. If we don't locate the parents, we're all going to be spending a lot more time with baby Merry."

"Count me in," Richard said. "I'm up for whatever it takes to find out who this baby belongs to."

Hermes yipped. Clearly he didn't like sharing the spotlight with anything that was cute and demanding, either.

Reese pinched the bridge of his nose. "I still say this should go through social services." His eyes rested on the baby, and he blinked a few times in quick succession. "But I've also seen how broken the foster system is, and I don't like the thought of her going into that."

Kate nudged me. "Mr. Law and Order is actually a big softie."

"If there isn't any more life-changing drama for today," Richard said, opening my door and pointing a finger at me and Kate, "I'll see you both tomorrow at the OWP holiday party."

I smacked a hand to my forehead. I signed us up for the Organization of Wedding Planners holiday party so long ago it had slipped my mind that it was this week. "I forgot all about that. Wait, why are you going?"

"I got roped into catering it, remember?" He gave me a pointed look, and I felt my face warm as it dawned on me that I'd been the one to do the roping. "Don't worry, darlings, after today a room filled with inebriated wedding planners will be nothing."

Kate and I exchanged a look. Somehow I doubted that.

CHAPTER 5

The glass elevator pinged open, and Kate and I stepped out in front of the National Cathedral. The massive Gothic building rose above us with its three main towers jutting pointed spires over three hundred feet into the air. The main entrance held three arched doorways adorned with intricate stone carvings and a stained glass rose window above the central arch.

Even though I couldn't see them from my vantage point, I knew the cathedral boasted gargoyles in the image of bishops, yuppies, and even Darth Vader. Flying buttresses extended off the sides like carved stone tent poles securing the sanctuary to the ground. The cathedral's ivory limestone reflected the light and made the building almost blinding in the midday sun, its silhouette stark against the clear blue sky.

Kate slipped on her oversized sunglasses while I raised a hand to shield my eyes as I pulled my green angora scarf closer to my neck. It was sunny but cold, with a biting wind whipping down the long stretch of Wisconsin Avenue and making me shiver.

"I can't get used to the idea of having parties inside a church," Kate said as we followed the sidewalk past some bare-limbed trees.

I grasped the handrail as we went up the short flight of steps leading to the front door. "Correction, a cathedral."

"Either way," Kate said, "it feels odd to get soused at church."

I glanced at my wrist even though I wore no watch. "Who says we're going to get soused? It's lunchtime."

The glass double doors stood open, and a pair of women smiled at us from inside the church foyer. Kate lowered her voice. "It's still a holiday party. You know how those get."

We stepped inside and said hello to the greeters who directed us to a table with name tags in the shape of wreaths. I unwrapped my scarf and attached the name tag to my red-and-black-plaid dress, feeling grateful the tags used magnets instead of pins that leave holes in fabric.

"Speaking of cocktails, how was your date?" I asked her. "Did you hit the H Street Corridor?"

"We ended up at the oyster bar in Union Market, but it's not too far from H Street." She picked up the wreath name tag with her name on it. "I have to tell you, Annabelle, there are so many new restaurants and businesses in northeast, it would be nearly impossible to sift through all the employees."

That's what I'd been afraid of. "Thanks for checking it out."

"You know me," she said. "It's always work, work, work."

Kate took off her coat, and I blinked a few times. "So you have an issue with drinking in church but not with wearing a micromini?"

Kate tugged the hemline of the red dress which was tight at her waist and flared out. "I wouldn't say micro."

I eyed the skirt which rested several inches above mid-thigh. "It barely covers your—"

"Hoo-boy!" Fern, our go-to wedding day hairstylist, rushed up to us. "I'm glad you two are here."

He took our coats and waved for us to follow him to the coat check station off to one side, handing us a claim ticket once he'd passed the coats to the tuxedoed attendant.

With his arms free, I was finally able to take in his outfit. Covered from head to toe in forest-green velvet, Fern wore both pants and a cropped jacket that were tapered and slim fitting. He'd tied a white silk ascot at his throat and pinned it with a garnet the size of a small egg, and he'd pulled his dark hair back in a low ponytail that barely dipped below his collar. Nothing about this ensemble surprised me since Fern considered dressing to the season and occasion the height of creative expression. I was just happy he hadn't dressed in bishop's robes.

"Why are you at an Organization of Wedding Planners party?" I asked, returning the air kiss he gave me. "Not that I'm not thrilled to see you."

Kate looped an arm though his. "He's my plus one."

Why hadn't I thought to bring a plus one? Not that I'd want to subject anyone not in the wedding industry to the experience.

We walked from the foyer into the sanctuary, and I paused for a moment. The wooden chairs that usually sat in rows and filled the long sanctuary were gone, replaced by an elevated, round DJ booth in the center, and both cocktail tables and food stations fanned out around it. Patterned green lighting had been projected up the stone columns and vaulted ceiling, giving the cavernous space an otherworldly feel.

Kate and I had coordinated several wedding ceremonies at the National Cathedral, each one with masses of traditional white flowers on the altar and a bride processing to sacred music. The rules for weddings at the cathedral were quite strict, and the vergers who ran the show carried long ceremonial staffs for pomp and enforcement (or so it always felt to me). It was strange to see the religious space decked out like a nightclub.

"Have you seen Richard?" I asked Fern as my eyes scanned the people mingling around tables draped in shimmering red cloths.

"He was by the poke' station earlier." Fern motioned to a long wooden table to the right topped with glass bowls.

"Poke'?" Kate asked. "That's the Hawaiian version of ceviche, right?"

I nodded as I looked for Richard around the busy station. "Raw fish, yes."

"I wonder how he's making that fit in with the holiday theme."

"Have you tried the smoked scallops, ladies?" Bambie Sitwell, or Boob Job Bambie as we called her, asked as she walked up to us. "They're literally smoking them at that table over there."

I glanced at the square table where a chef in a white jacket appeared to be placing small plates of scallops under smoke-filled glass domes. "Hi, Bambie. Are they good?"

She closed her heavily made-up eyes for a moment and brushed a strand of hair off her Botoxed forehead. "Divine." Her eyes popped open. "But not as addictive as these mistletoe margaritas." She held up a large glass coupe filled with lime-green liquid and garnished with a green sprig of what I could only assume was mistletoe.

Kate's head swiveled around. "Did you say margarita?"

Bambie waved a hand laden with rings toward a bar that appeared to be draped in ivy and red berries. Kate and Fern took off in that direction without a backward glance.

Great. Now I was stuck talking with Boob Job Bambie, whose only topic of conversation seemed to be her latest trip to the med spa or her latest well-heeled, long-in-the-tooth husband. And was Richard really serving tequila at noon inside a cathedral? I knew he was what he considered a lapsed Catholic, and the National Cathedral was an Episcopal church, but this seemed a bit sacrilegious even for him.

I looked past Barbie's teased blond helmet and spotted my best friend's dark, spiky hair above the crowd. I caught his eye as he came into view, and a look of relief passed over his face.

He rushed over and gave me a perfunctory hug, ignoring Bambie who didn't seem to notice as she floated off to talk to someone else. "You got here just in time."

"Why?" I asked.

He straightened his dove-gray tie layered on his dark-gray shirt. "I was desperate for some intelligent conversation, that's why. All the planners want to talk about is 'the list'." He made air quotes with his fingers.

"You mean the *Capital Weddings Magazine* list? Is that out yet?"

Capital Weddings Magazine published a list in their January issue of the top wedding vendors as voted on by the DC wedding industry. The issue was one of their best sellers, and brides-to-be and their mothers had been known to use the list as a bible. Making the magazine was a boost to business, and getting the coveted starred listing as the top vote getter was the jewel in any wedding professional's crown.

"Rumor has it early issues have just come off the presses, and an issue is floating around the party somewhere," Richard said, looking nonplussed. It was easy for him to be so nonchalant since his company, Richard Gerard Catering, had been a fixture on the list since it began, and he'd gotten the star next to his name more than once.

"Don't you want to get a peek at it?" I asked him, peering around and trying to spot someone flashing a bridal magazine.

"I suppose, but it's not like the list changes dramatically from year to year." Richard studied a passing waiter then nodded approvingly.

"We only made it onto the list two years ago," I said. "I just hope we don't fall off after all the . . ."

"Murders?" Fern asked as he and Kate joined us, each holding a bright-green margarita. "You didn't. I checked."

I put a hand to my heart. "You did? Wait, where did you see it?"

"Brianna has it," he said, wrinkling his nose.

So much for getting a sneak peek. Brianna, owner of Brides by Brianna and one of the newer wedding planners to join the scene, had hit our radar when she'd started spreading rumors about Wedding Belles in an effort to steal our business. Kate and Fern had retaliated by telling anyone who would listen that Brianna was, in fact, running a call girl business instead of planning weddings. From then on, we'd done our best to avoid each other.

I twisted around to see if I could glimpse our nemesis. Sure enough, she held court on a low tufted sofa setup near the DJ booth with a gaggle of twentysomething planners clustered around her, flipping through what was undoubtably the January issue of *Capital Weddings*. Before I looked away, Brianna caught my eye and glared at me.

"She does not look happy," I said, indicating her with a nod of my head.

Fern gave me an arch smile. "No surprise there. She's not on the list."

Kate sloshed some margarita on her sleeve. "She's not? I heard she campaigned hard this year. Cassie at the floral warehouse said she called them and begged them to vote for her."

"Sounds about right," I said, feeling more pleasure than I would have liked to admit that a planner like Brianna, who was short on substance and long on styled shoots, had been left off the list. "I'm surprised she didn't get her daddy to buy her way on."

Brianna's business had reportedly been bankrolled by her wealthy father, which meant she had money to splash out on advertising and expensive gifts for clients. There were whispers that's she'd recently passed out Louis Vuitton passport cases to all the hotel executives for the holidays.

"Money can't buy everything, darling," Richard said. "It certainly can't buy class."

"Congratulations," a young woman with glossy black curls said as she came up and gave Kate a hug. "Are you so excited?"

"Thanks, Sasha," Kate said, raising her cocktail in a salute. "It's always an honor to be on the list."

Sasha tilted her head at Kate then looked at me. "You don't know, do you?" She giggled and clapped her hands. "Wedding Belles got the star. You're top vote getter."

It took a moment for the news to sink in, but I felt my mouth drop open. Kate squealed as she bounced up and down, Fern taking the cocktail from her hand before it all spilled onto the marble floor.

Richard gave me a one-armed hug and cleared his throat. "Well, it could not be more well deserved."

"Thanks." I felt dazed. "I was afraid we wouldn't make the list because of all the drama at our weddings this year."

Fern waved a hand at me. "I mean, who doesn't have a few dead bodies pop up at their weddings?" He took a drink from Kate's glass.

"The important thing is you always saved the weddings, even if it meant bending the law."

I hoped he would never mention that to my boyfriend.

"I wonder who else got stars," I said. Now I was dying to see the list and maybe stare at our star for a few hours.

"This is ridiculous," Fern said, handing both glasses to Kate. "I'll be right back."

He sashayed over to the planners huddled around the magazine. After talking to them for a few moments, they all jumped up and rushed across the hall. Fern picked up the abandoned magazine and hurried back to us.

"How did you do that?" Kate asked.

"Simple. I told them there was an Instagram wall they could take pictures of their cocktails against, and that no one had posted a cocktail shot yet." He winked. "It should take them a while to search the Cathedral and realize I lied."

I took the magazine from him and flipped to the back section where I knew the list would be. I located the section on wedding planners and ran a finger down until I found the blurb about Wedding Belles along with a hot-pink star. I felt a rush seeing it with my own eyes.

"I can't believe it," Kate whispered as she gazed over my shoulder at the magazine page. "Look at all the names of all those older planners around ours. I wonder what they think about this."

It hadn't occurred to me what the reaction from our competition might be, but as I looked up I noticed a group of older planners a few feet away giving us the serious side-eye.

Richard took the magazine from me. "Let's take a look at the list of caterers. Probably all the usual suspects."

I nudged Kate and indicated the glaring planners with a jerk of my head. "I'm not sure this is going to make us the most popular people."

"When you're on top, people are always going to want to knock you down." Fern took his cocktail back from Kate and raised it. "But at least you're on top, sweeties."

"We should go out and celebrate," Kate said. "And not in a place where they serve communion."

I felt my phone buzz and glanced at the screen. Why did Reese need me to call him ASAP?

"I think I'm going to faint," Richard said, the magazine slipping from his hand and dropping to the floor.

I caught his arm as he staggered against me. "What's wrong? Do you feel ill?"

"I'm dying." His words came out in short gasps as the color drained from his usually tanned face. "It's over."

Kate stared at her nearly empty glass. "What's happening? Was he poisoned?"

"Worse," Richard said, his eyes wide and his voice a strangled sob. "Richard Gerard Catering is not on the list."

CHAPTER 6

"Put your head between your knees." Fern rubbed Richard's back. "It will help with the hyperventilating."

"We're in a car, you ninny," Richard said as he hitched in his breath. "I can't bend over that far without putting my head in the glove compartment."

I glanced at Fern in my rearview mirror and saw him make a face that Richard undoubtedly missed.

"Maybe that's where you should put it," Fern muttered.

Richard either didn't hear him or chose to ignore the comment. He slumped against the passenger side window of my car. "I can't believe this happened. My life is over."

I drove up the ramp of the National Cathedral underground parking garage and paused when we reached the top. Traffic on Wisconsin Avenue whizzed by us, allowing me to idle the car for a few moments. I cranked up the heat and put my icy fingers to the vents to warm them more quickly.

We'd rushed Richard out of the party and into my car so fast I hadn't had time to warm it up, so the air inside still felt like the air outside, and that seemed to be getting more frigid by the minute.

"Your life isn't over. Like I said before, I'm sure you were left off the list by mistake."

"It's a conspiracy," Richard insisted. "I've been blacklisted; I just know it."

"Why would anyone blacklist you?" Kate leaned her head between the front seats. "Have you made any new enemies lately?"

"Of course not," Richard said, then tapped his chin. "Define 'enemies.' And 'lately.'"

As my car warmed, I took a long breath. "Why does it suddenly smell like I walked inside a gingerbread house?"

"Since we left the party in such a fast and furious flurry, I barely had time to eat." Fern held up a basket filled with cookies. "I might have grabbed a few treats for the road. Want one?"

"A few treats?" Richard gaped at him. "That's an entire basket of cookies from the dessert station."

"I wouldn't mind a cookie, " I said, reaching a hand behind me.

Richard looked at me like I'd just kicked his dog. "I can't believe you can eat at a time like this." His eyes flitted to the dark-brown cookie Fern put in my hand. "And those molasses cookies are meant to be paired with iced vanilla latte shooters."

My stomach rumbled. "I'll risk it."

A car honked behind me, and I looked up at the light, which was now green. I waved an apology and turned left into traffic, glancing over at Richard, who'd dropped his head into his hands. "I can't believe someone would have it out for you enough to remove you from the list. Everyone knows you're the best caterer in town."

I took a bite of cookie. Not only did it smell like Christmas; the sugar-dusted molasses cookie tasted like it. I could almost hear the sleigh bells as I wolfed it down. Kate and Fern both crunched on cookies behind me as well.

Fern held up the magazine in question. "He's definitely not on it. I've gone through the entire thing a few times." He flipped to a page and held it up. "I, however, got mentioned as an 'editor's pick'. What does that even mean? It's not like I've done any of the editors' hair." He flipped a few more pages to the masthead. "Or have I?"

Richard whipped his head around. "You brought that thing with you? I never want to lay eyes on it again for as long as I live. *Capital Weddings* is dead to me." He waved a finger in the air. "Dead, I say."

"At least you're not overreacting," Kate said.

Even though I agreed that Richard was being his usual overly dramatic self, I also knew that being left off the list was a huge deal and could mean that a lot of brides wouldn't be calling him over the course of the next twelve months. Unlike Wedding Belles, Richard Gerard Catering did more than weddings, but brides made up a big chunk of his client list. Not only that, weddings kept him from being bored to tears with corporate luncheons and drop-off deliveries to law firms. I, for one, did not want to deal with a restless Richard with too much time on his hands. I'd had a glimpse of it when he'd been shut down under suspicion of poisoning once, and I did not want to relive that anytime soon. I veered right onto Massachusetts Avenue as the light changed from yellow to red.

Richard clutched the armrest. "Where are we going? Georgetown isn't this way."

"We're stopping by the District Two police station," I said.

Richard snapped his fingers. "Excellent idea, Annabelle. I should press charges against *Capital Weddings*. This is slander and defamation at the very least."

I sighed. "We're not going to press charges against the magazine. Reese texted me and said he had some information about the baby that Buster and Mack found."

"Are we still going on about that baby?" Richard fluttered his hands in the air. "It's not like the child knows she's been abandoned. She's probably better off now than she was before. I, on the other hand, have had my entire reputation destroyed."

I hooked another right onto a mostly residential street and turned into the District Two parking lot. "I promise you we're not making light of what's happened, but I also promised Buster and Mack we'd help them find out as much as we could about who left Merry."

"It's not like we can't do both," Kate said. "We've investigated enough crimes that we should be able to juggle the baby case and figure out why you got left off the list."

Richard twisted to face her. "I do not say this often. "He paused. "Okay, I've never said this at all, but you are a genius, Kate."

She grinned. "Thank you. It's nice for you to finally ackno—"

He cut her off. "Don't let it go to your head, darling. It was probably a one-off, but you're right that we need to investigate why *Capital Weddings* has it out for me the same way we would a murder at a wedding." A flutter of the hand. "Or an abandoned baby."

"Fine." I let my breath out in a huff and stepped out of the car. Everyone followed me as I hurried across the parking lot out of the cold and into the two-story brown brick building with blacked windows. Reese was going to love this. Not only was I showing up with a small posse, I'd gotten roped into a second investigation. Maybe I wouldn't tell him about 'The Case of the Blacklisted Best Friend' right away.

I stamped my feet a few times to warm them up as we stood in the utilitarian foyer of the station. A reception desk to the right stood guard in front of a series of battered wooden desks behind it. I could hear the sounds of typing and of people talking. I spotted Reese bent over a desk looking at a computer monitor.

"It's been a while since I've been here," Fern said, slipping off his green-velvet gloves. "Do you remember the time I gave all the officers makeovers?"

"I don't think any of us will ever forget that," Kate said. "Especially the officer who got the Dorothy Hamill pixie cut."

Fern grinned and touched a hand to his own low ponytail. "That was very flattering for his face."

I led the way to the front desk and gave the female officer on duty my most winning smile. "I'm here to see Detective Mike Reese."

She stared at me, then her eyes shifted to my friends. Her stony expression didn't change. "He expecting you?"

"He's probably not expecting all of this," Kate said under her breath.

"Tell him his friend Richard Gerard is here," Richard said.

We all looked at Richard.

He shrugged. "What? We did a lot of male bonding yesterday. You can really get to know someone when you pick out a Christmas tree with them."

After their exhaustive tree search, I was pretty sure Reese felt that he knew more about Richard now than he ever wanted to.

Reese looked up and saw us. I waved at him and assumed a look of oblivious innocence. As I saw him raise an eyebrow, I felt sure it hadn't worked.

"So," he said, walking over to us, "the gang's all here."

"We were at a party at the Cathedral when you texted me," I said. "It was quicker to bring them with me."

Reese pushed up his already rolled-up shirt sleeves. "Come on back. I want to show you something."

The female officer at reception grudgingly lifted the swing gate so we could follow Reese.

"So I pulled all the security camera footage from any business near the Born Again Biker Church." He rested a hand on my back as we gathered around a desk with him. "It's in a strip mall that hasn't gone through gentrification yet, so not all of the businesses have cameras, and those that do have them don't keep them on all the time. That being said, I did manage to get one feed that shows us the front of the church."

He typed something on his keyboard and a video began playing full screen. It was black and white and pretty grainy. It also appeared to only film every few seconds, so the footage looked jerky. We all leaned in to watch the view of the front of the church from a side angle. The glass double doors opened and closed a few times as churchgoers appeared to leave. I glanced at the time stamp. Around twelve thirty on Sunday afternoon. This would have been after the service ended, so we were probably watching the last stragglers. Several minutes passed on the video time stamp, and then a figure moved into the screen holding something. I heard myself suck in breath, and I saw Kate raise a hand to her mouth.

The figure, who wore a dark coat and a scarf covering their face, placed a baby carrier outside the door. Even with the delayed time and jerky footage, I could see the hesitation as the figure gazed down at the child before knocking on the glass and turning away quickly. Then the figure was gone from the screen, and the next thing we saw was the large figure of Mack coming outside and finding the baby.

Reese reached down and stopped the video. Fern sniffled and produced a handkerchief from his pocket, then dabbed at his eyes. I found myself blinking away tears as well.

Richard cleared his throat. "At least they had the good sense to knock on the glass. Considering how cold it was yesterday, the little thing could have frozen to death if no one knew to look for her."

"It was someone who cared about her." I leaned closer to Reese and felt comforted by the warmth of his hand on my back.

"Whoever it was, they had second thoughts," Kate said, her voice breaking.

I nodded. "You could see them hesitate."

"Too bad we can't tell anything about them from the footage," Reese said. "The face is completely covered, and they turn away from the camera when they leave."

"We know it was a woman," Fern said.

We all turned to him.

"We do?" Reese asked.

Fern pointed to the screen. "Back it up a bit." When Reese rewound the footage, Fern waved his fingers. "See? Right there. A bit of her hair flies out of the scarf when she turns."

Reese bent his face near the monitor. "Well, would you look at that?"

"Just because they have long hair doesn't mean it's a woman," Richard said. "Have you seen the hair on some of Buster and Mack's biker friends?"

Fern let out a short breath and pointed to the strand of blond hair on the screen. "It's also color treated. How many Harley riders get highlights done?" He held up his hands. "Not that I'm saying they couldn't use some face-framing color."

"Are you sure?" I asked.

Fern folded his arms over his green velvet jacket. "As sure as I am that you haven't had a haircut in six months, and Kate is about a week away from needing her roots touched up."

"I'd take his word as expert testimony," I told Reese.

CHAPTER 7

I ran the last few steps down the sidewalk and pushed through the glass doors of Lush, the bell above me ringing as I stamped my feet on the concrete floor to regain feeling in them. Kate and Richard were close on my heels, and I could hear Kate's teeth chattering as she unwound the scarf from her neck.

We'd dropped Fern at his salon on the way after he'd remembered he had a full afternoon of society matrons who needed cut and color. We'd promised to fill him in on any new information on the search for the baby's mama, and he'd promised Richard he'd keep his ear to the ground about any catering gossip.

"I haven't been here in ages," Richard said, walking further into the flower shop. "It's like stepping into a greenhouse."

I had to agree with him. Between the almost tropical heat, which must have been turned to full blast, and the heady perfume of flowers spilling out of the galvanized metal buckets lining the wall, it felt like we'd entered a hothouse. The back metal table held a bubble bowl with a partially finished holiday arrangement of red roses and holly leaves with remnants of trimmed flowers scattered around it. I noticed a pair of empty cappuccino cups on the table alongside a baby bottle.

Mack appeared from the doorway that led to the back of the shop. He was decked out in his usual black leather pants and leather vest with chains that jangled as he walked. The only addition to the outfit was a black baby carrier attached to his chest, and I could see Merry's chubby legs dangling beneath. Part of me was surprised the baby carrier wasn't leather with his biker club's emblem emblazoned on the front.

He held a finger to his lips. "She just fell asleep."

I tiptoed toward him and peered at the tiny face pressed sideways against his T-shirt. "How long will she sleep?"

Mack shrugged. "Two hours? Two minutes?" He rubbed his eyes, and I could see how bloodshot they were. "We haven't exactly worked out a sleeping schedule yet."

Richard sniffed. "It doesn't smell like a baby in here. You must be doing something right."

Buster emerged from the back holding a plastic container of Lysol wipes and rubber gloves. "We aren't getting much floral designing done, that much I can tell you."

"Are you positive you want to take this on?" Kate reached out and touched the baby's tiny pajama-clad foot. "There are some wonderful foster parents out there."

Mack's face darkened. "No foster care."

"We didn't come to talk about Merry," I said. "Well, not directly at least."

"If you're calling about the changes for Saturday," Buster said, holding up a yellow-gloved palm, "I already know. Darla called me an hour ago."

"Darla called you?" I pulled my phone out of my purse. "She didn't call me. What changes? It's only a few days before the wedding. There can't be any more changes."

Kate waved a finger at me. "That right there is why Darla didn't call you. I'll bet she knew you'd tell her no, but she thought she could sweet-talk the boys."

I couldn't imagine what additional changes they could have come up with only a day after we'd had the final meeting. I dropped my phone back in my purse. "Well? Did she sweet-talk you?"

Buster set the Lysol wipes on the metal worktable. "Unfortunately for her, sleep deprivation does not make me more open to last-minute changes." He took off his rubber gloves. "Who needs a coffee besides me?"

Kate and I both raised our hands.

"It makes him a bear," Mack said in a stage whisper with an apologetic smile to Buster. "Well, it does."

Buster grunted at him as he moved in front of the large cappuccino machine and began fiddling with nozzles. "Debbie saw some Instagram post about holiday margaritas and wanted to add some mistletoe for garnishing."

"I wonder what the bah humbug bride thinks about that," Kate said.

I turned to Richard who was staring down at his phone. "It must have been the mistletoe margaritas from the Cathedral party. I can't believe she saw posts from it so soon."

"Believe it," Richard muttered. "All anyone is posting is either closeups of their cocktails from the party or pictures of their listing in *Capital Weddings*."

Mack's face lit up. "Is the new list out already?"

"That's right." Buster turned from measuring coffee grounds. "I'd forgotten it should be hitting the stands soon."

Kate shook her head while I made a frowny face. Both floral designers looked confused.

Richard sighed. "Oh, for heaven's sake. My career may be finished, but I haven't gone blind." He glanced back at his phone screen. "That's it. I need to call my office."

He walked a few feet away and leaned against a high top table, his phone pressed to his ear.

"Richard Gerard Catering wasn't on the list," I said in a low voice, even though the sounds of Buster's fancy machine made it pointless for me to whisper.

"What?" Mack looked from me to Kate. "That's impossible. He's one of the top caterers in town. He's been on the list since they started it."

"It's true," Kate said. "Not only did he not get top vote getter like he did last year, but his name doesn't appear on the list at all."

Buster glanced over our heads at Richard. "I'm surprised he's so calm."

"He was less than calm when he found out," I said. "Actually, he shrieked and wailed so loudly we had to remove him from the OWP holiday party before security dragged him off."

"That sounds more like Richard," Mack said, jiggling the baby as she shifted in the carrier.

"So," I said, realizing we'd drifted way off topic, "what happened with Darla?"

Buster handed Kate and me each an oversized white cup topped with frothy white foam. "Before I could give her my answer, she got squirrelly and hung up the phone."

"I wonder if the bride busted her," Kate said as she blew on her cappuccino.

I wrapped my hands around the round coffee cup so my fingers absorbed the warmth. "All I know is that if the bride spots a mistletoe margarita, it's going to be a very one-sided wedding."

"What kind of lunatic plans a December wedding when they hate winter and winter holidays?" Kate asked.

"We don't know if she hates all winter holidays." Buster twitched one broad shoulder up and down. "Maybe she'd be up for using blue and white and decorating with dreidels. Hanukkah is very overlooked when it comes to design inspiration."

"From my short experience with this bride, I'm guessing that wouldn't fly either," I said, "although an ice-blue winter wedding would be stunning."

"That's it," Richard rejoined us. "My career in this town is over. I'm kaput, done, finito."

Mack thumped him on the back and he staggered forward. "It's only one issue of one magazine."

Richard waved his phone in the air. "I just called into Richard

Gerard Catering HQ and there has not been a single new inquiry since this morning."

I glanced at the modern chrome clock on the wall and took a tentative sip of coffee, so I wouldn't burn my tongue. "It's only one o'clock."

"But it's the holidays," Richard said. "These are our busiest weeks. We make more money in December than in any other month."

"Odd how your business picks up and ours slows down," Kate said.

"That's one good thing we can say about weddings," I said. "Not many in the dead of winter."

The Douglas wedding was an anomaly. Rarely did we take weddings around the holidays because it was the one time of year we weren't insanely busy. Of course, Darla and Debbie were repeat clients, and they never capped their budgets, two reasons we'd agreed to a wedding right before Christmas. Part of me wished we hadn't, though, because I didn't like having to finalize wedding details when I should be focused on decorating my tree and picking out presents. I hadn't even gotten a present for Reese, and I knew if I didn't act fast I'd be either paying for overnight shipping or giving him coupons for free hugs.

"But you have a lot of corporate parties coming up, right?" I asked as Richard paced small circles in front of me and muttered to himself.

Richard stopped pacing. "For now. What happens when the magazine actually hits the stands and word gets out I've been kicked off the list? This is a fickle town, Annabelle. One day you're hot and the next you're..."

"Listen." I set down my cup and put a hand on his arm. "None of your regular clients will stop using you because of some silly wedding list."

Kate added her hand to mine. "Don't forget that we promised to help you find out who's behind you getting taken off the list. If there's a conspiracy, we'll get to the bottom of it."

"That reminds me." I took my hand off Richard's arm and reached into my purse for the image Reese had printed off for me. I held it up to Buster and Mack. "Does this woman look familiar?"

Mack squinted at the grainy black-and-white photo. "That's a woman?"

"Fern confirmed it from the blond hair popping out of the scarf," Kate said.

Neither man questioned Fern's assessment as they leaned in to study the image.

"This is the person who left baby Merry in front of your church," I told them. "Reese pulled footage from a nearby security camera, and it shows this woman putting the baby down and walking away."

"This must be her mother," Buster said, touching his pointer finger to the image. "And she has blond hair."

Mack looked down at the tiny head lolling against his chest. "That makes sense. Merry has fair coloring, although her hair is just peach fuzz right now."

"Do you know anyone who could be this woman?" I asked.

Buster shook his head. "It's hard to say. Aside from the blond hair, there isn't much to go on. You can't see anything of her face except the tip of a nose and even that's blurry."

I looked at the grainy image. He was right. Although we now knew the person who abandoned Merry was a woman with blond hair, that only narrowed the field down to tens of thousands of people in the DC area.

"It was a long shot," I said, setting the photo down on the nearby worktable. "What we really need to do is what the cops do—inspect the scene of the crime."

"You mean the place where the little waif was left?" Richard asked. "What do you think you'll find? A driver's license the woman dropped and nobody noticed?"

I ignored Richard's snarky comments. "From the video, we can tell what direction she approached from. It would be helpful to see where that is and what's there."

"You want a tour of the Born Again Biker Church?" Mack asked.

"That can be arranged." Buster pulled out a key ring. "Since we're deacons, I have a key."

"What are we waiting for?" Kate rubbed her hands together. "I've never been to a biker church."

Mack motioned to Merry with his head. "I'll stay here with her and mind the shop. There's no way I'm taking her out of this carrier now that she's actually sleeping."

Buster led us toward the front door, but Richard didn't follow.

"You coming?" I asked, looking back at him.

"I'll stay with Mack," Richard said, throwing an arm around the florist's wide back and not reaching the other shoulder. "I have a few things to check out online anyway."

I couldn't help being suspicious. Since when did Richard voluntarily hang out with a baby and a florist?

"Suit yourself," Kate said, tugging me by the sleeve.

As I walked through the glass door Buster held open, I cast a final glance at Richard and Mack, an odd couple if ever there was one, and hoped my gut feeling was wrong.

CHAPTER 8

"This definitely doesn't look like any church I've ever seen." Kate peered up at the sign stretching across the storefront of the worn-down mini mall. "Born Again Biker Church" was written in dark block letters with a red cross on each end of the sign. This was a far cry from the picturesque wooden clapboard churches or impressive stone cathedrals we usually found ourselves working in.

I'd parked my CRV in one of the spaces that butted up to the glass-fronted church, glad not to have to parallel park on the street for once, and I joined Kate on the sidewalk. I twisted to look at the businesses around us. The area was still mostly low warehouses and strip malls with operations not looking for much walk-by traffic: commercial kitchens, car repair shops, off-site storage. I knew that rent in this area of the city was lower, so spaces were larger and a little run-down.

I pulled the photo of the woman out of my purse and arranged myself at the proper angle. "She came and went from this direction."

Kate held a hand over her eyes as she followed my gaze across the parking lot. A three-level self-storage complex and street parking were the only things in that direction. "Unless the woman lives in a storage unit, I don't think she came from there."

I put the photo back in my purse. So much for that bright idea.

Buster roared into the lot and angled his bike in one of the motorcycle spots at the end of the row. He took off his black skullcap helmet as he got off his bike and walked toward the double doors with keys in hand. We huddled behind him to block the wind as he jiggled the keys in the glass doors.

He finally pushed one side and held it open for us. "We don't keep the church unlocked if there's no service. Not that we have anything worth stealing."

"That's an understatement," Kate whispered to me as we hurried in out of the cold.

The inside of the church was as utilitarian as the outside with a dingy tile floor, metal folding chairs arranged in uneven rows, and a few sagging sofas around the edges of the room. Near the doors were a pair of spindly-legged rectangular tables stacked with pamphlets and Bibles, and a round table held a pair of coffee dispensers with paper "Caf" and "Decaf" signs taped on the front. Styrofoam cups held sugar packets and wooden stirrers, and a clear plastic bin of cookies looked to be mostly crumbs. The scent of coffee, evergreen, and sweat lingered in the air, which was quite a change from the aroma of incense and flowers I associated with churches.

Buster flipped a switch by the door and long rows of fluorescent lights on the ceiling flickered to life. "It's not much, but the folks who come here don't worry too much about appearances."

Despite the bare-bones decor and odd combination of smells, there was a warmth to the place I couldn't explain. A Christmas tree strung with popcorn chains stood in one corner, and shiny-gold garland hung in swags over the low stage at the front. I walked over to a large bulletin board hanging on the wall. Newspaper articles about the church's philanthropic activities were tacked up alongside fliers selling bikes and notes with messages of encouragement from one member to another. I turned and looked out the glass front of the building and noticed the transparent surface was hazy.

Buster saw me studying it. "We put an anti-shatter film over the glass."

"Why?" I asked, touching my fingertips to the cold surface.

Buster shrugged. "Some groups don't like the work we do. They don't consider us real Christians because it's our policy to love and accept everyone and not to judge."

"Who would have a problem with that?" Kate asked. "Love and acceptance sound pretty churchy to me."

He pointed to the newspaper clippings on the bulletin board. "We've gotten some press for the funerals."

Kate and I went over to the board. I scanned one of the articles. "So you set up human shields outside of funerals?"

Buster rocked back on the heels of his leather boots. "You know those churches that like to hold up hateful signs when it's a funeral for a suicide or a gay person or even a soldier? We make sure the family and friends don't have to see any of that ugliness."

"I had no idea you and Mack did that." I felt embarrassed I'd known them for almost five years and had never been aware of this part of their lives.

Buster shrugged. "Like I said, we don't believe in judging. We know what it's like to be judged. Most of our members have done plenty of things they aren't proud of, and most of the world would judge them harshly for. But we've all seen our way to the light. Now we're about spreading that light."

Kate pointed to an article on the wall. "You guys escorted this kid to school when he was being bullied?"

Buster grinned. "That was one of my favorites. His grandmother is one of our members and told us how bad he was being picked on. About thirty of us rode him to school and dropped him off so all the other kids could see. We even got him his own leather vest. I don't know if I've ever seen a kid smile so much."

I could imagine that an escort of over two dozen rough-looking biker dudes on Harleys would make most bullies think twice.

Kate reached for a napkin from the coffee station and dabbed it to her eyes then nudged me. "Why don't we do something like that?"

"That was a good day." A man with a grizzled gray beard and leather jacket came inside, stomping his feet on the doormat. A skinny woman with dishwater-blond hair was with him and as she took off her scarf, I noticed a colorful tattoo swirling up from the cleavage exposed by her leather lace-up vest.

Buster gave the man a handshake and one-armed hug. "Hey, Soul Man. I was showing my friends around. They're helping us find who left the baby." He kissed the woman on the cheek. "Hey, Shelley."

The older man nodded, his eyes going to us. "Welcome to our church." He stepped forward and held out his hand. "I'm the preacher. Everyone calls me Soul Man. And this is the missus."

The woman winked at us. "Call me Shelley." Her voice made her sound like a two-pack-a-day smoker, but she smelled like tea rose perfume when she leaned close.

"Annabelle," I said, shaking both of their hands. I motioned to my assistant who was blowing her nose. "This is Kate."

Kate waved as she wiped her nose with the limp napkin. "Buster was telling us about the work you do."

Shelley walked over to the coffee station and began straightening the supplies. She handed Kate another napkin. "How are y'all getting along with this baby thing?"

"We don't know much," I said. "Except that a woman dropped her off."

Shelley moved her head up and down. "Makes sense. It was probably the mama who got scared and didn't know what to do."

"You don't know any of the wives or girlfriends of church members who might have been pregnant, do you?" I asked.

"Not many come to services," Soul Man answered for her. "We might only have a handful of women each Sunday; ain't that right Shelley?"

"Sometimes it's just me and Christie Gail," Shelley said. "That's our daughter."

Buster and Soul Man moved across the room and started moving the folding chairs back into straight lines.

"Do you ever get together with the other wives and girlfriends?" I asked.

"When we do group rides, more of them turn out," she said. "And everyone shows up for the picnics. Me and Soul Man don't go out as much anymore, but some of the men play pool down at Bedlam."

"Bedlam?" Kate asked.

"A bar in Adams Morgan where a lot of bikers tend to hang out." She looked us up and down. "But you could go if you wanted to. They have a vegan menu."

I didn't ask why one look at us made her think we would be vegans, and I tried not to act surprised that a bar frequented by bikers would have an animal-product-free menu in the first place. These Harley riders were more complicated than I'd given them credit for.

Shelley jerked her thumb toward a pair of doors on the other side of the room. "I'm gonna hit the ladies."

When she disappeared into one of the doors, I turned to face Kate. "Are you thinking what I'm thinking?"

"That we have *got* to see what they put on a vegan menu at a biker bar?"

I waved one hand at her. "No, although I'd like to meet some of these vegan bikers. I'm thinking maybe we should find out more about their daughter."

"You think she could be the one who dropped off the baby?" Kate dropped her voice. "Wouldn't her parents have noticed?"

"You've heard of the teenaged girls who wear baggy sweatshirts and no one even knows they're pregnant," I said. "It's been sweater weather for almost four months now."

"You're only saying this because she's the only other female we've heard about who's associated with the church," Kate said.

"Probably," I admitted. "But it's worth at least checking out. If she looks anything like her mother, she'd have blond hair."

Shelley emerged from the bathroom, and I waved her over. "You don't happen to have a picture of your daughter, do you?"

She reached into the back pocket of her jeans. "Sure I do, hon." She pulled out a small rectangular picture and held it out. "This isn't all that recent, but you can see she takes after me."

Kate craned over my shoulder to see. "She's adorable. How old is the photo?"

I stared down at the school photo of a little blond girl who could not have been over ten-years-old.

"It's from the beginning of the school year," Shelley said. "She's cut her hair since then."

I handed it back to her. "She's your only daughter?"

Shelley sighed as she tucked it back in her wallet. "Soul Man and me got a late start, so she's all we got. She's enough though."

"She's not boring you with baby pictures, is she?" Soul Man asked, wrapping an arm around Shelley's waist as he and Buster rejoined us.

Shelley slapped his chest. "They asked to see a picture of Christie Gail."

Her husband raised an eyebrow.

"It's true," Kate said. "We love kids."

I made a point not to look at Kate and see if her pants were on fire.

"Well, I'd better get back to Mack." Buster jangled the keys in his hand.

I remembered that Richard stayed with Mack and the baby, and wondered what the three of them had been up to while we'd been away. I was almost afraid to find out.

We said our farewells to Soul Man and Shelley outside the church while Buster locked up. As Kate and I walked to my car, I felt my purse vibrating. I dug my phone out and looked at the screen. Richard.

"We're on our way back," I said when I answered.

"I'm not at Lush anymore," Richard said.

I hesitated at my car door. "Where are you?"

"I'm going right to the source, Annabelle." Richard's voice was a couple of octaves higher than usual.

"The source of what?" I asked, ignoring the sound of Kate yanking on her door handle on the other side of the car.

"I'm outside the offices of *Capital Weddings*," he said. "I'm about to march inside and demand to know who has it in for me."

I groaned. This was not going to turn out well.

CHAPTER 9

I spotted Richard on the corner of I Street looking up at a glass-fronted office building with his arms crossed. Even though the wind whipped down the street and swirled my long hair into my face, Richard's short spiky hair was unruffled.

"What are you doing out here?" I asked as Kate and I hurried up to him. "You're going to freeze to death."

"I can't feel a thing," Richard said, his eyes not leaving the building. "I'm fueled by outrage."

"That's not a good sign," Kate said.

I followed his gaze. "So what's the plan? Are you trying to hex the staff at *Capital Weddings* from out here?"

He gave me a sidelong glance. "Don't be absurd."

This from the man who'd been known to have voodoo dolls made to look like people who'd offended him.

The glass door to a nearby Starbucks opened, and the scent of coffee wafted over to us, along with a blast of heat, both welcome as we stood outside in the cold. A woman in a puffy black jacket passed holding a red cardboard cup covered in snowflakes, and I looked at the tall cup longingly. I wouldn't mind ducking inside and getting a peppermint mocha, but I couldn't leave Richard.

"What happened to hanging out with Mack?" I asked. "Or was that all a ruse so you could come down here before I could talk you out of it?"

"If I hadn't wanted you to know I was here, I never would have called you," he said. "But you know there's only so much baby I can handle at a time. Once the little creature woke up, it was time for me to go."

"Why don't we discuss your plans for revenge over coffee and scones?" Kate asked, taking a step toward the Starbucks.

"I've abandoned my quest for revenge," Richard said.

"That was fast," Kate said, giving me a look that told me she didn't believe him. Knowing Richard, I wasn't convinced either.

"Right now I just want to know what happened." Richard's brows pressed together to form a wrinkle between his eyes. "I couldn't have gone from top caterer to off the list in the course of a year without reason."

"I maintain it could have been an error," I said. "You know the magazine's been using more and more interns to do their fact-checking."

"Then I'd like to meet the intern who was so bad at their job they forgot to list the city's best caterer." Richard squared his shoulders and headed for the entrance of the building.

Kate and I rushed to follow him, more for the intern's sake than anything else. We passed through the glass doors of the office building and crossed mouse-gray marble floors to a bank of elevators. Richard threw his arm out to catch a set of closing doors, and we hopped on behind him. There were only two men inside with us, and they both wore dark suits and power ties. We all faced forward.

"Don't you want to know what we discovered at the Born Again Biker Church?" Kate asked Richard in a low voice as the elevator surged upward.

"Do I have a choice?"

Kate ignored his comment. "To be honest, it was a bit of a bust. There's nothing but self storage in the direction the woman came from, and Soul Man and Shelley couldn't think of any women they knew who'd been pregnant."

One of the men in the elevator glanced over at us, but Kate didn't seem to notice.

"Soul Man?" Richard asked.

"The preacher," I explained. "Shelley is his wife. They were both very nice."

"So you're back to square one?"

"I don't think we ever got very far off square one," Kate said. "Annabelle thinks we need to meet more of the church members."

The elevator doors opened and one of the men stepped off, glancing back at us as he left.

"It's clearly connected to the church or someone who goes there," I said. "You have to go out of your way to find the place, so only someone with a strong connection would seek out a biker strip mall church in Northeast DC."

The other man raised his eyebrows as he stared down at his newspaper.

"We're going to go check out Bedlam," Kate said. "It's a biker bar in Adams Morgan where some of Buster and Mack's church friends hang out."

Richard twisted to face me. "You're going to a biker bar?"

"You should come with us," Kate said. "They even have a vegan menu."

"Vegan food at a biker bar?" Richard shuddered. "Perish the thought."

The elevator dinged and the doors opened.

"This is us," Richard said, striding off without a backward glance.

We followed him to the right where he threw open a set of glass doors with the words "Capital Weddings" written across them in swirling black letters. A sleek half-moon reception desk sat in the small lobby with two groupings of white furniture and copies of *Capital Weddings* magazines scattered across a glass coffee table.

A blond receptionist looked up at us and smiled. "Can I help you?"

"I certainly hope so," Richard began. "I've come to lodge a com—"

I stepped in front of him. "We'd like to speak to your editor in charge of the 'Best of' list. We don't have an appointment."

Her smile had faltered when Richard had started in on what was clearly meant to be a tirade, but she regained her sunny expression. "Of course. Let me see if Marcie is available. Who should I tell her is here?"

Richard opened his mouth, but I cut him off. "Annabelle Archer from Wedding Belles."

She seemed to recognize the name and nodded as she picked up her phone. I motioned for Richard and Kate to follow me to one of the sofas.

"Why didn't you let me talk?" Richard asked.

"Because you would have made that poor girl cry, and she had nothing to do with the list," I said, keeping my voice to a whisper. "Besides, if there really is a conspiracy against you, we don't want them to know you're here. This way we still have the element of surprise."

Richard sniffed and brushed the arm of his jacket. "I guess living with a detective is rubbing off on you, darling. You're getting positively sneaky."

I'd take that as a compliment and as an indication that Richard was getting used to the idea of me living with Reese.

"Annabelle!" A tall woman with jet-black hair appeared from around the corner. "I can't believe it's actually you. This is such good timing."

I stood up and accepted her hug, even though I didn't think I'd ever laid eyes on the woman. "Is it?"

She bobbed her head up and down. "I was going to ship you a box of magazines since you were one of our top vendors. Congratulations, by the way."

"Thanks." I swept a hand behind me. "Have you met my assistant, Kate, and my friend, Richard?"

Richard extended his hand in front of Kate. "Gerard. Richard Gerard." He gave her a pointed look. "As in Richard Gerard Catering."

"So nice to meet you both." Marcie shook his hand and then Kate's, but didn't seem to register anything when Richard said his company name. "Why don't you come back to my office, and we'll get you those magazines."

Richard held me back as we followed Marcie out of the lobby and into an open floor plan office with a hive of cubbies. His face looked distressed. "She didn't even recognize my name."

"It's not like she actually works in our industry," I said to him in my softest voice. "They may have a magazine about weddings, but when have you actually seen any of these people out at our weddings or industry events?"

Richard scanned the room even though we saw mostly the tops of heads and a few clusters of people talking. "Then why are they making decisions that affect all of our careers?"

"That's the million dollar question," I said.

Marcie paused when she reached an office in the corner with glass walls and floor-to-ceiling windows overlooking I Street. She waved at a pair of chairs across from a wooden desk. "Have a seat."

Kate and I sat while Richard hovered behind me. Marcie walked behind her desk and pressed an intercom button on her phone. "Marcus, can you bring me a box of our January issue?"

"Marcus?" Richard asked.

"He's my right-hand man." Marcie sat in her leather chair. "He's been with me for a few months now, and I couldn't have put the last issue together without him."

"Was he involved with gathering information for the list?" Richard asked.

Marcie tilted her head at Richard. "Actually he was. He took over most of that, which was amazing since it's such tedious work. How did you know? Do you know Marcus?"

"Here are those issues you requested." A young man with wavy blond hair entered the office, holding a cardboard box.

"I do know Marcus," Richard said, his hands on his hips and his eyes blazing.

Marcus saw Richard and dropped the box. It landed on his foot with a heavy thud, and Marcus shrieked in pain.

CHAPTER 10

"So Marcus worked for you?" I asked after Kate had found us a small table at the back of the Starbucks on I Street. We'd hustled Richard out of the *Capital Weddings* offices after his screams had started to gather a crowd. Marcus rolling around on the floor clutching his possibly broken foot hadn't helped matters.

Marcie had stood gaping while Richard hurled accusations of slander and defamation at the injured man until Kate and I had finally managed to drag him off. I'd have to call her later and apologize for the chaos and thank her for the magazines. I pushed the cardboard box under the table.

Richard slumped into his chair. "For almost a year. I brought him on to try to ease some of my workload."

"He's cute," Kate said, then shrugged when Richard glared at her. "What? He is. I mean, from what I could see before he started screaming and rolling around."

"Why don't you get us some coffees?" I said to her and held out my Starbucks card.

She waved me off and tapped her phone. "I use the app. This one's on me."

As the warmth from the coffee shop defrosted my fingers and toes,

I slipped off my coat and hung it on the back of my chair. "So clearly it didn't work out. What went wrong?"

"It started when Babette began ordering too much food," Richard said.

I looked at him. "Babette?"

"From the movie *Babette's Feast*. That's what I called him when he ordered enough food to feed the entire city for a dinner party for ten."

"You don't have a nickname for me or Kate, do you?" I asked.

"You mean like Laurel and Hardy, Punch and Judy, Laverne and Shirley?"

I leaned back. "Yes, like that."

Richard straightened. "Of course not, darling."

I wasn't sure if I believed him, but I also wasn't sure if I wanted to know. "So he ordered too much food, and you fired him?"

"No. That was only the beginning, even though I had to talk our chef out of murdering him when our food costs went through the roof," Richard said. "He didn't take direction well and saw himself as a creative visionary instead of my assistant."

I could see how that would cause problems since Richard considered himself a creative visionary, and his company certainly wasn't big enough for two.

"So you guys didn't get along well. That's not unheard of in the wedding world. Why did it end so badly?"

"Do you remember my big corporate client?" Richard put his elbows on the small round table and rested his chin on his hands. "The one who gave me a few events every month?"

"I remember you mentioning them," I said. "Drop-off lunches, board meetings, annual holiday parties."

Kate returned carrying a cardboard holder with three large holiday cups covered with white plastic lids. "Peppermint mocha for Annabelle, a caramel brûlée latte for Richard, and a sugar-free nonfat no whip vanilla latte for me." She slapped a brown paper bag on the table. "And some scones. This occasion calls for carb loading."

Richard took the cup she proffered. "Do you think you could have come up with a more pretentious coffee order?"

"Absolutely." Kate winked at him. "I could have asked for soy milk."

"So, the corporate client?" I prodded, taking a sip of my minty mocha and enjoying the full-fat, sugar-filled, whipped-cream-topped coffee.

"Right," Richard said as Kate sat down. "I guess Marcus felt he wasn't getting the respect or creative license he deserved, so he changed one of my proposals that went out to my bigwig client."

"Changed it how?" Kate opened the paper bag and took out a scone.

"Added so much profanity it would have made a sailor blush."

I almost choked on my drink. "To a catering proposal?"

"Yep." Color filled Richard's cheeks. "Every other word was an F-bomb, and the descriptions of the food were so dirty I couldn't even understand half of them."

"That is dirty," Kate said with wide eyes as she put a piece of scone in her mouth and crumbs fell onto her lap.

"So you fired him?" I asked.

"Spectacularly," Richard said. "I told him he'd never work in the event industry again, but I guess I didn't consider that he'd go work for a magazine about the event industry."

Kate took a long sip and dabbed at her upper lip, even though she had no whipped cream to dab off. "Are we sure he left your name off the list on purpose?"

"You saw the way he reacted to seeing Richard." I tore a corner off of Kate's scone. "He looked as guilty as anyone I've ever seen."

"Marcus is smart, even if he can't cater to save his life." Richard drummed his fingers on the table. "It's clear to me he maneuvered his way into the magazine, made himself indispensable, and then took over the list. He played the long game without anyone knowing it."

I chewed on my bite of cinnamon scone and thought for a moment. Richard's version of how it had played out seemed pretty convincing to me, and it was the only reasonable explanation as to why Richard Gerard Catering would be omitted from a list they'd topped for years.

"So what can we do about it?" Kate asked.

"The better question is how can we make it look like an accident?" Richard asked.

I shushed him as Kate giggled. "You know we shouldn't even be joking about that."

"Just because people tend to drop dead around us?" Kate asked. "If you think about it, it's the perfect cover. The police are used to us finding murder victims. They never expect us to produce one."

I shot her a look. "I still don't think we should joke about murder. Especially not one in which Richard would be the primary suspect."

Richard frowned. "That does put a damper on my plans."

"I'll call Marcie and talk to her after things have cooled off a bit," I said. "I'm sure once I explain you were left off the list and why her assistant might have been motivated to leave you off on purpose, she'll understand."

"But what can she do?" Richard threw his hands in the air. "It's not like they can reprint thousands of copies." He paused. "You don't think they'd reprint it, do you?"

I shook my head. "Nope."

His shoulders slumped. "So that's it then. Even though I was knocked off the list by a vengeful former employee, there's nothing I can do about it. Even if the magazine issues an apology or prints an addition in a future issue, I'm still not on the list for an entire year."

I patted his hand. "I'm really sorry, Richard."

"You know what would make you feel better?" Kate said, her eyes bright.

"I'm almost afraid to ask," Richard said.

"You should come with us to Bedlam." Kate rubbed her hands together. "It'll take your mind off all of this."

"I'm sure the last thing Richard wants to do is hang around a loud bar with a bunch of bikers," I said.

Richard sat up. "I don't know. Maybe a biker bar would be fun."

I tried to keep my mouth from dangling open.

Richard tapped his chin. "The more I think about it, the better it sounds. How long have I been working myself to the bone to build up my business? Years." He snapped his fingers. "And it can all be taken away from me like that."

"It hasn't all been taken away from you," I said.

"First, I lost my biggest corporate client, and now I stand to lose a significant amount of wedding business." Richard smacked his hand on the table. "If anyone deserves a night to cut loose, it's me."

"That's the spirit." Kate smacked her hand on the table as well.

Richard stood up. "If we're going to Bedlam tonight, then I need to dash."

I glanced at the clock on the wall. "We still have a few hours."

"Not if I'm going to put together an appropriate outfit," he said. "I'm not sure what kind of shape my leather is in."

"Leather?" My voice came out a squeak.

Richard waved his fingers up and down in front of me. "If we're going to do this, we're going to do it right. Don't even think of wearing a sweater set and pedal pushers, darling."

I opened my mouth to say that I didn't own a pair of pedal pushers, but Richard was already flouncing out of the coffee shop.

"This should be fun," Kate said.

This should be a disaster, I thought.

CHAPTER 11

"I'm not so sure about this." I tugged at the shimmery-black miniskirt and felt glad I'd paired it with black tights. At least they kept my legs somewhat warm, which was more than I could say for the red sequined tank top. I rubbed my arms as I hurried along behind my assistant.

"You look great." Kate turned and flicked her eyes up and down my outfit as she walked ahead of me on Eighteenth Street. "My clothes almost look as good on you as they do on me."

I dodged a few people as I tried to navigate the sidewalk behind her in heels. "I still insist what I had on was fine."

Kate shot me a look over her shoulder. "Sure it was, if we were welcoming a classroom of first graders back to school." She swept an arm wide and almost belted someone. "This is Adams Morgan. Home of hole-in-the-wall restaurants and grimy bars."

I glanced around at the jumble of neon signs illuminating the dark and the lines snaking out of basement entrances. The air smelled of ethnic food and pulsed with the sounds of club music. I turned as we passed a townhouse with two lines—one leading upstairs to a brightly lit bar called "Heaven" and another twisting down to a dark club glowing with red light and a sign indicating "Hell." Eighties music spilled out of Hell along with college-aged kids.

"I'm definitely having second thoughts," I said, stepping over a puddle of something unidentifiable on the sidewalk.

Kate stopped as we reached a nondescript building with the word "Bedlam" hanging above the door in Gothic letters. "I thought you wanted to help Buster and Mack find the baby's mother."

"You know I do," I said. "I'm just wondering if there's a way that doesn't involve me showing so much skin."

"We usually do things your way." Kate patted my arm. "Tonight we're trying the Kate method of investigation."

Usually Kate's method of anything involved lots of flirting and not much else.

"As long as we actually do some investigating," I said as I eyed the dark bar with the heavy wooden door.

Kate winked at me. "Follow my lead."

I trailed inside after her and paused for a moment to let my eyes adjust. Even though it was nighttime, the street outside was bright with street lamps and neon signs and headlamps from passing cars. Inside Bedlam, the lights were dim and the furnishings were dark. Tall black leather banquettes lined the walls, which were made of dark wood paneling. A lamp hung over a pool table in the back, and a long mahogany bar stretched down one side of the place dotted with leather-topped barstools. I didn't notice any Harley-Davidson signs, but most of the patrons lounging at tables and clustered around the pool table looked like versions of Buster and Mack.

Kate sashayed up to the bar and hopped onto a barstool, ordering a beer for each of us before I'd figured out how to sit down without my skirt riding up to my belly button. I decided to lean against the bar instead.

The bartender, who had a gray mustache that curled up at the ends, set two bottles in front of us and his eyes settled on me. "You girls sure you aren't looking for Heaven and Hell?"

I laughed, trying to sound causal. It came out sounding strangled. "We're friends with Buster and Mack. And Soul Man."

The bartender raised a bushy eyebrow and nodded. "None of them are here tonight, but some of the other boys are." He gestured toward the group playing pool.

"Thanks." I took a swig of beer and tried not to grimace as I swallowed it. Beer was not my drink of choice and especially not domestic light beer. I pulled one of my heels off the sticky floor. I suspected more beer had been spilled on the floor at Bedlam than had been drunk.

Kate leaned in to me. "Good thing Richard isn't here. He'd run out of hand sanitizer within five minutes."

I feared she was right. "He said he'd meet us here, but maybe he changed his mind."

"I'll bet dollars and doughnuts he's home plotting revenge," Kate said.

"Dollars *to* doughnuts," I corrected, but without much enthusiasm. Richard had been as disheartened as I'd ever seen him this afternoon, and I hoped he wasn't home alone getting more depressed.

"Well, smack my tush and call me Judy!"

Kate and I both turned toward the familiar voice. I squinted at the men playing pool and shook my head. "Is that . . . ?"

"It sure is," Kate said, gaping at the lean man dressed head to toe in black leather. "How did Richard beat us here?"

"I don't know, but it looks like he's been here for a while."

Kate watched Richard high five the burly men he was playing with. "And I think he's winning."

I pulled her with me as I walked over to him. As we got closer, I could tell that his leather was shiny and unmarred, unlike the other men whose jackets and vests were worn and dull and covered in patches. There was a distinct possibility that Richard had gone out and purchased his outfit right after we'd left him. Not that I had any clue where you bought biker wear in Washington.

"Annabelle! Kate!" He beamed at us and raised a beer bottle. "You made it."

I was speechless. Not only was Richard dressed in leather and playing pool with a bunch of bikers, he was drinking beer out of a bottle without wiping the top first. Things were worse than I'd thought.

"Are you okay?" I asked.

He waved a hand at me. "I'm better than okay. I'm great." He jerked his head toward the three men standing with him. "Slim, Stray Dog, and Rubble have helped me realize that I was upset over nothing."

I glanced at the men and nodded greetings. "Thanks for helping him out, guys."

"Don't mention it," the biggest man said, thumping Richard on the back. "We know what it's like to be in a low place."

Had Richard told them details or had he been vague? I doubted men named Stray Dog and Rubble had ever fallen into a funk over a listing in a wedding magazine.

Richard grinned at the man. "Slim here is one of the deacons at Buster and Mack's church. He's very wise."

I noticed that Richard was slurring his speech and wondered how many beers he'd put away before we arrived.

"You two are friends with Buster and Mack?" A man with heavy stubble and a black T-shirt stretched tight over his belly switched his pool cue from one hand to the other.

"We're friends from work," I said. "Do you all go to the Born Again Biker Church?"

The men nodded. Jackpot.

"Crazy about the baby, isn't it?" Kate asked as she leaned one hand against the edge of the pool table.

The men murmured agreement.

"Any idea who could have left her?" I asked.

They shook their heads.

"We don't got many female members," Slim said. "And if any of our members got some girl in trouble, I hope he would have come to us. We don't judge each other. We get enough of that from the outside world."

The shortest and stockiest man leaned down on the pool table to take a shot. "Most of us got girlfriends or wives now."

"Rubble's right," the stubbly man said. "I can't think of a one of us who's still out there playing around."

"Any thoughts about who might have had reason to leave their baby at your church?" I asked.

Slim tilted his head for a moment before raising and lowering one beefy shoulder. "Can't think of anyone." He looked at the man with the five o'clock shadow. "Stray Dog? You're tight with the younger guys."

Stray Dog frowned. "You got me. I don't think I've laid eyes on a pregnant lady in months."

"So much for that," Kate said to me.

A cocktail waitress in black shorts and a spaghetti strap white top slapped a laminated menu on a nearby high top table. "Y'all want any food?"

Kate picked up the menu while the blond waitress tapped her toe impatiently. "I might give the grilled vegan wrap a try."

"Grilled vegans?" Richard made a face. "No thank you."

I looked over Kate's shoulder. "It's made with portobellos, not actual vegans."

"That sounds only slightly better," Richard said.

"We should probably be going," I said, noticing Richard leaning against Slim.

Richard blew a raspberry. "Nonsense. The night is young. Live a little, Annabelle."

"I, for one, want to see what Richard's like when he cuts loose." Kate handed the menu to the waitress. "We'll get the Mexican pizza to share."

Richard shook his hips. "Ole'!"

Oh boy.

"You sure we're not gate crashing?" I asked Slim.

"Naw," he said. "It's not like you're the only outsiders here." He pointed over my shoulder. "I think those two are lost."

Richard's glazed eyes popped open. "I must be losing my mind."

I swiveled my head and stifled a groan. Kate inhaled sharply beside me. "Is it too late to hide?"

"There you are, dearie!" Leatrice called out as she thrust a hand high in the air to wave as the other hand held Fern's arm.

"I'll race you out the back," I said.

CHAPTER 12

"What are you wearing?" I asked Leatrice when she and Fern joined us.

She spun around and the bright-red felt skirt belled out around her. The skirt was decorated with vividly colored sequined appliqués of nutcrackers, angels, and wrapped presents. "It's called a Christmas tree skirt. Do you like it?"

"You're wearing a Christmas tree skirt?"

Leatrice looked at me like I was a simpleton. "Well, it is the Christmas season. This is a very popular item on the Home Shopping Network. I'm sure you'll see other people wearing them around."

"I doubt it." I didn't have the heart to break it to her that the skirt was meant to wrap around the base of a Christmas tree. At least she was in season.

"Fern said we were going to a restaurant, so I thought I should dress up." Leatrice glanced around her, then lifted her red cowboy boots off the sticky floor one at a time. "Restaurants downtown sure have gotten casual."

"How did you know we were here?" I asked Fern.

He wore a pair of black jeans and a white T-shirt with what

appeared to be a pack of cigarettes rolled up in the sleeve. His hair, usually tied back in a bun or ponytail, was brushed up into a pompadour with a ducktail of dark hair flipped up at the nape of his neck. "Kate texted me."

I narrowed my eyes at her.

"What?" She dropped her voice. "I didn't know Leatrice would tag along. Or dress more like a drag queen than him."

I pointed at the cigarettes in Fern's sleeve. "Since when do you smoke?"

"I don't." He grinned and flexed an arm muscle. "This is my 'bad boy' look since my leather was at the cleaners."

Did everyone own leather except for me?

"What are you drinking, little lady?" Slim asked Leatrice.

She blushed. "Well, aren't you the gentleman? I'll have a Shirley Temple with extra cherries."

Fern winked at him. "Make that two, sweetie, but instead of extra cherries I'll have extra vodka."

Slim ambled off to the bar while Rubble and Stray Dog resumed their game of pool. As I cast a glance at my ridiculously dressed friends, I mentally declared the evening a bust. We'd only met a few members of the Born Again Biker Church, and we didn't have leads on any new blondes who may have left baby Merry on the doorstep. I had to admit to myself that the baby may have been left at random, and there was a distinct possibility we'd never track down the mother. I felt a twinge of sadness for the baby, but reminded myself that she was currently being spoiled to death by Buster and Mack.

"We're heading out pretty soon," I said. "Richard's probably reached his limit."

Fern did a double take as his eyes rested on Richard slumped against a pool cue. "I didn't recognize him without his schoolmarm posture."

"He's self-medicating," Kate said in a whisper that was anything but. "After the fiasco with C-A-P—"

"I may be bereft and without a reason to live," Richard interrupted her, straightening up, "but I have not lost my ability to spell, thank you very much." He tried to put one hand on the pool table in a jaunty stance but missed and stumbled against Kate.

As the pair almost tumbled to the floor, I shook my head and jerked a finger toward the bar. "Let me stop Slim from ordering those drinks. I don't want to have to carry anyone else out of here."

I sidled up to Slim as he leaned against the mahogany bar with one booted foot resting on the brass railing at the bottom. He nodded at me.

"Is it too late to cancel those orders?" I asked. "I probably should get my friends home."

"Nix those drinks, Francie," Slim called out to a thin woman at the other end. The burly bartender who'd been working when we'd entered must have gone on break. The thirtysomething woman now tending bar wore a bright-white T-shirt over tight jeans, and her lips shone with coral-pink lip gloss.

The woman walked down to our end and ran a hand through the frosted hair that fell in feathers around her face. "Even the club soda with lime?"

Slim gave a gruff laugh. "Naw. Keep that."

The woman winked at him, filled a rocks glass with club soda, dropped a lime in it, and passed it across the bar. "Don't drink it too fast, big guy."

Another laugh from Slim as he took a swallow.

"I'd better settle my tab," I told the woman, pulling out some folded bills I'd tucked in my pocket earlier.

Slim waved my money away. "I got it. Any friends of Buster's and Mack's are friends of mine."

"That's very sweet," I protested, "but you don't need to do that."

He nodded at the bartender. "It's done." He cut his eyes to Richard behind us. "And both of the drinks the nervous fella had."

"Richard only had two drinks?" I asked.

"The first one was a boilermaker, so that may have been the problem," Slim said. "Your friend isn't much of a drinker, is he?"

"Not unless it's champagne or fine wine," I said, wishing I'd been there to see Richard drop a shot of whiskey into a beer mug and drink them both. I could count on one hand the number of times I'd seen either beverage pass his lips. And I'd have fingers to spare.

Slim studied me for a second. "Buster and Mack haven't brought you on a ride along, have they?"

"A ride along?" I asked, shaking my head. "On their bikes?"

"We got a bunch more church members who aren't here but who'll be at our event tomorrow." Slim tossed back the rest of his club soda and spit the chewed up lime into the bottom of the glass. "Meet us at the church parking lot at ten a.m. and you can hop on the back with a couple of us and see what we do."

"What do you mean?" I asked, my heart already racing at the thought of riding on the back of a Harley. It made me nervous just to look at them, much less ride on them.

"We're providing protection for a funeral tomorrow." Slim thunked the glass on the bar. "You want to know what we're really about, that's where you'll learn."

"Okay," I said before I could think better of it. I did want to meet more church members, and after reading about what the church did to help people they thought were unfairly judged, a part of me wanted to see these reformed bikers in action. "We'll be there."

Slim grinned at me and then looked at the bartender. "We'll make her a biker chick yet, Francie."

The bartender looked me up and down as Slim walked back to the pool table. "You won't find better men than Slim and his boys."

"We're friends with Buster and Mack," I said, hoping their names gave me some instant street cred I was lacking.

Recognition flashed across her face, and she nodded. "They don't come in here much, but they're good people."

I watched her flick a pale strand of hair off her face. "Sounds like you've known the Road Riders for Jesus for a while."

"We get all kinds in here, but they're special." She popped the cap off a Bud Light bottle and slid it over to me. "On the house."

The last thing I wanted was another beer, but I raised it and thanked her as she moved off to the far end of the bar. I took as small a sip as humanly possible and stared at the woman's frosted blonde hair, wondering if there was any chance she'd been the one to leave the baby on the doorstep of the church she clearly admired.

CHAPTER 13

"Why is there so much light?" Richard groaned as he dragged a blanket over his head and rolled over on the couch.

I padded into my living room, dodging the hanging paper stars, and set a mug of coffee on the coffee table for him. "Maybe because it's morning?"

"Impossible," Richard mumbled from under the beige cashmere throw. "I just fell asleep. At least I think I did. The details are a little fuzzy."

I popped the top on one of the bottled Frappuccinos I depended on to give me my morning caffeine and sugar rush and sat across from him in the yellow twill chair, tucking my bare feet under me to keep them warm. "I'm sure they are. You refused to leave Bedlam without doing a shot of tequila with Stray Dog."

Richard threw the blanket back and sat up. "That's absurd. When have you ever known me to do a shot of . . ." He raised a hand to his forehead. "Oh, good heavens. Did I suffer a head injury last night?"

I took a swig of my cold mocha drink and let my eyes close for a moment as I swallowed. I may not have liked to drink regular coffee, but add chocolate, lots of sugar, and milk, and I was hooked. "Like I said, there was tequila."

He blinked a few times, moving his hand over his eyes to block the light streaming in from the tall windows on one side of the room. "Who's Stray Dog?"

"According to you, he's your new best friend," I said, grinning.

Richard flushed and his eyes caught the pile of black leather clothes folded over the far arm of the couch. "It's starting to come back to me."

I motioned to the coffee mug. "Reese thought you might still be in need of sobering up."

Richard began to reach for the coffee and froze. "Reese?"

My boyfriend walked into the room, his own travel mug in hand. He wore gray pants and a black half-zip sweater, and his hair still looked damp from the shower. "Look who's alive."

Richard pulled the throw up higher over his bare chest and managed a weak smile. "Good morning, Detective. Fancy meeting you here."

Reese took a drink from his tall cup, and the corner of his mouth twitched up. "Just what I was thinking."

Richard gave him a manufactured laugh, his cheeks reddening even more.

"You have to go in to work?" I asked Reese.

"In a bit." His eyes flitted to Richard. "I thought I'd head out and give you two some time alone."

"Very considerate of you," Richard said.

I drained the last of my bottled coffee and stood. "No need. Kate and I are heading out on a ride with the Road Riders for Jesus."

Richard blinked at me rapidly, taking in my jeans and snug-fitting white T-shirt with the Wedding Belles logo on the front. "You and Kate are riding Harleys now? How long was I out?"

"Are you sure about this?" Reese asked, taking hold of one of my belt loops and pulling me close. "Not that it isn't sexy to think of you on the back of a motorcycle, but are you sure this is safe?"

The thought of riding on the back of a Harley still made my stomach flutter, but I pushed aside my nerves and nodded with more confidence than I felt. "It's the best way to meet more people who're connected to the church. Anyway, I'm not going alone. Kate will be with me."

Reese raised an eyebrow. "That doesn't make me feel any better."

"Kate's better than you'd think in pressure situations," I said. "You can't work on weddings for so many years and not be."

A phone trilled and we all looked around. Reese touched his back pocket and shook his head. "Not mine."

Richard hunted around in the folds of the blanket until he found his ringing phone, cleared his throat, and answered it. "Richard Gerard Catering. This is Richard."

I turned to Reese as Richard began talking in his most official voice to someone who was clearly a client. "I thought of something last night. Is there any way to do a search of local hospitals and see who's given birth in the past month?"

"I'm assuming this means you've turned up nothing?" he asked. When I didn't answer, Reese angled his head at me. "You're kidding about the hospitals, right?"

"Why not? If we had a list, we could find out if each mother was in possession of her baby."

"First of all, there are quite a few hospitals in the metro DC area. More if you include the suburbs." Reese counted off a finger and then raised another one. "And secondly, there are privacy laws. I can't go pulling birth records all over the city for something that isn't even an official case. I'd like to keep my job if you don't mind."

Well, when he put it like that.

Richard hung up and dropped his phone on the couch. "Are you still going on about that baby?" He stood and wrapped the throw around himself, throwing one end over his shoulder. "I'm telling you, Annabelle, as much as I'd love to see the little poop machine exit our lives as quickly as possible, you're looking for a needle in a haystack."

"Richard's right," Reese said. "The chances of locating the woman who left the child are slim. She abandoned the baby for a reason, and she clearly doesn't want anyone to know. I hate to think of the child being orphaned, but if her parents don't want her, she may be better off finding a family that does."

Richard made a surprised little noise. "Would you look at that? The two men in your life agree on something."

I wasn't sure what it said about me that one of the most important men in my life stood wearing a cashmere throw as a toga, but I didn't dwell on it. If I was being honest with myself, I knew they were both right. So far we had almost no leads, and it felt like we were shooting in the dark.

"I promised Buster and Mack that I'd try," I said. "I owe it to them."

Reese crossed to the coat rack in the corner and plucked his leather jacket from one of the hooks. He held it out as I slipped my arms inside. "If you're going to do this, you should do it right."

Even though it was a little big on me, the well-worn leather held traces of my boyfriend's aftershave. I popped the collar. "Better?"

"Heaven preserve us," Richard muttered, scooping up his own leather clothes from the end of the couch.

Reese pulled me to him by the collar, and my body pressed against his. "I'm digging this bad girl look. You sure you have to leave right now?"

"At least wait until I do," Richard said as he clucked disapprovingly.

Reese kissed me a bit more intensely than usual, then released me. I tried to catch my breath as I felt the heat creep up my face. I cleared my throat and turned to Richard, trying to act like I wasn't flustered. "Are you sure you're okay about the whole *Capital Weddings* thing? You're not going to rush off and try to blow up their office while I'm gone, are you?"

"Old news, darling," he said with a wave of his hand. "I've got more things to do than plot revenge on my old employee Marcus."

I suspected revenge was still on the to-do list even if it had moved down a few notches. "Like?"

"For one, that was Darla on the phone, and she wants all the dishes with cranberries, nutmeg, and nuts to be removed from the menu. Actually, it's the bride who wants to commit this travesty. Now I have to figure out how to rework the menu so it isn't bland and boring."

Even though he was complaining, I knew he liked being tasked with a challenge. I liked the fact that it would take his mind off 'the list.' "If you've already prepped some of the food with festive flavors, we could always use it for our team holiday party on Thursday."

"Thursday?" Richard nearly dropped his armful of clothes. "We're throwing together a party in two days?"

"It's just our crew," I said. "Nothing fancy."

Richard gave me a disapproving look. "Just because it's small, doesn't mean it shouldn't be done properly." He tapped his chin. "It's too late for custom signage, but I could probably come up with a signature cocktail. And we need a theme. Maybe Christmas in Caracas or a Hannukah in Havana?"

"The theme is 'old wedding stuff,'" I said. "I've got an office filled with leftover cocktail napkins, stir sticks, striped paper straws, and favors that I never want to see again. We're going to use it all, so if you can come up with a drink that works with that, be my guest."

Richard looked aghast for a moment, then he cocked his head. "It's so horribly kitsch, it could work."

There was a knock on the door and Reese opened it. Kate stood in the doorway in hip-hugger jeans and a Wedding Belles T-shirt that matched mine peeking out from under a brown leather bomber jacket. Her usually smooth bob was tousled, and dark eyeliner made her eyes look smoky. "Ready to ride?"

Richard gave her the once-over. "The descent from Wedding Belle to Hell's Angel didn't take long."

Kate winked at him. "You should join us on the dark side."

"Not on your life," Richard said with a sniff. "I have to redesign the wedding menu for your Scrooge of a bride, plus the detective and I have plenty to do here to get this place ready for the holiday party."

Reese's head swiveled to him. "Wait? What?"

"I certainly can't do it all by myself," Richard called over his shoulder as he headed down the hall with his clothes, dragging the blanket behind him. "You do live here now. That makes you one of us."

"Look at the bright side," I said as I stepped into the hall with Kate. "You seem to be 'in' with Richard."

Reese let out a deep sigh as he watched me go. "Talk about a double-edged sword."

CHAPTER 14

"I'm starting to feel guilty," I said as Kate swung her car into the parking lot of the Born Again Biker Church. "Do you think I should have left Reese with Richard? You know how he gets when he's on a tear about something."

"Oh, I know how Richard gets." Kate turned off the car engine and opened her door. "If I were you, I'd be more concerned that Reese might shoot him."

"That's very comforting," I said, getting out and following Kate toward the people clustered around the shiny-chrome Harleys in front of the church. Each bike had a large American flag attached to its bumper that waved in the wind.

I felt a nervous flutter as I took in the number of tattoos, piercings, black bandanas, and leather in the group. Most of the men had either sun-weathered faces or beards, and the women showed cleavage or midriffs or both, despite the cold weather.

I spotted Slim, and he waved a hand in greeting as we approached. "You made it. Wasn't sure if the idea of a bunch of bikers might have scared you away."

"We're tougher than we look," Kate rested one hand on her jutted-out hip.

"We work with brides," I said. "Not much scares us anymore."

Slim chuckled. "Fair enough. You're with me and she's with Stray Dog." He handed us both black skullcap helmets before hooking one over his own head. He threw a leg over the seat of a low motorcycle and motioned behind him. "Hop on."

I watched Kate jump on behind the stubbly younger man from the bar as he revved his engine. I eyed Slim's bike for a second before taking a deep breath and straddling the seat behind him, the large flag at my back. He gunned the motor, and I threw my arms around his waist seconds before we lurched forward. As the other bikes around me roared to life and we left the parking lot in a double line, I pressed my eyes closed.

Since we were still in the city, I knew we weren't going very fast, but the heavy vibration of the bike and the throaty rumbling of the engine made me tighten my grip. I felt the wind whip my face and cut through my jeans as we accelerated. I opened my eyes long enough to see we were heading out of DC, then I closed them again. As I concentrated on breathing and trying not to freeze to death, I huddled behind Slim and felt grateful that he wasn't so slim.

After a while, the bike slowed, the wind died down, and Slim leaned into a turn. I blinked a few times as we pulled up to the entrance to a cemetery and tried to loosen my grip on the big man in front of me. I heard Kate whoop as the entire procession of bikes rolled to a stop.

"That was amazing," she said, running up to me and thumping me on the back. "Wasn't it?"

I pulled off my helmet and tried to force my frigid lips into a believable grin. "Amazing."

Slim twisted around and winked at me. "You don't look too worse for wear."

I peeled myself from the leather seat and held onto the back of the bike for a moment, feeling like my entire body was still vibrating. "I'm good. Thanks."

"Cheese and crackers! Annabelle? Kate?"

Mack's voice made me turn. "Surprise," I managed to say in a steady voice.

The burly florist gaped at us, his mouth a perfect circle surrounded by his dark-red goatee. "What are you two doing here?"

"What do you think?" I asked. "We're trying to gather more information about anyone who might have left baby Merry, remember?"

Mack's eyebrows lifted, then his eyes slid away from mine. "Of course. I guess I didn't know you were so determined."

Kate elbowed him. "You know Annabelle once she gets her teeth into an investigation."

"So no luck so far?" Mack asked.

"Not really," I admitted. "My only lead is Francie at Bedlam."

"The bartender?" Mack asked. "I don't know if you talked to her for long, but she's not the maternal type."

"All the more reason she'd want to give up a baby," I said.

Mack looked at me like I'd lost my mind. "If she'd gotten pregnant, maybe, but that skinny thing hasn't gained a pound in all the time I've known her."

I felt deflated, even though I knew she'd been a long shot.

Kate put an arm around my shoulders. "I guess it's back to the drawing room."

"Or the drawing board," I said and couldn't help noticing Mack trying to hide his pleasure.

Before I could ask him if I was wasting my time searching for this mystery mother, I heard loud voices from across the street.

Mack's face darkened. "Diddly darn, those people make me so mad I could spit!"

Knowing Mack and his aversion to cursing, these were harsh words. I followed his narrowed eyes to the small group of protestors across from us holding neon-hued signs and chanting behind a police barrier.

Kate put a hand over her mouth. "Those signs are horrible. What's wrong with those people?"

Mack's eyebrows pressed together. "That so-called church thinks they have the right to pass judgment on the entire world."

I glanced behind me at the gravesite with a dark-green tent erected over several rows of chairs. Sprays of white flowers on stands crowded the gravestone. "Whose funeral is this?"

"A soldier killed in combat," Soul Man said, joining us. His wife stood a few feet away talking to some of the other women.

I felt a lump in my throat and rising fury at the protestors. "So what do we do?"

The biker preacher crossed his arms over his chest and jerked his head toward the small but noisy group. "Since we've been invited by the family, we're going to move a row of bikes in front of them so the family can't see or hear the protest when they arrive."

I balled my hands into fists and felt my planner instinct kick in. "Let's do it."

Slim nodded at me and got back on his bike with me behind him. Stray Dog and Kate followed us and about ten other bikers as we positioned ourselves in front of the meager protest. The shouts were louder since they were right behind me, and I twisted to see a wiry gray-haired man shaking a sign so close I could have reached out and grabbed it. I fought the instinct to snatch it from him and whack him over the head.

"I'll stay on the bike and rev the engine as needed," Slim said. "You take the flag and stand in front of me to block the view."

As I jumped off the bike and pulled the flag from its holder, I glanced up and saw the woman next to the gray-haired man staring at me. Unlike the frenzied man beside her, she didn't shake her sign and she wasn't screaming. She looked like she wanted to be anywhere but there. But she was there, I reminded myself, and I wondered if she felt any shame at what she was doing. I gave her what I hoped was a look of disgust and returned to my task, lifting the flag and walking to stand in front of Slim.

Mack backed his bike next to Slim's and took his own flag from the back, standing next to me as the striped fabric snapped in the wind around us.

"I'm assuming Buster is watching Merry," I said, making my voice a near shout to be heard over the motorcycle motors and the protesters.

He nodded. "This is no place for a baby."

I agreed. I wondered how much longer they would be content juggling a newborn, a thriving business, and their Christian biker gang.

"Did you just poke me?" Kate's shriek rose above the noise.

I turned to see a protestor with a bad perm and dark roots that made her look like a blond skunk holding a sign inches from Kate. Before I could remind Kate that the Road Riders for Jesus were a nonviolent Christian biker gang, the woman jabbed Kate so hard she stumbled back and fell into Stray Dog's lap.

So much for a nice ride in the country, I thought as chaos erupted around me.

CHAPTER 15

"What on earth happened to you two?" Richard asked as Kate and I walked in the door to my apartment, his head peeking over the open divide between my living room and kitchen.

I sniffed the air and almost coughed as I inhaled the heavy scent of cinnamon. "Are you baking?"

He walked out holding a wooden spoon. "No, I'm mulling spices." He waved the spoon in the direction of Kate's face and the faintly purple mark on her left cheekbone. "Should I get a steak for that bruise?" He glanced at my filthy T-shirt. "And some Spray-and-Wash for that shirt?"

"Do I have steaks?" I asked, wondering if he'd taken it upon himself to stock my kitchen like he used to do back when I was single.

He gave a small snort as he shook his head. "Of course not. Your kitchen is a wasteland. It took all my creativity to pull together the mulling spices."

"I'm fine," Kate said, heading for the couch and shrugging off her bomber jacket. "You should see the other chick."

Richard raised a perfectly arched eyebrow. "I take it the ride didn't go well?"

"The ride was great," Kate said. "We just had a bit of a disagreement with the people protesting the funeral."

Richard looked bewildered, so I brought him up to speed on the funeral and the protesters and the melee that the police broke up and Slim and Stray Dog had to drag Kate out of.

"It sounds like you were on the side of right," Richard said, appraising Kate with a look of admiration. "Well done, darling." He turned his eyes to me. "And where were you while Kate was channeling her inner lady wrestler?"

"Annabelle tried to help, but she got tangled up in the bikes," Kate said.

That was a gracious way of saying I'd tripped and fallen flat on my face in the dirt. Mack had finally picked me up, rescuing me from being trampled to death by everyone running to the fight. By the time I'd gotten my bearings and recovered from being stepped on by more than one heavyset biker, the brawl had been over.

Richard patted my arm then wiped his hand on the Santa Claus apron tied around his neck. "Better luck next time."

As far as I was concerned, there wouldn't be a next time. As good as it made me feel to act as a human shield for the soldier's funeral, I'd come to one definite conclusion. Harleys were not for me. I could understand why people loved them, and I didn't deny the rush I'd gotten from the roar of the motor coursing through my body, but the bad-ass bikes made me feel a little *too* invincible. Another few rides on a cruiser, and I was afraid I'd be putting my difficult brides in headlocks.

I breathed in again as I slipped off Reese's leather jacket. "Do I smell curry?"

Richard spun on his heels and returned to the kitchen. "Like I said, I had to improvise. It did give me a brilliant theme for our holiday party though."

I wiped the last traces of dirt from my boyfriend's jacket as I hung it back on the coat rack and exchanged a glance with Kate. Every holiday season Richard decked out his offices in his own totally unique spin on a theme that over the years had ranged from Bolshevik glamour to Tibetan chic.

"Didn't we agree the theme was leftover stuff from past brides?" I asked.

"That doesn't have much of a ring to it," Richard called after he pressed the automatic ice maker, and I heard the freezer spit out a few cubes. "But Taj Ma-Holidays does, doesn't it?"

Taj Ma-Holidays? Kate mouthed to me.

Richard's head appeared over the dividing counter. "As in Taj Mahal. Get it?"

Oh, I got it.

"We can serve Curry Kwanza cheese puffs, Merry Mango lassies, and Dreidel Dreidel Dahl." Richard clapped his hand. "I've planned out a menu that covers every winter holiday."

Kate sighed. "What's wrong with crantinis and cutout cookies?"

Richard sucked in air. "I guess nothing if you want to be predictable."

"Do you remember what happened to your creative holiday decor last year?" I asked, flopping down in the chair across from Kate.

"You mean my Christmas in the Casbah, an Arabic interpretation of the holidays?" Richard marched out and handed Kate an ice pack wrapped in a red-striped dish towel. "It would have been worthy of *Architectural Digest* if Jim's insane flying squirrel hadn't destroyed it."

"Your catering captain brought Rocky to the office again?" Kate sat forward as she touched the ice to her bruise. "I don't think I heard this."

"Really?" I muttered. "He complained about it for weeks. At least it felt like weeks."

Richard shot me a look. "That flying rodent scattered the sand I'd put around the Christmas tree so it would look like it was sitting in the desert. The sand dunes were ruined. Then he ran up the tree and clung to the very top, bending it over until it almost touched the floor before he jumped off. Of course the tree snapped back, and my camel tree topper flew across the room and crashed into the bay window.

Not to mention the tiny Bedouin ornaments that fell all over the floor." Richard stifled a small sob. "It was awful."

"Which is why we should keep things simple," I said. "The party is in two days, and we have the Douglas wedding on Saturday. I, for one, would *not* like to add anything else to my plate. Let's do a grab bag gift exchange, drink some bubbly, and reminisce about our craziest brides of the year."

Kate raised a hand. "I second that. We also have this baby situation we promised Buster and Mack we'd help them with. There's no time to build a Taj Mahal out of sugar cubes or whatever you might be envisioning."

Richard opened his mouth to protest, then tilted his head. "I never thought of a sugar cube Taj Mahal. I wonder—"

"No!" Kate and I said in unison.

Richard jumped. "Fine. We'll do your repurposing theme and serve gingerbread and champagne with cranberries for garnish." He pretended to be snoring then jerked awake. "Oh, I'm sorry. Did I fall asleep out of boredom?" He turned and stomped back to the kitchen.

"I think we can cross 'tracking down the missing baby mama' off our list," I said, making a point of ignoring Richard slamming around in the kitchen.

"You're giving up so soon?" Kate asked. "It's only been a few days."

I looked down at my dirt-smeared shirt. "And we've gotten nowhere. No potential moms. No witnesses. No nothing. I'm starting to think whoever left baby Merry did it randomly and just got lucky Buster and Mack found her."

Kate didn't look convinced. "Maybe, but I still think a biker church in a run-down strip mall is an odd place to dump a baby."

"I also get the feeling that Mack doesn't want us to find the mom," I said. "He seemed practically pleased when I told him we'd had no luck so far."

"They do seem pretty attached to the baby," Kate said. "The longer she stays with them, the worse it'll get."

I held up both palms. "I'm not going to be the one who tries to take her from them."

Kate switched her ice pack from one hand to the other. "If we don't find the mother, they're going to have to notify social services. You can't just keep a baby like that."

Especially since my boyfriend was a cop and knew the entire situation. Even knowing how broken the system was, Reese wouldn't be able to look the other way for much longer. I guess I understood, even though it was hard to imagine two people taking to the role of instant parent better than Buster and Mack. I hated the thought of how broken-hearted they'd be.

"I guess we're going to have to wish for a Christmas miracle," I said.

Kate winked at me. "Here's Taj-Ma-hoping."

"I heard that," Richard yelled.

CHAPTER 16

"So explain this grab bag gift exchange thing to me again," Kate said the next morning as we strolled through Georgetown.

Wreaths made of fake greenery with a shiny-gold bow tied at the bottom topped each of the streetlights dotting the sidewalk down M Street, and the steady ringing of a bell told me a Salvation Army bucket was nearby. The sidewalks were crowded with shoppers, so I held my to-go peppermint mocha close to keep it from getting knocked out of my hand.

I stepped around a sandwich board sign advertising 30 percent off, hearing the holiday Muzak spilling out of the designer handbag store, and giving Kate a tug as she slowed to look at the pricey purses. "We each buy a present under twenty dollars and wrap it up, then at the party we sit in a circle, and the first person picks a present and opens it."

"Sounds simple enough so far."

I pulled the collar of my coat tighter around my neck, regretting not wearing a scarf to block the wind. "The next person can either 'steal' that present or open a new one."

Kate fell behind me to avoid a harried-looking mother pushing a double-wide stroller. "What happens to the person whose gift was stolen?"

"They open a new one."

Kate fell back in beside me. "Why do I have a feeling this is going to end in someone getting their knickers in a fist?"

"You mean knickers in a twist?" I asked as Kate mouthed the phrase to herself then shrugged. She made a good point. This had the potential for drama.

"Every time I've done it at a party, it's been fun," I said, taking a sip of my now-lukewarm peppermint mocha.

"Were Richard and Fern at any of those parties?"

I slowed as we passed Starbucks and breathed in the rich scent of coffee. "Well, no, but even without the gift exchange, there's a good chance one of them will flounce off in a huff about something."

Kate raised a finger. "Point taken. So we have to find something under twenty dollars that anyone at the party might like?"

"That's the idea." I looked down the brown paving stone sidewalk at the red-brick and cream-colored townhouses pressed up against each other in a row, their colorful awnings hanging over glass fronts. Some of the buildings rose two stories and some three, giving the rooftops an uneven, jagged look. I wondered if any of the stores contained a gift that would appeal to both Richard *and* Buster or Fern *and* Mack.

I ducked into The Paper Source and pulled Kate with me. "Let's look in here."

We pushed through the tall doors and past the rows of chic wrapping paper hanging on wooden rods. Tables were piled high with books, crafting kits, and oversized mugs, and it smelled of paper and ink.

Kate picked up an adult coloring book featuring sea creatures on the cover. "Does Reese like dolphins?"

"Very funny," I said, taking a final drink of my coffee and tasting the bitter dregs from the bottom of the cup. I'd almost forgotten my boyfriend would be at the party and that he'd mentioned it to his older brother, Daniel, a former cop we'd gotten to know during a few past weddings that had taken a turn for the deadly. I decided not to mention that to Kate since she'd been known to flirt shamelessly with Daniel and had even once planted a serious kiss on him. Knowing he might be at the party would distract her from the task at hand.

I held up a box of hands-free walkie talkies. "This might work for Leatrice."

Kate sighed. "That's right. Leatrice is coming."

"Do you really think we could sneak a party past her eagle eyes?"

Kate grasped my coat sleeve. "Do you think she's bringing Sidney Allen?"

I hadn't thought about that, but now that Kate mentioned it, I felt sure Leatrice would bring the prima donna entertainment designer she'd been dating. "There's a decent chance of it."

Kate held up a box with a colorful drawing of three llamas on the front. "How about Llamanoes? It's like dominoes, but with pictures of llamas in funny outfits." She picked up a small set of fabric dolls with yarn hair. "And these are like voodoo dolls. Richard would love them. I'm sure he's worn out the ones he has."

I was sure he had. "Let's not encourage Richard to stab imaginary people any more than he already does."

Kate replaced the dolls on the table. "Good point. So far Llamanoes are the gift to beat."

I raised an eyebrow. This was not going to be easy. I wandered around the store and was inspecting a set of stemless champagne flutes when Kate glided up to me.

"Pssst," she said without turning her head to look at me. "I think we're being followed."

I swiveled my head to her. "Followed? What are you talking about?"

"Don't look at me," she scolded. "Act natural."

I fought the urge to roll my eyes. "And standing next to each other and talking without looking at each other is natural?"

She motioned toward the large glass front of the store. "Don't be obvious, but I'm pretty sure that man was walking behind us earlier."

"So?" I peered across the open space at the short figure in a heavy brown coat and black knit cap standing outside and studying the window display. "It's Georgetown in December. There are a lot of people walking around."

"But how many of them also went into the Starbucks on Wisconsin Avenue like we did and are now at The Paper Source?"

I was impressed that Kate was so attentive to her surroundings and scolded myself for not paying more attention. I was a young woman living in a city after all. "Why would anyone be following us?" I asked. "Unless one of your dates is becoming too attentive."

"You think he's a stalker?" Kate tilted her head to one side as she thought. "Nope. None of the guys I've been seeing are that short, and I'm pretty sure none of them are whack-a-doos."

"Pretty sure?" I mumbled. "That's encouraging."

Kate shrugged. "It's DC. I can never be 100 percent sure if they're a bit unbalanced or just congressional staffers."

I couldn't see the man's face because his collar was turned up and he wore a black scarf around his neck, but he didn't seem to be moving on. I didn't know too many men who were that captivated by stationery and quirky gifts.

"Here's what we do," I said in a low voice, even though there was a hundred feet and a wall of glass between us and our potential follower. "We leave the store and walk back in the direction we came from, then duck into that alcove at the end of the block. If he stays here or walks the other way, he isn't following us."

"Sounds good," Kate said, "but we could also walk out and walk into the Sprinkles cupcake shop next door. That would be more of a win-win."

"And if he really is trailing us, he wouldn't need to move to keep an eye on us if we walk right next door," I said.

"Fine, we'll do it your way." Kate looped an arm through mine. "But once we ditch this guy, I'm coming back here to buy the Llamanoes. After I get a cupcake."

We walked out of the stationery store and made a sharp right, passing the man and taking long strides down the sidewalk. Neither of us turned to see if he was following us, but once we reached the end of the block, we hurried past the white picket fence attached to The Old Stone House and ducked through the low gate and into the gardens. I pulled Kate down low so we were crouched below the fence.

We didn't have to wait long. A minute later, the man appeared and paused at the fence, looking around. I felt my heart race, and Kate gripped my arm even tighter.

As he stepped through the gate and glanced around, I shot to my feet. "Why are you following us?"

The figure stumbled back and fell onto the ground, the thick scarf falling down to reveal bright-pink lips.

Kate leapt up beside me. "Our stalker is Leatrice?"

CHAPTER 17

"I'm not stalking you," Leatrice said once I'd helped her up. "I'm trailing after the person who *is* following you."

Kate glanced around us at the empty garden with bare tree branches and low scraggy bushes. "So you're saying someone is trailing us, and you're following that person?"

Leatrice bobbed her head up and down, the knit cap no longer hiding her distinctive Mary Tyler Moore flip. "I noticed someone loitering outside our building this morning when I did my usual security sweep of the neighborhood. I didn't think too much of it, even though I noted it in my activity log. I didn't think she was a covert agent. She didn't look the type, but you never know. The city has seen a definite uptick in sleeper spy activity."

"Yep," Kate muttered. "That sounds completely normal."

I shushed her. "Go on, Leatrice. When did you think this person started following us?"

"I heard you and Kate leave and happened to look out my window." Color crept into her cheeks, and I suspected she'd been watching us go. "Right after you headed down the street, the same woman from earlier started walking about a block behind you. Naturally, I followed."

"Naturally," Kate said. "Your disguise was pretty good, you know. We thought you were a man. I mean, a severely vertically challenged man, but still."

Leatrice beamed. "I didn't have much time to assemble my disguise. If I hadn't been in such a rush, I would have added a mustache or a wig."

"So then what happened?" I asked. "Did the woman stay behind us?"

"For a long time, yes." Leatrice looked toward the sidewalk. "But when you came out of the paper store, she walked down one of the side streets toward the canal."

"So if she dropped off, she may not have been following us," I said. "It could have been a coincidence that she was behind us."

Leatrice frowned. "I don't think so. She definitely watched you two for a while."

"That's odd," Kate said. "I've never had a woman follow me. Men, sure. That's nothing new."

"Did you recognize the woman?" I asked Leatrice. "What did she look like?"

"No, I'd never seen her before this morning." Leatrice nibbled on her heavily lipsticked lower lip. "I couldn't see much under her hat and scarf, but I could tell she was a woman from her shape."

"So we're looking for a woman-shaped woman," I said, trying to keep the exasperation out of my voice. "That narrows it down."

Kate stood up and clasped my hand. "You don't think it's one of our brides, do you?"

"Why would a bride follow us?" I asked, knowing very well that a bridezilla didn't need a logical reason to do anything.

"Who knows?" Kate threw her hands in the air. "Maybe we didn't return her phone call within the hour, maybe we weren't available for her wedding, maybe she's getting divorced and blames us."

"You're being ridiculous," I said, although I mentally reviewed our current client roster to see if anyone jumped out at me as a potential nutcase. No one sprang to mind, but that didn't give me much comfort. "Why don't we walk down the street she took and see if

Leatrice recognizes her? There must be some detail that sets her apart since she followed her all over Georgetown."

"Her coat is dark green," Leatrice said. "And she's wearing boots."

"That's something," I said. "Most people in DC wear black coats, so a dark-green one shouldn't be tough to pick out of a crowd."

"So we're going to stalk the stalker?" Kate grinned. "I kind of like that."

Leatrice rubbed her hands together. "This is so exciting. What if she's a spy?"

"If she's a spy, why would she be following me and Kate?" I said, leading the way out of the small garden and back to the sidewalk.

Leatrice stopped and stared at us. "What if you're both spies?"

"We're wedding planners." Kate patted her arm. "You should know. You've crashed some of our weddings."

Leatrice didn't seem convinced. "True, but wedding planning would be the perfect cover for an international spy. Just think of all the politicians you've worked for."

"Leatrice," I said. "You know us. We're not spies."

Leatrice finally nodded and squeezed my hand. "You're right. A spy wouldn't be as messy as you are, dear."

Kate muffled a laugh behind her hand and tried to assume a serious expression. "So which way did she go?"

My elderly neighbor pointed to a side street across from us that led down to the canal and finally to the Potomac River. "Down that street."

I pressed the button for the walk signal and watched the electric display across the street until it lit up with a green stick figure. "Let's go. There may be a chance she's still around."

Kate and Leatrice hurried after me, Leatrice jogging to keep up with my long strides and Kate taking short steps in her high-heeled boots. I waited at the intersection for them to catch up and held the collar of my coat close to my neck. Once they'd joined me, we headed down the sloped sidewalk and crossed over the canal bridge, the brown water flowing beneath us.

Kate put a hand on my arm to stop me. "There it is."

"You see a dark-green coat?" I asked, scanning the few people strolling down the street with us. "Where?"

Kate raised a finger and pointed to the pink-edged doors and windows of the shop across from us, a hot-pink old-fashioned bicycle with a flower-filled basket leaning against the lamppost out front. "You can't say no to a cupcake from Baked & Wired. They're your favorite."

She was right. The cupcakes from the Georgetown bakery and coffee shop were hands down my favorite sweet treat in the city, but I couldn't focus on buttercream at the moment. "Maybe once we locate this mystery stalker."

"I could go for a cupcake," Leatrice said. "Surveillance is hard work."

So much for my intrepid team.

Kate leaned on the bridge railing and lifted one foot to rub the instep. "Can we at least pop inside Lush and sit down for a second? These boots were not made for downhill walking."

I suppressed the urge to tell her that her shoes were never designed for any kind of walking. My eyes went to Buster and Mack's floral shop a few doors down and then scanned the rest of the street. No sign of a green coat anywhere. "Fine. But only for a minute."

Leatrice and I each took one of Kate's elbows to keep her from falling face-first on the downhill walk. I held open one side of the glass doors and let them walk in ahead of me. A bell jingled above us to announce our arrival as I was met with the distinct scent of fresh flowers and freshly brewed espresso. I would know Lush with my eyes closed.

I let the door fall behind me as I spotted a woman looking at a table set up with small potted fir trees, Jo Malone scented candles, and topiaries made out of cranberries.

Leatrice nudged me. "Dark-green coat at ten o'clock."

The woman turned at the sound of the bell and Leatrice's stage whisper and met my eyes. Well, this was a surprise.

CHAPTER 18

The woman who'd seemed so unhappy to be at the funeral protest the day before drew in her breath sharply when she spotted me. Now that I was closer to her and she wasn't bundled in a hat and scarf, I realized she was much younger than I'd originally thought. No way could she be the old guy's wife, unless he went in for child brides.

Her heart-shaped face was unlined, and there was a smattering of freckles across the bridge of her nose. The ash-brown hair that fell around her face indeed looked like it had been streaked with blond highlights at the ends, and her blue eyes blinked rapidly as she looked at me.

What was she doing here, I wondered, and why was she, of all people, following us?

Her shoulders curved forward, she lowered her head, and she shuffled toward the corner of the shop as if trying to slip out unnoticed. Luckily, my body blocked the doorway.

"I remember you," I said as she edged her way toward the door. "You were at the funeral yesterday."

Kate spun around. "What?"

I stepped in front of the woman. "You were with the protest. You were next to the man with the gray hair who seemed to be the leader."

"I'm sorry," she mumbled without meeting my eyes. "This was a mistake."

"You're one of those horrible protesters?" Kate's voice went up a couple of octaves. "Why were you following us? Did you want to get in a few more hits?"

The woman looked up at Kate's face, the purple bruise on her cheek still visible through her concealer, and flinched, shaking her head.

Mack emerged from the back of the shop wearing baby Merry in the black fabric carrier on his chest. Even though I couldn't see her head, from the direction of her flailing arms and legs I could tell the baby faced him.

"What's all the ruckus?" he asked, jiggling the baby up and down as he walked back and forth. "You woke up Merry."

The woman drew in her breath again, and her eyes fixed on Mack.

It only took a second for everything to click in my head. "You're the mother. You're the one who left the baby at the church."

The entire shop went still as every eye turned to her. Crimson flooded her cheeks, and her eyes darted around the room. I was afraid she was going to try to run through me and out the door, so I squared my body in anticipation. Instead, her shoulders sagged as if she were a puppet who'd had her strings cut, and she sank to the floor with her hands over her face.

Buster came out of the back and stood behind Mack. "What's going on?"

"I think they found the baby's mother," Mack said, his voice barely a whisper and his face crestfallen.

Buster gaped at the sobbing woman on the cement floor then looked up at me. "How did you track her down? I thought you didn't have any leads."

"Technically we didn't find her," I said. "She was following us, although I don't know why."

"And I was following her," Leatrice added. "I thought she might be a secret agent."

Buster walked over to the woman and lifted her up by the shoulders. "Why don't you come sit down? You look like you could use a cappuccino."

"I know I could use a cappuccino," Kate said, following Buster and the woman to the long metal table near the coffee station.

Buster sat the woman on a metal stool and took the one next to her, keeping his thick arm around her shoulders. "You're among friends now. Why don't you tell us why you're here and why you left your baby at our church?"

Mack hadn't moved from where he stood near the open door to the back of the shop, but he stroked the baby's head as she fussed. The woman swiped at her eyes and pushed a strand of hair off her face and turned toward the sound of the baby's tiny cries.

"Is she okay?"

"She's fine," Mack said, holding on to the tiny pajamaed feet with his large hands and gazing down at her head. "She's an easy baby, you know."

The woman nodded. "That's good. I thought she'd find a good home if I left her with you all."

I pulled out a stool across from her. "So it's true. You're the mother." Part of me couldn't believe we'd actually located her. Or, to be more accurate, she'd located us.

She took a deep breath and straightened up. "I'm Prudence, but I like to go by Prue. My father is the leader of our church and, well . . ." She met my eyes. "You've seen what he's like."

My memories of the gray-haired man screaming curses, his eyes blazing with hate, were fresh in my mind. "I take it he doesn't know you had a baby?"

She shook her head, her lips pressed together. "I'm only eighteen and still a senior in high school. He would kill me if he knew. My mother's been gone for a while, so it's just the two of us. He only became the way he is after she died." A pained expression passed across her face, but she gave a small shake of her head and continued.

"I didn't know I was pregnant for a long time, then when I realized it I wore baggy clothes to hide the bump. He doesn't like me wearing anything tight, so it wasn't hard."

Mack took a few steps closer, and I noticed his stern expression softening.

"I'd seen you all every time we protested a funeral." Prue's eyes filled with tears. "I hated going to them, but my father made me. You and your friends always seemed so kind. I figured any people who would come out and do what you do for strangers would take good care of a baby."

"So you tracked down their church and left Merry outside?" I asked.

She nodded. "I waited around the corner to make sure someone found her. I didn't just run off." A tear snaked down her face. "I almost ran back for her, but then I saw you two come out and pick her up." She looked between Buster and Mack. "You looked so happy, I figured I'd made the right decision after all, even though it was the hardest thing I've ever done."

Buster rubbed the woman's back, then stood and moved to the large chrome coffee machine.

Mack took Buster's place, lowering himself onto the stool so the baby's feet rested on his thighs. "I'm sure she's missed you. Do you want to hold her?"

Prue looked longingly at the tiny baby, then shook her head. "I can't keep her. I don't want to get any more attached to her than I already am. It nearly killed me to walk away the first time."

"Come on." Mack lifted the sleeping child out of the front carrier, keeping one hand on the back of her head. "I've been wearing her for hours. It would give me a break."

Prue accepted the now-sleeping baby and cradled her in her arms, tracing one finger lightly down the side of Merry's face. Mack cleared his throat and looked away, blinking hard. Buster faced the coffee machine as he fiddled with the nozzles and handles, but I saw him wipe his cheeks furtively.

"Isn't there anyone else you and Merry could stay with aside from your father?" Leatrice asked, hopping onto a stool and letting her legs swing beneath her.

Prue didn't look up as she shook her head. "Everyone I know is in the church. They won't help me. They're just like my father."

Kate touched a hand to her bruise. "No, they didn't strike me as the forgiving and accepting types."

"What about the baby's father?" I asked, suspecting the answer before she gave it.

"He's my age and doesn't want to deal with a baby," the girl said. "He freaked out when I told him, and now he won't even look at me."

Kate muttered some choice words under her breath, and Mack nodded in agreement, even though I knew he normally didn't approve of cursing.

Prue choked back a sob. "Even if I got away from my father, I don't have any way to support Merry. I haven't even graduated from high school." She closed her eyes and gave a shake of her head. "What kind of life would that be for her? I want her to end up better than me."

The steam nozzle hissed as Buster finished off a pair of cappuccinos. He turned and set one in front of Prue and another in front of Kate, then turned back to the coffee station before I could get a good look at his face.

"Then why were you following us?" I asked.

She looked up. "I just wanted to make sure she was okay. I saw you two yesterday and heard you mention Merry, so I figured you knew where she was and might lead me to her. I read your T-shirts, and it was easy enough to find your business address online."

Kate looked confused for a moment, then snapped her fingers. "We both wore our Wedding Belles T-shirts."

"Not exactly the marketing we'd imagined," I said.

"I waited outside of your building for a few hours before you came out," Prue said. "I almost gave up, but then you appeared."

Leatrice bounced up and down in her stool. "That's when I saw you and thought you might be a spy."

Prue's eyes drew together in obvious confusion, but I waved a hand. "Don't mind her. She thinks everyone is a spy at some point. So you thought we'd lead you to Merry?"

She shrugged. "I hoped, although I was about to give up when you started acting weird."

"That would be when we realized Leatrice was following us," Kate said.

"I thought you'd seen me, so I went the opposite way and happened to see the Harleys outside this shop." She gazed down at her baby. "I came inside here and pretended to be looking around in hopes that Merry would be here."

"That was quite a long shot," I said. "What if she'd been somewhere else?"

Prue bit her lower lip. "I guess I would have kept coming back."

"It doesn't sound like you want to give up your baby to me," Leatrice said.

The girl took a shaky breath. "I don't have any other choice."

"Of course you do." Buster drank a shot of espresso in a single gulp and turned back around. "You and Merry can live here."

Everyone's mouths dropped open, including Mack's.

Kate glanced around the industrial-style flower shop. "Are you planning to put a cot between the flower buckets?"

Mack sat up straighter. "He means the apartment upstairs. We've been using it for storage, but it's got two bedrooms and would be the perfect size for a mother and baby."

"It's the obvious solution," Buster said. "You don't want to lose Merry and neither do we. This way you'd have someplace to live, and we'd still get to see her."

Mack nodded. "We'll watch her while you're at school."

Prue's eyes lit up, then she frowned. "An apartment in this neighborhood would be expensive, and I don't have any money." She set her mouth. "And I can't take charity."

"Who said anything about charity?" Buster asked. "We all work hard, and so can you. We need extra hands around the flower shop, especially during the holidays. We'll pay you just like we pay our other employees, and you can pay a small amount back for your room and board. But you have to finish up school before you can start working full-time."

Prue looked at both men, her eyes narrowing as she took in the hulking figures with multiple piercings wearing black leather. "But I don't know you."

Kate crossed one leg over the other, and her coat fell open to reveal plenty of bare leg. "They took care of your baby happily and with no questions asked. What more do you need to know?"

I reached a hand across the table. "I've known Buster and Mack for years, and there aren't two people I would trust more."

Kate made an indignant noise, but I ignored her.

Prue held my eyes for a moment, then looked at Buster and Mack and smiled tentatively. "Are you sure? You don't know me."

Mack shrugged. "You came back. What more do we need to know?"

Leatrice pulled a tissue out of her pocket and blew her nose. "This is even better than busting open an international spy ring. Well, it's *as* good."

"Don't worry." Kate patted the sniffling Leatrice on the shoulder. "The day's still young."

CHAPTER 19

"Where is your wine opener?" Richard called from the kitchen over the sounds of opening and slamming drawers in rapid succession. Forget hearing the Harry Connick Jr. holiday music I had playing from my portable iPhone speaker on top of the bookshelf.

"Drawer next to the fridge," Reese called back from the stepladder where he stood wrapping white lights around the Christmas tree. He looked down at me holding a spool of string lights between my hands and dropped his voice. "I hope he's opening a bottle for himself. He definitely needs to relax."

"This is standard pre-event Richard," I said. "He won't unwind until people have tasted his food and declared it the best thing they've ever eaten."

"I thought we were keeping the food simple. Didn't you nix the three-foot snowman cheese ball and the gingerbread people made to look like each of us?"

"I think he gave up the gingerbread people only because he couldn't find a cookie cutter that looked like Hermes, but you know Richard doesn't do low-key." I inhaled the savory scents of baked Brie and the sweet and spicy nuts he'd put in the oven to warm. "Luckily, he's got holiday parties booked, and our wedding nixed all the holiday-themed food, so we're eating what he made for those. I'm just glad I'm not cooking."

Reese wisely didn't make a comment as he wrapped the end of the last string around the top of the tree and stepped down off the ladder. He stood back to admire his handiwork and wrapped an arm around my waist. "This place is starting to look pretty good."

I had to agree. My apartment—correction, our apartment now—usually erred on the side of minimalism, but the Christmas tree, pillar candles, and hanging paper stars made it look positively festive. And the combination of the fresh fir tree and Richard's cooking made it smell as good as it looked.

"That should be the last of it," Kate said as she appeared from the hallway with an armload of leftover items from our past weddings. She dumped it on the couch. "We've got a variety of cocktail napkins; striped straws in pink, gold, and lavender; and even some 'Eat, Drink, and Be Married' stir sticks."

"Perfect." I picked up a stack of cream "Heather and Jeff" napkins and fanned them out across my coffee table. "Once this party is over, I hope never to lay eyes on any of this stuff again."

"It was a great idea to have a party to use up all of this," Kate said, arranging the stir sticks and straws on the countertop between the kitchen and living room. "You know what we could have done to make it even more fun? Wear old bridesmaids' gowns." She waved a wooden stir stick at me. "Boy, do I have some doozies."

"So we'd be in awful bridesmaids' dresses and the men would be in regular clothes?" I asked. "That doesn't seem fair."

"I'll bet we could get Fern into a bridesmaids' gown." Kate wagged her eyebrows at me. "I have a burgundy velvet he'd look great in."

"Make way, make way," Richard cried as he appeared from the kitchen holding a large tray in front of him and set it in the center of the coffee table.

Kate leaned down and breathed in. "They smell amazing. What are they?"

Richard wiped his hands off on his Santa apron. "Pepper jelly palmiers and pimento cheese puffs. But no touching until everyone gets here." He spun on his heel.

Kate pulled her hand back and frowned, shooting a look at Richard's retreating back. "Fine. Why don't I get the drinks going since someone is being such a despot with the food?"

"Don't forget we need a nonalcoholic option," I reminded her as she followed Richard into the kitchen. "Not only are Buster and Mack teetotalers, but one of our guests is only eighteen."

"I'm on it," she said.

Reese pulled me closer and brushed a strand of hair off my forehead. "I'm glad everything worked out with the baby and her mother."

"Who knew the floral business was so lucrative that Buster and Mack could own their entire building?" I gazed up at him. "What would you have done if the mother hadn't found us, and Buster and Mack had wanted to keep the baby?"

He let out a breath. "I don't know. I couldn't in good conscience have put the child into the system right before the holidays, but you also can't just keep a baby you find. I'm glad I wasn't forced into an impossible decision."

"I'm sorry I put you in another difficult situation," I said. "I seem to do that a lot."

He grinned at me. "This time it wasn't actually your fault, and there was no dead body, so it really pales in comparison to all the other times you've meddled in police investigations or the many occasions I've had to save you from a violent criminal."

I swatted at him. "You wish you needed to save me."

He pulled me closer. "I do wish you needed me to save the day more."

"I never said I didn't need you." I felt my face flush. "There are a lot of other ways I need you."

He arched an eyebrow as he lowered his head and his lips brushed over mine. I wrapped my arms around his neck and let myself sink into the kiss, feeling it all the way to my fingertips.

"Yoo hoo!" Leatrice called as she opened the door without knocking.

Reese pulled away from me and sighed. "Tomorrow I'm going out and buying a dead bolt."

I eyed Leatrice as she walked into the room, the eight blue-and-white candles on her headband bobbing as she set a round tray down next to Richard's hot hors d'oeuvres display. She wore her brightly colored Christmas tree skirt with the plug dangling from the back and a red sweatshirt.

"Better get two just to be safe," I said.

Hermes, who she'd been watching while we prepared for the party, scampered in with her, jumping onto the couch and yipping happily as he ran from one end to the other.

Sidney Allen came in behind the small Yorkie, holding a foil-topped bottle in a shimmering red velveteen bag and two small wrapped presents. He wore a dark suit, like he did at every event, and the pants were hiked up high on his chest so the belt appeared to be nearly looped around his armpits. For once, he wasn't wearing the headset I was so used to seeing him scream into as he coordinated his performers.

"Glad you could make it," I said, taking the bottle from him. "We aren't quite ready, but we're getting there." I pointed to the tree in the corner. "Grab bag gifts go under there."

Leatrice waved a hand at me. "The only reason we're early is I wanted to get a good place for my pigs-in-a-blanket wreath."

I peered down at the circle of hotdogs wrapped in golden-brown pastry. With the bow at the bottom cut out of strips of red peppers, it did indeed look like a wreath. It smelled, however, like a plate of hotdogs. I couldn't wait until Richard saw it sitting beside his delicately shaped palmiers and cheese puffs dusted with finely grated parmesan.

Reese rubbed his hands together. "Now we're talking."

Richard came out of the kitchen holding the baked Brie topped with cherry compote and stopped dead in his tracks when he spotted Leatrice. He inhaled sharply when his eyes dropped to the hot dog wreath. "What in the name of—?"

"It's a pigs-in-a-blanket wreath," I said before he could make a snarky comment. "Isn't it clever?"

Hermes leapt off the couch, ran to Richard, sniffed his leg, then ran back to the couch. Richard's frozen expression didn't change as he nodded, setting the baked Brie on the counter between the living room and kitchen.

He came up behind me, giving Hermes a pat, and whispered, "What's on her head?"

"Interesting hat, Leatrice," I said. "Where did you get it?"

"Holiday sale last year at Filene's." Leatrice reached up and touched the stuffed fabric candles. "You don't see many Christmas hats with candles, do you?"

"That's because it's a menorah," Richard muttered.

"Who wants some bubbly?" Kate asked as she came out of the kitchen holding a tray of champagne flutes with cranberries floating on top.

"Yes, please." Fern walked through the open door taking small steps and barely moving anything above his knees. His crimson suit was skintight with gold piping along the edges, and he wore a snowy-white ascot with a jeweled star at his neck, making him look very much like a slimmed-down version of Santa Claus. A green-and-red gift bag hung from one wrist. "I had to walk two blocks. This suit is barely made for standing, much less walking distances."

"I wouldn't call two blocks a distance," I said, taking the gift bag from him since he clearly couldn't lift his arm to hand it to me.

"You would if you were trying to fit into your skinny suit." He let out a tiny breath, straining the one gold button on his jacket. "I hope you have some keto diet food."

I didn't even know what foods counted as keto, but I felt sure that anything Richard had made contained enough butter, cheese, and real cream to float a barge. "You're starting a diet *before* the holidays?"

Fern glanced at the trays of food and looked pained, either from the suit cutting off his circulation or the fact that he couldn't eat anything.

"Do like I do, and go on a liquid diet." Kate handed him a champagne flute and popped a gold-striped straw in it so he barely had to raise his arm to drink.

"Good thinking." Fern drained the glass in a single sip. "I feel thinner already."

I didn't have the heart to tell either of them that a liquid diet did not mean drinking only booze.

Fern scanned the group, his eyes settling on Leatrice, and he shuffled over to her. "Sweetie, did you know your skirt has a plug hanging from the back?"

"It lights up," she said, pointing to the tiny lights embedded in the fabric. "But it's not very practical. You have to stand right next to an outlet and not move a lot."

Only Leatrice would be undeterred by a plug dangling from her clothing.

Richard motioned to our tree. "Don't you actually need a Christmas tree skirt? I say we plug her in and lay her down under there."

I elbowed him. "Be nice. It's a holiday party."

"I'm always nice, darling." He gave Reese a simpering smile. "Right, Detective?"

Reese nodded a little too eagerly as Richard left us to return to the kitchen. "I think I liked it better when Richard ignored me."

"Too late," I said. "There's no going back now."

He laughed and entwined his fingers with mine. "Good."

I felt a flutter in my stomach and picked up a glass of champagne. I was still getting used to the idea of having a boyfriend, not to mention a hot one, and much less a live-in one. Sometimes I felt like pinching myself to make sure it was real.

"Look who we found on our way up," Mack said, walking in with baby Merry strapped to his chest and Buster and Prue both carrying armfuls of colorful boxes. Mack swept an arm behind him to reveal a tall, broad-shouldered man with dark hair flecked with gray at the temples.

"Daniel!" Kate nearly dropped the tray of glasses when she saw Reese's older brother.

"I take it you didn't warn her he was coming?" Reese asked me.

I shook my head. "I was afraid of what she'd wear if she thought there were going to be any eligible men here."

As it was, her white angora sweater left little to the imagination.

Kate set the tray down without spilling anything and hurried over to Daniel Reese. "I had no idea you were coming." She glanced over her shoulder and narrowed her eyes at me.

Daniel smiled, looking very much like his brother. "I wouldn't miss it."

"Come on in, everyone," I said, ignoring Kate's pointed look and waving everyone inside. "Presents for the gift exchange go under the tree."

I turned up the volume on the holiday jazz as Leatrice began walking around the room holding the tray with her hotdog wreath, the plug to her skirt bouncing around her legs. Richard passed glasses of booze-free punch over the counter, and I noticed Prue smile as she took one of Leatrice's pigs-in-a-blanket. Mack bounced the baby gently on his chest in time to "Deck the Halls", which she seemed to be sleeping through, and Buster produced several boxes of glass ball ornaments I recognized as one of the holiday items they sold in their shop.

Buster winked at me. "You did say the theme was leftover inventory purge, right?"

"Your leftover inventory is a lot fancier than mine," I told him as I eyed the blown-glass orbs.

Fern stutter-stepped over to me. "Baby-mama is cute." He angled his head as he stared at her across the room. "And young. You don't think she'll let me fix her hair, do you? I haven't worked on anyone young in forever."

I leveled my gaze at him, and he gave a nervous laugh. "Aside from you and Kate, of course. You know I don't mean that you two are old, sweetie."

"Thanks," I said.

"Don't mention it." He patted my arm and began making his way geisha girl-style to Prue.

I made a mental note to warn the girl not to give Fern free rein with her hair unless she wanted to end up with a transformation worthy of the witness relocation program.

I saw the door open and our cake baker friend, Alexandra, poke her head inside. I waved her in and tried not to stare when I saw whose hand she was holding as she pulled him behind her. "Is that the detective you worked with on our last case?" I asked Reese.

The mousy-haired man with the questionable combover smiled and nodded to us before turning his attention back to the tall glamorous woman next to him. He looked as shocked to be holding her hand as I was, although I'd thought they'd looked like they were getting cozy during the police investigation we'd met him on.

"It sure is," Reese said, shaking his head. "Doesn't Alexandra live in Scotland?"

"Yep," I said, watching the baker flip her long brown hair off her shoulder and set a pink bakery box on the coffee table. "She flies over to do our high-profile cakes a few times a year."

Reese pointed to the box. "Do you think she brought cake?"

"The oddest couple of the century just walked in and you're thinking about cake?" I asked him, secretly hoping Alexandra had brought some of her famous sweets as well.

He looped an arm around me and pulled me close. "Cake isn't all I'm thinking about."

I felt myself blush and looked around to see if anyone had heard. The nearest person was Buster who was unpacking ornaments and handing them out for people to hang.

Reese took a red-and-green-swirled glass ball and passed it to me. "Here, babe."

As I took the ornament from him and hung it on our first Christmas tree together, I felt happier than I had in a long time. Even knowing I had a wedding in a couple of days with a bride who rivaled the Grinch couldn't put a damper on the feeling of home I got as I looked around the room. Richard had left the kitchen and removed his apron, and he stood next to the couch petting Hermes on the head. He looked calmer than usual, and I felt surprised he wasn't scurrying around after Leatrice trying to get people to eat his hors d'oeuvres instead. Maybe he really was over the disappointment of being left off the list, although somehow I doubted it.

"Cheers to surviving another year," Kate said from her perch on Daniel's lap as she raised a glass of champagne. "Together."

Everyone raised their glasses and clinked them.

Reese locked eyes with me, his hazel eyes deepening to green. "I'll drink to that."

* * *

THANK you for reading MARRY AND BRIGHT!

Since it's the holidays, Richard has decided to share a couple of his party recipes on the next pages (most of them borrowed and adapted from *Southern Living*, which he loves and reads from cover to cover). Enjoy!

If you liked this cozy mystery, you'll love THE TRUFFLE WITH WEDDINGS, the next book in the series. An over-the-top Valentine's Day wedding. A poisoned box of chocolates. Will the most romantic holiday of the year become the most deadly?

One-click THE TRUFFLE WITH WEDDINGS Now>

"The twists and turns of this story don't disappoint. Plus the moments I laughed out-loud are priceless." Amazon Reviewer

* * *

This book has been edited and proofed, but typos are like little gremlins that like to sneak in when we're not looking. If you spot a typo, please report it to:
laura@lauradurham.com
Thank you!!

PEPPER JELLY PALMIERS

1 (17.3-oz.) package frozen puff pastry sheets, thawed
1 and 1/4 cup finely shredded Parmesan cheese
6 tablespoons chopped fresh chives
1/2 teaspoon kosher salt
1/2 teaspoon black pepper
2/3 cup hot pepper jelly
Parchment paper

Step 1
Roll 1 pastry sheet into a 12- x 10-inch rectangle on lightly floured surface. Sprinkle with half of cheese, 3 Tbsp. chives, and 1/4 tsp. each salt and pepper. Roll up pastry, jelly-roll fashion, starting with each short side and ending at middle of pastry sheet. Wrap pastry tightly with parchment paper. Repeat procedure with remaining pastry sheet, cheese, chives, salt, and pepper. Freeze for1 to 24 hours.

Step 2
Preheat oven to 375°. Line baking sheets with parchment paper. Remove pastries from freezer, and let stand at room temperature for 10 minutes. Cut each roll into 1/4-inch-thick slices, and place on baking sheets.

Step 3
Bake, in batches, 20 minutes or until golden.

Step 4
Microwave pepper jelly in a microwave-safe bowl on HIGH for 1 minute. Brush 1/2 tsp. pepper jelly onto each palmier. Serve immediately.

Make Ahead: Prepare Step 1 of the recipe, and wrap the dough in plastic wrap. Freeze up to 1 month. Resume with Step 2 about an hour before serving.

CHERRY WALNUT BRIE

1/3 cup cherry preserves
1 tablespoon balsamic vinegar
1/8 teaspoon freshly ground pepper
1/8 teaspoon salt
1 (8-oz.) Brie round, rind removed from top
Chopped toasted walnuts

Stir together cherry preserves, balsamic vinegar, pepper, and salt in a bowl. Drizzle over warm Brie round. Top with walnuts. Serve with crackers.

ACKNOWLEDGMENTS

As always, an enormous thank you to all of my wonderful readers, especially my beta readers and my review team. I never give you enough time, but you always come through for me. A special shout-out to the beta readers who caught all my goofs this time: Linda Fore, Tony Noice, Sheila Kraemer, Wendy Green, Carol Spayde, Katherine Munro, and Tricia Knox. Thank you!!

A heartfelt thank you to everyone who leaves reviews. They really make a difference, and I am grateful for every one of them!

I learned a lot about Christian biker gangs for this book and was very impressed by them. One of the themes I revisit often in my books is looking beyond appearances, and I think this fits perfectly with these tough guys (and ladies) with hearts of gold.

CLAUS FOR CELEBRATION

AN ANNABELLE ARCHER WEDDING PLANNER
MYSTERY #15

LAURA DURHAM

*For Cathy Jaquette,
the OC and an amazing friend*

CHAPTER 1

"I think we've made a huge mistake, Annabelle," my assistant, Kate, said as she walked into my apartment carrying several canvas tote bags slung over her shoulders. She dropped them on the floor, kicked off her high heels, and collapsed onto my couch.

"You couldn't find the ice-blue paper?" I asked, bending over and pawing through the bags with one hand while holding my bottled Mocha Frappuccino with the other.

"Oh, I found it." She flicked a hand through her blond bob. "Along with the ball ornaments and the 'naughty' and 'nice' signs for the drinks." She cast her eyes around my apartment, lingering on the sparsely decorated Christmas tree in the corner. "Good thing, too. This place needs a little oomph. I thought Richard was helping with party decor. Unless he's going through a minimalist phase again."

"He got delayed yesterday. Some important meeting that's going to change all of our lives." I padded back to the kitchen in my bare feet, taking a swig of my cold, sweet drink as I walked. I resumed buttering the toast I'd left on the counter when Kate had walked in, and I now peered at her across the opening between my kitchen and living room. "So what's this huge mistake we're making?"

"Taking on all this work. We usually slow down in December. All of our corporate planner friends get crazy and our hotel contacts are too busy to eat, but the holidays are usually the one time of the year when we can catch our breath." She motioned to the bags strewn across my floor. "Where's my break?"

I took a bite of toast, savoring the Irish butter my fiancé had gotten me hooked on, and chased it with a gulp of cold mocha-flavored coffee. Kate was right. December was usually downtime for wedding planners. Only the most stalwart brides wanted to compete with corporate holiday parties for event space or pay the holiday premiums. As the owner of Wedding Belles, Washington DC's most on-the-rise wedding planning company, I usually blocked off the month for rest and regrouping and catching up on sleep after the busy autumn and before the intense booking season that started in January. This year, however, my usual plan had flown out the window.

Carrying my plate of toast and drink out with me to the living room, I sat down next to Kate on the couch. "I know this month has been unusual, but might I remind you that the engagement party was your idea?"

She sat up and tilted her head at me. "Because we haven't had a free weekend all fall. If we don't have it now, you and Hottie Cop will never have a proper party to celebrate your engagement. I know you like to put off anything personal, but since you put me in charge of your wedding planning, we're throwing you and Reese a party." She flopped back again. "I just didn't know we'd have to work it around two weddings, including one on New Year's Eve."

"Neither did I," I said, holding out the plate and offering her a piece of toast, which she waved away. "Who knew we'd get a last-minute New Year's Eve wedding?"

"Don't get me wrong. The extra money will be nice, especially since they're paying our holiday wedding premium, but you know what a sacrifice it is for me to work on New Year's Eve, Annabelle."

I did know. As a champion dater, New Year's Eve was typically one of her busiest nights of the year. Kate had been known to fit in multiple dates on New Year's Eve, flitting between fancy restaurant seatings and over-the-top parties. Personally, I didn't know how she juggled it all, since I was more of the type to ring in the new year on my couch in my PJs.

"I promise I'll make it up to you," I said. "If anyone books a last-minute Valentine's Day wedding, I'll do it solo. And aside from lots of new meetings with potential clients, January and February are dead."

She gave me a side-eye glance. "I suppose I can survive until then. Fern is working on a new system to streamline my Valentine's dates this year, so hopefully it won't be as much of a disaster as last year."

I remembered the year before had involved wireless headsets, spreadsheets, and plenty of hysterics on our hairdresser friend Fern's part.

"I thought I remembered something about you wanting to slow down your dating pace and find someone to get serious with." I tucked my feet up under me. "What happened to that?"

She draped one arm across the back of the yellow twill couch cushions, drumming her pink, polished fingernails on the fabric. "There is one guy I could see myself with, but I'm not sure if I'm ready to settle down yet."

"The lawyer from Williams & Connolly?" I asked.

She shook her head.

"The guy who works at the White House?"

She wrinkled her nose. "No one dates White House staffers anymore. Anyway, I'm not into young guys who work on the Hill anymore. This guy's more . . .established."

Established? I knew what that was a code word for. I tried to remember her mentioning an older guy, but I'd always found it hard to keep track of her men. "Did you finally decide to get a sugar daddy?"

Kate gave me a scandalized look. "He's not *that* old, besides, I gave up that idea when Wedding Belles took off, and you raised my salary." She darted her eyes to me. "He's not your typical DC guy. He's older and not involved in politics or the government at all. Plus, he's completely different from me in almost every way."

I shrugged. "You know what they say. Opposites attract."

"Speaking of opposites." Kate craned her neck toward the hallway of my apartment. "Where is your very attractive opposite?"

"Reese?" I asked, glancing down the hall, even though I knew my fiancé wasn't there. "He went into the precinct early this morning. There's been an uptick in shoplifting and pickpocketing around Georgetown, and one of their prime suspects showed up outside the station tied up in gold Christmas garland with a bow around his mouth."

Mike Reese was not only my fiancé, he was a DC police detective I'd met when one of our clients had been murdered at a wedding. It had taken us a few years--and a few more dead bodies--before we'd started dating, but we'd been living together for almost a year and had been engaged for several months.

"So he was literally gift wrapped for them?" She flipped a hand through her hair. "Which proves that the city is crazy at the holidays, which is why we don't take weddings in December, which is why it's insane that we have a wedding at the Four Seasons on Saturday and your engagement party on Sunday, not to mention the last-minute planning for the New Year's wedding."

She gasped for breath.

"We can handle it." I took a final bite of now-cold toast and drained the Frappuccino, standing and heading for the kitchen with the empty plate and bottle. "It isn't like we've never had two events on a weekend."

"Yes." Kate stood and walked to the opening between the two rooms, leaning over the counter and poking her head into the kitchen. "But how wrecked have we looked the second day? I refuse to let you go to your own engagement party looking like you did at the Turner-Finley wedding."

I dropped the empty bottle in my recycling bin. "How did I look at that wedding?"

She waved a hand in my general direction. "Like this. Hair in a ponytail. Hardly any makeup. Like you don't care."

I touched a hand to my bare face and glanced down at the jeans and T-shirt I'd thrown on. "I *don't* care. It's barely ten in the morning, and we don't have a meeting until this afternoon. This morning is supposed to be about finalizing all the vendors for Saturday and putting together gift bags."

"Fine," she said. "But I hope you're planning on a cute outfit to go see Buster and Mack later. It's one of the few in-person meetings we're going to have with our New Year's bride before the wedding day."

I made a mental rundown of my closet and the size of my dry-cleaning bag. "Don't worry. I've got plenty of cute winter outfits."

Kate made a face. "You might want to rethink that." She cut her eyes to her own short black skirt and white button-down opened low at the neck. "Why do you think I'm not wearing a coat in December?"

I'd assumed it was so she could show as much leg and cleavage as possible. "What are you talking about?"

Kate made tsk-ing noises at me. "You never check the weather, do you? We got a warm snap. It's seventy-eight degrees outside and will be all week."

"In December?" I gaped at her. "But Saturday's wedding is snowflake themed. Everything is icicles and ice blue. We have an outside s'mores station and hot chocolate bar."

"Yeah, that's going to be a little weird."

I slumped against the kitchen counter, hearing my office phone ringing down the hall. If I was a betting woman, I'd have put money on that being Saturday's bride calling in a panic because her wintry wedding was now going to be pleasantly warm instead of cool and cozy. I knew I'd have to work some serious wedding planner Zen magic to convince her that her day wouldn't be a disaster. Even though I told all my brides the only thing I couldn't control was the weather, they still seemed to think I could whip out a mythical cure-all when it poured rain or when temperatures soared to near one hundred degrees in the summer.

The door flew open, and my best friend, Richard Gerard, staggered into my apartment, dropping a plastic crate on the floor with a loud thud. His gaze went from the scantily decorated Christmas tree to me, and he let out a tortured sigh.

"The next time I have another brilliant idea like this, will someone please shoot me?"

Kate grinned at me. "Dibs."

CHAPTER 2

"Neither this absurd warm weather nor you living on the fourth floor of a walk-up is getting me in the holiday spirit," Richard said as he fanned himself with two hands. "Thank heavens I didn't wear my cashmere. Much more of this, and I'm going to need to pull my summer wardrobe back out. Trust me when I say I do not have time to air out my linen suits right now."

He swung his black leather man bag off his shoulder and set it on the ground. As it tipped over, a tiny black-and-brown Yorkie popped out of the top and scampered out, yipping happily as he ran around sniffing.

"Poor Hermès can't even wear his sweaters," Richard said, fluttering a hand at the small dog. "What's the point of having Gucci if you can't wear it?"

"One of the great questions of the universe," Kate said under her breath as she scratched Hermès under the chin.

"Don't worry," I said, joining Richard in the living room as he brushed off the sleeves of his royal blue blazer with a lint brush that seemed to have materialized out of thin air. "I was just explaining to Kate that the week might be a little packed, but it's nothing we can't handle. We've all had multiple events on a weekend before."

"Indeed," he said absently, his gaze scouring my apartment while he frowned.

As the owner of Richard Gerard Catering, one of the premier catering companies in the area, Richard was adept at juggling parties. I knew back-to-back events were not enough to send him over the edge, although he did live most of his life close to it. Or, as Kate liked to put it, on the brink of insanity.

"Is it the rehearsal dinner or my engagement party that has you worried?" I asked. "Or are you still peeved the couple decided on a hotel for their actual wedding reception, because you know I can't force them to choose an off-premise venue. You did get their rehearsal dinner, and it's a pretty elaborate one."

"What?" He shook his head. "Of course not. I got over that ages ago."

I didn't point out that he'd been complaining about it only two days prior. I'd found with Richard it was better not to have a perfect memory.

I rested a hand on his sleeve. "I promise you it will all be fine. Tell him our new Wedding Belles motto, Kate."

"It's handled," Kate said, spreading her hands out in front of her as if she were unfurling a sign. "We're thinking of putting it on T-shirts."

I looked down at the crate at his feet. "We can set out the holiday decor you brought, and we'll be halfway to having this place decorated for the engagement party."

"About that," Richard said, not meeting my eyes. "I may have added a teensy little 'to-do' to your week."

"How teensy?" Kate asked, both hands on her hips as she eyed him.

"Don't be upset, Annabelle." He shifted from one foot to the other. "But I may have arranged for a photographer from *DC Life Magazine* to do a profile piece on Wedding Belles."

"Why would that make me upset?" I asked. "We've been dying to get into that magazine. A profile on our business would be huge."

He bent over his plastic crate and began pulling out holiday decor. "I'm glad you're pleased, darling. Now all we need to do is get your apartment in shape for the magazine's photo shoot."

My stomach tightened as I glanced around the slightly unkempt and severely unstyled living room. Client files were strewn across one end of the dining room table, and one of Reese's jackets was hooked over the back of a chair. Wedding magazines sat stacked high in a rack by the couch, and my glass coffee table held nothing but more paperwork and an unwashed coffee mug. "A photo shoot? In my apartment?"

"I tried to convince them to do it somewhere else." He sighed deeply as he scanned the space. "But they insist on capturing their subjects in their homes and offices. They want a real behind-the-scenes look."

I groaned. Unfortunately for me, my apartment also doubled as Wedding Belles headquarters, with the home office down the hall housing filing cabinets, a rarely-used desk, and a vast assortment of leftover wedding favors, gift bags, and programs. Despite planning over-the-top weddings for clients, my own design style was decidedly simplistic. I usually argued that I didn't have time to keep my life and my clients' weddings styled, but the truth was I wasn't a fussy person when it came to myself. I favored yoga pants and jeans over cute dresses, and would rather have a comfortable home than a fussy one. I was a substance over style woman, and I knew that did not lend itself to stunning photos.

Kate flopped back onto the couch, and Hermès immediately jumped up and began licking the hand draped over her head. "We're doomed."

"Nonsense," Richard said, adopting the take-charge tone he used when addressing his waiters or his dog. Accordingly, Hermès froze, his eyes on Richard. "All this place needs is a thorough cleaning, all new furniture, a fresh coat of paint, and some sort of design aesthetic."

"Oh, is that all?" Kate asked, propping herself up on her elbows. "And this is in between final preparations for this weekend's wedding, planning for our New Year's Eve wedding, and pulling together Annabelle's engagement party?"

Richard swiveled his head toward me, and his dark spiky hair didn't so much as quiver. "A New Year's Eve wedding? When were you going to mention this to me?"

"That's what you took away from all of that?" I asked.

He sniffed, looking slightly abashed. "Fine. Perhaps this isn't the best time to have a photography team descend on your apartment, but when opportunity knocks, Annabelle, you have to open the door."

"Yoo hoo!" A head popped around the front door that Richard had left standing open.

"And when you come *here*, you have to remember to close the door," I muttered to Richard as my downstairs neighbor Leatrice bustled inside wearing a reindeer sweater with three-dimensional googly eyes, her jet-black hair adorned with a blinking reindeer antler headband. "And lock it."

"I thought I heard barking," she said, making a beeline for Hermès.

For a woman who had cruised past her eightieth birthday, she had remarkably acute hearing. She also considered herself an amateur spy, so she possessed an apartment full of listening devices. It was anyone's guess which she'd employed today.

"What's up, Leatrice?" I asked. "We're kind of in the middle of a crisis here."

Her eyebrows popped up, and she pursed her bright-coral lips. "Another murder?"

"No," I said with a sigh. "It's not like we stumble over dead bodies every day."

"It's been months since we had anything to do with a murder investigation," Kate added, counting quickly on her fingers. "Over eight months. I think that's a record for us."

"You aren't counting the body you found on my wedding day?" Leatrice asked as she rubbed Hermès's belly.

Kate shook her head. "He wasn't dead. I'm only counting actual corpses."

"I think I know who you *shouldn't* have at the magazine interview," Richard said out of the corner of his mouth.

"As much fun as this is," I said, giving my assistant a pointed look, "we really need to get to work if we're going to get everything done before the weekend."

"That's why I popped by, dear," Leatrice said. "My honeybun wanted to see if you needed anything for your engagement party in the way of performers."

Leatrice had recently married Sidney Allen, an entertainment coordinator who provided costumed performers for events. The two had met when Leatrice crashed a Venetian-themed wedding I'd planned that had been filled with Carnival characters courtesy of Sidney Allen.

"Performers?" Richard sucked in a breath. "What type of performers does 'honeybun' suggest for an engagement party?"

"It is two weeks before Christmas," Leatrice said. "We thought elves could be fun."

"Elves?" Kate cocked her head to one side. "Like the hot Orlando Bloom, *Lord of the Rings* kind or the short jingle-bell hat, Santa Claus kind?"

Leatrice giggled. "The Santa Claus kind, of course."

"Oh, no." Richard held up his hands, palms out. "Just because this party is taking place in December does not mean we're going to have an apartment full of little people in pointy shoes running around."

"Sidney Allen doesn't actually use little people for his elves, does he?" I asked. "I feel like that isn't very PC."

Leatrice nibbled the corner of her bottom lip. "I'm not sure. They might not be little people. They might be children."

"Child labor," Richard mumbled. "Even better."

"I don't think we need any elves," I said to Leatrice, "but please tell Sidney Allen that we appreciate the offer."

"The party's pretty set," Kate added. "Food by Richard, décor by Buster and Mack. Annabelle doesn't want a fuss."

My elderly neighbor shrugged. "Probably for the best. My poor sugar muffin is stretched pretty thin with all the Santas he's providing for holiday parties. But don't worry. I can still bring my pigs-in-a-blanket wreath."

Richard clutched my arm for support, and I hoped he wasn't going into a full-on swoon.

"I think we're set on food, too," I said. "Richard's doing the catering, and you know his rules about outside food."

The official rule was that he preferred outside food not be brought to events he catered because he was responsible for the food safety of the party. The reality was that he would toss it out a window.

"Too bad," Kate said. "I love a good pig-in-a-blanket. Especially when said pigs are arranged to look like a Christmas wreath."

Richard shot her a look, but before he could say something, the door swung open.

Fern, hairdresser to the rich and famous of DC and our go-to wedding hairstylist, staggered into the room. His dark hair was pulled back into a low ponytail, and he wore cranberry-colored pants and a dark-gray turtleneck. A few strands of hair fell in his face as he leaned against the armrest of my couch. "Thank goodness you're all here."

"What's wrong?" I asked. Fern was always impeccably put together, rarely a hair out of place.

"It's Santa Claus," he said, pressing a hand to his throat. "He's missing."

CHAPTER 3

"Have I been sucked into an alternate universe?" Richard asked, looking from face to face. "Santa can't be missing because . . ." He darted a glance at Hermès. "Well, I don't want to say it out loud."

Kate put her hands over the small dog's pointy ears. "Because he's not real?"

"Not the *real* Santa Claus," Fern said. "Kris Kringle Jingle. The man who dresses up in a Santa costume and walks around Georgetown singing holiday songs to people."

Leatrice clapped her hands together. "Oh, I love him. He always compliments me on my hair and does the best version of "Jingle Bell Rock." Her face fell. "Did you say he's missing?"

Fern nodded, dropping into the overstuffed yellow twill chair positioned across from my couch. "At least according to my friend, Jeannie."

I headed toward the kitchen to get Fern some water, since his cheeks were flushed pink. I snagged a bottle from the fridge and leaned my head over the divider between the rooms. "How does Jeannie know he's missing and not just taking some time off? I'm sure wearing a Santa costume when it's almost eighty degrees isn't fun."

"Jeannie knows everything that goes on in Georgetown," Fern said, fanning himself with a linen handkerchief, his head tipped back against the cushion. "If she thinks he's missing, then he's missing."

I returned to the living room and handed Fern the bottled water, then perched on the arm of the couch, resigning myself to the fact that nothing was going to get done until Fern finished his story.

He winked at me. "You're an angel, Annabelle."

"Is this Jeannie someone you work with?" Kate asked. "Have you taken on a new stylist in the salon?"

Fern took a long drink of water, then laughed. "Aren't you a stitch? No, Jeannie is one of the housing challenged of Georgetown."

"Housing challenged?" Richard tilted his head. "Do you mean homeless?"

"Yes, but it's not like she lives on the streets. She moves from shelter to shelter," Fern said. "We met when she was sitting outside the salon one day, and I offered to give her a wash and dry. Now she comes in just about every week. And she's the one I save all my hotel toiletries for. Jeannie loves the little bottles."

"How often do you stay in hotels?" Kate asked.

Fern smoothed a loose strand of hair back into his ponytail. "I'm in hotels almost every weekend. I may not *stay* there per se."

"Are you telling me you take the toiletries out of the hotel rooms where our brides are getting ready?" I asked, caught between feeling scandalized and impressed.

He gave a half shrug. "Maybe. Trust me when I tell you that Jeannie gets more enjoyment out of them than anyone could."

Richard gave an impatient sigh. "So how did this street person decide that the singing Santa is missing?"

"Like I said," Fern gave Richard an equally impatient look. "She knows everything that goes on in Georgetown. She's the one who told me that Violet Drummond was having an affair with a diplomatic intern thirty years younger than her."

Richard's eyebrows shot up, but I jumped in before he and Fern could go down the rabbit hole of society gossip they both adored. "So how long does Jeannie say he's been missing?"

"At least a day." Fern sat up. "She claims that Kris Kringle Jingle told her he was nervous about something he'd seen the day before yesterday. He wouldn't go into more detail, but claimed he saw something he shouldn't have, and he hoped *they* hadn't seen him."

Leatrice's eyes were as round as the googly reindeer eyes on her sweater. "Hope who hadn't seen him?"

"That's what she doesn't know," Fern said. "But Jeannie hasn't seen him since then, and she's convinced something bad has happened to him."

"It does sound suspicious."

We all swung our heads toward the deep voice and the doorway where my fiancé, Mike Reese, stood listening.

I jumped up, my heart fluttering a bit seeing him. Even though we now lived together, I still got butterflies each time I saw my tall fiancé with dark hair and hazel eyes. "I didn't know you'd be home so early."

He scanned the crowd in our apartment, one eyebrow lifting slightly. He'd gotten used to my colorful friends coming in and out of our place—mostly work-related, since Wedding Belles operated out of our Georgetown apartment—but it wasn't every day so many of them were camped out in the living room.

Leatrice leapt to her feet, jostling Hermès, who gave a disapproving yip, and she rushed over to Reese. "It seems like we've stumbled into another mystery, Detective."

"No." I waved a finger. "No, we haven't. There's no mystery." The last thing I needed to add to my already jam-packed schedule was a criminal investigation. I knew from past experience that our investigations usually took over everything, and I could not afford the distraction this week.

Reese grinned at me. "I'm glad to hear you saying that. I don't know if I've ever heard you insist there *isn't* a case."

I resisted the urge to make a face at him. "There's a first time for everything. Besides, Richard just told me he arranged to have a Wedding Belles magazine shoot in our apartment this week on top of the wedding we have to pull together for Saturday and the party we're supposedly hosting on Sunday."

Reese ran a hand through his hair, and an errant curl flopped down on his forehead. "Maybe I should plan to clear out until next week."

"Don't you dare," I said, walking over and slipping my hand into his. "You're the only thing that's going to keep me sane."

He smiled and pulled me close to him. "We definitely don't want you going insane."

"So what do I tell Jeannie?" Fern asked, tapping one toe on the floor. "That it's bad timing for her friend to go missing?"

"You have to admit," Kate said, "two weeks before Christmas is not the time to get anyone's attention."

"Who is the missing person?" Reese asked.

"Kris Kringle Jingle," Fern said.

Leatrice bounced up and down on her toes. "You know. The fellow who dresses as Santa and walks around singing holiday songs in Georgetown."

A look of recognition flashed across my fiancé's face. "I do know him. He's been doing that for years. We keep him on our radar--like we keep any street performer--but he's never gotten any complaints. How long has he been missing?"

Fern stood. "At least twenty-four hours. Possibly more. My friend Jeannie can tell you more."

Reese nodded, then looked down at me. "Why don't I go talk with this Jeannie? That way you don't have to get sucked into an investigation, and I can file an official police report if we need to."

"You mean do things the official way?" Kate tapped a finger on her chin. "No hiding bodies or searching for evidence behind the backs of the police? Now that's a novel approach."

I ignored her comment and stared up at my handsome fiancé. "You sure you have the time?"

He kissed me on the forehead. "I'm sure, as long as it will keep you from running around trying to solve the case on your own. I'm on my lunch break, anyway. I'll just grab something quick while Fern and I are out."

"Lunch break?" I glanced up at the clock on my wall, preparing to tease him about taking such an early lunch, but swallowing hard when I saw the time. "It's after eleven already? Ugh! We have a floral meeting soon, and I'm not dressed."

Reese gave me a quick kiss and stepped back. "I'd better leave you to it, babe. I'll see you tonight." He beckoned Fern. "You're with me."

Fern trilled his fingers together as he followed Reese out the door, turning to wave at us. "This is so exciting. An official police investigation."

The butterflies in my stomach that my fiancé had produced had morphed into a tight ball. I hadn't gotten any of the confirmation calls made for Saturday's wedding, and I could only hope that the meeting with Buster and Mack would be quick.

Kate stood and steered me toward the hallway. "You get dressed while Richard and I talk about the photo shoot and the party."

"And why don't I take Hermès downstairs with me while you kids work?" Leatrice asked. "It's been ages since I babysat."

Richard's gaze went between his little dog and his crate of decor. "Fine, but no elf caps on him."

Leatrice's smile drooped, but she made a criss cross over her heart as she scooped up the Yorkie and headed out of my apartment. "You have my word."

I thought there was a much greater chance she had a matching set of reindeer antlers for him, but I didn't say anything as I hurried down the hall to get dressed. My mind went to the potentially missing Santa, then I shook my head. I'd been honest when I'd told Reese that the last thing I needed was to get pulled into another investigation, but I also felt a pang of guilt when I thought about Kris Kringle Jingle.

Just like everyone who lived in Georgetown, I'd grown used to the cheery sight of the slightly rumpled Santa who sang merrily as he strolled up and down M Street. He was as much a part of the neighborhood as the C&O Canal that cut through it and the colorful row houses lining the narrow streets. I forced myself not to think the worst as I pulled off my jeans and pawed through my dry-cleaning bag.

First a heat wave and now a missing Santa? The holidays weren't off to a great start.

CHAPTER 4

"That's not half bad for something you grabbed from the floor," Kate said as she appraised my black pants and hunter green top while holding open the door to Buster and Mack's flower shop.

The bell overhead tinkled as we walked inside Lush, and we were greeted by the store's familiar aroma of cut flowers and espresso, now mixed with the sharp scent of evergreen.

"I didn't grab it from the floor." I tried to sound indignant, even though, to be fair, the pants had been rescued from my dry-cleaning bag.

She plucked a strand of carpet lint from my pant leg. "I stand corrected."

"Fine," I said, under my breath, even though I didn't see any customers milling about the display tables that were stacked tall with holiday candles, glittering ornaments, and frosted-glass vases. "I may have gotten a little behind on laundry."

Kate held up her hands. "No judgment. I told you we needed some downtime. December is supposed to be the month where we get all our wedding day dresses cleaned and mended."

I sighed, knowing she was right. My dry-cleaning bag was jammed with black dresses, and my favorite black flats were in desperate need of a little love and a lot of shoe polish.

We stepped further inside and started to weave our way around the displays. Lush was usually what I would have called industrial chic, with concrete floors and metal shelves filled with galvanized buckets of fresh flowers lining the walls. Since November, however, it had transformed into a winter wonderland with a towering frosted Christmas tree in each corner, and the buckets of hydrangea and roses replaced with white birch branches and crimson amaryllis.

"Annabelle! Kate!" Mack appeared from the back of the shop, waving with one large hand and holding a tiny espresso cup with the other. "Make sure you pull the door closed tightly. I don't want the heat to wilt all of our evergreens."

As he lumbered toward us, I was reminded how incongruous a burly, leather-clad biker with a dark-red goatee, tattoos, and piercings was in a floral shop decked out with Christmas trees glistening with fake snow, pine wreaths hanging from velvet ribbon, and white twinkle lights dripping like icicles from the ceiling. When he reached us, I realized he wore a baby carrier strapped to his back, and a small, fair head poked around the side of his.

"Hey, Mack." I stood up on tiptoes to give him a kiss on the cheek, and then reached out for the child's chubby fist. "And hi, Merry."

"She's gotten so big," Kate said as the child unleashed a torrent of happy chatter and clapped her hands.

"Well, she is a year old," Mack reminded us, twisting his head and catching the little girl's eye.

"I can't believe it." Kate shook her head as Mack led us to the back of the shop and a long, high metal table surrounded by tall barstools. "Has it really been a year already?"

I thought back to the same time last year when Buster and Mack had found Merry on the doorstep of their biker church. A lot had happened since then, including Merry and her teenaged mother coming to live above Lush, and Buster and Mack becoming surrogate fathers to both of them. I looked at the chubby legs dangling from the metal frame carrier hooked on Mack's back. Only a few months ago,

Merry was traveling in a front-facing fabric carrier, and now the little girl with blond hair curling around her ears looked almost ready to walk.

"We were going to do a big birthday party," Mack said, downing the last of his espresso. "But you know how crazy December is for florists. Between the home installations and the holiday parties, we're stretched thin."

"And this year it's also crazy for wedding planners." Kate hopped onto one of the barstools and set her pink purse beside her.

"You two don't normally have more than one wedding over the holidays, do you?" Mack asked, waving a hand toward the elaborate, chrome espresso machine behind him. "Cappuccino? Espresso?"

"No, we don't, to the question about holiday weddings," Kate said, "and yes, please, to the cappuccino. I need all the caffeine I can get."

"Make that two," I said, taking a seat as Mack bustled around the machine, Merry bobbing behind him.

"Now which wedding are we meeting about today?" Mack asked, then swiveled his head around quickly. "Son of a nutcracker! It's not the bride for this Saturday, is it? I've already placed her floral order."

"No," I assured him. "We're all set for that one. This is for the New Year's Eve wedding."

"Thank heavens." He glanced toward the ceiling, and I suspected he was saying a small prayer of thanks. Aside from being the city's top event florists, Buster and Mack were also members of a Christian motorcycle gang and the Born Again Biker Church. They'd reformed their previous lives, and now they never drank, cursed, or took the Lord's name in vain. It also appeared that their creative alternatives to cursing were seasonally inspired.

"Don't get too happy," Kate told him, raising her voice to be heard above the screeching of the espresso machine's steaming wand. "We only booked the wedding recently, and we know almost nothing about it."

"Except that they fired their old planner and are throwing out whatever work she'd done for them." I shifted on the barstool and put the client's thin file on the table in front of me. "The bride isn't even joining us today. She just called us to say something came up and to go ahead without her."

Mack looked over his shoulder. "Do we have creative carte blanche?"

"As long as you stick with the theme of 'time,'" I said. "And the couple wants an Old World feel."

"So that's a no," Mack said, then shrugged. "That's fine. I'd rather have some direction than none at all."

I opened the file and stared down at the notes I'd taken when I'd talked to the bride on the phone. "Aside from keeping the venue and photographer and basic theme, we're starting from zero. I'd hoped to get the old floral proposals this morning so you could see what the client doesn't want, but we got a little derailed."

"By Santa Claus," Kate added.

Mack placed two oversized cappuccinos in front of us, then turned back to the machine to retrieve his own refilled demitasse cup. "Now this I want to hear."

"It's nothing really." I wrapped my hands around the warm cup and enjoyed the heat, even if it wasn't cold outside. "Fern is all worked up because a friend of his claims that Kris Kringle Jingle is missing."

Mack nearly dropped his small cup. "Missing? Is he sure?"

"We don't know," I said. "Reese went with him to interview the lady who insists he's disappeared."

Kate eyed Mack over the rim of her mug as she took a sip. "Why? Do you know Kris?"

"Kris Kringle Jingle?" Mack looked at her as if her question was absurd. "Of course we know him." He leaned his head back and bellowed for Buster, then turned back to us. "When it isn't the holidays, he's one of our local laborers. Mostly loading the vans and unloading shipments."

Buster appeared from the door leading into the back of the shop, his face lighting up when he saw us. "Sorry about that. I was on the phone trying to get more holly for Greta Van Strubbel's party." He pushed the black biker goggles further up on his bald head. "Although

I'm not sure how the holly and berry theme is going to play if it hits eighty degrees."

I didn't know how both men were still completely decked out in black leather pants and thick jackets emblazoned with Road Riders for Jesus patches when it was so warm. Just looking at them made me sweat, but I didn't say anything.

"Tell us about it," Kate said. "Saturday's wedding has an icicle theme, remember?"

"Did you know about Kris?" Mack said to Buster.

"Kris Kringle Jingle?" Buster asked, stroking one hand down his brown goatee. "No, what?"

Mack waved a beefy hand toward me and Kate. "The ladies say he's missing."

"To be perfectly accurate," Kate said, "Fern is the one who says he's missing. And he's getting his information from a woman named Jeannie."

Mack drained his espresso in a single gulp. "That would explain why we didn't see him yesterday. He usually passes by and belts out a verse of 'The Little Drummer Boy.'"

Buster blinked hard a few times. More evidence that Buster and Mack were softies, despite their intimidating appearance. "That song gets us every time." He swiped at his eyes. "Do they think something has happened to him?"

"Reese went with Fern to talk to this Jeannie woman."

Mack put a hand to his heart. "That's a relief. I know your fiancé will be able to find him."

"If he's missing," I said. "It's so warm, he might just be taking a break at home instead of having to be out in a heavy Santa suit in this heat."

"Home?" Buster cocked his head at me. "Kris doesn't have a home."

Kate's mug clattered on the table. "What do you mean he doesn't have a home?"

"An apartment then?" I asked, lowering my own mug before I took a drink.

Mack shook his head. "He moves around the shelters, and he

sometimes rents a cheap motel room, especially when it gets really cold or he works a lot of jobs for us, but Kris has been homeless for years."

I remembered that Buster and Mack often employed the neighborhood homeless when they needed extra labor, paying them under the table with cash and feeding them well throughout the day.

Buster shoved his hands into the pockets of his snug leather pants. "He can usually be found at one of the shelters. Have they searched all those yet?"

"I don't know." I glanced at Kate, who looked just as shocked as I was. I'd seen Kris Kringle Jingle charming people with holiday songs for years, and never once had I suspected he was homeless. Now that I knew the singing Santa lived on the street, I found my own stomach tightening with worry. Suddenly, our weddings didn't seem like the most important thing in the world.

CHAPTER 5

I pushed against my front door, but it only slid forward a few inches. Glancing back at Kate, who held her high heels in one hand after the climb up three flights of stairs, I sighed. "This is not a good sign."

"Hold on a second," Richard called out from the crack in the door. "I need to move this so you can get inside."

After a notable amount of heaving and groaning, the door opened. If I weren't absolutely sure I'd walked into the correct stone-fronted apartment building and up the right number of stairs, I would have thought I was in the wrong place.

"Holy holly berries," Kate whispered as she stared through the doorframe, obviously still under the influence of Buster and Mack.

Even though Kate and I had only been gone a couple of hours, my apartment didn't look remotely like I'd left it. The single plastic crate Richard had arrived with had been joined by a stack of glass racks, more plastic crates, and piles of empty cardboard boxes all pushed into the hallway. Richard had clearly gotten a few deliveries after we'd left, and I was both impressed and shocked he'd actually had rental furniture hauled up to my fourth-floor apartment. At least, I hoped it was rental.

The yellow twill sofa and overstuffed chair that comprised the bulk of my living room furniture were gone, as was the beige rug that covered the hardwood floors. In their place were a stylish gray sofa and a pair of pickle wood French chairs upholstered in a gray-and-white chevron pattern. My glass coffee table remained, but the paperwork was gone. It was now topped with a pair of rattan trays arranged with stacks of slipcovered books, bowls of moss balls, and milk glass vases filled with white orchids.

My dining room table had been cleared, draped in a linen I recognized as "White Etched Velvet" from Party Settings rental company and fully set as if I were having a dinner party for eight. Matte silver chargers were topped with white plates, and a gray hemstitched linen napkin was banded around the top plate. Cut glassware and ornate silverware completed the look.

The Christmas tree, which had been sparsely decorated, now stood covered from tip to trunk in ivory, silver, and gold. An ivory crushed velvet ribbon wrapped around the tree as a garland and glass ball ornaments reflected the twinkle of the white lights. Even the base was swathed in a silver crushed velvet skirt and surrounded by boxes wrapped in gold paper.

"I thought you were adding a few design elements," I said, hearing my voice crack. "Where's all my stuff?"

"Not to worry, darling." Richard bustled forward and took me by the elbow. "Your furniture is still here. It's in the back."

"The back?" Kate stepped inside tentatively, as if she wasn't sure about the new version of my apartment. "Where in the back? On the fire escape?"

Richard gave her a side-eye glance. "Of course not. As much as that tired, old stuff might deserve it, I did not relegate it to the fire escape. The couch is in the bedroom and the chair is in the office."

I cast a glance down my hallway. Neither the bedroom nor the office had tons of extra space, so I was afraid to see where exactly the furniture had gone.

"And all this is for...?" I prompted.

"The photo shoot, of course." Richard threw his arms wide. "If the magazine is going to photograph you in your Georgetown apartment, we can't have pictures of you and Kate sitting on a saggy old couch covered in pizza stains."

I understood his logic, but the new furniture looked too chic to sit on. And what kind of person kept a dining table fully set? I knew I would have a hard time looking like I was at home in a place that was decidedly not me.

He patted my arm. "Trust me. All the magazine shoots are like this. No one actually lives in houses that look like the ones in *Architectural Digest*. Everything is staged to some degree."

"This is definitely some degree," Kate mumbled.

"So I'm supposed to live with this until the photo shoot?" I asked, wondering what Reese would think when he saw the new and improved look. This was definitely not a living room where you kicked your feet up onto the coffee table anymore. I twisted around as I scanned the room. "Where's the TV?"

Richard jerked a thumb behind him. "In your bedroom. It made the room look too butch."

"Problem solved," Kate said, poking at one of the glassless silver geometric terrariums on the coffee table. "This is definitely where testosterone goes to die."

"You won't have to suffer very long," Richard said, flouncing off toward the kitchen. "The shoot is tomorrow morning, and I can have everything removed by the afternoon."

"Tomorrow morning?" I repeated. "You didn't tell me the shoot was so soon."

"No need to drag things out, am I right?" Richard said. "Anyway, tomorrow was the only time slot the photographer had. If we'd waited, you'd miss getting into the next issue."

I did a quick mental rundown of the week's schedule. We didn't have any meetings scheduled the next morning, but I worried that the confirmation calls for Saturday's wedding were getting pushed off again. I usually blocked out a full day leading up to a wedding just so Kate and I could focus on the last-minute details and go over the paperwork for a final time.

Kate shrugged. "I guess it's better we get it out of the way. Do we know what we're wearing?"

I almost smacked my forehead as I thought about the jam-packed dry-cleaning bag hanging in my closet. Did I have anything clean to wear? Come to think of it, did I own anything stylish enough for a magazine feature? "Should we go with all black, since that's what we usually wear on a wedding day?"

Richard groaned loudly. "Black again? I'm sure you two can come up with something a little less predictable than black."

"But it's DC," I said, knowing that a black dress might be my only unwrinkled option. "Everyone in DC wears black, even to weddings."

Richard's head appeared in the open space between the kitchen and living room. "Which is why you need to wear something else. *Anything* else."

Kate leaned close to me. "Don't worry. I'll take care of wardrobe."

I eyed her. "Do I need to remind you that microminis and J. Lo necklines do not scream 'elite wedding planner'?"

Before my assistant could make a face at me, I heard a sharp intake of breath behind us.

"I would ask if you've been robbed," Fern said as he walked in, "but it's rare that burglars leave the place looking better than before."

Reese followed him, his eyes wide. "Um, babe?"

"I know, I know," I said, before he could ask. "It's all Richard's doing for the magazine shoot, but it will be gone by tomorrow."

"You're doing a magazine shoot tomorrow?" Fern asked, fluttering his fingers at his throat. "And you didn't ask me to do your hair?"

"Richard just told us about it," Kate said. "Are you free tomorrow morning?"

"For a magazine shoot?" Fern grinned. "Of course I am. If I have any society hussies booked at the salon, I'll just reschedule them. They can get bleached blonde another day."

"You know, the people who said things would get routine after we moved in together could not have been more wrong," Reese said, letting out a breath.

"Not everyone has my friends," I reminded him, taking his hand in mine. "How did it go with Jeannie?"

His expression went from bemused to serious. "I took a statement from her. She seems pretty credible, and I feel confident she told us the truth."

"So Kris Kringle Jingle is missing?"

"It seems so, and Jeannie is convinced that something bad has happened to him," my fiancé said. "She says he was acting nervous the day before he vanished, and he told her that he'd seen something he shouldn't have."

"But he didn't say exactly what?" I asked.

Reese shook his head. "It's not much to go on, but I issued a BOLO for Kris. Luckily, people take a lot of photos with him during the holidays, so I have a good description and a decent image."

"Be on the lookout," Fern mouthed to Kate, with a nudge.

"I know what BOLO means," she said. "We do have cops show up to about half our weddings, remember?"

I tried to ignore her statement, and the fact that it was sort of true.

"Did you know he was homeless?" I asked Reese. "Buster and Mack use him as seasonal labor and they told us he usually rotates through the shelters, but occasionally gets a motel room."

"I knew. Did you know he refuses to take money for singing Christmas carols? Jeannie says it was his way of thanking people for helping him out during the year."

Now that I thought about it, I'd never noticed him asking for money. It was probably one of the reasons I hadn't guessed he was homeless. Concern for the singing Santa gnawed at the back of my mind again, but I told myself that Reese was on the case.

"Is that the office phone?" Kate asked as a muffled ringing came from down the hall.

"Yep," I said, hurrying toward it and pushing open the door to Wedding Belles headquarters. My mouth fell open when I realized that the overstuffed chair that used to sit across from my couch now took up almost every square inch of floor space in my home office.

The room had not been spacious to start with--the desk, office chair, high bookshelf, and tall filing cabinet leaving enough room on the floor for us to store client supplies and assemble gift bags. Richard had shoved the chair far enough into the room so the door could close, and had stacked everything from the floor into the chair. The only way I could get to the ringing phone on the desk was to dive for it or somehow clamber over the chair that faced away from me.

"Remind me to kill you later," I yelled to Richard as I gingerly stepped onto the back of the chair and attempted to keep my balance. Edging from the back to the arm, I managed to crab walk my way from the upholstered chair to my swivel office chair, collapsing into it and picking up the phone.

"Wedding Belles," I said, steadying my breath. "This is Annabelle."

"You're dead," the voice on the other end said.

My stomach churned as I realized that I knew the voice. Very well.

CHAPTER 6

"You're sure it was Brianna on the phone?" Kate asked, sitting on a stool next to mine the next morning and sipping from a to-go cup of coffee.

We'd positioned the high stools in front of my living room window to get the most natural morning light, and because the sliver of space was the only place in my apartment that wasn't overly staged and styled. My living room had been transformed from frumpy and functional to ornate and over-the-top, and I hardly recognized it.

"Of course I'm sure." I held a bottle of cold Mocha Frappuccino in my lap as Fern sprayed a puff of hairspray on the back of my hair. "First of all, it sounded exactly like her, Southern accent and all. Secondly, who else hates us enough to threaten murder, and probably most damning, I heard someone in the background say her name."

"Amateur," Fern muttered.

"Who's Brianna?" Carl asked as he peered at Kate's face through black-framed, hipster glasses, then began dabbing foundation on her cheeks.

"I forget you've been out of the wedding scene," I said, sliding my gaze over to the makeup artist with short, dark hair and colorful tattoos swirling down both arms.

Although Carl had been one of my original go-to makeup artists, he'd stopped taking weddings for several years in order to serve as the first lady's personal makeup artist. Because the job had involved traveling around the world with her, locking in weddings months out had been impossible. But since the change in the administration, he was now available for weddings again, and we'd even been able to pull in this last-minute favor.

It was a Wedding Belles rule to only hire nice people--sometimes easier said than done in a business with plenty of divas--and Carl fit that bill to a tee. Not only was he a talented makeup artist, he was as sweet and humble as they came, despite his famous client catapulting him into the limelight.

"You're lucky you don't know her," Kate said, her eyes closed as Carl patted something over her lids. "She's all Instagram smoke and mirrors."

He straightened up and assessed Kate's face. "And she threatened to kill you? Why?"

"We have a bit of a complicated relationship with her," I said, shifting on the stool as Fern pulled a round brush through my hair.

Fern let out another blast of hairspray. "That floozy is just jealous of our girls. She's been trying to spread rumors about them ever since she arrived."

I fought the urge to twist around and gape at Fern. Bold words from the man who'd spread the story of Brianna using her wedding planning business as a front for a high-end call girl service. Although I appreciated his loyalty, Fern had only fanned the flames of our feud.

"It's complicated," I said, "but she does seem to have it in for us."

"But why call out of the blue and threaten your life?" Kate asked.

"She called the Wedding Belles line," I reminded her, taking a swig of my cold coffee as Fern stopped brushing. "The threat might not have been just for me."

"Thanks for that," Kate said. "But why now? Most people get *less* vindictive over the holidays."

"Speak for yourself," Richard said, emerging from my kitchen behind us. "Anyone who's waited in line for a photo with Santa deserves to be homicidal."

"I doubt Brianna was having a bad reaction from waiting in line to see Santa." Especially since she was a single twentysomething. "Wait a second. How do you know anything about waiting in line to get a photo with Santa?"

"You don't think I'm going to let the fisherman's sweater I got Hermès in Ireland go to waste, do you? He's very photogenic, you know."

"Who's Hermès?" Carl whispered as Richard bustled around the dining table, no doubt putting the final touches on the completely unrealistic tablescape.

"His dog," Kate whispered back.

"If we eliminate holiday stress from the equation, there must be a reason for her to be mad enough to call and threaten us," I said, trying to get back on topic.

"And she didn't say *why* we were dead?" Kate asked, coughing as Carl dusted her face liberally with powder.

I shook my head. "Just that we were dead and she'd get us back."

"And nothing unusual has happened in the past few days?" Carl asked, bending over his pop-up table arranged neatly with palettes and pencils.

I nibbled the corner of my mouth. "I wouldn't say that. We did book a last-minute New Year's Eve wedding."

"And learned that Kris Kringle Jingle might be missing," Kate added.

Richard clattered a plate behind me. "The New Year's Eve wedding. Didn't you say the couple fired their first planner?"

Kate snapped her fingers. "He's right. They did, but they didn't tell us who the first planner was."

A feeling of dread came over me. "I'll bet it was Brianna. She probably heard we were taking it over and thinks we stole the wedding from her."

"It's not your fault that she has no clue what she's doing," Richard said. "Just because you can take a decent photo of yourself in cute shoes holding a cup of coffee, does not mean you can plan a wedding. What is wrong with these Millennials?"

"Hey," Kate said. "Not all Millennials are as awful as Brianna."

"If it is Brianna, what do we do about it?" I asked, gulping down the last of my chocolately, cold coffee and feeling grateful for both the caffeine and the sugar.

"Do about it?" Richard huffed out a breath as he came to stand in front of me, both hands on his hips. "You don't do anything. It's not like you're going to turn down the wedding, and you can't let petty people change the way you live your life. The more successful you become, the more jealous people you'll have to deal with. Trust me, darling. It's a cross I've had to bear for years."

I grinned at him, comforted by both his faith in me and my continuing success and his pep talk. "You're right. I can't let one person affect me so much."

"That being said," Richard waved one hand in the direction of my front door, "I might consider adding an extra dead bolt or two and perhaps one of those doorbell cameras."

"You should add that just for Leatrice," Kate muttered.

"I'm sure your hunky fiancé has it under control," Fern said. "I know I wouldn't worry if I lived with a cop that looked like that. You just know he's packing."

My cheeks warmed as Richard rolled his eyes and flounced back into the kitchen.

"I'm sure you're worrying over nothing," Carl said, his voice low and calm as he swirled pink blush over Kate's cheeks. "Most people are more bark than bite anyway. You just keep doing the good work you always do and don't worry about the rest. Karma will take care of that."

I smiled at Carl. I'd missed his even-keeled manner over the past few years, although it was easy to understand why the first lady had loved having him around. "You're right. Thanks."

"Anytime." He squeezed my shoulder. "Now, did you say something about Kris Kringle Jingle being missing?"

"Do you know him?" I asked.

He nodded as he stepped back, sizing up Kate's face and adding more blush to one cheek. "I worked at a Georgetown salon for years, remember? Kris Kringle Jingle always popped into the salon in December to say hello and sing a quick song."

Fern chuckled. "He does that in my salon, too. You should see my old society ladies light up."

I closed my eyes as Fern unleashed a cloud of spray over my head. "Did you know he's homeless?"

"No." Carl sounded surprised. "I don't think he ever asked us for money."

Fern stopped spraying. "He doesn't do Kris Kringle Jingle for money. It's his way of thanking the Georgetown residents."

"Speaking of Georgetown residents," Kate said as Buster and Mack bustled in behind us, the jangling chains on their leather clothing alerting us to their arrival.

"Sorry we're late," Mack called out. "It's been a crazy morning."

"Don't worry," I said. In truth, I hadn't known they were coming over at all.

"Thank heavens," Richard said. "I was worried I'd have to fashion some sort of candle centerpiece if you didn't get the flowers here in time."

I twisted around to see that Mack and Buster held a massive floral centerpiece between them. I shot Richard a look. "You made them bring flowers?"

Richard pressed a hand to his heart. "You expected me to set a table without fresh flowers? Really, Annabelle."

I'm sorry, I mouthed to my burly friends before Fern turned my head back so I faced forward.

"We're happy to do it," Mack said. "We were just running short on labor this morning, so it took twice as long to load the delivery trucks."

Even though I couldn't see, I could hear the two men setting the arrangement on the dining table and Richard fussing over it and moving glassware.

"Our usual guys were involved in the search," Buster added.

Mack let out a long sigh. "Once we drop this off, we're going to head back and join them."

"The search?" I wanted to turn back around but Fern held my head in place.

"For Kris," Buster said. "The homeless in Georgetown have organized their own search party to look for him."

I thought about the BOLO my fiancé had issued for Kris. I hoped between law enforcement and the search party, they'd locate him soon. It wouldn't feel like the holidays in Georgetown without the singing Santa.

"Well, this isn't good," Kate said.

"Agreed," I said. "I'd hoped Kris would have turned up by now."

"Not that, *this*," Kate stared down at the phone in her lap as Carl leaned over his makeup table, swirling an eye shadow brush in a small pot of pale pink powder. "You know how our New Year's Eve bride already had her venue set? Well, I just got a text from the space manager, Trista. She comes to the wedding planner assistant happy hours. Apparently, Brianna signed the contract for the client, so it's technically *her* rental, and she just told them that the New Year's Eve event is no longer a wedding, it's a party for Brides by Brianna."

My stomach dropped. "Can she do that?" I asked, even though I knew that she could. If she signed the contract, she was the client. I'd thought our new bride and groom had signed all their own contracts, but it looked like Brianna ran her business differently than we did. I assumed she did it so she could mark everything up, a practice I'd never believed in, but I knew some of our colleagues made a pretty penny doing it.

"According to Trista, it's already done," Kate said with a groan.

Fern made a disapproving noise in the back of his throat. "Looks like it's time to revive the tales about Madame Brianna."

I was too worried to even attempt to talk Fern out of it. With only three weeks to go, our new wedding was back to square one. How were we going to find an available venue for New Year's Eve on top of everything else?

CHAPTER 7

"Try not to look like you're being held at gunpoint," Richard said, standing a few feet away as Kate and I posed on the sofa.

I sat on one end, wearing the surprisingly appropriate pale green wrap dress Kate had chosen for me, while she perched on the armrest in a not-too-short winter white sheath. We both wore significantly more makeup than we usually did--including false lashes--but I knew it wouldn't look as dramatic in photos.

"Which one of us are you talking to?" I asked, trying not to let my smile falter.

"You," Kate, Richard, and Fern all said at once.

I let out a breath and allowed my shoulders to sag. "Sorry. I can't stop thinking about the New Year's Eve wedding."

"It's okay." The female photographer lowered her camera. "Take a minute while I readjust the lights."

Fern rushed over holding a hair pick and a can of hairspray. "At least your style is holding up, sweetie."

I gave him a quick once-over. Instead of the black pants and shirt he'd been wearing that morning, he now had on beige pants tucked into high black boots, a matching belted jacket, and a black beret. "Did you change?"

Richard emitted an exasperated sigh as he joined us. "This is not a movie set, and you're not an old Hollywood director." He turned to face me, as Fern huffed something about Richard not having vision, then began fluffing Kate's hair. "I told you, darling. Don't worry. I'm making calls around town. If there's an available venue for New Year's Eve, I'll find it."

"But what if there isn't? It's bad enough that we're going to have to reprint invitations and have them rushed, but now we might not have a location to put on the invitations."

When I'd talked to the bride earlier, she'd been livid that her former planner had taken her venue. I'd been able to calm her down, but knowing brides the way I did, that calm wouldn't last long if we couldn't find a new site. Fast.

Richard took my hand and gave it an awkward pat. "You worrying and making the photo shoot take even longer than it should isn't going to help anyone. I know it's hard, but you need to channel some of that patented Annabelle Archer Zen. Focus on nothing but getting these photos right. Then you can worry about the wedding venue."

"And the wedding on Saturday and my engagement party?"

"Both of which are already planned," Kate reminded me.

"That's why you have a team, right?" Richard asked. "No one can do everything single-handedly, even though you like to think you can."

I managed a smile. Richard knew me too well. I did have a tendency to try to take on everything myself, even though time and time again I needed my friends to pull it all off. "You're right. Sorry I freaked out. I'm just rattled that a colleague would go after us and a client so blatantly."

"Brianna is a not a colleague." Richard's voice was low. "If you ask me, she's a wannabe who's gotten too big for her britches."

"Whatever she is," Kate said as Fern sprayed a final cloud of hairspray over her bob and moved away, "she's a horn in our side."

I suppressed an urge to laugh at the mental image of horns sprouting from our sides. "Or a thorn."

"Intolerable." Richard waved his hands in front of his face to disperse the high-end spray, although he could have just as easily been referring to Kate's habit of mangling expressions, which I sometimes suspected she continued to do just for his benefit.

Kate shrugged. "The only reason she can take over the venue and have a personal party there is because she doesn't have a New Year's Eve wedding. I'm sure no one important will go to her party."

"Not when we hire them for your client's wedding," Richard said with a wicked grin. "And Miss Malaprop is right. Brianna doesn't have any business. I mean, she's never once called me, and I'm the best caterer in the city."

I knew that Brianna would never call Richard because she knew we were best friends, but I didn't want to remind him that I was a reason he was missing out on business, even if he was correct and there wasn't much to be had.

"Ready?" the photographer asked from a few feet away.

I straightened my shoulders. "Let's do this."

Richard moved quickly out of the shot, standing next to Fern and Carl behind the light stand. He returned to tapping away on his phone, and I knew he was sending out his feelers for a venue. Richard had been in the DC wedding industry for far longer than I had and knew all the movers and shakers, as well as those who were off the radar. If anyone could track down a venue in a matter of hours, it would be him.

"We need to do something about Brianna," Kate said between shots, her face frozen in a smile. "She's gone from annoying to problematic to disastrous for our business."

"Chins down, ladies," the photographer said, moving in closer.

I lowered my chin as the shutter clicked rapidly. "Like what? We had no idea she was the planner our new client fired or that she'd signed their contracts. I feel like this is an isolated occurrence."

"What about all the times she spread rumors about us being murder magnets?"

"To be fair," I said, "that's kind of true."

The photographer moved to the right as she continued snapping. "Now turn your heads toward me."

"We haven't been involved in a murder in months," Kate said, sounding affronted. "Practically a lifetime."

I almost giggled. What did it say about us that we considered eight months without finding a dead body to be a good run?

"Perfect," the photographer called out. "Those are great smiles!"

"I agree that Brianna has been nothing but trouble for us, but it's not like we can run her out of town on a rail," I said.

"I don't care what she's on, as long as she leaves," Kate said. "Fern will have some ideas, I'm sure."

I glanced at Fern, fully expecting him to be holding a megaphone by his side and yelling 'Action'. "We don't have time to add 'blood feud' to this week's to-do list."

"Fine," she sighed. "But don't expect Brianna to back down. That Southern belle is a Southern bi--"

"That's it, ladies." The photographer lowered her camera. "I've got what I need."

"Thank you," I said, sinking back on the couch.

Kate flopped down next to me, her eyes sweeping the room. "This new look is kind of growing on me, although this couch is definitely not as comfortable as your old one."

"That's called structural integrity," Richard said, walking over. "Which those sad, old, yellow couch cushions barely have."

"Say what you will about my furniture," I said. "It's comfortable. I don't think I could live in a place as perfect as this."

"Pearls unto swine," Richard muttered, turning on his heel and walking over to thank the photographer.

"I hope you have plans to do something fun later," Carl said, joining us on the couch. "You're all made up for date night."

Kate raised her hand. "I do. I'd never let these long lashes go to waste."

"Every night is date night for some people," I said.

Kate twisted to face me. "If you tell me you and Reese are staying in and ordering Thai again, I'm going to go ballistic."

"I don't know what we're doing. I didn't think I'd be so done up, so we didn't even discuss it."

Carl nudged me. "Make him take you somewhere fabulous. You've got the smoky eyes to pull it off."

Kate held up a warning finger. "And not a sports bar. I've seen how much your fiancé loves ESPN."

It would be a shame to sit at home after having the former first lady's makeup artist do my face, although I didn't know how Reese would react to seeing me with such dramatic eyes. He was used to seeing me with barely a swipe of mascara and just a touch of face powder.

"Speak of the very attractive devil," Kate said as the door opened, and Reese stepped inside.

His eyebrows lifted as he took in the lights stands positioned throughout the room, Richard standing off to the side on his phone, Fern chatting with the photographer as she packed up her camera, and the multiple makeup cases and stools gathered by the door.

I gave him a wave, and his eyes widened.

"Is that your fiancé?" Carl asked in a hushed voice.

"Mmm hmm," Kate answered for me. "And he's a cop. A detective, actually. He doesn't always look so scary, though."

I stood as I registered the intense look on his face. We hadn't been living together for too long, but I knew when he was concerned.

"How did the shoot go?" he asked, forcing a smile as I took his hand. "You look really pretty."

"Thanks," I said. "It was good. What's wrong?"

He released a breath. "That obvious, huh?" He scraped a hand through his hair. "It's about Kris."

"Buster and Mack said they were joining all Kris's homeless friends to search for him. Maybe having all those people looking will help the search."

Reese tightened his grip on my hand. "Actually, we found something."

My stomach lurched. "Kris?"

"Not exactly," he said. "We found his Santa suit covered in blood."

CHAPTER 8

"I should tell Jeannie," Fern said, holding a cold compress to his head as he reclined on the couch.

We'd all been upset to learn that Kris Kringle Jingle's Santa suit had been found covered in blood, but Fern had taken it especially hard, slumping to the floor and having to be carried to the couch, where he lay sprawled from one end to the other. Kate had rescued his fallen beret from the floor and was now fanning him with it.

Amid the hysteria, both the magazine photographer and Carl had made their excuses and left, so it was just the five of us.

"I suspect she's heard by now," Reese said, sitting on the edge of one of the upholstered armchairs, his elbows leaning on his knees. "Word spreads pretty quickly on the streets."

Fern emitted a choked sob and mumbled something as Kate patted his shoulder and fanned faster.

"Tell us again where you found it," Richard called from the kitchen where I knew he was quietly packing up his supplies. Not even a bloody Santa suit could slow Richard's instinct to tidy, although I knew he was trying to be discreet.

Reese glanced down at his pocket-sized notebook. "Shoved in a dumpster in one of the alleys off M Street. It appeared sometime between late last night and this morning, because the beat cop didn't report seeing it on his patrol last night, and it was hanging out of the top."

I paced a small circle behind the couch. "Just because the suit was found doesn't mean Kris is dead."

Reese nodded solemnly. "No, but there was a lot of blood. If whoever was wearing the suit isn't dead, they're severely wounded."

Fern made another strangled sound.

"Why would someone hurt him, then dump the suit separately from the body?" I asked.

My fiancé shrugged. "Maybe they're hoping his body won't be identified when it's found."

"So you guys are searching for a body or a person?" Kate's voice was low and her brow furrowed.

Reese didn't answer.

My throat constricted, and I blew out a breath. Who would want to hurt or kill a man who dressed as Santa and sang songs to cheer people up? It wasn't like he was panhandling, so he wouldn't have any cash on him for muggers. And according to Reese, he didn't have any sort of criminal record, so it wasn't like his past was catching up to him. As far as I could tell, Kris was innocent. If this had to do with something he thought he saw, whatever it was must have been pretty bad.

"This is awful. The holidays won't feel the same without Kris Kringle Jingle," Kate said, giving voice to what we all probably felt. "They should just cancel Christmas in Georgetown this year."

I knew what she meant. Knowing that Santa was missing and might be dead didn't put you in the holiday spirit.

Richard inhaled sharply from the kitchen. "Cancel Christmas? Are you out of your mind? I've got a half dozen holiday parties to cater in the next week. People overeating during the holidays is the only thing that gets my business through the horrific month of January when everyone is on a diet."

Fern bolted upright and the cold washcloth flopped onto his lap. "I hate to admit it, but Richard is right. Canceling Christmas is the last thing Kris would have wanted. He was all about getting people into the spirit of the season. Besides, we don't know he'd dead."

"Who would have had it in for him?" I asked, walking around to face Fern.

Fern stood, and the damp cloth fell from his lap to the floor. "I'm not the person who knew him best."

Reese flipped a page in his notebook. "Jeannie insisted he didn't have any enemies. She said he got along with everyone--business owners and homeless alike."

"So it has to be connected to whatever it was he thought he saw," I said.

"I need to see her." Fern unbelted his beige jacket and tossed it onto the couch. "She'll be upset."

Reese stood. "I'll come with you."

"You're not going without me." I looked around the apartment for my purse. Where had Richard hidden it when he'd purged the space of anything practical?

"Dressed like that?" Kate waved a hand at my celadon-green dress made of silk shantung, then her gaze dropped to my heels. "You'll break your neck in two seconds."

I wanted to argue that I could walk in heels, but I knew she was right. I never wore heels for any significant stretch of time anymore, and the three-inch pumps would have me limping after only a block on the uneven Georgetown sidewalks. Plus, I was dressed for a society garden party, not to go traipsing around the city. I headed down the hall. "It will only take me a minute to change."

Richard poked his head out of the kitchen doorway as I passed. "I suppose you're leaving me here to clean up?"

"You *are* the only one who knows which rentals came from which company," I said.

He let out a sigh. "Fine, but frankly, this new look is growing on me. You're sure you don't want to leave the furniture as is?"

I opened my bedroom door and crawled over the couch that now took up every bit of floor space, my feet sinking into the sagging cushions. Even though my original furniture was worn and many years from stylish, it was comfortable. The furniture Richard had brought in for the shoot may have looked chic, but it was not the kind of stuff you cuddled up on.

"I'm sure," I called out, clambering over the back of the couch and opening my closet door as I untied my wrap dress. As promised, I quickly changed into a pair of jeans and a T-shirt and climbed back over the couch, holding the photo shoot dress I'd tucked back into the garment bag it had arrived in.

"I believe this is yours." I met Kate in the hallway outside the kitchen entrance and handed her the bag.

"Technically, it belongs to Rent the Runway, but who's quibbling? It's mine for another twenty-four hours."

Although I understood the concept of renting designer fashion--after all, men had been doing it with tuxedos for years--it still gave me pause that so many stylish young women in DC didn't own a thing they wore. According to Kate, some of her friends had virtually empty closets but a monthly subscription plan to Rent the Runway. They wore designer clothes that they could never afford, yet owned none of them.

"Do you mind staying here and catching up on the confirmation calls for Saturday?" I asked her.

"Consider it done." She looked down at her white dress. "Besides, I didn't bring good crime investigation clothes."

"We aren't investigating," I said, but stopped when I noticed that both she and Richard wore disbelieving looks on their faces. I cast a quick glance at my fiancé, who stood near the front door. "I'm with Reese. Even if I wanted to, how much poking around could I do?"

Richard stood in the doorway to the kitchen, his hands on his hips and one toe tapping on the linoleum. "If there's a way, you'll find it."

I held up three fingers. "I'm not doing anything but supporting Fern as he talks to Jeannie. No investigating. Scout's honor."

"You know," Kate said, tilting her head at me then glancing at Richard. "I think she actually believes what she's saying."

"Which goes to support my belief that anyone who works with brides day in and day out can't help but be delusional," Richard said.

"I'm not delusional," I said. "And I'm not getting sucked into another investigation, especially not this week. We don't have time for it."

"That's what you say every time, Annabelle." Richard shook his head. "And before you know it, we're all poking around for clues, breaking into suspects' hotel rooms, and running from deranged killers."

Kate held up a finger. "One hotel room, and we had the key, so technically it wasn't breaking and entering."

I motioned with my hands for both of them to keep it down. "Not so loud. Reese doesn't know all the details about our trip to Ireland, and I'd like to keep it that way."

"I'm sure you would," Richard said. "Just remember. It's two weeks before Christmas, and you've got a big wedding on Saturday with a lavish rehearsal dinner the night before, as well as a wedding to plan from start to finish by New Year's Eve." He took a gulp of air. "Not to mention the fact that you still don't have a venue for it. This is no time to play Nancy Drew."

My pulse raced at the thought of how much work we had to do. He was right. I had no time to spare. "Don't worry. I'm with my fiancé. You know how he feels about me poking around in his cases."

"I don't know, Annie," Kate said, tapping one finger on her chin. "He seems to have gotten so used to you meddling that he doesn't even notice it anymore. He even planned one of our criminal-catching schemes."

Richard nodded solemnly. "It's Stockholm Syndrome."

I shot him a look. "Stockholm Syndrome? You mean when a captive becomes sympathetic or emotionally attached to their captor. Who's the captor in this scenario? Me?"

Richard shrugged, his face the picture of innocence. "I'm only saying that you may have used your feminine wiles to make your fiancé more tolerant of your crime-solving fetish."

"My feminine wiles?"

"Yeah, I'm not sure about that," Kate said, tilting her head at me. "Generally speaking, Annabelle doesn't have feminine wiles."

"Thank you." I hesitated. "I think."

I glanced over at Fern standing with Reese, his face ashen. "Listen. I'll be back before you know it, ready to focus on work."

I joined Reese and Fern, giving a backward wave to my friends as we left the apartment. I would show them that I could stay out of a case, I thought. Then again, this was Santa we were talking about.

CHAPTER 9

We stopped at the corner of M Street, and I jumped back so a lady with a double stroller wouldn't run over my toes. It was afternoon in Georgetown and the weather was sunny and warm, which meant everyone was out. The streets bustled with shoppers and tourists, people weaving around each other down the brick sidewalks holding colorful paper shopping bags with ribbon handles. Wreaths topped each of the tall lampposts, and shop windows featured holiday displays, although the icy blues (and even the bright greens and reds) seemed incongruous with the almost summertime weather.

Despite the temperature, the neighborhood looked decked out for the season, and holiday music drifted out from various shops. The tinny notes of "Santa Baby" mingled with the sound of a Salvation Army bell ringer at the end of the next block. I inhaled deeply and could smell the rich aroma of coffee, reminding me that in DC, I was never more than a few feet away from a Starbucks at any given time. Or at least it felt that way. My stomach growled. I wouldn't mind a peppermint mocha, even though I knew we were not here to get coffee.

"So where does Jeannie usually hang out?" I asked.

"Depends." Fern scanned the crowds. "At the holidays, she likes to stay out of the way since it's such a madhouse, but Clyde's is a favorite. They give her coffee and lunch most days."

"That's where she was yesterday," Reese said, pulling me close as a group of giggling teenaged girls barreled by us without looking up.

"Then Clyde's it is." I started heading toward the popular restaurant, using the massive nutcrackers they put outside their restaurant each December as a visual guide.

We passed Starbucks, and I sucked in the addictive scent, promising myself that I'd treat myself on the way back. I would need the caffeine for the rest of the day, anyway.

"Annabelle!"

Mack's deep voice made me turn as he came out of the chain coffee shop behind us, carrying a cardboard holder filled with to-go cups and a handful of paper bags I assumed were filled with pastries.

"Hey," I said, noticing his eyes were rimmed red. "I didn't expect to see you here. Don't you usually go to Baked and Wired on your block, that is if you aren't brewing your own?"

He took a shaky breath. "I'm getting coffees and snacks for some of Kris's friends who were helping with the search. They're right around the corner, so I didn't want to make them wait." He dropped his voice. "Don't tell Buster I didn't shop local."

I mimed zipping up my lips. "You can count on me."

"Since we've stopped to chat," Fern said, looking longingly in the glass window, "I need a coffee and maybe a scone." He waved a hand in front of his brimming eyes, his voice cracking. "I'm so upset, I'm craving carbs."

Mack watched Fern hurry into the Starbucks. "I know how he feels. I can't believe what they found."

"How did you hear?" Reese asked. "We were going to come find you after we talked to Jeannie."

"One of the fellows who helps us out sometimes, Stanley, was the first person to happen upon the bloody suit."

"Is he okay?" Reese asked.

"A little shaken up," Mack said, shifting from one leg to the other, his leather pants groaning in response. "He and Kris are friends, and they usually worked as a team when they helped us out."

"Has he given a statement already?" Reese asked.

Mack shrugged. "I don't know, but I can ask. Everyone's pretty upset. It would be one thing if they'd found a body, but his Santa suit drenched in blood just makes us all worry about what happened to him and where he is. None of us believe he's dead, but if he was the person in that suit, he must be hurt."

"That's a pretty safe bet," I said. "If he was hurt, do you know anyone he'd turn to or anyplace he might hide?"

Mack rubbed a hand down his goatee. "Aside from Jeannie? I like to think he'd come to us if he needed help, but we haven't seen him."

"And you don't know anyone who would want to hurt Kris?" Reese asked.

Mack shook his head firmly. "He didn't have an enemy in the world. Everyone loved Kris. The police are sure it wasn't another Santa?"

Now it was Reese's turn to shake his head. "His name was written on the inside of the suit in Sharpie."

"You're still looking for him, right?" Mack said, staring intently at my fiancé. "I mean, even though Kris was homeless."

Reese put a hand on Mack's thick, tattooed forearm. "Of course. This case will get just as much attention as any other. I'll make sure of it."

A small smile cracked Mack's face, and he cleared his throat. "Well, I'd better get back to the group."

"Can you let Stanley know I'd like to talk to him?" Reese asked as Mack started to back away.

"We'll probably go back to Lush if you want to stop by later," Mack called out over the din of the crowd before he disappeared around the corner.

"Did you know Buster and Mack employed so many homeless people?" Reese asked.

I thought about it. "I've definitely seen them use homeless crew to unload their vans at churches, especially at New York Avenue Presbyterian and St. Matthew's Cathedral. I didn't know they used them so often at the shop, but I usually don't see the back end of their operation. Knowing Buster and Mack, I'm not surprised."

"Me either," Reese said. "Those two certainly aren't what you'd expect when you first look at them, are they?"

"Is anyone?"

"That's it," Fern said, pushing open the glass door and emerging from the coffee shop. Crumbs fell from his mouth as he thrust a cardboard drink holder and small paper bag at me. "This day is officially a disaster."

"What happened?" I asked. "Are they out of skim soy milk?"

"What happened is that I just chugged a full fat latte and ate a blueberry scone." Fern pressed his fingers to his lips. "All this with Kris has pushed me over the edge. I won't be able to fit into my skinny holiday pants if I keep this up."

"You already drank your coffee?" I glanced down at the three paper cups. "So this is...?"

"For you two, of course. And Jeannie." He rolled his eyes at me. "As if I don't know your coffee order, sweetie." He patted Reese's arm. "I pegged you as a plain coffee guy, but I did get you a cake doughnut. You know, since you're a cop."

The corner of Reese's mouth quirked up. "Thanks."

"You're very welcome." Fern spun on his heel. "Now let's go talk to Jeannie before I go back in there and get another scone."

Fern started walking ahead of us toward Clyde's, and I hurried to catch up, pulling the coffee out of the holder and passing it to Reese, along with the doughnut bag. I balanced the holder while dislodging my own hot mocha and dodging the aggressive shoppers. I took a sip as I walked, trying not to spill the warm drink all over me and groaning out loud as I swallowed and realized Fern had asked for extra mocha syrup. He knew me so well.

Fern barely paused at the intersection with Wisconsin Avenue, barreling across only moments before the walk signal started blinking its warning. Reese and I ran to make it before the stream of traffic resumed, my foot touching the other side of the sidewalk as I heard cars rush by behind me.

"If this is what he's like when he drinks regular milk and eats carbs, I'm glad he's usually on a diet," I said to Reese. "I don't know if I could keep up if he was full octane all the time."

I spotted the giant nutcrackers ahead of us, flanking the entrance to the popular restaurant. Towering at least fifteen feet high, the glossy, brightly colored figures jutted out onto the sidewalk in front of the large glass windows of the restaurant. Fern stopped when he reached the wooden and brass doors, waiting for us to catch up. Even before he threw open the door, I could smell the aroma of crab cakes and french fries, probably the place's most popular menu items.

"She should be at the bar," Fern said, holding the door open for us.

I stepped inside and my eyes adjusted to the rich wood of the long bar and the burgundy of the booths stretched down one side of the narrow room. I didn't know what Jeannie looked like, but a quick scan of the bar told me the businessmen and tourists in bright shorts and fanny packs weren't her.

Fern bit the corner of his lip as he took in the restaurant. "Let me talk to the hostess."

He approached a petite woman dressed in black and talked to her in hushed tones.

"Was she at the bar yesterday?" I asked my fiancé, noticing that he hadn't touched the coffee or doughnut.

He nodded, his face set in an unreadable expression.

"She's not here," Fern said when he returned to us. "Hasn't been here all day."

"Is that unusual?" I asked.

"Very." Fern fluttered a hand over his neat ponytail. "The manager slips her cash to sweep the sidewalk every morning. Today's the first day she didn't show."

"Really?" Reese's face turned grim. "In how long?"

"Years," Fern said, his voice quavering as he clutched my arm. "Oh, Annabelle. I have a horrible feeling something's happened to Jeannie, too."

CHAPTER 10

The overhead bell jingled as we walked into Lush, and I breathed in the distinctive scents of pine and cinnamon. Even though the weather outside was far from frightful, Buster and Mack's festively decorated shop smelled every bit like Christmas.

"We're back here," Buster called, and I saw an arm waving above the arrangements of frosted branches and miniature fir trees on the display tables.

As I passed an artfully stacked collection of trendy Homesick candles in colorful boxes, I was reminded that I hadn't even started shopping for gifts for my friends. I wondered how many of them would enjoy a "Jewish Christmas" or "Grandma's Kitchen" scented candle. I picked up a pink box that read "Single, Not Sorry" and described the candle inside as smelling like freedom and fun. I'd have to remember to come back and buy that one for Kate.

Replacing the quirky candle, I led the way to the back of the store where Mack stood at the espresso machine and the long metal table was surrounded by people on the high stools. Some of the faces seemed vaguely familiar, and I suspected I'd seen them unloading the florals at past weddings.

Prue waved at me while bouncing a giggling Merry on her lap and flipping her dirty-blond ponytail out of the baby's reach. "You all look like you need some hot chocolate."

The last thing I needed was another hot drink, but I smiled at Merry's young mother and nodded. "Sure, thanks."

Fern sat on one of the last available barstools, slumping over the table, and Buster looked up at me from where he sat comforting a man in an unseasonably thick flannel shirt. "Is he okay?"

"We struck out with Jeannie," I said.

Fern raised his head. "Because she's gone."

"Gone?" Mack fumbled with the mug he was holding. "What do you mean gone?"

"The staff at Clyde's hasn't seen her today," Reese said. "But that could be because she's been out looking for Kris."

Mack nodded his head, a bit too eagerly. "I'm sure that's it."

Fern gave a sharp shake of his head. "It isn't like Jeannie to be a no-show. Even if she was going to look for Kris, she would have swept the front of Clyde's first."

"Her friend's disappearance could very well have thrown her off her usual routine," Reese said, using his calmest police detective voice. "She was clearly distraught when we talked to her yesterday. That kind of anxiety can cause people to do things they wouldn't normally do or forget things they usually do."

Fern pressed his fingers to his throat. "I hope you're right. She's supposed to come by the salon tomorrow morning before I open for her wash and style, although she only ever wears her hair in a long braid, which is *not* a style."

"I'm sure she'll be there," I said, feigning more confidence than I felt. "She probably heard that Kris's suit was found and is shaken up."

There were mumbles around the table that told me not everyone agreed with me, but Fern sat up straighter. "Maybe you're right. The old girl never misses her hair appointment. It's when she fills me in on all the Georgetown gossip."

"So is that how you know what everyone in Georgetown is up to?" I asked.

Fern smiled. "Of course. Jeannie sees everything that goes on around here."

Mack lumbered over to me and Reese, handing both of us steaming mugs. "We've been talking about what could have happened to Kris. We have quite a few theories about how his suit could have gotten blood on it."

"It could be tomato sauce," a woman with frizzy gray hair said. "Kris loves spaghetti."

I noticed Reese's eyebrow lift. Even the most rookie cop wouldn't mistake spaghetti sauce for blood, but he didn't respond.

"Or he might have gotten a bunch of paint on him and thrown out the suit," someone else called out.

"Does anyone know where he might have gone if he did get hurt?" Reese asked. "Does he have any family in the area?"

"Kris didn't have any family that I know of," Mack said, then turned to the people gathered around the table. "Did he ever mention family to you all?"

Head shakes and low murmurs told us no.

"If he had any family that was still alive, they didn't live here," Prue said. "I think he was originally from somewhere up North. The last time he was in the shop he mentioned that he'd never gotten used to the heat south of the Mason-Dixon."

Reese took his notebook out of his jeans pocket, flipped it open, and began scribbling. "Did he say anything else about his past?"

"Kris didn't focus on the past," a man said from the end of the table. "He always said he was moving forward."

"And paying it forward," a woman with bushy brown hair said, blowing her nose into a tissue. "That's why he put on the costume and sang to people. He liked to give back."

"Not everyone agreed with him on that," a small man with a grizzled beard said almost so quietly I couldn't hear him.

I stepped closer to the man, who seemed to shrink into himself as I approached. "What? What do you mean?"

The man's gaze darted around the group. "I'm saying what we all knew. Not everyone thought Kris should have been taking all the attention and making us look bad."

Heads dropped around the table, and there was a murmur of both agreement and dissent.

"How did he make you look bad?" Reese asked.

The man shrugged, not lifting his head. "He didn't ask for money, so it made it harder for those of us who did. And the Salvation Army bell ringers *really* didn't like him."

I stared at the man even though he wouldn't look up at me. "The other Santas had it in for him?"

Another shrug as he shifted on his stool. "You know they get part of the money they collect. It was hard for them to compete with Kris's singing. I've seen a few of them try to run him off or try to drown him out with their bell."

I exchanged a glance with my fiancé. I'd never given a thought to how Kris Kringle Jingle might impact other Santas or other homeless people, but I supposed it made sense. You could never make everyone happy.

"Thanks," Reese said. "That's helpful. I can also check if he's in the system," Reese said, "but I'm guessing Kris Kringle Jingle wasn't his legal name."

"It's all I ever knew him as," a heavyset, balding man said, his voice high and chirpy.

"I'm assuming you didn't put him on your payroll," Reese said to Mack, "so you never needed any official documents."

Mack shifted from one foot to the other. "That's right. He was strictly freelance and paid in cash."

Reese nodded. "Don't worry. The metropolitan police department has bigger things to worry about than a flower shop helping out the local street population with under-the-table payments."

"That's why you're our favorite cop." Mack let out a breath, but I noticed several of the people at the table stiffen.

"Don't worry," I said. "He's only trying to help figure out what happened to your friend."

"That's right," Reese said. "I want to find Kris."

Fern nudged the bushy-haired woman next to him. "I've worked with him on more than one murder case. He may look like a pretty face, but he'll find our Kris."

Reese ignored Fern's comment, but a flush crept up his neck. "Now, which one of you is Stanley?"

Mack scanned the room, then exchanged a look with Buster. "He was here earlier. Where did he go?"

"Are we talking about the guy who discovered the suit?" I asked, glancing at Reese's pinched face. "Didn't you tell him we needed to talk to him?"

"We did," Buster said, disappearing through the doorway that led to the back office and designer workspace. After a minute, he returned shaking his head. "He's not in the back or in the loading dock or alley."

Mack ran a hand over his bald head. "He looked nervous when we mentioned that a policeman would be stopping by to take his statement. Maybe we shouldn't have mentioned the cop part."

"I don't know why that would be an issue," Buster said. "He already talked to the cops when he gave his statement. Plus, an officer was there when they found the Santa costume. Helped calm him down. An Officer Rogers, I think. I remembered because it reminded me of Mr. Rogers."

"We watch a lot of Mr. Rogers reruns with Merry," Mack said, pressing a hand to his heart. "We love Mr. Rogers."

Reese flipped his notebook closed. "It's all right. Maybe he didn't want to give his statement twice. I can review what he said when I get back to the station."

"That's two people," Fern said.

"Two people?" Prue asked as Merry slapped her chubby palms on the table.

"Two people connected to Kris who are now missing," Fern said, holding up two fingers. "First, Jeannie who said that Kris was nervous because he saw something suspicious, and now Stanley, who was the first person to find the bloody suit."

"We don't know they're *missing* missing," Mack said, his voice quivering.

"Maybe you don't," Fern said, shivering and making the sign of the cross over his chest, "but I have a strong premonition that they're both in trouble."

"He's dressed up as a priest one too many times," I whispered to Reese.

"Agreed," my fiancé said, his voice low so only I could hear him. "But, for once, I agree with your dramatic friend. I have a bad feeling that there's more to this whole mess than we know."

CHAPTER 11

"Where have you been?" Richard's head popped over the divider between my living room and kitchen as Reese and I walked into the apartment. "Didn't you get my texts?"

I dug my phone out from the bottom of my purse, cringing when I saw that my ringer had been off and the screen was filled with Richard's messages, which were punctuated with significantly more exclamation points and question marks as I scrolled down. "Sorry. We were preoccupied."

Richard's head disappeared into the kitchen with him mumbling something I was glad I couldn't hear, as his tiny black-and-brown dog scampered over to us, sniffing our legs and yipping happily.

I was surprised to see that our apartment had been returned to its usual state, and impressed that Richard had packed up every linen, plate, and fork. Even the plastic glass racks were gone, which meant that some unhappy delivery guys had carried everything down three flights of stairs. The chic and uncomfortable furniture had vanished, and my old furniture was back in place, although the room did look a little frumpy in comparison to its earlier look. At least Richard had left the Christmas tree decorations up, so the overall look was festively frumpy.

Perfectly embodying the theme, Leatrice sat on the yellow twill couch in a green sweatshirt printed with a fake pointy collar and wide, red belt to make it look like she was an elf. The green cap on her head, however, was genuine, and the bells jingled as she moved.

"What are you doing here, Leatrice?" I asked, hoping I didn't sound unhappy to find her parked in my living room. "I thought you'd be with your hubby."

Since her wedding over the summer, Leatrice and Sidney Allen had become even more inseparable, which meant I saw much more of the quirky entertainment diva, but it also meant that my nosy neighbor spent much less time poking into my life. It was a trade-off I'd take any day of the week.

"Returning Hermès," she said. "Besides, my love muffin has a party tonight. A troupe of sugar plum fairies down at the Willard Hotel. I thought I'd see what you were up to."

Richard's head reappeared over the divider. "I told her we were insanely busy."

"Hey, Hermès." Reese leaned down and rubbed the dog's furry head. "Your daddy doesn't seem to have calmed down much."

"I heard that," Richard called out. "How could I have calmed down when you abandoned me for hours to do everything solo?"

"Hey!" Kate leaned out from the office down the hall. "You weren't solo, and you also didn't do that much work, unless you consider chopping food work."

"Actually, I do," Richard said, "and so do my many cooks and pantry staff." He waved a wooden spoon in my direction. "You know cooking calms me, darling, and with everything going on, I thought I'd whip up a little grouper with tarragon shallot cream sauce to help me think."

Some people used meditation apps or miniature sand gardens to calm them. Richard cooked.

"Well, it smells amazing." Reese headed for the kitchen. "I was expecting to order takeout for dinner."

Richard shot me a look. "Please tell me that you and Annabelle do more than order takeout every night."

"We do," I said. Sometimes we went out to eat, and sometimes we ate cereal on the couch.

"Good news." Kate walked down the hall waving her phone. "I just heard back from Autoshop."

"Is your car in the shop?" Reese asked. "Brakes again?"

Kate was unquestionably a horrible driver, and slammed on her brakes so often when driving around downtown DC that she went through brake pads like some people went through paper towels.

"No." Kate laughed. "Autoshop is an event venue down at Union Market."

"It used to be an actual auto body shop, so it's got a cool industrial vibe, and has been completely refurbished," I told him then turned to Kate. "I can't believe they're available on New Year's Eve."

"Cancellation," Kate said. "We got lucky. How did it go with Jeannie?"

"Not so lucky." I saw my fiancé's brow crease. "Jeannie hasn't shown up at her usual place today."

"Do you think she heard about Kris's bloody Santa suit and wanted to be alone?" Kate asked.

"I might think that if she hadn't disappeared before the suit was found," I said. "And then the homeless guy who was one of the ones who found the suit was gone when we went to find him at Lush."

Kate put one hand on her hip. "That's weird."

"Did you say bloody Santa suit?" Leatrice moved faster than any eighty-year-old I'd ever met and was standing next to us in mere seconds, bouncing up and down on her toes.

"Oh, no." Richard joined us, pointing his wooden spoon at each of us. "I know exactly where this is headed, and I won't have it."

"What are you talking--?" I began, but Richard silenced me with a flourish of his spoon.

"Don't play coy with me, Annabelle. You know perfectly well what I mean. First it starts with a seemingly innocent discussion of the case, then it moves to someone thinking it sounds suspicious, and before you know it we're running amateur sting operations and running for our lives from deranged murderers." He heaved in a breath, his face red. "I'm telling you right now, we barely have time to pull off these weddings and your engagement party. There is no room in our lives for a murder investigation."

"Murder?" Leatrice's eyes danced. "I was wondering when you'd get another one."

"There's no murder," I said, although I didn't have high hopes the police would find Kris alive considering how much blood he--or someone--had lost.

Richard swung his spoon around, nearly whacking her in the elf cap. "Exactly. There is not, I repeat not, 'another one'."

"Of course not, dear," she said. "You seem very agitated. Do you need to lie down for a second?"

"If I'm agitated, it's only because Miss Marple here can't seem to stop meddling in investigations."

"If you remember," I said, "I was the one who insisted that we didn't have time when Fern first mentioned that Kris was missing."

Richard glared at me and ignored Leatrice. "It always seems to start out that way, and then you slowly get sucked in. You can't resist the urge to fix things. You never have. Mark my words, this case will be just like the others. You hunting for clues while you pretend you aren't, all of us ending up in danger, and me a nervous wreck."

That did sum up the last few criminal investigations we'd been involved in.

Reese put a hand on Richard's shoulder. "Now you know how I feel."

Richard sighed. "She used to be much worse, you know."

"Hello?" I waved my hands. "I'm standing right here."

My fiancé steered Richard back into the kitchen where I could hear them commiserating about how stubborn I was. I was sincerely regretting all the effort I'd put into getting them to be friends. Apparently, I'd done *too* good of a job.

Leatrice tugged me by the sleeve back toward the couch. "Where did you find the victim?"

"There is no victim," I said, keeping my voice low. "It was just his Santa suit covered in blood."

Leatrice tilted her head, and her bells jingled as the cap slid down her jet-black hair. "So you don't know if Kris Kringle Jingle is dead or not?"

I shook my head. "We're hoping he abandoned his suit, but there was a lot of blood."

"Who would want to hurt a man who dressed up like Santa and made people happy?" Leatrice asked.

"Well, according to some of his friends, not everyone was happy with all the attention he got, especially the bell-ringing Santas." I glanced toward the kitchen. "And Richard's right. This Santa turf war —if that's what it is—is one case we need to leave to the police. We have our hands full as it is."

"So are you going to tell Richard or let him twist in the wind a little longer?" Kate asked.

"Definitely twist," I said with a grin.

Kate grabbed her pink purse from the overstuffed chair and slung it over her shoulder. "As much as I'd like to watch him spiral out of control, I have a date tonight."

"A date?" Leatrice rubbed her palms together. "Tell me about your young man."

"Well, for one, he isn't all that young."

"You're going out with the older guy?" I asked, my interest immediately piqued. "I thought you weren't going out with him because you didn't want to settle down."

She held up both palms. "It's just a date. We're not hitting a wedding chapel after dinner." She pulled out her car keys. "You want me to pick you up tomorrow morning?"

"Tomorrow morning?" I thought for a moment before snapping my fingers. "Delivering our icicle-themed gift bags to the hotels in eighty-degree weather. Yes, pick me up. I have a really great parking space I don't want to lose."

"Have fun, dearie." Leatrice waved as Kate walked out, closing the front door behind her.

Reese emerged from the kitchen and gave me two thumbs up, which I took to mean that he'd calmed down Richard.

"Dinner will be ready in five minutes," Richard called out, confirming my assumption with his chirpy tone.

I walked over and took my fiancé's hand. "You're the Richard Whisperer."

"If only that was a paid position," he said with a wicked grin. "I feel like I could pull in a decent amount of overtime."

My phone vibrated in my hand and I glanced down at it, surprised to see Kate's name pop up. "Second thoughts about the date?" I joked when I answered.

"No," she said. "But I won't be able to pick you up tomorrow morning after all."

"Why not?"

Kate exhaled loudly. "Because someone flattened all my tires."

CHAPTER 12

"Can you believe that?" I asked Reese after we'd returned back upstairs from waiting with Kate for a tow truck. We'd deposited Leatrice in her first-floor apartment just in time for an episode of *Matlock*, and I was looking forward to some quiet time with my fiancé.

"What's not to believe?" Richard asked, walking out from the kitchen holding a plate in each oven-mitted hand. "Potential murder? Sabotage? Just another day in the life of Wedding Belles."

I exchanged a look with Reese. From his expression, I suspected it had slipped his mind that Richard was waiting with dinner.

Richard hesitated when he saw us staring at him. "What? You don't think I'm going to let this perfectly lovely sauce go to waste, do you? Even if you did take so long the fish could now be mistaken for high-end jerky."

"It still smells great," I said, in an attempt to mask my surprise.

Richard put the plates on my dining table, which was devoid of the elaborate decor from earlier. The handblown crystal had been replaced by my basic wine glasses; the eight pieces of sterling silver flatware per plate had been pared down to my stainless steel knives and forks, and instead of silk napkins in gilded napkin rings, there were plain plaid napkins folded in rectangles. The only reminder that there had been a photo shoot was the colorful floral arrangement that stretched down the middle and gave off the faint scent of lilies.

"I suppose you got Kate off to her date and her car off to the shop?" he asked, oven mitts on his hips. He seemed oddly calm about the whole thing, which made me nervous.

I nodded. "She was late for her date and pretty upset about having to get four new tires, but her car should be ready some time tomorrow."

Richard spun around and headed back to the kitchen, talking over his shoulder. "Any idea who did the deed, detective?"

"No clues that would pinpoint who did it," Reese said. "Definitely intentional, though. It looked like a sharp object--like a screwdriver--was used to poke a hole in each tire."

"I wouldn't have been surprised if Kate had popped one tire, considering how many curbs she runs up onto and potholes she nails, but even she couldn't have hit four all at once," I said. "This was definitely the work of Brianna."

My fiancé put an arm around me. "You can't know that for sure, babe. No one saw her, and the only CCTV camera pointed in the direction of Kate's parked car is the one at the store across the street, and the manager said it wasn't recording."

I felt a fresh wave of frustration that I'd lost the chance to have a recording of our arch nemesis Brianna committing a crime. "Why have a camera if you don't turn it on?"

"Deterrence," Reese said, giving me a squeeze.

Richard returned carrying a final plate. "Speaking of deterrence, I don't suppose this little incident has convinced you to leave well enough alone?"

"This had nothing to do with the investigation into Kris Kringle Jingle's disappearance," I said. "This is 100 percent Brianna. She's the one who called me and made the threat, and she's the one who popped Kate's tires."

Richard shrugged as he set the final plate on the table and whipped off the oven mitts. "Maybe. Maybe not. You can't tell me it's another wild coincidence that someone goes missing at the same time you and Kate are sent a very clear message."

"Of course I can. The message is don't work with brides who fire Brianna. If I followed your logic, we shouldn't have taken the New Year's Eve wedding, which we are now in the position to ask you to cater. You still think I should leave well enough alone? Maybe tell the client to find someone else? Another planner who doesn't use Richard Gerard Catering, perhaps?"

Richard's mouth dangled open. "I hadn't thought of it from that angle." He sniffed and smoothed down the front of his apron. "You know I'd never advise you to abandon a client, darling."

I gave him a pointed look. "What about the threats and sabotage?"

He straightened his shoulders. "We must soldier on, of course. We can't let some upstart like Brianna interfere in our work, especially when we only have a couple of weeks to pull it all together." He waved a hand at the table. "Sit, sit. I'll get the wine."

"Well played," Reese whispered as we took our seats at the table.

"I know his pressure points," I said, keeping my voice low. "He can't stand the thought of not being part of a big event. He might take a bullet himself if it means a big enough check and a magazine feature."

Richard returned with a bottle of cold Chardonnay, which he handed off to Reese. "You're absolutely sure the tire slasher couldn't have been connected to the Kris Kringle case?"

"How could they be?" I asked as my fiancé poured the wine. "Kate hasn't been involved so far and neither has her car. But Brianna knows the kind of car Kate drives, and she made a threat. Besides, we don't know what happened to Kris."

"Whatever it was, it wasn't good," muttered Richard.

I sighed with a bite of fish halfway to my mouth. He was right about that. "So there's no proof Brianna popped Kate's tires, and we don't know who killed Kris or why."

Reese raised an eyebrow and swallowed a mouthful. "We?"

"Yes, Annabelle." In Richard's case, both eyebrows were raised. "What do you mean we?"

"Nothing," I said, focusing on my plate.

Reese put one hand over mine. "Why don't we make a deal? I know you're physically incapable of letting things go." He held up a hand when I started to protest. "Babe, I know you. You can't *not* try to fix things. It's in your DNA. It's one of the maddeningly charming things I love about you."

"Maddening is right," Richard mumbled, ignoring the look I shot him.

"If I promise to keep you looped into the case the entire way--which I'm not supposed to be doing with a civilian, by the way--will you promise not to interfere?" Reese asked.

"You'd have better luck tying her up and keeping her in a closet until you've found Kris," Richard said, again avoiding my eyes.

"I can do that," I said, shooting daggers at Richard and smiling sweetly at my fiancé. "As long as I can tell Fern and Buster and Mack that you're doing everything you can to find Kris."

"Trust me, babe. I want to find him alive as much as anyone. He's a Georgetown institution. The holidays aren't going to feel the same without him."

My throat tightened, and I reached for my wine. "If the temperature doesn't drop, it will feel like Christmas in the Sahara."

A few file folders sat stacked by Richard's plate, and he tapped them with a finger. "Speaking of our unfortunately themed wedding this weekend, I know I'm only doing the rehearsal dinner," he let out a tortured sigh, "but I'm going to have to rework this après ski motif."

"You know I can't stop clients from having hotel weddings," I said, for the umpteenth time. "The bride's family loves the Four Seasons. Just be glad I talked them out of having the entire weekend there. Plus, their rehearsal dinner is more elaborate than some weddings."

"Yes, but it isn't the event that gets top billing, is it?"

I shook my head. "When you say rework, what do you mean? The menu cards are already printed."

"I've resigned myself to the ridiculousness of our cheese fondue station and apple cider shooters in eighty-degree weather, but I cannot have my waiters walking around in alpine sweaters. I know it was my idea to make them look more festive, but that was when I thought it would be chilly. Now we're going to be able to use the outdoor space, and I do not want waiters dropping from heatstroke in December."

"That's fine," I said. "Have them wear tuxes."

Richard made a face. "I'm sure I can come up with something a bit more special than tuxedos, darling."

"I still have to decide if we should scrap the hot cocoa station at the valet station on Saturday night," I said. "We already have the cardboard cuffs for the to-go cups embossed with icicles, but I can't imagine people will be lining up for a hot drink when it feels like summer."

"Put it inside and crank up the AC," Reese said. "Can't you get a fake snow machine to pump out some snow? People would go for it if they got snowed on at the same time."

Richard gaped at him. "You know, that's not a bad idea." He nudged me. "You didn't tell me he has an instinct for events."

"Detectives do have problem-solving skills," Reese said.

I noticed Richard studying my fiancé and leveled a finger at him. "Don't even think about it."

"What?" Richard widened his eyes and attempted to look innocent.

"You know what," I told him. "You're scheming to think of ways you can put him to work for you."

"Nonsense," Richard said. "But if he happens to be around when we discuss our events, far be it from me to stop him from sharing his ideas."

"Be careful you don't end up on his payroll," I said to Reese. "Or serving apple cider shooters in an alpine sweater."

"Don't be silly, darling." Richard laughed, before cutting his eyes to Reese. "Although he would look good in a sweater, and you know I like my servers to be attractive."

Reese had ping-ponged his head back and forth without saying a word. Finally, he swallowed and shook his head. "I appreciate the vote of confidence, but I'm happy on the force, and frankly, I think it's less stressful than wedding planning or catering."

"Isn't that the truth?" Richard said, draining his glass of wine.

My fiancé's phone buzzed, and he pulled it out of his pants pocket, looking down at the screen and frowning. "Hobbes just responded to an anonymous call and found an apartment filled with stolen electronics."

I swallowed a bite and dabbed my lips with my napkin. "That's a good thing, right?"

"Sure." Reese absently scratched the stubble on his chin. "But the guys who apparently lived there and stole everything were tied up with Christmas tree garland and wearing Santa hats."

Richard raised his wine glass. "I've said it before and I'll say it again, the holidays make people crazy."

CHAPTER 13

"That was the third bellman that's laughed at our welcome bags," Kate said as she slid into the passenger seat of my car. I'd idled in front of the Georgetown Inn with my flashers on while she'd run inside the redbrick hotel with two armloads of ice-blue bags embossed with shiny silver icicles. Even the tissue paper was iridescent silver and the name tags were white snowflakes.

"Ignore them," I said, turning off my flashers and pulling back into traffic. "How could we know we'd get a heat wave when we ordered everything?"

Kate swiped a hand across her forehead and leaned one arm out the window. "Heat wave is right. This is ridiculous. I was so excited for boot weather, and I really should be pulling out my flip-flops."

I couldn't argue with her as I let the breeze from the open car window hit my face. I was wearing a sleeveless red plaid dress I usually paired with a turtleneck, but now wore solo. "We can only hope the weather turns, and everyone who laughed at us will be eating crow."

"Fried crow," Kate said under her breath as she fanned herself. "You know, I much prefer being the wheelman than being the delivery girl."

"Sorry," I said, although I was not sorry Kate wasn't behind the wheel of my car. "Any word on the new tires?"

"What's there to say about tires, except for the fact that they're now my Christmas gift to myself?" She shook her head. "I can't believe Reese couldn't fingerprint the ones that were popped."

"I doubt the person touched them when they did it," I said. "Plus, if Brianna did do it, I don't think she's in the system."

Kate snorted. "Don't be so sure." She glanced over at me as I headed out of Georgetown, passing the harbor and going underneath the highway. "Where are we going now? We're out of welcome bags and hotels to deliver them to."

I stopped at the red light at the top of K Street. "Autoshop. I thought we should do a walk-through before we have the clients sign the contract."

"So we're actually spending the whole day doing wedding work?" Kate gave me an approving look as she nodded slowly. "I'm a little surprised."

"What else would we be doing?" I asked, gunning the engine as the light turned green.

"Oh, I don't know. Poking around in your fiancé's case, organizing a secret search party for Kris Kringle Jingle, having Leatrice hack into the police computers to check on the case's progress. You know, the usual."

"Very funny." I breathed in the smell of exhaust and food trucks as we headed down K Street. "Even if I did want to do those things, I've been threatened under pain of death by Richard. Reese and his guys are still searching for Kris and questioning the Salvation Army bell ringers, and he promised to let me know as soon as they find anything, although he's now also working on the case of the burglars who were tied up and wearing Santa hats."

"That is weird, but I'll bet some of their criminal buddies turned them in and decided to get creative with it. There's no honor among thieves, but there might be a sense of humor."

"At least it closes some of the robbery cases Reese was working on.

Apparently, the thieves had hit a bunch of Georgetown houses in the past month."

"So now they're trying to find out who turned them in?" Kate asked.

"Yes, but more to thank whomever did it. Reese is still focused on finding Kris."

"What do you think the chances are they're going to find him alive?" Kate asked.

"You never know. As long as they don't have a body, there's a chance he survived whatever happened to him." I repeated Reese's words, although I suspected I believed them about as much as he did.

"It's pretty weird there was no body. I mean, we've been involved in more than our fair share of murder investigations, and never have we just found bloody clothes."

She made a good point.

I drummed my fingers against the steering wheel. "Which means there's a chance it wasn't a murder and Kris ditched the Santa suit after being wounded."

"Or someone took it off him and dumped the body where it wouldn't be found," Kate said.

A less pleasant option.

"Either way," I said, "Reese is on the case. Not to mention Buster and Mack and their homeless crew. When we left them yesterday, they were heading out to sweep the area again. If anyone knows places to stash a body, it's the people who know the streets."

"Although if it was another homeless person or Salvation Army Santa, they'd know all the spots, too."

"Hmm." I hadn't thought about that. Our only suspects were other people who knew the streets.

Kate gave me a side-eye look. "I'm glad to see you taking a back seat on this one. If you really want to solve something, you should focus on proving that Brianna popped my tires."

I entered a busy traffic circle and exited onto Massachusetts Avenue. "We both know it was her even if we can't prove it. Who else would do something like that?"

Kate held her hands palm up. "And what did I ever do to her?"

I cut my eyes to my assistant. "You mean, aside from spread the rumor that her business is a front for a prostitution ring?"

She shook a finger at me. "I only did that after she told everyone that we were murder magnets."

To be fair, saying we were murder magnets wasn't totally off base. It wasn't nice, but it wasn't completely wrong.

"I'm not thrilled that she's escalated from trash talking to vandalism," I said. "But she seems to think everything we do is a personal attack on her."

"We didn't even know she was the planner the New Year's Eve client had fired," Kate said. "Maybe she should focus on being a better planner instead of lashing out at the rest of us."

"I wonder if they have a greeting card for that."

"A greeting card is not what I was thinking of sending her," Kate muttered. "More like the bill for my tires."

I was glad it was December, and Kate would be getting her holiday bonus from me soon. After last night, I knew what it would be going toward. "Are we doing a holiday party for the gang this year? I know it's kind of crazy right now, but we always do something."

Kate twisted in her seat to face me. "I meant to ask you, how do you feel about combining your engagement party with the Wedding Belles holiday party?"

"Since I wasn't the one who wanted an engagement party in the first place, I'm fine with anything." I smiled at the idea. "Actually, I think it's great. It will make it less like an engagement party."

Kate let out a long breath. "You have to have an engagement party, Annabelle. You're a wedding planner. This is your business. How are we supposed to convince our clients they need all these fabulous things for their weddings if you and Reese run off to the courthouse?"

"We're hardly running off to the courthouse," I said, sighing almost as loudly as she had. "We just haven't had time to focus on planning yet."

"Which is why I took over and became your official wedding planner, but it would be helpful to get some feedback." She held up two fingers. "I'm this close to booking bride and groom llamas for your cocktail hour."

I laughed. "You know how Richard gets about livestock at events. I do not want to see him running around with a pooper scooper and rubber gloves again."

"Okay, that's a no on the llamas."

"But a yes to the holiday party/engagement party mash-up," I reminded her. "Most of our guests would have been at both anyway. The only difference this time will be the addition of Reese's cop buddies. It will be like a Wedding Belles holiday party that's being raided."

Kate snapped her fingers. "And there's our theme!"

Before I could tell her the many reasons why that was not a great engagement party theme, I spotted a woman with a long white braid hurrying across the street, an overstuffed IKEA bag hanging off one shoulder. She disappeared into a brick building with large wooden doors.

I grabbed my phone from the center console and pressed one of my pre-programmed speed dial numbers.

"Annabelle, what a lovely surprise," Fern said when he answered.

"Quick question," I said. "What color hair does Jeannie have?"

"Jeannie? White. It's quite pretty, although it would look even better if she let me cut it and give her layers, but she's about as open to change with her hair as you are, sweetie. Why do you ask?"

"I'm assuming she didn't show up for her wash and style this morning?" I answered his question with one of my own.

"How did you know?"

I jerked my car to the curb in front of the building the woman had run into. "Because I'm pretty sure I just saw her halfway across town."

CHAPTER 14

"Whoa," Kate said as I hopped out of the car. "Where are you going? What happened to our site visit?"

I hitched my purse over my shoulder and looked up at the three-story brick building with tall windows lined up in a grid. "I just want to pop in here and see if the woman I saw was actually Jeannie."

Kate jumped out of the car on her side, slamming the door as she followed me. "I thought we weren't going to get involved with the case. I thought we were laser focused on our events."

I paused to let her catch up to me in her highheeled mules. "This isn't getting involved. This is doing a favor for Fern."

"Really?" Kate muttered as she wobbled up the steps toward the large double doors with an imposing brick and stone archway overhead that read "Gales School." "Because this feels an awful lot like getting involved."

I put a hand on the metal door handle as I read the sign printed on the glass--"Central Union Mission." "You know Fern is worried sick about Kris and Jeannie. If we can tell him that one of them is safe, wouldn't that be a good thing?"

"I feel like you're sneaking this through on a technicality, Annabelle, but I'll let it slide. But only if this is an in-and-out operation. If we end up cowering in a storage closet or rummaging through someone's office for evidence, I'm out of here, *and* I'm telling Richard."

I exhaled, shaking my head. "Since when are you on his side?"

"Since his side became the one where I don't get nearly arrested."

"Fine, but I'm telling you, this is perfectly innocent." I peered through the glass top of the doors, seeing another set of doors and a wide hallway beyond that. "We look for Jeannie, maybe talk with her, and then we leave."

"So you say." She yanked open one of the doors and held it open for me.

"When did you become the voice of reason?" I asked, grinning at her.

We walked inside, passing through the second set of double doors and pausing. Although the outside of the building indicated the shelter had been a school in its former life, the inside had a long, well-lit hallway and the walls looked freshly painted, even if the paint choice was a gray on gray. I smelled food and realized it must be around lunchtime as people disappeared through a doorway to the right. I didn't know if the mission was a residential shelter or if it only provided meals and services, but it seemed to be bustling.

"Do I smell fried chicken?" Kate asked, sucking in a deep breath.

"Since when do you eat fried food?"

She inhaled again. "I don't, but I love to smell it."

I rolled my eyes, motioning for Kate to follow me as I peeked my head into the well-trafficked doorway.

The room had windows along one side and long fluorescent lights in the ceiling, with tables and attached benches stretching the width of the space. In the corner was an entrance to a kitchen and what appeared to be a buffet line and stacks of green trays.

Kate nudged me. "Is that her?"

I followed her line of sight and spotted the woman with the white braid down her back. "She matches Fern's description."

Kate tapped her wrist, even though she didn't wear a watch. "Then let's do this and get out of here. Autoshop is waiting."

I wound my way to where the woman sat with her back to us. She wasn't eating, but seemed to be nursing a Styrofoam cup of coffee. Walking around the table, I took a seat directly across from her.

She glanced up and her pale-blue eyes flickered something--concern, fear, confusion? "Who are you?"

"We're friends of Fern's," I said.

She sized us both up as Kate sat next to me. "That makes sense." She motioned her head toward Kate. "Especially her."

I tried not to take that as a passive-aggressive comment about my messy ponytail. "You're Jeannie, right?"

She nodded and took a sip of coffee.

"He's worried about you," I said, when I realized she wasn't much of a talker. "You missed your usual appointment this morning."

Her eyes darted around the room, then dropped to her cup. "Can you tell him I'm sorry about that?"

"He'd rather hear it from you," Kate said. "You know how Fern worries."

Jeannie let out a small laugh. "That man sure is a mess of nerves."

A pretty accurate assessment. When she didn't say more, I continued. "And the folks at Clyde's are worried, too."

She shifted on the bench. "Can you tell them I needed a few days off? I'll be back soon."

I leaned closer. "Why do you need a few days off? Is this about Kris?"

Her head jerked up. "Are you here about him?"

"No," I said. "We're here because Fern was worried about you, but everyone is pretty concerned about Kris, too. You heard they found his Santa suit, right?"

Jeannie pressed her lips together and nodded.

"I know you told my fiancé that Kris was worried about something before he disappeared. Something he saw. Do you think that could have gotten him killed?"

She eyed me warily. "Your fiancé? You mean that good-looking cop Fern brought around? You're engaged to him?"

I tried not to be offended for the second time in the conversation. "Yes, he's my fiancé."

"She looks a lot better when she tries," Kate said. "You should have seen her yesterday. She had fake lashes and everything."

Jeannie cocked an eyebrow at me as if she was trying to imagine me with false eyelashes.

I sighed. "Back to Kris. Did he seem to be afraid for his life?"

Jeannie dropped her gaze back to her cup and shrugged. "He seemed concerned, but Kris doesn't like to let anything upset him too much. He says he can't sing if he's in a bad mood."

"And you don't know of anyone who would want him dead?" I asked. "Or what he saw?"

She shook her head sharply. "Everyone loves Kris."

"Not everyone," I said. "We heard that some of the bell ringers weren't crazy about him, and even some of your homeless friends didn't like his policy of not taking money."

Jeannie looked over her shoulder and dropped her voice. "Those Salvation Army Santas can get real competitive. It's not a big secret they don't like Kris, but kill him?" She shook her head. "And none of our people would do that either. Even if they didn't like his singing shtick. It had to be someone else."

It seemed to be the general consensus that no one would have hurt Kris, but clearly *someone* did. A man sat next to me, the smell of fried chicken and macaroni and cheese wafting up from his plate. My stomach growled, reminding me of my banana and coffee breakfast.

"So if it wasn't an angry Santa trying to knock off the competition, what about what he saw? He didn't tell you anything more about it?"

Another shake of her head. "Just that they shouldn't be doing that sort of thing around the holidays." The corner of her mouth quirked up. "He's touchy about people messing with Christmas."

I guess that made sense. He did dress up like Santa and sing carols just to make people happy, so he had a certain claim to the holly jolly holiday.

"And he didn't want to go to the cops about it?" I asked.

Jeannie shrugged.

I wondered if he thought he wouldn't be taken seriously because he was homeless or because he dressed up like Santa and sang carols. None of us said anything for a few minutes.

"This seems like a nice place," Kate finally said, swiveling her head around. "The food smells good."

Jeannie nodded and took another tiny sip of coffee.

I twisted my head to take in the quickly filling dining room, as well. "It's not all that close to Georgetown, though."

"I like to move around," she said.

I nodded but knew that contradicted everything Fern had told me about the woman. She was a Georgetown institution, much like Kris Kringle Jingle. I looked at the tight set of her jaw and the thin line of her mouth. No way was this woman going to talk to us, even if she knew something. I suspected her being halfway across town—and the nervous way she scanned the room—had something to do with Kris. Was she avoiding Georgetown because, despite what she said, she considered one of the other homeless there a threat? Was she avoiding being seen by a murderous bell ringer? Was she afraid that her connection with Kris put her in danger? Whatever the reason, the expression on her face told me she wasn't going to tell us.

I stood. "My fiancé is determined to find out what happened to your friend. The forensics unit is inspecting the recovered Santa suit for clues, so hopefully we'll have more information soon."

Her head snapped up, her brows pressed together forming a hard crease between her eyes. "They can know things just from that bloody suit?"

"Sure," I said. "Forensics is pretty impressive."

Kate stood next to me. "But don't think it's like CSI. None of the forensic techs are even remotely as hot in real life."

I didn't want to know how my assistant knew the "hotness" of the DC forensics department.

"Thanks for talking to us," I said. "We'll tell Fern and the folks at Clyde's you're okay."

Jeannie gnawed on her bottom lip. "Tell that cute cop of yours thanks from me. Not everyone takes us seriously, but he didn't look at me like I was crazy when Fern brought him around and told him about Kris."

"Of course he didn't think you were crazy," Kate said. "He's friends with Fern."

That got a small smile from Jeannie. "Sometimes I think that one might be a sandwich short of a picnic."

"Most creative geniuses are," I said.

"Which explains the entire wedding industry," Kate said under her breath as we left Jeannie.

When we'd gotten outside, I looked over my shoulder. "I'm glad she's okay."

"Too bad she didn't tell us anything."

I let Kate hang onto my arm as we walked down the concrete steps. "What do you mean? She gave us a huge clue."

"Just now?" Kate glanced back at the building. "Was she talking in code?"

I shrugged. "She told us that Kris isn't dead."

"She did?"

"Didn't you notice how she referred to him in the present tense? Most people have assumed he's dead when they hear his suit was found soaked in blood, but she didn't seem all that concerned and she talked about him as if she knows he's alive."

"Maybe she's an optimist," Kate suggested, opening her side of the car and leaning against the top of the doorframe.

"Or maybe she knows something we don't." I nibbled the corner of my lip as we both got into the car. "I hope she isn't in danger."

"Either way, I wouldn't worry about her too much."

I cut my eyes to Kate as I started the car and eased it into traffic. "What happened to your Christmas spirit?"

She shook her head and jerked a thumb behind her. "I mean, I wouldn't worry because it looked like the cops were keeping an eye on her."

"The cops?" I craned my neck around quickly, but we were already a block away.

"Didn't you notice the two guys in the unmarked car parked a few spaces in front of us?"

I hadn't. "How do you know they were cops?"

Kate gave me a withering look. "Have I ever been wrong about predicting a man's profession by his clothing?" She didn't wait for me to answer. "Trust me, they were cops."

So someone in the police department was keeping an eye on Jeannie, but my fiancé clearly had no idea. This got more interesting—and baffling—by the second.

CHAPTER 15

"So are we back to wedding business?" Kate asked as we walked up the metal stairs leading into Autoshop.

I dropped my phone back into my purse. "Absolutely. Fern is happy to hear that Jeannie is okay, and I told Reese so he wouldn't worry about searching for her as well as Kris. Now if we only knew what happened to the homeless man who found the Santa suit."

Kate paused at the wide entrance to the long room with exposed brick walls and steel beams running along the ceiling. "But in a detached curiosity way, right?"

"Of course. I promise to be completely focused on our walk-through." I scanned the space, which was the embodiment of industrial chic and made me feel like I should be wearing hipster glasses and have the tips of my hair dyed pink.

"Good, because we don't have long to figure out a design plan for the space," Kate said. "But don't you think it's perfect?"

"It *is* a blank slate." I stepped into the room, my shoes tapping on the concrete floors, and gazed down at the tall windows that ran across the far end of the space. "We could do just about anything with it."

"Exactly." Kate walked into the middle of the empty room and spread her arms out wide. "Since the bride wants a time theme, we could hang clocks from the ceiling over each table."

I turned to look at the rough, redbrick walls as my mind raced with ideas. "I wonder if we could rent grandfather clocks to position along the walls."

"And look at this elevated space we could use for cocktails." Kate strode to the other side of the room where more black metal stairs led to a long, narrow space that ran parallel to the main room and had whitewashed brick walls.

I followed her up the stairs until we were standing in the cocktail space, which featured more large windows and doors to an outdoor terrace. "We could put two bars against the walls inside and maybe another outside."

Kate snapped her fingers. "That reminds me. I need to think up a name for our specialty cocktail."

"This wedding is having a specialty cocktail?" I asked.

"Annabelle." She patted my hand. "All weddings should have a specialty cocktail."

"You've really drunk the Instagram Kool-Aid, haven't you?"

"For the right party, *that* could be a cute name for a custom cocktail," she said, winking at me. "But for a time-themed New Year's Eve wedding, I was thinking about the Melon Ball Drop or the Thyme After Thyme with actual thyme sprigs for garnish."

"Cute," I admitted. "How long have you been brainstorming those?"

Kate grinned. "Since the bride signed the contract."

I crossed to one of the windows overlooking the terrace and spotted the top of the Capitol in the distance. "Normally, I wouldn't think a terrace would be very useful for a New Year's Eve wedding, but this year we could actually use it."

"Don't remind me." Kate slipped on her oversized sunglasses as sunlight streamed through the windows. "I hate sweating in December."

"At least this wedding isn't stuck with a snowflake theme," I said.

"You have got to be kidding me," Kate said as she slid her sunglasses to the end of her nose and squinted over them.

"I never kid about themes, Kate. You know that. Complain about them, yes. But kid..."

She elbowed me to cut me off. "It's the tire slasher."

"The what?" I watched as her face hardened into a scowl. "Wait. Do you mean Brianna?" I followed her gaze and saw the blond wedding planner flouncing into the event space from the other side. "What is she doing here?'

"Stalking us," Kate said, not taking her eyes off the woman.

I instinctively put a hand on Kate's arm. "You know you can't run over there and accuse her of slashing your tires."

"Why not?"

"Because then she'll know she's getting to us," I said. "The last thing we want is for someone like her to think she's winning."

"Good point." Kate took a deep breath. "Can I kick her? Accidentally?"

"No," I said. "Remember, revenge is a dish best served cold."

Kate made a face. "That doesn't make any sense. What tastes good cold? Are you sure you're saying it right?"

"Positive," I told her. "Now let's go make sure that two-bit tramp knows she isn't getting to us."

Kate grinned. "I love it when Fern rubs off on you."

We walked down from the cocktail area and crossed the room toward Brianna, who stood next to a pair of young women who looked like they could be in high school and were both engrossed in their phones. When the tall blond saw us, her smile froze and she muttered something under her breath that made both women's heads snap up.

"If it isn't the crime-fighting duo themselves," she said in her syrupy Southern accent, laughing at her own joke.

"What are you doing here?" Kate asked, putting her hands on her hips and rapping the toe of her shoe on the floor. "I know you don't have a wedding booked here."

"Styled shoot," one of the girls said. "At least that's what we're trying for."

Brianna's cheeks flushed pink, and she shot daggers at the girl.

"You're so lucky to have the time on your hands to do styled shoots," Kate said, her voice dripping with fake sincerity. "That's the problem with having so many paying clients, like our wedding at the Four Seasons this weekend and the Ritz last weekend. We barely have time to breathe, much less dream up fake events to photograph."

"That's because y'all are too busy stealing other planners' weddings," Brianna said, her eyes flashing.

Kate held up her hands. "We had nothing to do with the bride bailing on you. She didn't even call us until she'd fired you."

"She didn't tell us who her planner had been," I added. "We had no idea it was you."

Brianna glared at both of us. "Like I'd believe that. You've been trying to destroy me ever since I came here."

"Us?" Kate gaped at her. "You're the one who told everyone we were the wedding planners of death."

"Well, you are," Brianna practically screamed. "How many dead bodies have y'all found at your weddings? Ten? Twenty?"

The women with Brianna stared at us.

"Not twenty," I assured them, although I was fairly certain the number was higher than ten.

"Well, while you're running around like chickens with your heads cut off on New Year's Eve, I'm going to be hosting an industry party so over-the-top that no one will be talking about anything else for years." She wagged a finger at us. "Everyone will see just how much better a planner I am than you two."

"Listen, Brianna," I said, thinking that maybe our feud had gone on long enough. "That's silly. You don't need to spend a ton of money on a party to prove you're good."

"Silly?" She tossed her hair off her shoulder. "My daddy always says there isn't any problem that enough money can't fix."

I sighed. Someone wasn't going to win father of the year.

"I'm not sure how we got off on such a bad foot," I said, "but why don't we talk this out?"

"There's nothing to talk about." Brianna folded her arms tightly across her chest. "I'm sorry y'all are making me get ugly, but I'm done being sweet."

Kate folded her own arms. "This has been you being sweet?"

"Ladies," I said, making a last-ditch effort to diffuse the situation. "Let's all calm down."

"You call slashing my tires being sweet?" Kate asked, taking a step forward.

Both of Brianna's assistants swung their heads toward her, but she just smiled.

"Did your tires get slashed? Well, isn't that a shame?" She batted her eyelashes. "Maybe you made the wrong person angry."

"Maybe *you* did," Kate said, her voice menacing.

Brianna stepped back, clearing her throat. "I've had about enough of y'all threatening me."

Kate leaned forward, flicking her fingers at the three women. "Then I suggest you leave, sweetie."

Brianna spun on her heel and the other two women scurried after her, their shoes pattering as they hurried down the stairs.

"Well, that went well," I said.

"What?" Kate gave me her most innocent face. "I said 'sweetie'."

CHAPTER 16

"This is an odd way to go back to Georgetown," Kate said as I veered off Wisconsin Avenue and headed down Massachusetts Avenue.

Since it was still in the mid-seventies, I had my car windows down instead of cranking the AC. It just seemed wrong to use air conditioning in December, even if the weather called for it. I rested my arm on the window sill and breathed in. "We're not going back to Georgetown."

"Are we leaving the city to make our fortune elsewhere now that that crazy Brianna is after us?" Kate asked, reaching for the Blue Bottle coffee she'd gotten when we'd walked through the Union Market food stalls on our way out of Autoshop. "Because I'm okay with that plan. I think we could do well planning weddings on the beaches of Mexico."

"After we just pulled after a major coup and found a new wedding venue in a matter of days?"

"Good point," she said. "The bride was pretty thrilled just now when I told her the contract was in the works."

Kate had called the bride while I'd pulled the car around. Delivering good news to a client was something we never delayed.

She took a gulp of coffee. "But Mexico is never a bad option considering our track record."

I made a face at her. "Ha ha. We're not running off to Mexico. We're going to swing by the police station."

Kate took a sip from her to-go cup. "Is this your way of sneaking in some alone time with Reese?"

"No," I said, reaching for the blueberry lemonade I'd snagged from the Village Cafe, "but we're going to pretend it is."

"I'm confused."

"The guy who found Kris's Santa suit may be missing, but the cop who was with him isn't," I said, sipping my drink and puckering my lips at the tartness.

"So we're going to the police precinct your fiancé works at to see someone other than him?"

I made a right turn and slowed down as I entered a more residential street. "You got it."

"And when he catches us questioning a cop connected to the case, our excuse is going to be temporary insanity?"

"He won't catch us," I said. "He's supposed to be out looking for Kris."

"And we're supposed to be planning two weddings and an engagement party," Kate muttered.

I slowed down as we approached the square, two-story brick building that housed the police precinct, swinging my car nose first into a parallel spot on the street. "It's just a few questions. If I ask Reese, he'll think I'm trying to poke around in his case."

"Aren't you?" Kate took a final sip and placed her coffee back in the center console.

"Hardly." I opened my car door and stepped up onto the curb. "I'm trying to help him."

Kate got out and joined me on the sidewalk. "Explain."

"Kris's friend Jeannie was hiding something. Stanley, the only other witness of any kind, disappeared. If this case isn't what it seems, Reese could be wasting his time. The cop who was with Stanley might have some insight. I mean, he must know something or have some thoughts about why Stanley would have disappeared."

"So you're trying to prevent your fiancé from spinning his wheels?"

I pointed a finger at her. "Exactly. He's got his hands full with all the weird holiday-related crimes."

She nodded thoughtfully as we walked toward the dark glass front of the station. "Not bad. Not totally believable, but I've heard worse. What holiday-related crimes, aside from a singing Santa going missing?"

"Apparently there was a home invasion in upper Georgetown that went wrong late last night. The guy who was trying to break in ended up tied up with a holiday wreath shoved down around his waist. He was rolling around on the people's front porch when the cops arrived."

Kate gave a snort of laughter. "So the homeowners fought back? Good for them."

I pulled open one side of the tinted glass doors. "They insist it wasn't them. Said they heard scuffling and when they opened the door, the guy was struggling to get up, but couldn't because the wreath had his arms pinned down."

"So someone out there is helping the police catch bad guys? That's a good thing, right?"

I shrugged as Kate stepped into the building in front of me. "Technically, they aren't supposed to encourage citizens taking the law into their own hands, but I know Reese isn't complaining. He's been talking about crime in Georgetown being on the rise for a while now, as well as his suspicions that it's being run by a group and not just random perpetrators. I think he's grateful for any help in cracking the crime ring."

Kate hesitated. "You don't think my tire slashing was done by this crime ring, do you?"

I followed her inside, my shoes tapping on the dingy linoleum as we headed for the reception desk to the right. "From what Reese has told me, they don't do random vandalism."

"You're right. It has Brianna written all over it." She sucked in a breath, her face brightening. "Maybe Brianna is involved in the crime ring. Maybe she's actually a crime boss."

I raised an eyebrow at her. "Don't give her that much credit. She can't even plan a wedding properly. How would she run a criminal organization?"

"You make a good point." Kate winked at me. "That doesn't mean I can't spread the rumor that Brianna has gone from being a Madame to being a crime boss."

"That should help diffuse the situation," I said under my breath.

When we reached the faux wood desk, I smiled at the female officer standing behind it. My eyes flicked to the battered desks that extended behind the counter and the closed office doors at the far end. I saw a weathered coffee pot on a small table to one side with a trash can next to it filled to the rim with discarded sugar packets and plastic creamer pods. The building held the distinct scent of stale coffee and cigarette smoke, even though I knew you couldn't smoke inside.

"I'm Annabelle Archer," I said, keeping my smile wide as the woman leveled her gaze at me.

"She's engaged to Mike Reese," Kate added, leaning on the desk and flashing the woman, and the entire office, her cleavage. "Detective Mike Reese."

The female cop glanced at me, gave me the once-over, and nodded. "He's not here."

"Shoot," I said, trying to sound disappointed. "By any chance is Officer Rogers available?"

"Rookie Rogers?" She looked over her shoulder. "Hey, Rogers. You available?"

A cop with wispy, sandy-brown hair and a round, baby face rose from a desk in the back. He walked forward, his look of confusion turning into a smile as he got closer and no doubt got a better look at Kate. The female cop rolled her eyes and stepped away.

"How can I help you, ladies?" he asked, his attention on Kate.

I darted a quick look to my assistant. After working together for so many years, I liked to think we had an unspoken shorthand.

She blinked at me. "What?"

Stifling a groan, I widened my own eyes, which I cut in the direction of the cop.

"Ah." Understanding crossed her face, and she nodded her head almost imperceptibly before bestowing one of her most alluring smiles on the young cop. "Aren't you the one who found the Santa suit?"

His own smile dimmed a bit. "How did you know that?"

Kate jerked a thumb at me. "She's engaged to Mike Reese."

"Oh." He sounded relieved as he looked quickly at me then back at Kate and her low-cut top. "Yep. That was me."

"It must have been shocking," Kate leaned closer, "to find a bloody Santa suit like that."

"Actually, I didn't find it. I came up on the homeless guy as he was pulling it out of the dumpster. As soon as I realized what it was, I took control of the evidence and called it in."

"I'll bet you took control," Kate said, winking at him.

The rookie cop's cheeks flushed pink, and I hoped he wouldn't pass out before we could finish questioning him. This was one drawback to using Kate's charms to extract information.

"What happened to the homeless guy?" I asked.

Officer Rogers pulled his gaze away from Kate and thought for a second. "Stanley? I took his statement, but he didn't have much to say. He saw the suit hanging out of the dumpster and pulled it out."

"Did he seem nervous or upset?"

"Both, I guess, but that wasn't a surprise since Stanley has some mental issues and he knew the victim," Rogers said, smoothing his thinning hair to one side.

"Victim?" Kate tilted her head at him. "How do you know Kris is dead if you only found the suit?"

Rogers shrugged. "I don't, but there was a lot of blood. No one loses that much blood and survives."

"Shouldn't there be a body?" I asked.

"Lots of things could have happened to the body." His voice took on a more authoritative tone. "It could have been thrown in the river or driven out of the city, or maybe we just haven't found it yet."

All of this was true, so why did I have such a hard time believing Kris was dead? Was it because I didn't want to believe it despite all hard evidence to the contrary? I nodded, but I wasn't convinced.

"Why?" Rogers asked. "Does Reese think the Santa is still alive?"

The officer's question jerked me out of my thoughts. "What? No, I didn't say that."

He exhaled, rubbing two fingers down the bridge of his nose. "I know a lot of folks in Georgetown liked the guy, but sometimes living on the streets can be dangerous. And the homeless community isn't always so friendly to each other."

That wasn't what Jeannie had told us, but then again, she wouldn't want to make her community look bad by saying they didn't get along.

Kate flipped her hair off her face. "In what way?"

Rogers puffed his chest out a bit. "They fight over stuff and the best spots. Just like any group of people."

"Do you know a lot of the homeless people in Georgetown?" I asked.

He nodded. "It's my beat, so I know most of them by name."

"So you knew Kris personally?"

Another nod. "He was a good guy. Never bothered people. Always stopped to talk to me." He dropped his eyes. "I'll miss the fella."

"And you don't have any leads on what might have happened?" Kate asked, her now voice less coquettish.

"Living on the streets isn't good for your health, but I got the feeling that Stanley either knew more than he wanted to say or that he was involved."

"You think Stanley might have killed him?" My voice rose and I saw a cop glance over, so I lowered it quickly. "I thought they were buddies."

"Most homicides happen between friends and family," he said. "Anyone who draws attention to themselves like Kris did was bound to have haters. They could have gotten into an argument that got out of hand. Who knows? We'd also gotten complaints from some of the bell ringers in Georgetown. They thought he was poaching their donations."

"But he didn't take money," I said.

Rogers raised his palms. "I know. They still complained. But I'm just guessing about all this. Kris might have just been at the wrong place at the wrong time."

Kate tugged on my arm and inclined her head to the back of the room. "Speaking of being in the wrong place."

Crap. My fiancé had emerged from one of the back offices. So much for him being out. I ducked down and pretended to tie my shoes, even though they had no laces.

"Thanks for talking with us," Kate said above me, her voice low. "We can keep this visit just between us, right? I'll bet a good-looking guy like you knows how to keep a girl's secret."

I could only imagine the looks she was giving him to make him agree so enthusiastically.

"Gotta run," Kate said, hunching over and pulling me with her as she blew a kiss over her shoulder. "I'll call you."

I didn't look back until we were outside and halfway to my car. "Do you think Reese saw us?"

"He's not out here scolding us, is he?" Kate asked, not slowing down until we'd reached the car.

We jumped inside, and I quickly pulled away from the curb, not breathing easily until the police station was in my rearview mirror. "Well, that was interesting."

Kate reached for her coffee. "If you say so."

"Officer Rogers seemed convinced that Kris is dead, but Jeannie seems to think he isn't." I took a long sip of my blueberry lemonade. "Obviously, one of them is wrong."

Kate kicked off her heels and stretched out her legs. "And even more obviously, you want to find out which one."

CHAPTER 17

I jumped when my phone trilled in my purse. Please don't be Reese, I thought, as I pulled it out. I was not ready to explain why Kate and I had been sneaking out of the police station, especially after I'd promised to stay out of his case.

Kate snapped her head to me. "You don't think that's him, do you? Driving to Mexico is still on the table, you know."

Pulling the phone from my purse, I glanced at the screen and let out a loud sigh. Not Reese. "We don't have to make a run for the border. It's Richard."

"I'm not sure if that's much better. Let's not take Mexico off the table just yet."

I answered, trying to sound as cheery--and innocent--as possible.

"Would you care to explain why all my caterer friends are getting requests for a sizable proposal for New Year's Eve, and I'm not?" Richard asked, before I'd finished saying hello.

My car's Bluetooth was acting up, so I held the phone against my ear with one shoulder while I drove. Not the safest thing, but safer than ignoring Richard's call. "Because the proposal request is coming from Brianna, and you're guilty by association."

"Not the worst association I've been a part of," Richard said with a sniff.

Kate and I had left the police station and were almost back in Georgetown, with my assistant scrolling through emails at a blinding pace, as I navigated the traffic down Constitution Avenue.

"Tell him he'd be better off working with us on New Year's Eve," Kate said. "Brianna is crazy."

"Did you hear that?" I asked Richard, pumping the brakes as a traffic light turned red and the BMW in front of me gunned it through.

"Of course she's crazy," Richard said. "She's one of those bottle blondes from the South who's sniffed too much bleach and bourbon, but she's the kind of crazy who has daddy's money to back her up. Do you know what she's asking for in these proposals?"

"No," I admitted, although I couldn't help being impressed by how quickly the woman had sent out feelers.

"Lobster, King crab legs, caviar, the works. She even wants her after midnight snacks to be Kobe beef sliders."

So it really would be a party the wedding industry would be talking about for years. "Like you said, she's got her daddy's money to pay for it."

Richard let out a deep sigh. "It's too bad I'm past the point of hitching my cart to a sugar daddy."

"And get rid of PJ?" I said. "No way. Not after we finally met him. Trust me, a sugar daddy is not the answer."

"Depends on the question." Kate glanced over at me. "Is this still about Brianna?"

I nodded slowly, without dropping the phone. "She's sparing no expense for her party."

Kate shrugged. "But who's going? All of our crew will be with us, and I know some other planners who have events, not to mention all the hotels. The only people who will be available to attend are the ones without a party on the biggest party night of the year."

"Which is usually us," I reminded her, since we rarely took weddings over the stretch between Christmas and New Year's Day.

"And weren't you just complaining about working too much over the holidays?"

Kate winked at me. "A girl can change her mind, can't she?"

"Kate has a point," Richard said. "New Year's Eve is not the night to snag all the event people. She should have picked a random Thursday, like everyone else does."

Because our industry work week focused on the weekend, all of our networking events were held on weeknights. And if a wedding planner wanted to host a social event, they never picked a Friday or Saturday. Those dates were for people who worked regular nine-to-five jobs.

"If she'd picked a different night, she wouldn't have gotten to screw over our new client and her former bride," I said. "And perhaps more importantly, she wouldn't have gotten to screw over us."

"I hope she and her five guests have fun," Kate said under her breath.

I slowed down as I merged onto M Street and headed into Georgetown proper. "We're almost at my apartment. Can I call you later?"

"We still need to discuss the menu for our New Year's Eve event, Annabelle, although I don't suppose I need to worry about Brianna snatching up all the King crab legs?"

"No," I told him. "Crab has not come up with the bride, nor have Kobe beef sliders. Sorry."

"Tell him if he plays his card right, we might be able to swing a dessert station," Kate said.

"Be still, my beating heart," Richard drawled, obviously hearing Kate's snarky comment. "I'll alert the pastry chef to start pumping out annoyingly tiny tartlets."

The line went dead, and I slid the phone down to my lap.

"I take it the industry is already buzzing about Brianna's party?" Kate asked.

"Apparently. I have to give the woman credit, she always seems to land on her feet."

"It's easier when you're landing on piles of cash," Kate said.

She had a point. Brianna did seem to keep herself afloat, not from good press she earned but from PR she bought.

"Hey." Kate nudged me. "Is that who I think it is?"

I followed her line of sight and her outstretched finger. There--walking along the sidewalk of M Street--was a Santa Claus who appeared to be singing. I rolled down my window and slowed the car. Yep. That was definitely "We Wish You a Merry Christmas" I heard wafting through the air.

I fumbled for my phone. "I should call Reese and tell him we found Kris Kringle Jingle."

"I can't believe he's strolling down the sidewalk like nothing happened." Kate shook her head. "And where did he get a new suit?"

Although we could only see the back of the Santa, we could hear him pretty clearly as he belted out the last few bars of the song. "It's December. Santa costumes can't be too hard to find, although he looks a lot skinnier from the back than I remember."

When Santa took a breath and started singing "Grandma Got Run Over By a Reindeer," Kate and I turned to each other.

"That's not Kris," she said.

I agreed with her, wishing I could get through the traffic and get a good look at the front of this imposter Santa. "Who else would walk around Georgetown singing in a Santa costume?"

"Maybe one of the Salvation Army bell ringers decided to poach the gig now that Kris has disappeared."

"That doesn't seem very Christmassy," I said. "Then again, neither does 'Grandma Got Run Over by a Reindeer.'"

"And it's going to be stuck in my head for the rest of the day," Kate grumbled, grabbing the door handle. "Slow down. I'm getting out."

"What?" We weren't going very fast, but we were moving, and we were in the left lane. I slammed on my brakes as she opened the door. "You're getting out in the middle of the street?"

"I need to give this guy a piece of my mind." She closed the door behind her and scooted through the other cars, waving as they honked at her.

I slid down in my seat, glad once again that I didn't have a

Wedding Belles sticker or magnet on my car. Keeping my eyes on Kate as she reached the sidewalk, I drove slowly to catch up with the stopped cars at the light.

She was too far away for me to hear, but I could see Kate walk up to the Santa and wave a finger at him, then stop, gape, and burst into laughter. That was not what I expected. What was even more of a surprise was when Santa turned around and waved at me.

Correction. Fern, dressed from head to toe as Santa Claus, waved at me.

CHAPTER 18

"I'm assuming you have an explanation for why you were wandering around Georgetown singing dodgy Christmas carols," I said to Fern as Kate and I followed him into his salon.

Up close, it was easy to see that Fern's version of Santa was a far cry from Kris Kringle Jingle, or most Santas. His costume had slimming darts at the waist and the wide shiny black belt served to cinch his midsection instead of ring it, with the jacket belling out beneath the belt like a miniskirt. His red velvet pants had a wide white cuff but were not wide-legged and baggy. Somehow, Fern had acquired the only pair of slim-fit Santa pants known to man.

"I beg your pardon." The bells on Fern's costume jingled as he flounced across the highly polished floors and deposited his red sack beside one of the two stylist chairs. "What was wrong with my songs?"

Kate cocked an eyebrow at him. "Grandma Got Run Over by a Reindeer?"

He pulled off his fake beard and deposited it on the ornate wooden credenza in front of the red swivel stylist's chair, his enormous blue topaz ring flashing in the opulent gold mirror on the wall. "A momentary lapse, sweetie. I'd already gone through all the favorites and that little ditty popped into my head."

"I guess a better question is why were you singing carols dressed as Santa in the first place?" I asked, noticing that the usually extravagantly decorated hair salon was even more ornamented than usual, with a frosted Christmas tree glittering at the back and red-and-gold wire ribbon garland draped in swags across the walls with massive bows topping each of the carved gold mirrors. Even the crystal chandeliers were swagged with red ribbon. Along with the usual scent of high-end hair products, the salon smelled faintly of fir tree and cinnamon, and Mariah Carey sang about all she wanted for Christmas faintly in the background.

"For Kris, of course," Fern said, removing his Santa hat and inspecting his hair in the mirror. "His singing is a tradition, and I, for one, don't want to see it lost. These are dark times, girls. We can't lose Santa Claus on top of everything else."

Kate shrugged and exchanged a glance with me. "He's not wrong."

I'd never known how fond of Christmas Fern was or how attached he'd been to Kris Kringle Jingle's carols. "That's a really nice sentiment, but how do you plan to take up Kris's job and do yours? I assume your clients aren't taking the holidays off."

"Sadly, no." Fern sighed, hiking up his shiny black belt as he headed to the mini refrigerator he kept behind a folding, tufted screen covered in red silk. "The holidays are prime time for blowouts and updos for parties, not to mention every floozy in town needs her roots done before New Year's."

Kate touched a hand to her own hair and walked closer to one of the mirrors to look at it. "Don't remind me."

Fern disappeared behind the screen, only his red velvet derrière poking out as he bent over. "Remember, Kate, we aren't coloring your hair, we're merely restoring it back to its original shade."

"Maybe when she was five," I muttered.

Kate ignored me and flopped into one of the red chairs and swiveled it in a circle. "Should I remind Fern how long it's been since you got a haircut?"

I didn't have to look at my long, auburn hair pulled up into a high ponytail to be reminded just how long I'd let it grow. "You know I don't pay attention to my hair when we're busy."

"Which is always," Kate said. "I'm surprised he hasn't thrown a smock around you already."

To be honest, so was I. Fern usually relished any excuse to drag me into his chair and give me a trim, since I never remembered to schedule appointments. Today, he seemed to be too preoccupied by the Santa drama to give my split ends a second thought.

Fern emerged from behind the screen with a bottle of champagne in one hand and three glass flutes in the other. "I'm hoping I can get some substitute Santas to take the shifts I can't."

I eyed the champagne. "I hope this isn't your way of buttering us up, because we really don't have the time--"

"Don't be silly." Fern let out a peal of laughter. "I know you two can't do it, plus I've heard you sing."

I tried not to take too much offense at that, but I was relieved he wasn't going to try to sweet-talk us into donning Santa suits.

"Let me guess," Kate said as she took one of the champagne flutes from Fern. "Is one of your stand-in Santas short with jet-black hair?"

Fern beamed as he handed me a glass. "Did the old girl tell you?"

"I'm a good guesser," Kate said as Fern poured her some bubbly, and the cranberries that had been in the bottom of her flute bobbed to the surface. "Who else loves dressing up as much as you do?"

I gave his outfit the once-over. "I hate to be the one to tell you, but I don't think this suit will fit her. Not unless she wears platform boots."

Fern poured champagne into my glass and giggled. "She's not wearing my suit. I had this custom-made, sweetie. Leatrice has her own Santa suit."

Why was I not surprised about either statement?

"So you and Leatrice are going to pick up the slack from Kris Kringle Jingle and sing carols all the way until Christmas?" Kate asked.

"Only until Kris returns," Fern said, "and I doubt he'll lay low until Christmas. This is his favorite time of the year."

I took a sip of champagne and the bubbles tickled my throat as I swallowed. "You're the second person we've talked to today who seems sure Kris is alive."

"You know me. I'm an optimist." Fern filled his own glass and set the bottle on the nearest credenza.

Kate raised an eyebrow at me. Fern was usually the first person to predict the sky was falling or take to his bed over the new Pantone color of the year being a shade that was horrible for his complexion.

"You were convinced that something awful had happened just yesterday," I reminded him. "What changed your mind?"

Fern's gaze darted around the shop as he drained his glass and reached for the bottle of bubbly. "I decided to get into the Christmas spirit and think positive thoughts."

I narrowed my eyes at him. "What aren't you telling us?"

Fern poured himself another glass, his hands trembling slightly. "Can't a jolly old elf change his mind?" He upended the bottle completely and shook the last few drops into his glass. "Better get us another."

When he'd slipped off the chair and bustled off to the back of the salon, I turned to Kate. "What's gotten into him, do you think?"

"You know this season makes people crazy, and Fern's already got a head start." Kate spun herself around in the chair. "Maybe he can't deal with the idea of Kris being seriously hurt or dead and has decided to be delusional instead of realistic."

That made some sort of twisted sense, although I couldn't help thinking that Fern's about-face was sudden. "You don't think he'd keep something from us, do you?"

"Fern?" Kate laughed, stopping her spinning chair with one foot. "When have you ever known him to be able to keep a secret?"

She had a point. If you wanted the world to know something, you told Fern.

A shriek from the back made us both freeze, exchange a quick look, then run off to find the source of the screaming. We pushed through a heavy brocade curtain dividing the salon from the back storage area and found Fern standing with his hands pressed to his cheeks.

"What's wrong?" I asked.

Fern swung around to face us both, waving a hand at the door that led to the back alleyway standing ajar. "I've been robbed."

CHAPTER 19

My fiancé strode to the door that still hung open, running a hand through his hair. "So this was standing open when you came in?"

Fern nodded, his fingers pressed to his lips. "I only use the back door for the occasional delivery. I don't use it to come in and out."

Kate stood next to him, rubbing his arm while she held a freshly opened bottle of bubbly in her other hand. She'd been refilling both of their glasses since Fern had discovered the break-in and called the police.

Reese hadn't been the first to arrive. His partner, Detective Hobbes, had beaten him there, and a pair of uniformed officers were checking the back alley.

It had been a while since I'd seen my fiancé's partner. Since he'd started a long-distance relationship with our go-to cake baker who lived in Scotland, he'd been using lots of accumulated time off. Despite his frequent overseas trips, not much had changed with the slightly paunchy and slightly frumpy detective. Every time I saw him in his rumpled clothes, I was amazed he was dating our glamorous baker friend. But I'd seen lots of odd pairings in my years planning weddings--nothing should have surprised me anymore. One thing I knew for sure, you couldn't use reason or logic to explain love.

"And you're sure you didn't leave it open?" Hobbes asked, bending down to inspect the lock and smoothing a palm over his light-brown comb-over. "It doesn't look forced."

Kate topped off his glass, and Fern tossed it back. "I've had no reason to open it over the past few days, but I also don't remember checking it."

Reese looked over from where he stood next to Hobbes. "And no one else has a key?"

Fern cleared his throat. "Well, I've given keys to stylists who've worked for me so they can accept deliveries when I'm not here, and I had a receptionist for a hot minute and she still has a key, and I gave the shop owner next door and Leatrice a copy just in case I ever locked myself out."

We all stared at him.

"And then I keep a spare on top of the doorsill."

Reese dragged a hand over his face as he shook his head. "So pretty much anyone could have walked in here?"

Fern held his glass out to Kate, who promptly filled it. "But why would they? I don't have anything to steal except industrial-sized bottles of shampoo."

"And champagne," Kate reminded him, holding up the bottle.

The two uniformed officers walked inside from the back door. I recognized one as the rookie we'd talked to at the station and felt my cheeks warm as I saw a flash of recognition when he spotted Kate and me.

"Nothing outside to tell us who might have done this," he said. If he did remember us, he didn't say anything.

"Thanks," Hobbes said, waving for them both to follow him out front as he glanced at his partner. "We'll leave you to wrap this up."

Reese nodded, thumping the detective on the back. I could tell from the quick look exchanged between the two men that they thought the call had been a waste of time. I was starting to agree with them.

I noticed the rookie cop look at Kate as he passed, blushing when she winked at him. I wanted to thank him for not mentioning that he'd met us before, but I hoped Kate's wink conveyed our gratitude. If Reese noticed the exchange, he didn't remark on it. Of course, it wasn't unusual for Kate to flirt with cops. Or firemen or paramedics or security guards. Come to think of it, it would have been more unusual if she hadn't.

"So what *is* missing?" Reese asked once the rest of the police had left.

Fern swiveled his head to take in the storage area and the floor-to-ceiling shelving units. Fluffy beige towels were scattered in one corner along with a cellophane-wrapped family-size pack of toilet paper. "Not much. The towels have been strewn all over the floor, but I don't think any are gone. It looks like someone flattened my toilet paper, and I seem to be missing a box of biscotti."

Reese's gaze flicked to me, and I could tell he was battling between frustration and amusement. "So we're not looking for a hardened criminal, just someone who was in the mood for cookies and likes to squeeze the Charmin."

Fern slid his eyes to my detective fiancé. "Are you saying this isn't a crime?"

"Not a violent one, and if the intruder used a key, it was barely a B and E."

Fern blinked at him.

"Breaking and entering," I said in a low voice.

"Thank you, Annabelle." Sarcasm dripped off Fern's voice.

Kate tapped one high-heeled foot on the tile floor. "I would suspect Brianna, but if it was her, I'd have expected her to do more damage."

"Kate's right," I said. "Given her recent track record, Brianna would have broken mirrors or trashed the place. The intruder didn't even appear to leave this storage area. They clearly didn't intend to vandalize or steal."

Reese eyed the towels. "If it was cold out, I'd think it was someone sneaking in to get warm."

Fern's face lit up. "What if it was Kris?"

Now it was my turn to study the towels with interest. "Then where's the blood? His Santa suit was pretty bloody. If he was injured badly enough to bleed like that, wouldn't he be dripping blood?"

We all looked at the clean floor and unblemished towels. Fern's shoulders sagged.

"I don't think we should rule it out," Reese said. "We haven't gotten the results back on the bloody Santa suit yet, and we can't be sure the blood belongs to Kris."

"You think someone else was injured that badly while wearing Kris's Santa suit?" I tried to keep the disbelief from my voice, but it didn't work. It seemed out of character for Kris to let someone else wear his beloved suit and even stranger that person would then get severely wounded in it. "Then why did Kris disappear?"

"And where's the naked, injured person?" Kate asked. "Because whoever was in that suit, ditched it and managed to run off."

"I checked all the hospitals," Reese admitted. "None of them report a patient with injuries consistent with that amount of blood loss in the past few days."

I swallowed hard. That meant that either the person was lying low or they were dead. I turned to Fern. "I think now would be a good time to explain why you're so sure Kris is alive."

Reese walked over to stand next to me, putting a hand casually around my waist. The heat from his body sent a small jolt of pleasure through me, and I almost forgot what I'd asked Fern.

Fern let out a long breath and shrugged. "If you must know, I learned a little more about Kris after you left yesterday."

"From the other homeless people?" Reese asked.

Fern nodded. "Did you know that Kris served in the Navy, and he did two tours in Vietnam?"

"No," I said, leaning back into my fiancé. "I don't know much about him, aside from the fact that he has a nice singing voice and gives great compliments."

"Well, he didn't talk about it much, but he did a bunch of covert ops with naval intelligence over there."

"Wow." Kate shook her head. "I never would have guessed."

"I doubt it's something you advertised much when you came back," I said. "So what does him being in the military have to do with your changing your mind?"

"If Kris survived a war, he's smart enough not to get killed here," Fern said.

Kate took a swig from her champagne flute. "He has a point. If he was involved in covert ops, he must know how to lay low."

I glanced around the storage room. "And how to sneak into a building."

Reese leaned down and whispered in my ear. "I wouldn't call it sneaking if the key is kept over the doorsill."

"You know Kris isn't the only person missing," I reminded Fern.

"At least we know Jeannie is safe," he said.

I'd told Reese soon after he'd arrived, but I'd forgotten to ask him about Kate's claim the cops were watching her. I looked up at him. "Would there be any reason a couple of plainclothes cops would be keeping an eye on her?"

He tilted his head at me. "As far as I know, I'm the only cop who even knows who she is."

He had a point. I turned my attention back to Fern. "There's always the possibility that Stanley might have had something to do with Kris's disappearance."

Reese arched an eyebrow at me. "You think?"

I remembered that I couldn't explain why I thought that or that I'd gotten the inside scoop from one of his fellow cops. "He did find the suit. Maybe that was because he was dumping it."

Fern gasped. "What an awful thought. You think he's missing because he's a killer on the run? I don't want *him* coming in my salon and squeezing my Charmin."

"We don't know for sure," I said, quickly, avoiding my fiancé's piercing gaze. "It's just a theory."

"Which you promised not to come up with," Kate said out of the corner of her mouth.

"It came to me on the fly," I said, more for Reese's benefit.

Reese laughed. "I'm surprised you only have one theory at this point."

I didn't know whether to be offended or flattered.

Fern closed the back door and straightened his white fur collar. "Be that as it may, I'd better get back to caroling. Leatrice isn't starting her shift for another hour."

"Do I want to know?" Reese asked me, his low voice tickling my neck.

"Probably not," I told him, glad that he'd taken my murder theory in stride. "Just don't be surprised if you see a really short Santa around Georgetown."

I felt Reese's phone buzz in his jeans pocket and he retrieved it, looking quickly at the screen before answering. "Mike Reese here."

I watched as his face became solemn and then grim. He thanked the person on the other end and hung up, sliding the phone back into his jeans.

"Bad news?" I asked.

"I'm not sure. One floater they pulled out of the river, which is never fun. And a beat cop just found a guy knocked out cold and hog-tied down near the harbor with enough meth on him to kill an elephant."

"How could that be good news?" Kate asked.

Reese rubbed a hand down his scruffy cheeks. "The guy who was tied up runs a seedy strip club. We've suspected him of using the club as a front for drug trafficking for years, but have never been able to get anything to stick."

"Why do you look so conflicted?" I asked, knowing my fiancé's expression.

"Not so much conflicted as perplexed," he said. "The guy was wearing a Santa suit when they found him."

CHAPTER 20

I checked my phone again before dropping it onto the couch next to me. No text from Reese, although I didn't really expect one. I knew he was busy processing a murder scene, and I cringed as I thought about the body pulled from the river. Then I thought about the man found in a Santa suit, and wondered about all the criminals turning up decked out in suits or hats. First Kris Kringle Jingle goes missing, then his suit is found and the guy who found it goes missing, then criminals start turning up wearing Santa garb. Either someone had a thing against Santa or a weird Santa fetish. Reese had made us all promise not to read too much into it, making me swear I wouldn't take this as a reason to get more involved in the case.

"You don't have to tell me twice," Kate had told him as he'd left for the waterfront and the dead body they'd pulled out. "I've had enough of floaters, thank you very much."

Fern had agreed with her, looking a bit green as we'd walked him out to one of his stylist chairs.

I wanted to remind them the one body we'd found floating in a pond could hardly have been considered a floater since she'd barely been in the water for half an hour before we'd spotted her, but I thought it best not to remind my fiancé about the latest murder investigation we'd meddled in. Like Kate and Fern, I'd promised Reese to leave this case to the DC police and had given him a quick kiss as he'd dashed out the door. And I'd meant it. Of course, that was before I had so much time to mull things over.

Sinking back into my couch, I let out a deep sigh, soaking up the quiet. For the first time in days, there was no one in my apartment but me, and the silence was blissful. As bad as I felt about my fiancé being called to a murder scene, I was grateful for the rare moments of solitude. I didn't even have an urge to think about why Kris was still missing.

It wasn't that I didn't love living with Reese. I did. But after living by myself for so many years, I was still adjusting to having someone around who never left. My evenings watching trashy TV while I caught up on paperwork had fallen by the wayside, and I never ate cupcakes for dinner anymore.

Propping my bare feet up on the coffee table, I glanced at the alphabetized rehearsal dinner place cards stacked next to the ceremony programs all folded and tied with ivory ribbon. Not only did I finally have the place to myself, Kate had helped me knock out most of the weekend's wedding prep before she'd dashed off to meet her mystery man for dinner. The panic that had been fluttering in my stomach all week had lessened somewhat after we'd finished some of the tedious work that always took hours the week of a wedding.

We'd both learned our lessons years ago and would never dream about leaving place card alphabetizing and program tying until the last minute. It was bad enough when clients gave us changes to the seating the day of the wedding, but after being burned by one too many procrastinating brides and being forced to stay up until the wee hours the night before the wedding, we now insisted on their seating plans a full week before the wedding day. It made my heart sing to see the neat stacks of paper products all ready to go for the weekend.

"One down," I said to myself, knowing we still had plenty to do to plan the New Year's Eve wedding and pull together my engagement/Wedding Belles holiday party.

A quick peek out the darkened windows told me it was later than I'd realized, and my growling stomach reminded me that I'd survived the day on snacks and champagne. I didn't bother checking the fridge as I contemplated what type of takeout I should order and pulled my phone out of my pocket.

Would Reese be back in time to join me? My mind wandered to the drug dealer dressed up as Santa. Was it possible the man was connected to Kris?

I knew I was under strict orders not to get involved in the case, but I couldn't help wondering why someone would put the low life in a Santa suit and dump him for the police to find. I seriously doubted the strip club owner happened to be dressed as Santa before he was tied up, but what if he was? Was someone out to get Santas in DC? I thought about what Fern had told us. Kris had been involved in covert ops in Vietnam. Was it possible that Kris wasn't a victim? Could he be some sort of Santa vigilante? But what about Stanley? No one saw him actually find the bloody suit. What if he had been trying to ditch it when the cop appeared, and he'd had to pretend he'd found it? He might have knocked off Kris—either accidentally or in the heat of the moment—and gone on the run out of fear and guilt.

Shaking my head, I stood up. No way. I much preferred to think Kris had snuck into Fern's storage room than a killer was on the loose.

As I put the neatly stacked place cards and programs back in their boxes, I heard a sharp rap on the door. So much for my peaceful evening. I resigned myself to the high probability of it being Leatrice fully dressed in a Santa suit and eager to pump me for information on the murder she'd no doubt heard about over her police scanner. I opened the door and blinked a few times.

"Richard," I said as he pushed past me into the apartment. "Did we have plans?"

"Not per se." He dropped his man bag on the couch and set a paper bag with handles on the floor. Hermès spilled out of the leather bag and began scampering from one end of the couch to the other, sniffing vigorously.

"Do I smell food?" I inhaled the savory aroma that seemed to be emanating from the paper bag.

"I'm assuming you haven't eaten yet, am I right?" Richard answered my question with one of his own, his eyes flitting to my boxes of paper products on the coffee table.

"You assume correctly. Kate and I were knocking out some of the work for the wedding, and you know my rule about food and drink near paper products."

Richard picked up the paper bag and headed for the kitchen, giving me a quick look over his shoulder. "You mean the rule I taught you? Yes, I'm familiar with it, darling."

"Right." It was hard to remember all the things Richard had taught me over the years, since he'd taken me under his wing from almost the moment I'd moved to DC and opened Wedding Belles, sharing all his tips and tricks for surviving the world of events.

His dark choppy hair appeared over the divider between the kitchen and living room. "Fern told me that our detective was called out to a murder. I knew that meant you'd be left to your own devices for dinner, and we all know what that means."

Our detective? I wondered when *my* fiancé had become our detective, but I decided not to say anything. The bromance Richard had going on with Reese was better than the thinly veiled hostility he used to have for the man he'd once considered his usurper.

"You know I'm fully capable of feeding myself," I said, perching on the back of my couch and petting Hermès absently on the head as he settled into a spot.

Richard snorted from the kitchen. "I've seen your refrigerator, Annabelle, and it's barely changed since you started cohabitating."

"We both work a lot," I said, in my own defense.

"You know I'm not one for gender stereotypes," he said, coming out of the kitchen wearing a pink toile apron and carrying two pasta bowls. "But one of you two is going to have to learn how to cook. I thought it might be the detective, but I didn't take into account his erratic schedule and how often you'd be solo."

I followed him to the dining table, breathing in the rich scent as he set down the bowls. "Maybe you can be our live-in cook?"

He arched a perfectly coifed brow at me. "Not with the way you keep house."

"And we might not have room for PJ, as well," I said, referencing the significant other we'd met for the first time at Leatrice's wedding.

Richard's cheeks colored, and he hurried back to the kitchen. "If three's a crowd, four would be a disaster."

"You are bringing him to the party on Sunday, aren't you?" I asked as I sat down in front of one of the steaming bowls of pasta.

Richard returned with a tiny ceramic dish he placed on the floor, and Hermès immediately leapt from the couch and rushed over, while Richard bustled back to the kitchen, skillfully dodging the eager dog and my question.

I leaned over and peered at the contents of the dish. "Your dog eats pancetta?"

"He has very discerning taste," Richard said as he emerged from the kitchen again, this time with two wine glasses and an opened bottle. "Tell me if the nutmeg is too much in the carbonara. Nigella swears by it, but she is British."

I decided not to call Richard out on changing the subject, as I swirled my fork in the lightly sauced spaghetti. I suspected he was keeping his personal life close to his chest because he didn't want PJ getting a sense of how crazy our crew was and running for the hills. Not a bad plan. I'd been lucky Reese had a high tolerance for crazy.

"I didn't know you and Fern talked often," I said. "What else did he tell you?"

Richard shrugged as he filled my glass halfway with white wine. "Just that he'd had a break-in, and Reese had been called away early because they'd found a body."

"Did he tell you about the other guy they found?" I took a bite and savored the rich flavor of the crunchy pancetta.

"Some lowlife club owner tied up like he'd gotten on the wrong side of a dominatrix." Richard wrinkled his nose. "Fern's words, not mine."

"He was found wearing a Santa suit."

Richard's fork froze halfway to his mouth. "That explains it."

"Explains what?"

"Why Fern called me and was so insistent I come over here and keep an eye on you. He kept saying it was his fault that you were going to be sucked back in like Michael Corleone in *The Godfather III*."

I swallowed a too-hot mouthful and washed it down with a cold gulp of wine. "He compared me to the Godfather?"

"I thought it was a bit much considering our latest run-in with the mob, but now I get it." He eyed me. "Frankly, I'm surprised you're sitting here so calmly."

I rolled my eyes. "I promised Reese I wouldn't meddle."

"And you were serious about that?"

"Of course," I said, twirling spaghetti around my fork. "I've turned over a new leaf. Besides, Reese is still looking for Kris, so I know it's in good hands. And if there's a connection with all the other Santa crimes, he'll find it."

As if on cue, the door opened and my fiancé stumbled inside, his clothes disheveled and dirty.

Richard's mouth dropped open. "You didn't personally drag the body out of the Potomac, did you?"

Reese didn't even register surprise at seeing Richard in our apartment as he collapsed onto the couch, and Hermès scampered over and began licking his hand.

Richard sucked in a sharp breath. "Hermès! You do not know where that's been."

"You were saying something about his discerning taste?" I said, earning myself a pointed look as I got up to join Reese on the couch.

"You look like you need some pasta," Richard headed for the kitchen, wagging a finger at the little Yorkie who followed him. "And now *you* need a good teeth brushing, young man."

"How did things go with the body?" I asked, sitting next to Reese and brushing a loose strand of dark hair off his face.

"Well, it wasn't an accident." Reese rubbed a hand across his forehead. "The guy was strangled before he was tossed into the river."

My stomach turned. "What about the drug dealing Santa?"

He shook his head. "It's not my case."

"But shouldn't you be involved since it might be connected to the other Santa cases?"

Reese sighed. "The way things are going, I won't sleep if I take on all the cases with a Santa element to them."

"But what if the Santa crimes are connected?" When he didn't answer, I shook my head. "Someone needs to be working that angle."

Richard let out a tortured breath behind us. "Why do I feel like I know who that someone will be?"

CHAPTER 21

"He has a point, you know," Kate said as we walked along M Street the next day.

I'd insisted we spend the morning wrapping up the details for Saturday as well as calling potential vendors for our New Year's Eve wedding, then Kate had convinced me that we needed a break to stretch our legs and do some holiday shopping. As usual, I'd been too caught up in work to find presents for anyone, and, as of that morning, Kate had added a Secret Santa present to my long list.

"Who has a point?" I asked, glancing at a brightly decorated store window flocked with white paint to make it look like snow. Ironic, since I was almost sweating in the spring-like weather, even though I only wore a white button-down and jeans.

"Richard, of course. If Reese isn't working all the Santa cases, aren't you going to be tempted to connect them yourself? I know it's already killing you that Stanley is missing and we don't know why."

I shook my head as I dodged a group of giggling college students attempting to take a selfie while they walked down the sidewalk. "I do have some self-control, you know."

"Mmmhmm." She sounded far from convinced. "Have they given up looking for Kris?"

I shrugged. "Reese hasn't, but I think only as a favor to our friends. They haven't made much headway with that, although I want to side with Fern. He's not dead even though he hasn't turned up."

"But another guy in a Santa suit has turned up. And some in Santa hats."

"Yep," I said. "I guess it could be a coincidence, but that seems unlikely."

"But what's the connection, aside from both being Santa? A homeless vet and a dodgy club owner don't seem like a likely pairing. And then a couple of thieves?"

"Your guess is as good as mine," I said. "Maybe this club owner was involved in whatever Kris saw that made him freak out enough to go into hiding. Kris could be hiding to avoid falling victim to the same fate. Maybe someone is picking off Santas one by one."

"And you think that someone is Stanley?"

"Well, I hadn't before, but now I do."

She spun on me. "See? I knew you'd been thinking about it."

"Thinking about it? Sure. But I don't have the time to do anything about it. Our to-do list is a mile long. When would I fit in a murder investigation?"

Kate gave me a sidelong glance. "You're very resourceful, Annabelle. And sneakier than you look."

"Thanks, I think."

"We did get a lot done today," she admitted. "Once our New Year's Eve bride signs the contracts we requested, it's only a matter of confirming details."

"We got lucky she was so burned out from working with Brianna that she gave us carte blanche in picking vendors."

Kate held up one palm. "Do *not* say that name again. I still haven't come up with the proper retribution for that tire slasher."

I wanted to tell her that we weren't 100 percent positive Brianna had been the one to pop her tires, but not even I believed that. "Maybe we should put the brakes on this feud. I think we've come out on the losing end, so far."

"So far," Kate said, her eyes narrowed.

I sighed. I guess we weren't going to take the high road, so I decided to change the subject. "I have no idea what to get for Secret Santa this year. It's so hard to find something that anyone from our group would like, and now we're going to have a bunch of cops in the mix."

Kate paused in front of The Paper Source, tapping her chin. "I forgot about the extra guests for the engagement party. Maybe we should do the Secret Santa just for our crew after the party."

"That's a good idea," I said, glancing at the large paper nutcrackers and ballerinas perched atop shiny, gold boxes in the store window. "I'd hate to invite Reese's friends to an engagement party and ask them to bring a Secret Santa gift, too. That seems like a lot."

"Agreed." Kate held open the tall glass doors framed in pink. "I don't know how you're going to top the Llamanoes you gave last year."

We walked into the store, the usual tables of gifts piled high with holiday-themed offerings--a stack of mistletoe tea towels next to a red, felt pom-pom Christmas stocking, and an entire table devoted to colorful advent calendars, some of them three-dimensional and one of them featuring "Twelve Days of Christmas" socks. Instrumental holiday music played overhead, and the store smelled like paper and cinnamon air freshener.

Kate stopped at the end of the ramp leading into the shop. "I may have found something to beat the Llamanoes." She held up a box featuring a June Cleaver look-alike. "An inflatable turkey."

"What if Richard ended up with that?" I asked.

She frowned. "Good point. He might not be amused. He's never appreciated food humor." Her expression brightened. "But here's a set of tea towels of dogs dressed in pajamas."

"He might like that *too* much."

Kate grinned at me. "Another good point. We probably shouldn't encourage the dressing the dog like a human thing."

I picked up an inflatable set of antlers with rings to toss over them, labeled "Reindeer Games." "I'd say this might be fun if I didn't think Leatrice would want to wear them twenty-four seven."

"Then it's down to the Screaming Goat." Kate held up a box that contained a plastic goat standing on a plastic stump, pressing a button that made the thing let out a high-pitched scream.

I gave her a look.

"What?" She pressed the button again. "I feel like this goat every time Meltdown Maddie calls."

One of our spring brides had a tendency to overreact about everything and often ended up hyperventilating over the phone while we listened to her hunt for a paper bag. "Maybe we should go with something less hysterical."

Kate looked at the goat. "You're right. It sounds too much like Richard when his waiters fold the napkins wrong."

I caught a glimpse of a pair of fully dressed Santa Clauses walking past the store, but quickly realized it wasn't Kris and felt a pang of sadness. The Salvation Army Santas still worked in Georgetown, and it was most likely a couple of them. I remembered what Jeannie had said about the jealous Santas, and a shiver went through me. I hated thinking of every chubby man in a red suit as a potential murderer. It really put a damper on my Christmas cheer.

"I think I need some caffeine and sugar before I can handle any more cheesy holiday gift ideas," I said, feeling my sadness shift into shopping malaise.

"Cheesy?" Kate pretended to be affronted as she held up a set of elf drink markers with the beefy plastic elves wearing nothing but red-and-green hot pants and suspenders.

I laughed. "I feel like you own that outfit."

She cocked an eyebrow at me. "You might be right." She put down the sexy elves and linked her arm through mine. "It's not too early for a cupcake, is it?"

"I don't think it's ever too early for a cupcake, since they're just muffins with a fancy topping."

We headed out of the store, and I was grateful to be walking again. Shopping had never been my thing, which was one reason I bought most of my clothes online, to Richard's eternal horror. We turned down Thomas Jefferson Street, the road sloping down toward the canal and further on to the Potomac River and the harbor. I spotted the pink bicycle tied up outside our favorite bakery with flowers brimming from its basket, and I quickened my step. Baked & Wired cupcakes always improved my mood.

After crossing the bridge over the canal and seeing one of the old-fashioned canal boats tied to the shore, we ducked inside the glass-fronted bakery. I breathed in the heady aroma of coffee and icing, my gaze instantly drawn to the long counter covered in cupcakes, cookies, and cakes topped with glass domes. One tall shelving unit held holiday gift sets along with cellophane bags of peanut brittle and their trademark Hippie Crack granola tied with festive red ribbon.

"I'll grab coffees," Kate said, pointing to the coffee bar on the other side of the store. "Can you get me a uniporn cupcake?"

"Uniporn?" I repeated.

She winked at me. "The full name is 'uniporn and rainho', but they'll know what you mean."

This would be fun to order, I thought as Kate walked away, and I proceeded to the bakery counter. After inspecting the day's offerings, I ordered Kate's uniporn--which appeared to be funfetti with pink icing--along with a razmanian devil, dirty chai, chocolate doom, red velvet, and coconut.

"Hungry?" Kate asked as I met her at the door with a box of half a dozen cupcakes.

I took the paper cup of coffee she held out to me. "These aren't all for us. I thought Buster and Mack might need some cheering up. The holidays are always crazy for them, and Kris is still missing, which I know worries them."

"Good idea." She squeezed my arm. "Cupcakes always make me feel better."

We stepped outside, and I rested the box and my coffee on one of the empty French wire tables. Opening the box, I handed Kate her pink cupcake with heart sprinkles on the top and plucked out the razmanian devil with white frosting and single sugar heart perched on top.

Kate tapped her cupcake's wax paper wrapper against mine. "Cheers."

I took a bite of my cupcake, savoring the burst of flavor as I bit through the thick lemon buttercream and reached the raspberry jam center. She was right. Even though I'd gotten no shopping done, Kris Kringle Jingle was still missing, and now one of his friends was dead, the rush of sugar made me feel better. At least we had the New Year's Eve wedding well in hand and hadn't sustained any further property damage. If the temperature would dip below seventy degrees, I might consider the day a success.

Looking over Kate's head, I saw another Santa crossing the street at the intersection with M. Now that Santas were missing and Santa crimes on the rise—and in my mind, they were also suspects in Kris's disappearance—I seemed to see them everywhere. I felt a small surge of hope as I squinted at the red-suited figure a block away. Even from the distance, I could tell it wasn't Kris, and my heart sank. Santa glanced our way, then jerked back around, quickened his pace to a near run, and disappeared down M Street.

"Did you see that?" I asked Kate, but she was too involved in her cupcake to have noticed. Was I imagining things or had this Santa been wearing hipster glasses?

"What?" Kate mumbled through a mouthful.

"Nothing." I dismissed the feeling that Santa had been spooked by something, glancing around me and seeing nothing but a few tourists. Tucking my partially eaten cupcake back into the box, I closed it again, balancing the cupcake box and my coffee as we crossed the street toward Lush. The bell jingled overhead as we pushed through the front door, but instead of cheery Christmas carols, we were met with the sound of shrieking.

"That's no screaming goat," Kate said, wiping a dab of icing off her mouth. "And it doesn't sound like baby Merry, either."

We followed the sounds to the back of the shop where Buster sat with his head in his hands and Mack paced behind him, his hands in the air as he wailed. When he saw us, he stopped.

"You got my message?"

Kate looked at me. "What message?"

"We just called your office," Buster said. "We were about to call your cells."

"What's going on?" I asked, feeling a nervous flutter in my chest.

Mack began pacing again. "The flower order for this weekend's wedding? It's gone."

I stared at him. "Our wedding at the Four Seasons?"

Buster nodded, mutely.

"What do you mean, gone?" Kate said.

"When our guys went to the wholesaler this morning to pick it up, they said one of our other guys had picked it up already," Buster said. "As soon as they opened."

"We don't have other guys," Mack said, throwing his hands in the air again. "Someone stole our flowers and there's no time to get more, even if the entire city wasn't sold out."

Kate turned to me. "We're going to need more cupcakes."

CHAPTER 22

"I don't understand," Kate said, pacing next to Mack. "How can someone just waltz in and take an entire flower order?"

"The person apparently had our vendor number and knew enough to be convincing," Buster told her. He now stood at the cappuccino machine, a red velvet cupcake in one hand and the machine's metal coffee basket in the other. "And had a U-Haul van."

"So it had to be someone who had insider information into your business." I took a sip of the hot mocha Kate had gotten me, as I perched on one of the metal barstools around the long, high table. "Did the people at the warehouse recognize whomever picked up the flowers?"

"They were wearing a Santa suit," Mack said.

"What?" I nearly slipped off the stool.

Kate threw her hands up. "This is ridiculous. Are we the only people *not* wearing Santa suits?"

"Why?" Buster asked. "Who else is wearing them?"

"Aside from Fern and Leatrice as they try to fill in for Kris, only every criminal who's getting caught recently," I told them, giving them a brief rundown of all the Santa-related busts.

"That's pretty odd," Mack admitted, "but I doubt a criminal would have any use for our flowers."

"True." I settled myself back on the stool. "So we're back to someone who knows your business. Do you have any disgruntled employees who've left recently?"

Mack gave me a scandalized look. "Disgruntled? I would hope not. We take good care of our staff."

Buster fired up the milk frothing wand, which screeched for a moment before he turned it off again. "But we do have freelance staff that works for other florists. Maybe all this was a big misunderstanding and one of our freelancers got confused."

Leave it to my Christian biker friends to always look for the best in people. I wished he was right, but my gut told me his hope was misplaced.

"Then why haven't you gotten a call?" Kate asked, spinning on her heel and walking a brisk path across the width of the room. "By this point, whichever florist got the order should know it isn't theirs, right?"

Buster nodded reluctantly. "Right. We had an unusually large amount of birch branches and white hydrangea. It wasn't your typical Christmastime order."

Since we were trying to recreate a winter wonderland inside the Four Seasons hotel, everything about the decor was white. This wasn't a case where we could substitute a bunch of potted poinsettias and call it a day.

Mack paused his pacing for a moment as Buster thrust a cappuccino at him. "Where are we going to find that much large head white hydrangea by Saturday?"

"I would suggest we creep into people's gardens," Kate said, "but December isn't the season for it."

"And the wholesaler doesn't have any more or can't rush any more to you?" I asked, eyeing the open box of cupcakes in front of me. I'd finished my razmanian devil, but the stress of the situation had the coconut calling my name.

Buster returned to the table, cradling an oversized round coffee cup. "Not by Saturday. Most of the product we ordered was Dutch, so there isn't time for it to fly over and clear customs. I called around for anything local, but there's nothing."

I tore my gaze from the cupcakes and took a deep breath, inhaling the rich aroma of Buster's freshly brewed cappuccinos. "What are our options? Change the look?"

Kate shook her head. "The bride will freak."

"Agreed," I said. "Two days before the wedding is not the time to spring this on a bride. I know none of us want to use silk."

Mack sucked in a breath so sharply I looked around to see if Richard had walked in. "Lush does not use fake flowers."

I held up my hands. "It was just a last-resort suggestion. Silks have come a long way, you know."

"Even if we bought out every craft store in the area, I doubt we'd have enough white hydrangea," Buster said.

I took a gulp of coffee and sat up straighter. "Then we need to find your flowers. Someone clearly has them. Someone who has a grudge against you."

"Or against us," Kate said, slapping her hand on the metal table and making me jump. "This has Brianna written all over it."

Before I could tell her that was a ridiculous thought, I paused to really consider it. Brianna did know we used Lush almost exclusively. She also knew we had a wedding at the Four Seasons on Saturday, plus it wasn't out of the realm of possibility that she could have hired one of Buster and Mack's freelancers. The guy might not have even known he was doing something sneaky if she'd told him it was for her wedding. Brianna's smarmy Southern accent seemed to work like a charm on most men. And I wouldn't put it past our rival to try to sabotage us so dramatically. If she was resorting to vandalism, she was already pretty unhinged.

"You might be right," I said.

Mack's mouth gaped. "You think another wedding planner is behind this?"

Buster adjusted the motorcycle goggles perched on his bald head. "I know she's never used us before, but this seems extreme."

"It's not about you," Kate said. "It's about us. She's livid because her New Year's Eve bride fired her and hired us last week. She refused to turn the venue contract she'd signed over to the bride, and is holding her own party there instead on New Year's Eve just so we'd have to scramble for a last-minute venue. We're also pretty sure she's the one who slashed all four of my tires outside Annabelle's apartment."

Buster's mug clattered to the table. "She slashed your tires?"

"It sounds like we need to add her to our prayer list." Mack shook his head, his expression solemn. "All that hate in her heart must be a burden."

"You need to pray that I don't kill her," Kate muttered.

"If Brianna did take the flowers, where would she put them?" I asked.

Kate drummed her manicured fingers on the table. "Didn't she open that office space down near the intersection of M and Key Bridge?"

"You're right," I said. "It's upstairs over a bicycle shop or something. I'm sure the rent still costs her father a fortune since it's in Georgetown. It wouldn't look suspicious for a business to get a large flower delivery in Georgetown, but it would raise eyebrows if she had a truck full of flowers delivered to her apartment, wherever that is."

"Capitol Hill," Kate said. "She has a townhouse in Capitol Hill." When she noticed us all staring at her, she added, "Her assistant comes to our wedding assistant happy hours, remember? She told us in the group text that she used to go to Brianna's place on Capitol Hill before they got an office space."

I was both impressed and baffled by the wedding planners who rented expensive office space when so much of our job entailed meetings at venues or other vendors' studios. I knew in Brianna's case, it was more about the status of having a swanky Georgetown address for her business than any real need.

Pulling my phone out of my pocket, I glanced at the time. It was already midafternoon. "Does she go there every day?"

Kate shrugged. "If she does, I doubt she stays late, especially now that she doesn't have any weddings coming up to plan. She's always posting about having dinner at the newest, trendy restaurant, anyway."

"You follow her on social media?" I asked.

She grinned at me. "Only under my Instagram alias, Natasha Moosensquirrel."

Buster nearly spit out a mouthful of coffee, coughing loudly as he attempted to swallow.

"I like to follow some people without having them know it's me," she explained. "And Natasha is my alias when I use my Russian accent at bars to scare off men I'm not interested in."

"And that works?" Mack asked, taking a seat next to Buster.

"Da, darling," she said in a thick accent that brought to mind Rocky and Bullwinkle's cartoon nemesis. "It works like a charm."

I gave my head a shake. "Okay. So we know she probably won't be at her office space after hours. That's when we should go look for the flowers."

"Look for the flowers?" Mack looked from me to Kate as he nervously stroked his goatee. "Do you mean break into her office?"

I grabbed the coconut cupcake and took a bite, closing my eyes to savor it before opening them again and nodding. "If we have to. It isn't stealing if they don't belong to her in the first place."

Buster tilted his head at me. "I guess you're right."

"You don't have to be involved," I said, realizing that not only would it create a crisis of conscience for them, but that we wouldn't exactly be stealthy if we brought the two enormous bikers. Kate and I might be able to pass unnoticed in the back alleys of Georgetown. Buster and Mack were never unnoticed.

"Are you sure?" Mack asked, although I could see he was relieved by the idea of not being involved in a potential crime.

Buster frowned. "Won't you need a way to transport the flowers if you find them?"

"If we find them, we'll call you, and you can bring your van," Kate said. "That way you're only involved in the recovery part of the mission."

Mack put his hands to his cheeks. "What is your fiancé going to say about all this?"

I hadn't thought about Reese. He wasn't going to like this one bit. *If he found out.* "Let's hope he's so pleased I'm not meddling in a criminal investigation that he doesn't notice the rest. He is working late tonight, so hopefully we'll be back before he even notices I'm gone."

"Another foolproof plan," Kate said in her Russian accent. "You'd better be getting him a really good Christmas present, comrade."

CHAPTER 23

"I know I wanted to get back at Brianna," Kate said as she stood in my living room wearing head-to-toe black that looked like it had been painted on. "But I'm not sure if I want to go to jail for it."

"We aren't going to jail." I glanced outside my windows as I pawed through my wedding emergency kit. It was already dark, although I knew Georgetown would be bustling until late into the night. My stomach roiled from nerves, and I regretted that two cupcakes were the bulk of what I'd eaten during the day. Richard was right. I really needed to eat better.

"I can't believe my mini flashlight got swiped."

Kate didn't look surprised. "You know bridesmaids."

It was true that bridesmaids were known for pillaging our wedding supplies, but I couldn't imagine why one had needed a flashlight. Safety pins, hairspray, breath mints, sure. But, a flashlight?

"I guess we'll have to rely on our phones," I said, snapping my boxy metal case shut after retrieving a few bobby pins.

Kate tugged a black knit cap over her hair. "Should I ask what the bobby pins are for?"

"Picking locks," I said as I jammed them into the pocket of my black jeans.

"You can do that?"

I couldn't. "Technically, no, but I figure we should have them just in case."

"In case one of us needs to put our hair up into an emergency French twist?"

I made a face at her. "It can't be that hard. We've learned a lot of things on the fly before. Tying bow ties, folding pocket squares, making a bird of paradise out of a napkin."

"Call me crazy, but I don't want to be covertly watching a how-to YouTube video as we're crouched in front of a door trying to pick the lock."

The first time we'd had to tie actual bow ties for a bridal party, Kate and I had taken turns watching a tutorial on her phone behind one of the enormous pillars in the National Cathedral as we dashed back and forth to the getting-ready room, attempting to make the ties look even. I knew it was a feeling neither one of us ever wanted to repeat, although we'd become experts in tying bow ties since that harrowing day years ago.

"I doubt we'll need to pick a lock," I said. "Doors in Georgetown are notoriously old and rickety."

"So we're going to kick it in? That does not make me feel any better."

I pulled my own hair up into a high ponytail. "I don't know what we're going to do. All I know is that we need those flowers, and if Brianna has them, we're getting them back."

Kate made a fist and punched it into her other hand. "Yeah, we are. But let's go before your fiancé comes home and busts us."

"Good idea." I grabbed my car keys out of my purse, deciding to leave it and any other identification at home. I was looking at the keys, wondering if we should just walk instead of drive, when there was a knock on the door.

"Who do you think it is?" Kate whispered.

"It can't be Reese. He has a key."

"We all have keys," Kate said, reminding me again I should probably change my locks.

"Maybe it's Fern?" I had a good feeling it wasn't Richard, since he'd mentioned giving Hermès a bath when we'd talked earlier. I knew the little dog's bathing ritual included a hot oil treatment and a blowout, so Richard's evening was booked solid.

"Yoo hoo," the voice called through the door.

"Leatrice," Kate and I said at the same time.

Kate motioned to the door. "If you don't open it, she'll just use the key you gave her."

"I didn't give her a key," I reminded her. "She made one using her spy key mold."

Kate rolled her eyes. "You know I don't know any of my neighbors on a first-name basis. You should try it."

"I think that ship has sailed," I said as I opened the door.

Leatrice clapped her hands when she saw us. "Oh, good. You're both here. I need you to give me your honest opinion on my caroling costume."

Her green velvet hoop skirt swung from side to side as she entered my apartment, causing us to move out of the way. The matching cape was lined in white fur, as was the ruffled velvet cap that flopped around her face, and her hands were buried inside a white fur muff.

"It's very..." I began.

"Green," Kate said.

"Too green?" Leatrice asked. "My honeybun is wearing a red velvet suit and a red ribbon around his top hat, and I was going to put Hermès in green and red."

"Hermès is going caroling?" I asked.

Leatrice bobbed her head up and down, and her cap sunk lower on her forehead. "He loves Christmas carols. I haven't run it by Richard yet, but I'm sure he'll agree once he sees the tiny top hat I found."

"As long as you make sure I'm there when you ask him," Kate said.

Leatrice looked us up and down, taking in our attire for the first time since walking inside. "Where are you two off to dressed like Johnny Cash?"

Kate looked down at her outfit and mouthed, *Johnny Cash?*

"Just a work thing," I lied.

My neighbor narrowed her eyes at me. "Kate would never wear this much clothing for a work event."

She had a point. Even though Kate's black pants and scoop neck long-sleeved bodysuit were tight, they did cover her from ankle to wrist. With the black knit cap covering her blond hair, she looked every bit the cat burglar. Emphasis on cat.

Leatrice rubbed her hands together. "You're doing something covert, aren't you?"

"No," I said, at the same time Kate nodded her head.

"I knew it." Leatrice bounced up and down on her toes, making her hoop skirt swing back and forth. "Is it a stakeout? You know I'm excellent at stakeouts."

"It's not a stakeout," I told her. The last time we'd staged an unofficial and probably illegal stakeout, it had ended in my car getting torched and the wrong person being arrested.

"We're trying to find some stolen flowers," Kate said, shrugging when I shot her a look. "What? She would have dragged it out of us, anyway. I'm just saving us all a few tedious steps."

"Stolen flowers?" Leatrice rubbed her chin. "Do you have an idea where they are?"

"We have a guess," I admitted. "But we aren't certain, so we're going to scout it out."

"Understood." Leatrice spun around and headed for the door. "Give me five minutes, and I'll be ready to go."

"Wait," I said, waving my hands. "You can't go with us."

"Why not?" she asked. "I have all the spy and surveillance gear you could ever need, plus I can be your wheelman."

"We don't have a wheelman," Kate said.

"We don't *need* a wheelman," I insisted.

"What if we can't find parking or have to park blocks away?" Kate asked. "This is Georgetown, after all."

"See?" Leatrice beamed before turning and hurrying out the door and down the stairs, holding up her voluminous skirt as it filled up the width of the staircase. "You need me."

I sighed, shooting Kate a look. "What I need is to have my head examined."

"You plan weddings for a living, Annabelle," Kate said. "That's a given."

CHAPTER 24

"Why are we turning here?" I asked Leatrice, clutching the passenger side door handle as she took a wide turn in her ancient Ford Fairmont, the back of the long car seeming to swing around a few seconds after the front.

"To pick up Fern, of course," Leatrice said, adjusting her black fedora and craning her neck around as Kate slid from one end of the back seat to the other. "You okay back there, dear?"

Kate gave a thumbs-up as she righted herself, leaning her head between the driver's and passenger's front seats. "Glad I skipped dinner."

Leatrice glanced over, her face lighting up. "Should we stop for a bite to eat first?"

"We're on a mission to steal back an entire floral order," I said, trying to keep my impatience in check as I eyed the petite woman in a trench coat. "We're not going to the theatre. And tell me why we're picking up Fern."

"He's an excellent lookout." Leatrice didn't slow the car as we bumped up and down over the cobblestoned street and occasionally ran up onto the old trolley rails. "Don't you remember what a help he was when we staked out that murder suspect?"

"I remember him napping," I said.

Leatrice ignored me, pointing ahead of her to a figure all in black standing on the sidewalk. "There he is."

Fern waited outside his salon, although the lights inside the narrow, glass-fronted shop were out and it looked locked up tight. I blinked a few times as we slowed down next to him.

"Did you tell him to dress like a cat?" Kate asked.

Leatrice stopped the car, waving at him through the window. "I told him we were going to be cat burglars."

"That explains the dominatrix outfit," I said as Fern hopped in the back seat in his skintight black catsuit complete with Catwoman face mask with small pointy ears.

"Nice suit." Kate nodded appreciatively. "I might have to borrow it from you someday."

"It's a perfect size eight." Fern smoothed one hand over the shiny fabric. "Just like me."

I twisted around to face the back seat as Leatrice pulled away from the curb. "Just to be clear, we are going to Brianna's office to look for the flower order that was stolen from the wholesaler this morning. It's crucial that no one sees us and even more crucial that no one tells my fiancé about this."

Fern mimed zipping his lips closed. "You can count on me, sweetie. I'm the soul of discretion."

Coming from Georgetown's biggest gossip, this was rich.

"Are you sure you should keep secrets from your fiancé?" Leatrice asked, darting a glance at me as the car bounced over a dip in the cobblestones. "My sugar muffin and I tell each other everything."

"Your sugar muffin isn't a cop," I said. "If you were secretly part of an acting troupe that competed with his business, it might be a different story."

Leatrice tapped her chin. "I never thought of that."

"It's not that I like sneaking around behind Reese's back," I said. "But he has to do everything by the book, and if we wait for things to go through the proper channels, our flowers will be dead and our client's wedding will be ruined."

Kate popped her head between our two seats again. "Nothing motivates Annabelle like the possibility of a wedding disaster and an unhappy client."

She was right. Not only was an unhappy client bad for business, I couldn't stand the idea of not being able to solve a problem. The urge to fix things seemed to be baked into my DNA.

"I'm with you, sweetie." Catwoman reached up and patted me on the shoulder. "I can't do a bride's hair while she sobs uncontrollably about having no flowers for her wedding. It would stunt my creativity."

"So what's the plan?" Leatrice asked, hooking a left and pumping the brakes as the car dipped down a steep side street.

"The building is around the corner on the right," I said, "but I'd park around here."

Leatrice veered down a narrow alley, and we all sucked in our breath as the car barely missed scraping against one of the brick buildings. She jerked to a stop before hitting a green dumpster.

I braced my hand on the dashboard. "This works." I peered up at the back of the four-story buildings pressed close to each other. "This must be the back of Brianna's building."

"She's on the top floor of one of them," Kate said. "I know it from the front, but they all look the same from back here."

I caught sight of Fern's mask in the rearview mirror. "Maybe we should approach it from the back. That way we won't be seen."

Kate nodded and pointed to the metal stairs clinging to the buildings. "The fire escapes."

Leatrice shuddered. "Again?"

We'd had to hurry down three flights of my rusty fire escape on her wedding day, and I knew it wasn't her fondest memory of the day.

"You should stay here," I told her. "I need you ready to fly when we come out. Just in case we set off alarms or there are guard dogs."

"Guard dogs?" Fern put a hand to his black, leather chest. "Kitty doesn't like dogs."

"I doubt there are dogs," Kate said. "It's Georgetown. Everyone has purse dogs like Hermès. The most they could do would be piddle on your shoes."

I turned and leveled a finger at Fern. "You'll stay outside and be our lookout while Kate and I go inside."

"And how are we getting inside?" Kate asked. "And please don't say bobby pins."

Leatrice held up a wallet-sized leather pouch. "Use my lock-picking set."

I stared at her. "Should I ask where you got this?"

She beamed at me from under the brim of her fedora. "Amazon. They aren't illegal."

"I'll bet using them is," Kate said under her breath.

I reluctantly took the pouch, feeling like I was falling farther down the rabbit hole. "Let's hope we don't need it."

Kate opened her car door. "Let's do this before I come to my senses or lose my nerve."

"We'll be back," I told Leatrice as I followed Kate's lead, joining her and Fern at the bottom of one of the fire escapes. Although the metal stair systems were no longer required for buildings in DC, most of the older buildings still had them, and Georgetown was chock full of old buildings.

"Here goes nothing." Kate clambered up onto the hood of Leatrice's yellow car, then onto the top of the dumpster before climbing the ladder to the first landing of the fire escape.

I followed her, my arms shaking from both nerves and exertion as I pulled myself rung over rung, and Fern brought up the rear. Climbing the stairs was easier, but I was still breathing heavily when we reached the top. Luckily the lights were off in the building, since it wasn't residential and the businesses had closed for the day, so we didn't need to worry about anyone seeing us.

Kate's hands were on her hips as we gathered around the tall windows at the top. "I'm pretty sure this is it."

I squinted to see inside, but all I could see were dark shapes. "I don't see the outlines of branches or bunches of hydrangea, but they could be in another room."

Kate tugged at one of the windows, and it lifted with a groan. "It's open!"

I paused with a hand on her arm, waiting for the sound of an alarm, but none came. "And there's no security system."

"At least not one we can hear," Fern said in a stage whisper, glancing around us as if there was anyone else in the alley to overhear us.

I stole a quick glance down at Leatrice's car, her hat clearly visible through the windshield, and instantly regretted it. Four flights felt a lot higher than it sounded.

Kate pulled the window up all the way and ducked her head inside. "I'm going in."

"Stay out here and keep watch," I told Fern, who nodded solemnly and folded his arms over his chest, before I crawled into the building behind Kate.

When I was inside the room, I paused to let my eyes adjust to the dark. "Where are you?"

"Over here," Kate said.

I tracked her voice to the open door and saw her silhouette appear. We left the room that appeared to be storage, with nothing but a few boxes and a bookshelf, and proceeded down the hall. I heard Kate's shoes tapping on the hardwood floors and realized that even her black boots had heels.

As we approached the front of the building, lights from M Street spilled in through the large windows, and it was easy to see sleek desks against the walls and a large drafting table in the middle of the room. No surprise that even in the dark, the furnishings looked chic and cutting-edge.

"No flowers," Kate said.

Crap. My initial nervousness was replaced with disappointment. If the flowers weren't here, where were they? I was still convinced Brianna had taken them, but now I had no idea where she'd stashed them.

"Now what?" In the shadowy lighting, Kate's face looked fierce as she scanned the office space. "Time for a little payback?"

"No. All I wanted was our flowers. We aren't here for revenge. It's not our style."

"It might be *my* style," Kate mumbled, thumbing through a pile of papers on one of the desks. "You aren't the one whose tires were slashed."

I understood Kate's desire to extract a pound of flesh, but we weren't criminals, despite all current evidence to the contrary.

"Psssst."

I hurried back down the hallway to where Fern's head protruded into the room. "What's up? Is someone coming?"

"I hoped you two were coming," he said. "I'm getting bored out here."

I glanced back to Kate coming down the hall. "There's nothing here. We're ready to go."

Fern held out a hand for both of us as we crawled out the window and slid the glass back down. Despite the fact that we'd come up empty, I was glad we'd managed to get in and out of Brianna's office without anyone being the wiser. Reese would never even need to know about tonight, I thought as I wiped my hands on the front of my black jeans.

"Um, Annabelle," Kate said, leaning over the metal railing. "Where's Leatrice?"

CHAPTER 25

I followed Kate's gaze over the side of the fire escape. Leatrice's car was still in the same place, but even from four stories up, I could see that she was no longer sitting in the driver's side.

"Where could she have gone?" Fern asked. "She was just there a second ago."

I made a quick scan of the alley but didn't see my neighbor's trench-coated figure anywhere. I tuned back to Fern. "You didn't see her leave? Or hear anything suspicious?"

He shook his head, his eyes wide behind his mask. "I did poke my head inside the building when I called for you, but before that, nothing."

My pulse quickened as I started down the escape. "She couldn't have gotten far."

"She wouldn't have wandered off," Kate said, falling in step behind me. "You know she takes her job as wheelman seriously."

That was what scared me. I knew Leatrice wouldn't have walked off. Not when we were relying on her as our getaway driver. At least we weren't in need of a fast getaway.

When I reached the bottom, I descended down the ladder and dropped onto the dumpster.

"Annabelle?"

The muffled voice came from beneath me. I crouched down as Kate landed beside me, her boots making a loud echoing sound on the metal lid.

"I think she's inside the dumpster," I said, holding a hand above me to stop Fern from jumping down.

"What?" Kate dropped to her knees. "Leatrice? Are you in there?"

"Yes, dear. I'm so glad you're back," she said, her voice faint through the steel.

I waved for Fern to join us, then we all hopped from the dumpster onto the hood of the car. We lifted the lid and peeked in. Sure enough, Leatrice stood in the dumpster, along with piles of birch branches and bundles of white hydrangea.

"Our flowers!" Kate nearly dropped her side of the lid as she gaped inside.

I coughed from the putrid scent of garbage and flowers that had been sitting inside a metal box all day, while Fern put a hand over his mouth and gagged.

"Brianna stole them all right," I said. "She just didn't bother schlepping them up to her office."

"She put thousands of dollars worth of imported flowers in a dumpster," Kate said, shaking her head with a hand clamped over her own nose. "Now I'm really sorry we didn't trash her office."

"How did you think to look in here?" I asked my neighbor.

"It was the strangest thing," Leatrice said. "I was sitting in the car waiting for you when this Santa walked up and tapped the top of this dumpster."

Kate exchanged a look with me. "A Santa?"

Leatrice nodded. "I didn't see his face because of the beard and hat, but he made sure to catch my eye before pointing to the dumpster. I got out, but he was running away, so I peeked inside and found all of this. Unfortunately, the lid was too heavy for me to hold up and I leaned over too far."

"Brilliant, sweetie," Fern said, through his hand. "Too bad we're going to have to wash you in tomato juice to get rid of this smell."

"Are you okay?" I asked.

She nodded with a smile. "Just fine, dear. The flowers cushioned my fall."

"At least she found them," I said under my breath to myself as much as to anyone, as Fern and I held out hands to pull her out.

"I think you mean Santa found them," Kate muttered.

I was pretty sure Leatrice didn't hallucinate seeing Santa, but why was someone dressed up as Santa creeping around Georgetown at night, and how had they known something was in the dumpster? Something we were there to find? My first instinct was that it had been Kris, but his Santa suit was still with the cops. Of course, he could have gotten a new one, but just how many Santa suits were floating around in the city for everyone to be turning up in one?

Leatrice passed us a bundle of branches wrapped in brown paper. "Let me hand you the flowers before you pull me up."

Kate took the bundle and jumped down from the hood. "We can put these in the trunk."

"I told Buster and Mack that I'd call them if we found the flowers," I said. "They can bring their van."

"Do you really want to hang out in the alley any longer than we need to?" Kate asked as she leaned into Leatrice's car and popped the trunk. "Besides, have you seen how big this trunk is?"

Knowing the overall dimensions of the old car, I suspected it was sizable. "Okay. I guess the flowers can't get banged up any more than they already have."

The branches looked fine, although the hydrangea looked dangerously wilted. I hoped Buster and Mack could work their magic on them.

Leatrice handed up another bundle, followed by a tightly wrapped cluster of hydrangea. I handed them down to Kate, who proceeded to put them in the trunk. After a few minutes, Leatrice was passing up the last of the flowers, and then Fern and I were hauling her out.

We both stepped back once we'd deposited her onto the hood of her car and let the heavy, metal lid slam shut. The scent of the dumpster seemed to linger even though she was outside, and I suspected it had permeated her clothes. None of us probably smelled great at this point.

"Are you sure it was Santa you saw?" I asked Leatrice. "Not just someone in red and white. The lighting isn't great back here."

Leatrice looked askance at me. "I know my Santas, dear. He was in the full suit--shiny belt, white beard, and all."

Kate shrugged at me. "Looks like we're the only people not wearing a Santa suit around here. I mean, it is December."

"Did my lock-picking kit work upstairs?" Leatrice asked once we'd all gotten off her hood and into the car. A few bundles of flowers that hadn't fit in the trunk were stacked up between Kate and Fern in the back seat, and Fern had his window open and his head out.

"We didn't need to use it," I said. "The window was open."

"That was lucky. So you didn't leave any trace that you'd been there?" Leatrice reached over and patted my hand. "I knew you'd be a natural."

Although Leatrice thought she was paying me a compliment, I really didn't want to be a natural at breaking and entering. "I'm just grateful we have the flowers back."

"I'm texting Buster and Mack to tell them we're on the way," Kate said, tapping away on her phone in the back seat. "They're going to need to make room in their cooler."

"They have a cooler in their floral shop?" Leatrice asked, twisting around as she started the car and put it in reverse.

"A big one," Kate said. "I've had smaller apartments than their floral cooler."

Leatrice accelerated backward, slamming on the brakes when we reached the street. "Anyone coming?"

Fern poked his head out farther, swinging it from side to side. "Nope. You're all clear."

Leatrice pulled the car out backward, barely missing a car parked too close to the alleyway entrance before turning back onto the steep street leading toward the river. "In and out and no one saw us."

"Rock on wood," Kate said.

Leatrice cocked her head, mouthing the phrase to herself.

"She means 'knock on wood,'" I whispered.

"Can we please talk about the fact that one of our wedding planning colleagues stole a flower order and dumped it in the garbage?" Kate said. "I know we've had friendly competitors before, but this is getting out of hand."

I agreed with Kate, but from watching Reese put together his cases, I knew proving our accusations would be difficult. "I don't know what we can actually do."

"I have some ideas," Kate said.

"That we can do legally," I clarified.

Kate leaned forward. "Now you want to keep things legal?"

I pointed to an intersection ahead. "We're going to make a right up there, Leatrice."

"Obviously, the rumors about Brianna being a call girl weren't upsetting enough," Fern said. "What if we tell people she's a Russian spy?"

"Getting her shipped off to Moscow would be good," Kate said.

I sighed as I turned to face the back seat. "We're not going to accuse someone of being a traitor, even if she deserves it."

"Wrong street, Leatrice," Kate said, looking over my shoulder and out the front windshield.

"Oops." Leatrice giggled. "I'll just swing in here and then back us up."

"Besides," I said, "we don't know anyone who could ship Brianna off to Russia."

Kate gave me a sinister smile. "Speak for yourself. I'm pretty sure one of the guys I dated last year was CIA. You know when they say they're State Department, but are vague about specifics, that they're actually CIA."

Leatrice pumped the brakes and twisted her head around. "Is that true?"

I shook my head as Kate bobbed hers up and down vigorously.

"What's that all about?" Fern asked, lifting his cat mask and leaning forward to peer past me.

I spun back around and saw that we'd turned down another narrow alley, this one filled with a pair of box trucks and a bunch of thick-necked guys unloading them into a building. When they saw our car, one of the men started taking long steps toward us.

"Uh oh," Leatrice said, as the man's jacket flapped open revealing a gun in a holster.

"Get us out of here," I told her, sliding down in the passenger's seat. "Fast."

CHAPTER 26

"Is he still chasing us?" I asked, craning my neck to peek into the back seat.

Fern popped his head out his window, then ducked back inside. "No sign of him."

"Keep driving," I told Leatrice, waving one hand at the street. "We should go the back way to Lush."

Leatrice nodded, her hands clutched tightly around the steering wheel that seemed to dwarf her. "Goodness me. Wasn't that exciting?"

"Which part?" Kate asked, sinking into the beige, velour upholstery. "It's been a busy night."

The air coming into the car from the open windows was cool, and I hoped that meant the heat wave was breaking. I also hoped the air could help dissipate some of the lingering aroma of garbage. It was bad enough that the back seat was piled high with wilting flowers. As delicately perfumed as flowers were when they were fresh, they smelled awful once they started to wilt.

Leatrice flicked her eyes to the rearview mirror. "Why do you think that gentleman was chasing our car? You don't think he knew what we were up to, do you?"

"Doubtful," I said, putting a hand to my heart and feeling it hammer away. "I think he was afraid we'd see what he and his pals were up to."

Kate pulled her black cap off and ran a hand through her hair. "You think something criminal was going on?"

"Why else unload stuff in the middle of the night and have a bunch of neckless guys with guns doing it?" I asked.

"Maybe because it's impossible to park in Georgetown during the day?" Fern said. "I know I despise delivery trucks blocking the road during rush hour. I wouldn't mind a few more making deliveries in the evening."

"I'd say it's later than 'evening.'" I glanced down at the simulated wood dashboard of Leatrice's car before realizing there was no clock, just knobs to tune the radio and small levers to adjust the air conditioning. There wasn't a single digital thing in the car. Not shocking considering she'd probably purchased it during the Reagan administration.

"Who makes deliveries at midnight?" Kate said, clearing up my question of what time it was.

"Spies," Leatrice said in a hushed voice, tipping her slightly stained fedora back on her head. "I always knew Georgetown was a hotbed of spy activity, but who knew how much crime went on around here at night?"

"Makes you glad you live with a cop, right?" Kate asked.

"Yes," Leatrice answered, bobbing her head up and down.

I pointed to a street ahead of us. "Turn here."

"Scary guys aside, does anyone think the Santa who tipped us off about the flowers might have been Kris?" Kate asked, as Leatrice made the turn, and she and Fern slid to one side of the car.

"Possibly," I said. "There's no way to know for sure since Leatrice didn't get a good look at his face."

"And he wasn't singing," Leatrice said. "I would have recognized the singing."

"We could ask Kris," Fern said.

I spun around to face him. "Are you telling me you know he's alive and you know where to find him, because if you've been keeping this from me and from Reese then--"

"Unclench, sweetie," Fern said with a loud exhale. "I'm not saying any of that. I did, however, leave the key to my storage room over the sill in case Kris needed a place to sleep. I also left out some Christmas cookies."

"He's not *actually* Santa," Kate said.

"I know that." Fern straightened his cat mask. "It's not like I left out reindeer food, too."

"Reindeer food?" Leatrice shook her head. "What will you kids think of next?"

"I could always leave a note in case it's really him," Fern continued. "Maybe he'd be willing to talk to us."

"What if it's not him?" I asked. "What if it's Stanley?"

Fern ran his fingers down his long whiskers. "Then he won't answer. Can't hurt to try."

As much as I hated to admit it, leaving a note out for fake Santa Claus was the best option we had at the moment. Even thought I'd promised not to get sucked into the case--and meant it--I also wanted to see Kris Kringle back singing. If it couldn't feel like Christmas yet, at least it could sound like it.

I pointed to a barely visible driveway. "We'll go into this alley behind the shop to unload."

"Another alley?" Fern asked. "I'm starting to have post traumatic stress at the mention of alleys."

"This one should be safe," I said, holding the door handle again as Leatrice swung the car wide to make the tight turn. "Besides, Buster and Mack will be waiting for us."

Fern let out a dramatic sigh. "Good. We should really bring our biker gang muscle with us more often."

Not a bad plan, until people realized our friends were with a *Christian* biker gang and their answer to most problems was a prayer chain.

"Nothing happened," I reminded everyone. "We didn't damage Brianna's office; we found the flowers, and we hightailed it away from the scary guys in the alley. I'd call tonight a success."

"We might have seen something illegal going down." Leatrice slowed as we drove down the narrow alleyway. "Are you sure we shouldn't call your fiancé and tell him?"

"No," I said a little too forcefully. "He pulled a double shift, so I don't want to wake him."

The real reason was that I didn't want to explain why we were dressed in black from head to foot, and in Fern's case, mask. As sympathetic as I knew he'd be to our flower crisis, those feelings wouldn't extend to breaking and entering, although technically we'd only done one of those things. Telling him we might have happened upon a connection to the Kris Kringle Jingle case might make him think we'd been looking for it, which we hadn't, but he seemed to be skeptical of coincidence.

"Suit yourself," Kate said, "but you know he'll find out sooner or later. The man's like a human polygraph machine."

Leatrice pulled to a stop, and I spotted Buster and Mack standing at the back entrance to their shop. I knew they often burned the midnight oil, so I didn't feel bad about having them meet us so late.

"I can't believe it," Mack said, rushing over as we got out of the car. "You found our flowers."

"In a dumpster?" Buster asked, shaking his head as if he couldn't quite believe it. "How did you know to search dumpsters?"

"We didn't actually search dumpsters," I said. "Someone dressed as Santa tipped off Leatrice."

"Then I fell in," she said with a giggle. "I'm glad these three finished breaking into that wedding planner's office and found me. It was getting awfully stuffy in there."

Mack's mouth fell open. "A Santa? Was it Kris?"

"Leatrice couldn't tell," I said. "We didn't break in, by the way. We merely had a look around. Her office happened to be open."

Fern held up a finger. "Office window."

I shot him a look. "Cat burglars never tell their secrets."

Buster peered into the back seat, inhaling sharply when he saw the bundles of wilted flowers wrapped in brown paper. "We'd better get these hydrangea in water."

Kate opened the trunk and waved a hand at the birch branches. "Voila. Your winter wonderland."

Mack lumbered around to stand next to her. "I can't believe it. We were about to start gathering fallen branches and paint them with streaks of white."

Kate wrinkled her nose. "We would have had to turn the lights very low to make that work."

Buster filled his arms with flowers. "I'm glad you're all safe. Mack and I activated our emergency prayer chain this evening. You've had dozens of Road Riders for Jesus sending up messages for you."

"We weren't specific, of course," Mack added.

"Well whatever you did worked," I said. "Not only did we find the flowers, Leatrice might have spotted Kris, and we possibly witnessed some criminal activity."

"In addition to our own," Kate said, stacking the branches high in Mack's outstretched arms.

"I don't suppose you feel like sharing that with the police?" Mack asked, peering over the branches at an unmarked car driving down the alley toward us, the portable light on its roof flashing.

I swallowed hard as I looked at my crew--Leatrice dressed like a vintage spy, Fern in a Catwoman costume, and Kate and I in black from head to toe. This was going to be a tough one to explain.

"What a relief," Leatrice said as the officer stepped out of the car. "It's Reese."

I almost groaned out loud.

CHAPTER 27

"I know you're mad at me," I said, as Reese and I trudged up the last few steps to our apartment. "You've barely spoken to me since we left Buster and Mack's, and you won't hold my hand."

He flicked a glance at me as he opened the front door and held it open for me. "Babe, you smell like a garbage truck, and your hands are filthy."

I raised an arm to smell my shirt and cringed from the pungent smell as I walked inside ahead of him. "That may be true, but that doesn't mean you're not upset at me."

"Upset?" He tossed his keys on top of the bookshelf by the door. "Why would I be upset? I only came home from a really crappy day to find you gone and your phone on the coffee table. Then that phone starts blowing up with concerned texts from Mack about your covert mission, and when I come to find you, I see you and your cohorts dressed like you stepped out of a bad spy movie mixed with a really bad superhero movie."

I was glad Fern wasn't there to hear that. He took great offense when someone implied his outfits weren't authentic.

"How did you find me, anyway?" I picked up my phone from the glass coffee table and saw the series of increasingly hysterical messages from Mack scrolling down the locked screen. "You couldn't use the 'Find My Friends' app since my phone wasn't on me."

He cocked an eyebrow at me. "You think your phone is the only one I track?"

I wasn't sure if I should be disturbed or relieved that my fiancé kept tabs on my friends, too.

"I'm sorry I didn't leave a note," I said. Not that I knew what that note would have said. *Off to break into someone's office and rescue our stolen flowers* didn't seem like it would have made the situation any better. I was sorrier that I'd left my phone behind.

He went into the kitchen, and I could hear him opening the refrigerator. When he returned, he handed me one of his beers with the cap already twisted off. "I know you're not a beer drinker, but you probably need this."

"Thanks." I took a tentative swig of the microbrew, trying not to make a face as I swallowed. Nope. Still not a beer person.

"You want to tell me why you all smelled like you'd been rooting around in a landfill?"

I'd managed to avoid telling Reese the entire story when he'd arrived to find us behind Lush, partly because I knew having Leatrice and Fern around during the retelling would not help my case, and partly because I'd been so relieved to see him after the stressful evening that I'd wanted to do nothing more than go home.

"The long and short of it is that one of our unfriendly competitors stole the floral order for this weekend's wedding, and we found it in a dumpster behind her office building. Actually, someone dressed as Santa tipped off Leatrice, and then she found it by falling into a dumpster. It took all of us to get the flowers--and Leatrice--out and loaded into her car, and they smelled pretty bad after sitting in a big, metal container all day." I took another drink of the beer, wishing it was one of the crisp sauvignon blancs Richard preferred and often stocked in my refrigerator. "So, if you think about it, we were merely righting a wrong."

"Did you say Santa tipped her off?"

"I know," I said. "More Santas. There must be a sale on Santa suits somewhere. We don't know if it was Kris or not. Leatrice couldn't tell, but if it was, he got his hands on a new suit."

"Speaking of that, I heard back from the lab about Kris's bloody costume." He paused to tip back his beer. "It wasn't human blood."

"Not human?" I ran a hand through my hair and got another unpleasant whiff of garbage. I needed a shower.

"It was bovine."

"Cow's blood." I made a face. "How do you get that?"

"Butcher's shop? Grocery store meat department? Restaurant kitchen?" Reese suggested. "I'm sure someone living on the streets would know where to source it."

"That doesn't happen by accident," I said. "So it was staged to look like he was hurt or killed?"

"Looks like it."

"That explains Fern's storage room and Jeannie being so confident her friend wasn't dead. He's not," I said.

"But he wanted someone to think he was." Reese took another long pull from his beer. "It feels like someone's trying to make a point with all the Santas, and maybe that someone is Kris."

"You think Kris Kringle Jingle staged his own murder and is now running around framing criminals and dressing them up as Santa?" I asked, thinking it didn't sound like such a crazy idea once I'd said it out loud. "That means Stanley isn't a killer on the run. Then why is he still missing?"

"Maybe he knew about Kris staging his death."

I snapped my fingers. "Because he planted the suit. But why disappear?"

"Everyone who seems to know something about Kris's disappearance has gone underground. They must think that knowing about it puts them at risk."

"At risk from whom?" I started pacing a small circle. "If Stanley isn't a killer and the other Santas didn't knock him off, then we're back to whatever it was he saw. And what's up with all the Santa-related crimes?"

"Richard was right when he said the holidays make people crazy."

He folded his arms over his broad chest. "Speaking of crazy, do you want to explain what you and your motley crew were wearing tonight?"

I considered not mentioning our little expedition inside Brianna's office an omission and not a lie. Besides, we hadn't *broken* in, although we'd been intending to. "We didn't want to stick out while we searched for the flowers. We thought all black would make us blend in."

"If you wanted to blend in, you shouldn't have taken Fern or Leatrice," he muttered from behind his beer.

"Believe me, it wasn't our plan to bring them." I set my nearly full bottle on the coffee table and headed down the hall, pulling off my shirt as I walked. "But you know how hard it is to get out without Leatrice seeing you."

"I've considered rappelling before," Reese said, watching me disappear into the bathroom.

I laughed as I peeled off the rest of my clothes and turned on the shower. "Our neighbors would love that."

Reese appeared in the open bathroom door as I stepped into the shower and pulled the curtain closed. "If you're right about this Brianna being the one to threaten you, then pop Kate's tires and steal Buster and Mack's flowers, it seems like she's escalating pretty quickly."

"Do you think we should press charges?"

"Maybe if you hadn't taken the evidence out of the dumpster behind her offices," he said. "But now it might be tough to prove anything."

I let the water pour over me and hopefully wash away any trace of rancid flowers. "If we'd left them any longer, there would have been no chance to save them. As it is, they're not in great shape, but hopefully Buster and Mack can nurse them back to health in time for Saturday. I'll have to find a different way to deal with Brianna."

"I hope that doesn't mean taking things into your own hands and going vigilante."

"Do I strike you as the vigilante type?" I asked, as the warm water pounded against the knots in my shoulders.

"I was thinking more about Kate," he said.

"I can't make any promises when it comes to Kate. She did suggest having Brianna shipped off to Siberia. I'm pretty sure she can't actually pull it off, though."

"You're only pretty sure?"

I poured some coconut-scented shower gel into my hands and lathered it over my body. "She has a lot of ex-boyfriends in the government. I make no promises. Usually it comes in handy, like when we need to get special permits for elephants parading down Constitution Avenue or group tickets for tours of the Capitol."

He chuckled. "I hope your clients appreciate everything you two do for them, babe."

I poked my head out of the curtain. "If we do our jobs well, they'll never know any of this ever happened."

"And this other planner has no idea you rescued the flowers?"

I turned off the water. "Nope. No one saw us getting the flowers out of the dumpster. The alley was deserted. Aside from Santa." I hesitated as I pulled back the curtain, wondering whether or not to mention what we'd seen when we'd inadvertently driven down the wrong alley. I decided since I was busted, I might as well. "But we were spotted by some unsavory characters when we were driving to Lush."

"There are a lot of unsavory characters late at night in Georgetown," Reese said, handing me a towel.

I wrapped the towel around my chest then grabbed another for my hair. "Yeah, but these guys had guns, and one chased our car out of the alley."

He frowned. "You were chased at gunpoint and you're just now mentioning it?"

I flipped my head over and twisted the second towel around my wet hair, flipping it up and making it into a turban. "It's been a pretty busy night. Besides, it happened pretty fast, and Leatrice got us out of there before anything happened." I let out a breath. "I knew if I told you we saw something suspicious, you'd assume we were meddling in the case, which I promise you we're not."

My fiancé dragged a hand through his hair. "The case?"

"Kris Kringle Jingle said he saw something suspicious in Georgetown, and then he disappeared. What if we saw the same thing?"

He opened his mouth as if to argue with me, then clamped it closed. He dragged a hand through his hair. "How do you and your friends manage to stumble into crimes wherever you go?"

"I honestly don't know."

He shook his head. "It's really hard to stay angry at you when you're wearing nothing but a towel." He took another steadying breath. "Okay. Where did this happen?"

I thought back to the street we'd accidentally turned onto. "An alley down near the water. I think it was off of Thirty-first." I took a step closer. "Are you saying you think my hunch might be right?"

He narrowed his eyes at me. "I'm only saying it might be worth checking out."

"Can you investigate if there's not an official report or request?"

Reese wrapped an arm around me and pulled me close. "You're not the only one who can follow a hunch and disobey orders."

My pulse quickened as his hazel eyes deepened to green. I loved it when he talked dirty.

CHAPTER 28

"So he's going rogue?" Kate asked, as we stood at the back of Western Presbyterian Church the next evening.
"Not exactly," I said. "But he's going to poke around off the books."
Kate nudged me. "I think we're rubbing off on him."
"I don't know if that's a good thing or not."

After a hectic week, we'd both taken the day off to prepare for the weekend's wedding, and now we were waiting for the bridal party to arrive for the ceremony rehearsal. As usual, we were early, and, as it was with most rehearsals, the bridal party was late.

The church was lit at the front of the sanctuary, the light wood wainscoting and carved wooden arch overhead illuminated with lights behind the choir loft. It was already dark outside, so the stained glass windows along both sides of the church were muted, although the hanging pendant lamps over the pews shone down.

"It could have been anything, you know." Kate walked from the church foyer into the sanctuary, stepping on the wine-colored carpeting that ran down the center aisle. "Just because the guy had a gun, doesn't mean he's a criminal. Half the people in the country are packing, and some of them walk around with semiautomatics strapped to their backs just because they can. Of course, if you ask me, those guys are compensating for something."

I glanced around the quiet church, hoping a minister wasn't within earshot. "You're right. It could have been a regular, law-abiding citizen who just happened to be unloading a truck of perfectly legal goods in the dead of night."

Kate smirked at me. "Well, when you say it like that, it sounds silly."

I breathed in the scent of lilies, noticing two aging arrangements of white blooms at the altar. I knew Buster and Mack would be replacing those with their own stunning arrangements of blooming branches and hydrangea—as long as the flowers had sufficiently recovered. If anyone could pull off a wedding miracle, it was my florists with the super-charged prayer chain and faith as expansive as their biceps.

"I'm going to go look for the minister," I said, with a glance at my phone. "It's one thing for the bride and groom to be late, but we can't start rehearsing without her."

"Don't leave me here." Kate hurried behind me as I started to walk up one side of the sanctuary.

I looked back at her. "It's a church. I think you're safe."

She rubbed her arms. "Empty churches feel spooky, and they echo too much."

I shook my head as we snaked our way through the sanctuary and along a corridor to the administrative building attached to the church. It was quiet here, too. No doubt, the staff had all left early for the weekend.

"I don't see her," Kate said, sticking close to me as we continued down a softly lit hallway.

I found the minister's office, but the door was locked and the lights were off. So much for that. "You called and confirmed the rehearsal time, right?"

Kate bobbed her head up and down. "I talked to the reverend herself. Confirmed the time and date. I'm sure that's why the sanctuary is open and the lights are on."

She was right about that. If there wasn't anything going on in the sanctuary, the front doors would not have been unlocked for us.

"Where could she be?" I asked. "I know we're early, but this thing is supposed to start in fifteen minutes. The entire church is deserted."

"Not the *entire* church. There's Miriam's Kitchen."

"Miriam's Kitchen? You mean the soup kitchen?"

Kate let out an impatient breath. "It's a bit more than that, and it's inside the church."

I pointed to the floor. "This church?" How had I not known that? Although, to be fair, Kate had done all the work coordinating with the church on this wedding.

More nods from my assistant. "Yep. I think it's still open for a little while longer."

"Maybe the reverend is there," I suggested, heading off down the hall again.

Kate caught my arm and tugged me in the other direction. "This way, boss."

She led me through the church and outside. We walked down the side of the stone building to a stone arch with iron gates standing open.

"How do you know about this?" I asked.

"I came here to drop off the couple's application, remember?" She smiled as she ducked past the gates. "I got a full tour."

I followed her into a large room that had fluorescent lighting running overhead and reminded me a bit of the other shelter we'd visited, although this one had paper snowflakes hanging down from the ceiling. The tables were round instead of rectangular, circled with gray, metal folding chairs. The room was warm and smelled like food, the lingering scent of lunch and coffee hanging in the air.

It was clear that Miriam's Kitchen was preparing to close for the evening. Only a few people were scattered around the tables, but my gaze faltered when I saw one figure crouched over a far table.

"No reverend," Kate said with a sigh.

I nudged her and pointed to the man in red and white. "But we found another Santa."

"You don't think it's . . . ?" Her words trailed off.

"What are the chances of us finding Kris at a shelter all the way across town that happens to be in our bride's church?" I asked as I led the way through the tables toward the man, my heart pounding.

He looked up as we approached, and my heart sank.

"Apparently, not great," Kate said, sounding as defeated as I was.

It wasn't Kris. This man was gaunt with dark circles under his eyes and had none of the merry twinkle that the singing Santa did.

"You're not Kris," I said to answer the questioning look in his eyes.

His face contorted for a moment, and he shook his head vigorously. "Nope."

I watched his cheeks color beneath the gray stubble covering them. "Are you Stanley?"

He rubbed his nose and answered quickly. "Nope."

"Now, why are you lying to these nice ladies?" A burly man with thick arms and a deep baritone voice asked as he wiped off a table nearby.

Kate and I both turned to the man who wore a white apron over his T-shirt.

"This is Stanley?" Kate asked, jerking a thumb toward the Santa squirming in his chair.

"He sure is." The man with the apron gave us a wide smile as he walked back toward the kitchen. The clattering of pans told me there were more people cleaning up back there.

I pivoted to face Stanley, who'd scooted a few chairs away from us. "We're not here to turn you in."

He blanched. "Why would you turn me in? I haven't done nothing wrong." He looked from me to Kate. "Who are you?"

I thought for a second about the best way to sell ourselves. "We're friends with Buster and Mack."

His face relaxed a little bit. "Why are you here?"

"Believe it or not," Kate said, putting her hands on her hips. "It's a total coincidence. We're running a wedding rehearsal here."

"A lot of people have been looking for you," I said. "People are worried about you."

He gave a snort. "I'll bet folks have been looking for me."

"We know Kris isn't dead," I said, hoping I was right and hoping this would get him to talk.

He pressed his lips together. "You don't know nothing."

"Why are you dressed up like Santa?" Kate asked. "Taking over your friend's beat?"

Stanley shook his head. "It's not like that."

"Tell us then," I said. "Whatever's going on, we'd like to help."

"She's engaged to a cop," Kate said. "If you need protection, I'm sure Annabelle can arrange it."

Another derisive laugh. "You two are in over your heads."

"Always a possibility," Kate muttered, pulling her phone out of her purse as it vibrated. She elbowed me, and I glanced over at the text. The bride had arrived and now *she* was the only person in the sanctuary. From the liberal use of exclamation marks, she wasn't taking it in stride.

"We'd like to talk to you more . . ." I began as I turned back to Stanley.

"That was fast," Kate said, twisting around to take in the now-empty room.

Stanley was gone.

CHAPTER 29

I surveyed the rehearsal dinner space with my hands on my hips as waiters scurried around filling water glasses and lighting candles.

"No mentioning any of this to Richard," I warned Kate.

She nodded, fluffing a faux burlap linen on a high-top table. "You mean the homeless Santa who might or might not have something to do with Kris Kringle Jingle, who might or might not be dead?"

I let out a steadying breath. "Yes, that."

We'd made a cursory attempt to find Stanley, but he'd ducked out through the kitchen and disappeared into the night. After that, we'd been focused on calming the bride and getting the rehearsal going. The reverend had arrived late, as well as the church wedding coordinator, and Kate and I had been able to race over to the rehearsal dinner venue ahead of the bridal party.

Kate mimed zipping her lips. "The secret is safe with me."

Richard came up behind us with an electric lighter in one hand. "What are we keeping secret now?"

I put a hand to my heart. "Don't sneak up on me like that. You scared me half to death."

Richard eyed me. "A little jumpy, darling?"

"Just excited to put this weekend in the rearview mirror." I turned to him as Kate stepped away to fluff more linens. "It looks great."

We'd ducked out of the wedding rehearsal at the church--after lining up the processional and being shooed out by the rather territorial church lady--and rushed over to the Dockmaster Building at the DC Wharf. The two-story space perched on the end of the long dock and had three walls of floor-to-ceiling glass, giving it wide views of the Potomac River and a distant view of the monuments. When we'd booked it for December, we'd never imagined being able to use the balcony, but I noticed high tables scattered near the glass railing that ringed the second level.

Even though it didn't feel wintery outside, the après ski lodge decor made the inside look as cozy as a chalet in Aspen. A fake fur runner ran down the middle of both long dinner tables, topped with glass-encased pillar candles and freestanding antlers. A bar made with frosted logs sat off to the side with evergreens towering behind it, and chic brown leather furniture groupings were positioned on either side of the tables, cashmere throws draped over the love seats. The room even smelled like a Christmas tree.

"You'd never know it's T-shirt weather outside," I said.

Richard frowned, giving my sleeveless black dress a quick once-over. "You could have dressed more to the theme."

I noticed that he wore tweed and wondered how he wasn't sweating bullets. "I don't own anything that screams ski lodge in summer."

He sniffed and arched a brow. "More's the pity. I have the AC cranked as high as it will go, so you might be wishing for a sweater soon."

"None of the guests are dressed for cold weather," I reminded him. "Do you really want people shivering their way through dinner?"

"That's what the throws are for." He waved to the clear chivari chairs around the dinner tables, and I noticed cream-and-brown plaid pashminas draped over the backs.

Leave it to Richard to create a practical problem and solve it in the most stylish way.

"I checked the weather app," I said, holding up my phone. "The temperature is supposed to drop tonight."

Richard sniffed. "A lot of good that does me."

"Well, it makes the wedding reception a bit less ridiculous." I tucked my phone back into my dress pocket, as I spotted the event photographer leaning close to a place setting and snapping away. "And no one can tell how cold it was in photos."

Richard tapped a finger to his jaw. "You make a good point. This will still look fabulous on the Richard Gerard website."

"See? Lemonade out of lemons."

"I would love some lemonade," Fern said, dashing across the room from the entrance and wheeling his small black suitcase of hair supplies behind him. "It's perfect lemonade weather."

Richard scowled at him and I glanced around quickly, hoping he didn't have Leatrice in tow. Sometimes Leatrice manages to sweet-talk her way into my weddings, and Fern was usually the softest mark.

"What are you doing here?" I asked.

He fluttered a hand at me. "The bride wanted me to meet her here for touch-ups after the rehearsal."

Kate walked back up. "She needs touch-ups already? Didn't you just do her hair an hour ago?"

Fern shrugged. "I don't ask questions, sweetie. I just nod and smile."

Not a bad policy for working with brides.

"How did the rehearsal at the church go?" Fern asked, touching a hand to his low ponytail. "I tried to calm her down at the hotel when she was getting ready."

"Not bad," I said. "She was a little nervous when she got there, but by the time we lined up the bridal party, she seemed more relaxed."

"That's because I gave her some wine," Kate said.

"Wine?" I looked at her. "When? Where?"

"In the holding room at the back of the church while you were talking to the reverend."

My stomach tightened. "Where did you get the wine?" I wouldn't have put it past her to carry travel-sized bottles with her, but I suspected this wasn't the case.

"It was in the holding room," she said. "I didn't give her much. Just enough to take the edge off."

Richard stared at her. "You gave the bride sacramental wine?"

Even though he considered himself a lapsed Catholic, I could see a swoon coming.

"Let's just be glad the bride is happy and calm and in a good mood," I said, taking Richard's arm. "We like happy clients, right?"

"Of course," he muttered, still goggling at Kate.

"And she'll never know she almost had a floral-free wedding," Fern said, with a giggle that made me wonder if he'd gotten into some wine somewhere. "No amount of church wine could fix that."

Richard swung his attention to Fern. "What do you mean?"

Fern's eyes grew wide as the realization hit him that he'd get to share a juicy tidbit of gossip. "Didn't you hear? That Botoxed Barbie wedding planner made off with the flowers for the reception tomorrow, and we rescued them from a dumpster."

I closed my eyes for a moment, bracing for Richard's reaction.

"I beg your pardon?" he said, his voice eerily calm.

"It was so thrilling," Fern continued as Kate shook her head furtively. "I was the lookout while Annabelle and Kate looked for the flowers in Brianna's office, and Leatrice was the wheelman. Or wheellady, to be more accurate."

Richard pivoted his head to me. "Annabelle?"

"To be fair, you warned me not to meddle in the murder investigation. This had nothing to do with any murder or any of Reese's investigations."

"I thought it went unsaid that you shouldn't break into your competitor's office."

"First of all," Kate said, holding up a finger, "we didn't break in. She left her window open. And second, you would have done the same thing if your top rival had stolen all the food for one of your parties."

He opened his mouth, then paused. "You're right, although I might have done it in broad daylight so I couldn't be accused of subterfuge. What if she'd caught you?"

"Well, you don't have to worry," I said. "No one saw us and we didn't leave a trace that we'd been there. We didn't even touch anything. There's no way she'll ever know we were snooping around."

"She's going to know you got the flowers back," Richard said, holding up his phone. "Unless you plan not to post any photos from the wedding day."

I groaned and looked at the pained expression on Kate's face. "We could survive not posting any Instagram stories of this wedding, right?"

She gnawed on her lower lip. "But our brides love it when we post about their weddings and use their custom wedding hashtag."

"If you don't post, someone will," Fern said. "You can't have a social media blackout on the wedding."

He was right. As soon as a post went up with the wedding flowers in it, Brianna would know we'd been scrounging around in her dumpster.

"At least she won't know we were in her office," I said, although I suspected she would not be pleased that her plans to ruin our wedding were foiled.

Richard shrugged. "Unless she has security cameras."

I swallowed hard. I hadn't thought about that, since we didn't have a security system in Wedding Belles HQ, aka my apartment. But a wedding planner bankrolled by her rich father might very well have cameras in her office. From the stricken look on Kate's face, I could tell she was thinking the same thing.

Fern took Richard's hand and patted it. "That's enough helping from you, sweetie."

CHAPTER 30

"No, I don't think she's going to come after us while we're sleeping," I told Kate over the phone as I walked toward my apartment building. I saw a quick flash of a man in a hoodie and glasses leaving the building, so I ran to catch the door, glancing back at the slim figure and wondering if he was a new neighbor. I knew I'd seen him before. "We don't know she has cameras in her office space."

Kate let out a breath. "That's true."

I trudged up the stairs and paused at the door to my apartment. Not a comforting thought since Reese was still at work. "Just lock your doors and park your car someplace safe."

"Oh, I'm not staying at my place tonight," she said. "It's too hot."

"Hot?" The weather had finally dipped down, and there had been a chill in the air when we'd left the Dockmaster's Building.

"You know, dangerous. I'm going to stay someplace else until things cool off."

I rolled my eyes and was glad she couldn't see me. Our recent encounter with a few members of the mob had definitely made an impression on Kate. "Do I want to ask where you're staying?"

"Let's just say, I'll be very safe."

My money was on her bunking with one of her exes who was potentially CIA or the firefighter she'd gone out with a few times after my car had been burned to the ground by a Molotov cocktail. "Don't forget we start bright and early tomorrow at the Four Seasons."

"I still don't get why we have to be there for hair and makeup," she grumbled. "All we do is sit and watch the bridal party get ready."

"Because it's better than being at home and getting hundreds of texts and calls from the nervous bride. Our presence is like a comfort blanket, and it usually keeps them from going off the rails."

"If you say so, boss." There was a second, deeper voice in the background. "I'll see you tomorrow."

She clicked off, and I slipped my phone into my dress pocket. At least I didn't need to worry about Brianna coming after Kate tonight. Reese was right. The woman was escalating, and I didn't trust her not to do something crazy.

I opened my door, hesitating before going inside. Had I left the lights on? The living room was fully illuminated, making me wonder if Reese had gotten off earlier. I called his name, but the only response was Hermès scampering up and sniffing my ankles.

Okay, I knew I didn't have a dog in my apartment when I left. "Leatrice?"

My petite neighbor bounded down the hall, her black Mary Tyler Moore flip bouncing. "I'm so glad you're home. We've been too scared to go back downstairs."

I glanced back at the completely quiet stairwell then back at my neighbor in her brown footie pajamas with bear ears. "Scared of what?"

Leatrice didn't answer but instead, turned around and called behind her, "It's okay, honeybun. It's just Annabelle."

Honeybun, aka Sidney Allen, appeared from the far end of the hall. He was almost as petite as his wife, but with much less hair. Where Leatrice was all bones with skin that hung off her like flesh-colored chiffon, the entertainment diva was shaped like an egg with no discernible waist. He almost always wore a dark suit with the pants hiked up nearly to his armpits, and his thinning hair seemed to have a perpetual crease from the headset he wore when he was coordinating his performers at an event. This evening there was no headset, and burgundy velvet pajamas replaced the suit, but the elastic pants were tugged up nearly to his chin.

"Hello, Annabelle," he said in his gentlemanly Southern drawl, as if him padding down my hallway in his PJs was the most normal thing in the world.

"Were you in our bed?" I asked, wondering if I was going to need to get new sheets or move.

Leatrice giggled. "Don't be silly, dear. My sugar muffin was heading down the fire escape."

I shut the door behind me. "What's going on? Why are you going down the fire escape in your pajamas?"

"Because of the men who tried to get into our apartment," Sidney Allen said.

I looked at Leatrice, who was bobbing her head up and down. "What men?"

"Well, if we knew who they were we wouldn't be running from them, now would we?" Leatrice shook her head at me. "We'd just turned on Perry Mason when we heard someone jiggling the front door."

"We had the lights off," Sidney Allen said, "so they may have assumed we weren't home."

"Wouldn't they have heard *Perry Mason*?" I asked.

Leatrice blushed. "We were watching the TV in the bedroom. It's the fancy flat screen my sweetie pie brought over from his place."

"Okay. So you heard someone trying to get in your front door," I prompted. "And then what?"

"We ran out and turned on the lights," Leatrice said. "I looked out the peephole and saw two men running out the front door of the building. So we decided to hide out here in case they came back. That was a couple of hours ago."

"Well, I suggested we stop waiting here like sitting ducks and go to the cops," Sidney Allen said, his eyes flitting to my back door that led out onto the fire escape.

Leatrice shot him a look. "But I insisted we wait for the detective. I left him a message, but apparently he's out at a crime scene."

Another crime scene, I thought. So much for the holidays being about peace and goodwill toward men. Lately, Reese seemed to spend all his time at crime scenes.

I dropped my black Longchamp bag onto the floor next to the sofa and headed toward the kitchen, with Hermès close at my heels. "Do you think someone was trying to rob you?"

It seemed like a bad plan for burglars to pick the apartment on the first floor closest to the front door. Anyone could see what they were doing from the street, since the building's wooden front door was half glass. I peered inside the refrigerator and groaned when I realized there was nothing to drink but Reese's microbrews and one opened can of Diet Dr Pepper. I picked the opened can.

"I think someone saw my car last night and they're coming after me," Leatrice said, her head poking over the counter dividing my kitchen and living room.

Leatrice did have a distinctive car, but even if they spotted it near our building, they'd have no way to know which apartment was hers. "How could they track you down by your car?"

Hermès ran in circles around my feet and I patted his head. "Sorry, buddy. No more prosciutto."

He gave me a disgusted look and flounced out of the kitchen. It was scary how much the little Yorkie reminded me of Richard. I took a drink of the flat soda as I headed back to the living room.

"Easy," Leatrice said. "License plate records."

I sank onto the couch. "But those aren't public record, are they?"

Leatrice looked at me like I was a simpleton. "Cops can access them, along with anyone who can hack into their system."

Leatrice didn't need to remind me that she'd once used some friends she'd made on the dark web to hack into the DC police computers. I'm sure she didn't want Sidney Allen to know every sordid detail about her past, or have to explain why she was online friends with guys called Boots and Dagger Dan.

I took another sip of the syrupy sweet drink, making a mental note to go shopping soon. "So you think these guys somehow got into the records, used your license plate to get your address, and came here tonight to ...?"

"Intimidate me, scare me into silence, eliminate me," Leatrice said, listing the options off on her fingers as the color drained from her honeybun's face.

"It's not like you witnessed a crime," I said, thinking Leatrice's imagination and desire to see a conspiracy around every corner might be making her jump to conclusions.

"Maybe we did," Leatrice said. "Sure, we think we didn't see anything, but they don't know that. What if we caught them in the middle of a drug deal or a smuggling operation? Why else would a guy with a gun chase after us?"

I agreed with her that the guy chasing the car hadn't been normal behavior, but it seemed like a big leap to think that they'd tracked down Leatrice and were now after her. Although, knowing that Leatrice seemed to land in as many sticky situations as I did, I couldn't discount the possibility altogether. "Why don't I call Reese? He'll know what to do."

Leatrice sat down next to me and Hermès jumped up beside her, both tucking their feet up under themselves. Sidney Allen took the chair opposite, teetering on the edge as if he might need to leap to his feet at any moment.

"Thank you, Annabelle," he said. "Tell Mike we appreciate any help he can give."

Sidney Allen had unexpectedly bonded with my fiancé, and Reese had even been the best man in his wedding to Leatrice. I found it amazing that both Sidney Allen and Richard had a bromance going with Reese, and hoped there wouldn't be a brawl between the two divas one day.

I pulled out my phone and speed dialed my fiancé.

"Babe," he said when he answered, sounding out of breath. "I'm glad you called. Are you okay? Are you at home?"

"Yes, I'm at home. Why wouldn't I be okay?"

"I'm on the way to the building now. Don't leave our apartment."

"Okay." I sat up and put the empty soda can on the coffee table. "Now you're scaring me. What's going on?"

"I was just called to a crime scene in the alley behind our building."

CHAPTER 31

"Are those the two men you saw outside your apartment?" I asked Leatrice and Sidney Allen as we peered down the fire escape to the alley below.

Even though we were three stories up, I could tell that the men tied with their hands and feet behind their backs were broad-shouldered with dark hair and equally dark clothes. Several uniformed officers walked around the scene, and I saw my fiancé squatting next to the unconscious men. Apparently, the police had received an anonymous call that two criminals were tied up in the alley behind P Street. It appeared that they'd been knocked out as they were walking to the white paneled van that was parked off to the side.

Leatrice squinted and leaned over the metal railing. "It's hard to say, dearie. I really only saw their backs as they were running away, but it could be them. They look wide enough."

"It doesn't matter," I said, repeating what Reese had texted me. "These guys were already wanted by the police, so they'll be going to jail regardless."

"That makes me feel better," Leatrice said.

"What's on their heads?" Sidney Allen asked, taking a step back from the rail, his face pale.

"Santa hats." I thought I recognized one of the officers as the rookie Kate and I had talked to at the station. I stepped back from the railing in case he looked up. I didn't want him to be reminded of our visit, especially since it didn't seem like he'd mentioned it to Reese.

"Isn't that nice they're getting into the spirit of things?" Leatrice smiled. "Not enough people dress for the season anymore."

Since Leatrice had a special outfit for every holiday, including the minor ones like Flag Day and Arbor Day, I'm sure she felt the rest of us were slackers.

"I'm pretty sure they didn't decide to wear those hats," I said, rubbing my hands over my arms to warm them. "Santa paraphernalia has been turning up at a lot of crime scenes lately, mostly on the criminals."

"Fascinating," Leatrice said, flipping up the hood of her footie pajamas.

Sidney Allen waved us toward the door. "Why don't we go inside? It's getting cold out here."

He was right. It was getting cold. I felt like cheering as I realized the temperature had dropped significantly since earlier in the evening. Maybe our winter wonderland wedding wouldn't feel so out of place after all.

We went back into my apartment, and I double-checked that the door was bolted. I'd installed heavy-duty locks on my back entrance after a break-in a couple of years ago. Even though the memory shouldn't have been a good one, it always reminded me of my fiancé, since the murder case connected to the break-in was the reason we'd met. It was also the first time I'd meddled in his case, or as I liked to think of it, the first time we'd worked together.

"How about some hot chocolate?" I asked, heading to the kitchen.

"You have that?" Leatrice asked, padding after me in her pajamaed feet that looked like bear claws.

I tried not to be offended by the surprised tone. "Of course I do. And some gourmet ginger cookies."

"Goodness." Leatrice rubbed her hands together. "I'm not used to fancy food at your apartment unless Richard is around." She paused at the doorway to the kitchen, her eyes wide. "He's not hiding in here, is he?"

"No. I do not have Richard stashed in the pantry." I didn't explain that I could offer them such a luxurious treat because I'd received both the Williams Sonoma hot chocolate and the cookies as a holiday gift from one of our favorite photographers.

One of the nicest parts of December, aside from the fact that we were usually less busy, was getting thoughtful gifts from the vendors we sent business to all year. I'd gotten everything from a Four Seasons bathrobe to spa gift certificates to designer purses. The purses were always from Richard because he lamented my dearth of designer bags. Receiving the gift box today had reminded me that Kate and I had yet to order the holiday gifts *we* sent to vendors. One more thing to add to my to-do list, I thought, before pushing that aside and reaching for the red cylindrical tin of hot chocolate.

"Who do you think did that?" Sidney Allen asked from the living room.

I poked my head over the dividing counter from the kitchen. Hermès was curled up in a brown-and-black ball on the couch, and Sidney Allen sat perched on the edge of my overstuffed chair, rocking himself back and forth and wringing his hands. He reminded me of Humpty Dumpty, and I hoped he wasn't about to take a great fall.

"I think your husband might need a little comforting," I whispered to Leatrice, who still lingered in the doorway.

She immediately hurried over to him and began rubbing his back. "I'm sure Reese will get to the bottom of it, whatever happened. He's such a smart young man."

Sidney Allen smiled and nodded. "That's true."

I pulled down three "Twelve Days of Christmas" mugs from an overhead cabinet--part of a set from the Willard Hotel last Christmas--and began scooping dark chocolate shavings into each one. "If you ask me, whoever tied up those guys is the hero in all this."

"Really?" Sidney Allen asked.

I checked my fridge for milk, then finding none, filled my tea kettle with water and put it on the stove. Hot chocolate with hot water wouldn't be so bad, I thought, adding milk to my mental shopping list.

"Sure," I said. "I'm willing to bet that the guys tied up in our alley have a record or an outstanding arrest warrant or something. Everyone who's been tied up and turned in to the police dressed in Santa getup has turned out to be guilty as sin."

"So someone's cleaning up the city for Christmas?" he said, his voice sounding less shaky.

"Fern thinks that someone is Kris Kringle Jingle," Leatrice added.

I opened the round tin of Moravian Ginger Spice cookies and arranged a few on a plate, inhaling the sweet aroma of the thin cookies shaped like bells, snowmen, and stockings.

"What does Reese think?" Sidney Allen asked.

"You know him," I said, looking over the divider at my two elderly neighbors. "He doesn't want to say anything until he's positive."

"And he doesn't want to give Annabelle any more reason to get involved in his case," Leatrice said in a stage whisper.

I decided not to argue with her on that because I knew she was probably right. "Like I told Reese, I haven't been meddling this time. *We* seem to be stumbling into connections to Kris and all the Santa crimes."

I made a point not to mention talking to Stanley dressed as Santa. Not only would Leatrice read too much into it, nothing he'd said made sense. It was one of the main reasons I hadn't mentioned it to my fiancé. That, and he'd never believe Kate and I had run into the man by chance.

Leatrice flushed. "I suppose it was a Santa Claus who tipped me off to the stolen flowers in the dumpster, but how is Kris managing to do all these things?"

I decided it wouldn't hurt to tell Leatrice what I knew about the singing Santa. "Since he's lived on the streets for a while, he clearly knows how to get around without being seen. Plus, he served in Vietnam. Naval intelligence."

Leatrice gasped. "He's a veteran and he's homeless?"

"I'm afraid there are quite a few homeless vets in the city," I told her.

She shook her head. "I don't like that one bit."

"I don't think anyone does." I plucked the kettle off the burner as it started to whistle. "I had no idea he'd served until Fern told me."

"Well, we have to find him," Leatrice said, slapping the side of the chair and making both her fiancé and Hermès jump.

Stifling a laugh, I poured steaming hot water into the mugs and watched the chocolate shavings dissolve. "That's what we've been trying to do, but he's been pretty good at hiding so far."

"There must be a reason he's hiding," Sidney Allen said.

"Well, if he's the Santa vigilante, he's ticking off a bunch of pretty dangerous people." I carried two mugs out to the living room and handed one each to Leatrice and Sidney Allen. "I might be hiding too if I were him."

"Just think, sugar pie." Leatrice nudged Sidney Allen. "We've got our own crime-fighting Santa."

I returned to the kitchen for my mug and the cookies, walking back to the living room and sinking onto the couch next to Hermès, who gave me a disdainful look out of one eye before rearranging himself and going back to sleep. Taking a sip of the rich chocolate, I thought how much better it would be with milk. And maybe whipped cream on the top.

"You don't think he takes requests, do you?" Leatrice asked, her eyes sparkling over the rim of her mug. "I'm still convinced the guy in 2B is a sleeper agent for some foreign government."

I thought about Brianna slashing Kate's tires and stealing our flower order. "If he does, get in line."

CHAPTER 32

"Who knew you'd have a more exciting night than me?" Kate said the next day as we stood side by side in the Four Seasons ballroom and watched as large icicle lights were hung from the ceiling.

"It might be a first." I turned to take in the room, feeling pleased by the transformation of the room from hotel chic to winter wonderland.

The walls had been draped from floor to ceiling in white gossamer fabric with blue twinkle lights strung behind the layers of fabric. The dance floor was transparent and blinked with blue pinprick lights every time someone stepped on it. Clusters of birch branches ringed the room and were uplit so shadows of the branches crisscrossed the ceiling. Long, rectangular tables were draped in a sparkly white linen, and tall arrangements of branches cuffed with white hydrangea-- successfully rehydrated by Buster and Mack--ran the length of each table. Silver base plates sat at each place, and round mirrored menus fit perfectly in the center, the words written in swirling white calligraphy. The ladder-backed chairs were clear, and large snowflake tags hung off each one with a guest's name written in silver ink—our creative alternative to a place card.

"So the bad guys got hauled off to jail, and Kris is still on the loose?" Kate asked, walking over and straightening a white linen napkin on the nearest table. "Along with Santa Stanley?"

"We don't know that Kris did it," I said. "We just know that the guys were wearing Santa hats."

"Come on." Kate narrowed her eyes at me. "Who else would be doing this? Who else is obsessed with Santa Claus?"

"Aside from millions of children? Besides, these deliveries or reports of criminals in Santa gear started before Kris disappeared."

"But not long before, and maybe that's why he staged his own murder and went into hiding." Kate shifted from one ridiculously high heel to the other. "Of course, it could be Stanley. We saw him dressed as Santa and he seemed pretty wired. I wouldn't put vigilante past him."

"I don't know why either man doesn't come out of hiding now. It's not like they'd be in trouble for helping the police lock up a bunch of bad guys."

"Maybe Kris can't," Kate said with a shrug. "Maybe he feels like he's still in danger. I doubt he's rounded up all the criminals in town, and some of the big guys might be a little upset that their colleagues have been arrested. Stanley seemed to think it wasn't safe."

"Stanley said a lot of strange stuff," I reminded her.

"Is this spacing good?" Our lighting guy, John, called down from the top of a tall ladder.

I gave him a thumbs-up. "Perfect. These will be on a dimmer, right?"

He nodded and went back to hanging the icicle lights.

"At least the weather finally fits our theme," I said, waving for Kate to follow me out of the ballroom. "We won't have to crank up the AC to make people think it's winter."

Kate rubbed her hands together. "Finally my boots won't look ridiculous."

"It wasn't so much the boots that looked ridiculous. It was that they were paired with shorts. Really short shorts."

"Because it was really hot. If I'd worn boots and pants, I'd have been baking." She shook her head at me. "Don't blame me for the heat wave."

We walked into the foyer and across to the Dumbarton room, where Buster and Mack were setting up cocktail hour. Instead of white decor with touches of blue, this room was all ice blue with accents of white. The linens on the scattered high-top tables were a frosty blue, and the round bar in the center of the room was white acrylic lit from inside with blue LEDs. A curtain of white lights hung from the ceiling, filling it from end to end.

I spotted Mack installing a massive arrangement of white branches in the middle of the bar, his plus-sized leather pants and jacket a sharp contrast to the pale colors around him.

He waved at us. "What do you think?"

"The bride will love it," Kate called back.

Mack grinned then dropped a branch. "Elf on the shelf!" He ducked behind the bar to retrieve it, mumbling more sanitized holiday curses.

Buster walked up behind us, holding a pair of small square bowls jammed with fluffy white hydrangea. "Thanks to you. I don't know what we would have done without our flowers."

"All in a day's work." I patted his thick arm.

"One of our days, at least," Kate said. "Probably not your normal wedding planner's day."

I tried not to take offense since she was right. I liked to think Kate and I were a few levels above average, and our crew was definitely not your typical wedding planning team.

Buster laughed. "I delivered the bouquets. The bride loved them."

"How's she doing?" Kate asked. "When we left her to check on the ballroom, breakfast for her and the bridesmaids had just arrived."

As planned, Kate and I had arrived when hair and makeup had started, checking in on a tired bride still bubbling about the ski lodge rehearsal dinner the night before. Richard's food had been a huge success, as had his "to go" s'mores favors tied with miniature ski poles. The bridesmaids were still munching on the chocolate bars this morning, while they walked around the spacious suite in powder blue bathrobes with their names embroidered on the back. As we'd ducked out to check on setup, a waiter had been wheeling in a cart filled with bagels, muffins, and plates of sliced fruit.

Buster bit the corner of his bottom lip. "She seemed happy. Fern was making all the orange juice into mimosas."

I sighed. "How long until the mimosas become straight glasses of champagne?"

"And how long after that until Fern starts teasing everyone's hair too high?" Kate asked.

Knowing Fern when the bubbly and his creative juices got flowing, he could decide to make all the bridesmaids' hair resemble Christmas trees complete with blinking lights.

"We'd better get up there," I said. "You know how peeved he gets when we make him redo hair."

"Go." Buster shooed us away. "We've got everything under control down here."

We thanked him, waved to Mack, and headed out of the room. I paused at the large round table at the bottom of the stairs and touched a hand to the fake snow that covered it. Tucked into the faux snowdrift was a guest book and family photos in silver frames.

"You don't seem stressed about Brianna anymore," I said to Kate. "All I'm picking up is normal wedding day stress."

"Didn't I tell you?" She twisted to face me. "I texted one of Brianna's assistants. The one who comes to the assistant happy hours. She told me they don't have cameras in the office."

"And you waited all this time to tell me?" I shook my head. "Did the assistant think your question was strange?"

"I doubt it. I told her we were considering a security camera system and asked if they had one she could recommend."

I nodded at her. "Not bad."

Kate kept walking and glanced back over her shoulder, winking at me. "Does this mean I can get out of doing escort cards?"

"Nice try." I looked at the towering frosted Christmas tree positioned next to the table. "Don't you mean escort ornaments? And we have to wait until Buster and Mack add the silver ribbon garland to the tree first."

Instead of traditional cards to let guests know at which table they were seated, we'd come up with the idea of glass Christmas ornaments with names written on them in shiny silver calligraphy. It had seemed like a fun idea when we'd thought of it, but now we were tasked with hanging over a hundred breakable balls on a tree in some semblance of alphabetical order.

Kate groaned. "Setting them out might be my least favorite part of the wedding day. After lining up the bridal party for the processional."

"What about loading people onto shuttle buses?"

She snapped her fingers. "I almost forgot how much I loathe that. That's still number three after the processional and place cards. Thank you for reminding me, Annabelle."

I grinned at her as I joined her at the base of the stairs. "Anytime."

Kate's mouth dropped open, and she grabbed my arm. "Did you just see that?"

"See what?" I followed her gaze out the glass walls to the canal terrace.

"Santa." She touched a hand to the side of her head. "I could have sworn I just saw Santa Claus run by."

CHAPTER 33

"Doesn't the hotel have a Santa?" I asked as we reached the hotel's lobby, which was filled with at least a dozen towering Christmas trees, each one uniquely decorated. The hotel went all out for the holiday, so a roaming Santa didn't seem out of the realm of possibility.

"Only for special parties." Kate paused as a group of tourists passed us, so distracted by the ornately decorated trees that they almost ran into us. "And why would Santa be running around the outside of the hotel?"

We'd rushed to the glass walls that overlooked the C&O Canal, but there had been no sign of a Santa. We'd even ducked outside and looked up and down the canal. Nothing.

"Is it possible you're imagining Santa since so many have been popping up?" I asked, inhaling the heady scent of Christmas tree and leading the way through the busy lobby toward the elevator bank.

"Like PTSD?" she said. "Post Traumatic Santa Disorder?"

I gave her a withering look. "Post Traumatic *Stress* Disorder is a real thing. This is not."

As we passed a pair of upholstered chairs tucked against one wall, a deep throat clearing made me turn my head. "Daniel? Is that you?"

My fiancé's older brother stood. He had the same dark hair as Reese, although it was flecked with gray at the temples, and was only a fraction taller. Both men were handsome enough to turn heads, and I saw a woman near us do a quick double take.

"What a coincidence," I said, glancing around. "Are you working?"

Daniel Reese had been a DC cop before leaving to open his own private security firm. He now worked with an elite clientele, so it was easy to imagine his client would be staying at The Four Seasons.

Daniel looked at Kate. "You could say that."

"He's our bodyguard," Kate said, sidling up next to him. "I thought with everything going on with Brianna, we could use some extra muscle."

Even though it was widely known that Kate had a special talent for determining if people were dating with a single glance, it didn't take a relationship guru to know that something more was going on. Was this the older man she'd been talking about? I never would have called him "older," but I suppose he was older than Kate by about a decade. I decided to leave that topic for later.

"You hired security for our wedding without mentioning it to me?"

She smiled up at Daniel. "I wouldn't say hired."

"I'm doing this pro bono," Daniel said, pushing up the sleeves of his black blazer.

"And it's not for the wedding as much as it's for us," Kate said. "You said yourself that Brianna's obsession with us was turning violent. She knows we have a wedding here today. She might know we got the flowers back. She could know we snuck into her place."

"We don't know that for sure."

She flapped a hand in the air. "The long and short of it is that we need someone watching our backs."

She might have a point. Things with Brianna had gotten ugly, despite my initial efforts to make peace. If the planner really was behind the damage to Kate's car and the pilfering of our flowers, she was out of control. I wouldn't put it past her to show up and try to sabotage our wedding or even hurt one of us.

"Fine," I said. "You might be right."

Kate looped her arm through Daniel's. "I sent him a photo of Brianna, so he can keep an eye out for her while we focus on the wedding."

"I'll be discreet," he said.

In his black suit, I knew he'd look just like a wedding guest. A handsome, muscular wedding guest. Our bigger problem might be keeping the bridesmaids off him once they'd had a few drinks.

"Thanks." Since Daniel and I would be family one day, I wasn't sure if I should hug him or what, so I squeezed his arm. I still hadn't gotten used to the idea that I would have a brother-in-law. I'd barely adjusted to the concept of a fiancé.

We left him in the lobby while we proceeded to the bride's suite. As we rode the elevator up, I tapped the toe of my black flat.

"So you and Daniel?"

Kate swung her head to me, her cheeks splotched with pink. "Maybe. Why? Do you think he's too old for me?"

I held up both palms as the elevator doors pinged open. "Not at all. I think he's great. I'm marrying the slightly younger version, remember?"

She laughed nervously. "Right. Of course. He's a lot more laid-back when he's not working, you know."

"You don't need to convince me. As long as you're not just playing around with him. I doubt he's the kind of guy who's casual about anything."

"That's the weird thing." She nibbled the edge of her thumbnail as we walked down the hallway toward the bride's suite. "I've lost my urge to date around since I started seeing him."

I fought the urge to check if she had a fever. "That's a good thing. It shows you may be ready to stick with one guy and maybe settle down in the near future."

She didn't say anything else, and a few seconds later, we'd reached the propped-open door to the bridal suite. A haze of hairspray had drifted out into the hall, making me cough as we approached. I could hear the din of hip-hop music along with lots of female voices and one very distinct male voice.

"All right, tramps," he called out over the music. "Who's next to get bedazzled?"

I glanced at Kate. "That's not a good sign."

Pushing the door open, I spotted a blond bridesmaid dancing by in her monogrammed robe. As she turned around, I clutched Kate's arm for support. "Is that...?"

"A braid around the back of her head that looks like a Christmas wreath?" Kate patted my hand. "Sure is."

Fern had woven green ribbon through the circular braid and tied a red bow at the bottom. It would have been ideal for a flower girl, but looked silly on a grown woman. I suspected that everyone in the room had imbibed too much champagne to realize that a wreath on the back of their heads was not a style that would age well in photos. A French twist? Classic. A wreath made of hair? Not so much.

I led the way through the room, dodging a conga line of bridesmaids and passing the picked-over breakfast cart along with multiple bottles of champagne on end tables, coffee tables, and ice buckets. One look at the dancing bridesmaids told me they were all empty.

I saw Fern set up by the windows with the bride sitting in front of him on a stool. He wore a red velvet suit with white piping and his favorite black Ferragamo belt.

"Maybe this is who I mistook for Santa," Kate said.

"You're back." Fern beamed when he saw us, waving with the hand holding a champagne flute. "What do you think of the bridesmaids?"

"I think it isn't what we discussed," I said through a plastered on smile so the bride wouldn't think I was upset. I gave her a quick hug and told her she looked stunning.

"Do you mind if I take a quick bathroom break?" she asked, slipping off the stool.

"Take your time, sweetie," Fern said, smiling as she hurried off, then leaning in to me. "I'm not surprised she has to go again. That girl's been drinking like a fish all morning."

"That would explain why she's fine with the hair wreaths," Kate muttered.

I cut my eyes to a passing bridesmaid, then narrowed my eyes at

Fern. "Explain."

Fern fluttered a hand at me. "I got a burst of creative inspiration. Besides, it's a Christmas wedding."

"Actually, it's a winter wonderland wedding. Everything is blue and white."

He frowned then shrugged. "Well, it's almost Christmas. It will look marvelously festive at the church. I can change up their hair for the reception. Maybe put crystals in instead."

"Don't even think about doing anything but the classic updo you did at the bride's hair trial."

He let out a deeply wounded sigh. "You're no fun when it comes to themes, sweetie. What about some sprigs of holly? No? Fine, but those wreaths make a statement."

I folded my arms over my chest. "Yes, and it's 'Don't drink and do hair.'"

"Hurtful," Fern said, touching a hand to his chest, his enormous topaz ring flashing at me.

"Where's Carl?" I asked, scanning the room for our makeup artist.

"He had to run out to grab more mascara." Fern made a tsk-ing noise in the back of his throat. "He ran out of waterproof."

You couldn't put a bride in regular mascara unless you wanted her to look like a crying banshee.

"Love the suit," Kate said, waving at Fern's outfit. "It fits you better than the Santa suit."

"It's hard to get a slim fit Santa costume," Fern said, pulling a brush through the bride's hair and taking a drink of champagne. "Besides, my Santa costume disappeared. Didn't I tell you?"

"Disappeared?" I asked. "Do you mean it was stolen?"

Fern twitched one shoulder up and down. "I left it in my storage room, and I left the key over the doorsill for Kris, so I assume he's borrowing it."

"Or a drug kingpin is wearing it bound and gagged," Kate muttered.

"You probably should start locking your back door," I told Fern. "Just in case it isn't Kris."

"But then I never would have gotten this note from him," Fern said, producing a crumpled piece of paper from his impossibly snug pants pocket.

I took the paper and unfolded it, reading the note written by Fern at the top in which he asked Kris if he'd been the Santa at the dumpster. Below Fern's swirling handwriting was a hastily scrawled response.

Not me. Look for 4263.

"What's 4263?" Kate asked, leaning across me as she read the note.

Fern shrugged. "No idea. An address?"

I stared at the paper, the ink smudged. "But what street? This could be anywhere."

"And those numbers don't exist in Georgetown addresses," Fern reminded me. "Not Georgetown proper, at least. An address with 4263 would be much higher up Wisconsin or deeper into downtown."

I let out a breath, frustrated that the tip from our renegade Santa was so vague.

"Why be so cagey?" Kate asked. "Why not just tell us?"

I folded the paper and tucked it into my pocket. "Maybe he doesn't trust us."

Kate opened her arms wide. "Then why say anything at all? He clearly wants us to find something at 4263 or he wouldn't have mentioned it."

"But he felt he couldn't say it directly." I shook my head, more confused than ever.

I felt my phone buzz in my pocket and I pulled it out, turning to Kate before answering. "Keep an eye on the hair while I take this."

She stepped closer to Fern, taking the glass of champagne from his hand and stealing a sip.

I pressed the talk button as I walked toward the door, expecting it to be one of my wedding vendors checking in. "Annabelle Archer speaking."

"Babe, it's me," Reese said.

"Oh, hey." I felt a rush hearing his voice. "Guess who I just saw in the lobby of The Four Seasons."

He sighed deeply. "That's what I was calling to tell you. I told her not to bother you."

"Her?" I stepped out into the hallway, pulling the door almost closed to block out the sound of Beyoncé singing about all the single ladies.

"As I was leaving for work, Leatrice was heading out in her Santa suit to sing carols around Georgetown and insisted she was going to surprise you at the Four Seasons."

"That explains the Santa Kate saw running around outside the hotel," I said, shaking my head. "I have *got* to stop telling her where I'm working. I didn't know you were working today."

"Got called in." He sighed. "I just walked into the precinct."

"You might be able to help with this." I walked a few steps down the carpeted hallway, the sound of bridesmaids' laughter becoming fainter. "Fern got a note--most likely from Kris--telling him to look for 4263. Does that ring any bells? Is it the location of someplace notable in the criminal underworld?"

He chuckled. "4263? The criminal underworld? Not that I know of. I can do a search for addresses and see what I come up with."

"Thanks. I don't know why he's sending us code. Why not just tell us?"

"He's former military," Reese reminded me. "And it sounds like he's scared. Maybe he thought the note would be seen by the wrong person and get him into deeper trouble."

"Who's Fern going to show aside from us? The president of the Junior League?"

Another laugh from Reese. "Did you say Kate saw a Santa running around the Four Seasons? When was this?"

"About twenty minutes ago."

"I hate to break it to you, but that couldn't have been Leatrice. She only left our building twenty minutes ago."

I rubbed a hand across my forehead. "So you're telling me I have to deal with multiple Santas, a cryptic code that makes no sense, and a huge wedding?"

Reese chuckled. "'Tis the season, babe."

CHAPTER 34

"So I wasn't seeing things?" Kate asked as we stepped off the elevator at the lobby level.

We were greeted by piped-in holiday music and the low hum of visitors admiring the Christmas trees. I knew that in an hour or two the sun would set and the hotel's restaurant would also get busy. Hotels in December were always bustling--another reason we usually avoided holiday weddings.

"I'm not saying that," I said. "Just that between Fern's missing Santa suit, Leatrice in a Santa suit, and the fact that it's almost Christmas, there's a good chance we might see more than one Santa today."

I glanced at the empty upholstered chair where we'd left Daniel. "Where do you think he ran off to?"

"He's probably doing a perimeter sweep."

I raised an eyebrow at her. "Look who knows the security team lingo."

She gave a nervous laugh. "I've heard him talking to his guys a few times. You pick it up."

I understood that. After hearing Reese talk to Hobbes on the phone, I felt like I was learning the various codes they used to shorthand their conversations. "Let's forget about Leatrice and the fact that we have a private security guard and just focus on the wedding. We still need to hang those escort ornaments."

"No time like a present," Kate said.

"*The* present," I said under my breath, knowing she didn't care.

She twitched one shoulder up and down. "My version is more Christmassy."

As we crossed the lobby toward the stairs going down, I glanced over and saw a Santa coming through the glass front doors of the hotel. I tugged Kate along behind me. "Move it. I think I see Leatrice."

"You know she'll track us down eventually," Kate said as we hurried down the stairs. "You're just delaying the inevitable."

"If she can get past the hotel security," I said. "Short Santa with lots of makeup should send up some red flags."

We reached the ballroom level, and I saw that Buster and Mack had added the silver ribbon garland to our escort card tree. Behind the tree, a bright red leg and shiny black boot disappeared into the meeting room we'd set aside as the bride and groom's quiet space for when they arrived at the hotel after the ceremony and before they joined cocktail hour.

"Who was that?" I asked, fighting the urge to rub my eyes.

"Who was who?"

"Okay, I could have sworn I just saw the leg of a Santa go into the bride and groom's holding room."

"It couldn't be Leatrice. We just saw her upstairs." Kate clutched my arm. "We're being stalked by Santas. It's like a terrifying holiday horror movie."

I rushed over and peeked inside the room. Nothing. Of course the Santa could have gone out the back of the room that led to the hotel kitchens and prep area, but why would a Santa be sneaking around the bowels of a hotel?

"We're not being stalked by Santas," I said, joining Kate in the foyer again. "The hotel probably has one appearing in the restaurant or a private party or something. You know corporate holiday parties love their Santas."

"You know who would know?" Kate snapped her fingers. "Sidney Allen. Doesn't he supply most of the Santas around DC?"

"You're a genius." I pulled out my phone and searched up the entertainment diva's number, calling him and waiting until he picked up. "Hi, Sidney Allen. It's Annabelle."

"Hi, Annabelle." He sounded surprised to hear from me, and I could hear the worry in his voice. "We aren't working together today, are we?"

"No. Not today. I have a quick question for you."

"Okay. Hold on one second. Dickens carolers, I need you on the balcony pronto." He was clearly talking into the headset he always wore when coordinating entertainment at events. "Waifs, I need you to emote more. I need more waif from you. Okay, Annabelle, I'm back; what can I do for you?"

"Do you have any Santas at the Four Seasons today?"

"Today?" He went quiet for a moment. "Nope. We're at the Fairmont, the Park Hyatt, and the Mayflower. We're not at the Four Seasons again until a holiday party on Wednesday."

"Thanks. Sorry to bother you."

"Don't mention it," he said, then sucked in a sharp breath. "Carolers from the eighteenth century did not wear digital watches, Kenneth. Did you miss my email on historical accuracy? I have to run, Annabelle." And with that, he clicked off.

"So?" Kate asked.

"He doesn't have any Santas here, and I feel really sorry for Kenneth." I let out a breath. "We still have a wedding to run and ornaments to hang. Let's try to forget about the Santa sightings and focus on that."

"Agreed." Kate led the way to the meeting room next door that we were using to store all of our supplies and details for the wedding. "Our wedding is the one thing that's been smooth sailing."

When we walked in, Mack stood at the long table that held the drinks and a silver punch bowl filled with ice. Later in the evening, it would hold a buffet of sandwiches, pasta salad, chips, and cookies for all the vendors. For now, it was empty save the assortment of miniature bottles of sodas and waters.

Mack looked up from pouring himself a Sprite. "There you are. Did you see the tree?"

"It looks great," I said as Kate joined him at the table, and I headed for the stacks of boxes along one wall. "Now all we have to do is hang these in alphabetical order without breaking any."

"You know guests are going to take forever trying to find their names, right?" Kate asked, twisting the top off a Diet Coke.

"That's why you'll be standing there to help them."

She rolled her eyes. "Why me?"

"Would you rather be in charge of wrangling the bridal party into order for the introductions?"

She cringed. "Never mind. I'll take tree duty."

I knelt down and read the sides of the cardboard boxes, searching for the box we'd labeled "A-F." I stood up and turned around. "Did we bring all the boxes from my apartment?"

"Of course. We read off the letters as we loaded them into your CRV."

"That's what I thought." I counted the boxes again. "And we definitely unloaded everything from my car?"

"You know we did." Kate walked over to join me. "What's going on?"

"The 'A-F' box isn't here."

"Impossible." Kate bent over and walked down the row of boxes, reading the side of each one. She glanced over her shoulder at Mack. "You guys didn't take it by any chance?"

Mack shook his head. "This is the first I've been in here all day."

My pulse quickened and I tried not to panic. This wasn't a situation where we could fix it with back-up escort cards. We didn't have twenty-five spare ornaments or the time to paint names on them.

"Brianna," Kate said like she was uttering a curse.

So much for our wedding setup going smoothly.

CHAPTER 35

*A*s soon as she said it, I knew she was right. Who else would have any use for Christmas ornaments with other people's names on them? Only someone who wanted to sabotage our wedding, and Brianna knew we had a wedding at the Four Seasons today. She'd already tried to sabotage it once by stealing the flowers, and now she'd stolen some of our escort cards.

"She's Santa," Kate said.

"What?" Mack stared at her.

I nodded. "You're right. The person who stole the flower order was dressed like Santa. What better way to move around in December without people recognizing you than a Santa suit?"

Kate pointed to the doorway that led into the back of the hotel. "And she's moving around through the back of the house."

"The loading dock," I said. "I'll bet she's heading for the loading dock."

Mack shook his head. "Our trucks are blocking the way out. We thought it was her who tried to steal candy from your Valentine's wedding last year and had to abandon it because she couldn't get out of the loading dock. I don't think she'll make that mistake again."

"If it was me, I'd walk right out the front door," Kate said. "Who's going to stop Santa?"

"I'll head upstairs," I said, waving to Kate. "Can you text Daniel and tell him to be on the lookout for a Santa with a box?"

"On it," Kate said, her fingers already tapping away on her phone.

"I'll go tell Buster," Mack said, walking out of the room with me. "He'd love an excuse to chase down Brianna."

I took the stairs to the lobby two at a time, grateful I wore sensible flats on wedding days and grateful Kate wasn't running behind me this time, trying to keep up in her very insensible heels. When I reached the lobby, I swung my head from side to side. The place was brimming with people, but I didn't see a Santa. Not even Leatrice dressed as Santa. I pushed through the tourists ooh-ing and aah-ing over the decor until I'd reached the glass doors.

"Annabelle, dear!"

I spun to see Leatrice sitting on a cream-colored couch in the lobby's sitting area. As expected, she had on a Santa suit--sans the beard--and a full face of makeup. A uniformed police officer stood next to her looking less than pleased.

"Is everything okay?" As much as I wanted to catch Brianna, I didn't want Leatrice to get arrested, although I couldn't imagine what the octogenarian had done.

"Fine and dandy," she said, straightening her red-and-white hat.

"You know this Santa?" the officer asked. "We got a call from hotel security about some unauthorized Santas wandering around the hotel."

"I know her," I said. "She's my neighbor and she's harmless, if a little excited about the holidays. You can check with Detective Mike Reese. He'll vouch for her, as well."

The cop's eyebrows went up. "Thanks." The corners of his mouth curved up. "So when she threatened to give her detective friend my badge number, she wasn't kidding?"

I gave Leatrice a stern look, but she merely shrugged, holding up a slip of paper with numbers written on it along with a name.

"I'm sorry, officer." I scanned the lobby again. "Neither of you have seen another Santa come through here by any chance?"

Leatrice's garishly coral lips curled up into a wide smile. "Actually, I did. Just a minute ago."

"Where did she go?"

"She?" Leatrice blinked rapidly. "There's another lady Santa in Georgetown?"

"It's not a real Santa. It's Brianna, dressed as Santa, trying to sabotage our wedding."

Leatrice frowned. "That's not very Christmassy of her." She pointed at the glass doors. "She walked right out the front of the hotel."

"Thanks." I waved at her as I ran out of the hotel. Brianna didn't live here, and her office was all the way at the end of M Street, so I doubted she was walking all the way there carrying a big box. She had to have a getaway vehicle.

It was already dusk outside, and I squinted as I looked around. The hotel valets were busy running back and forth as cars swung into the circular drive that fronted the hotel, but I didn't see a Santa in any of the cars. I glanced back through the glass doors to the police officer, and I almost gasped out loud.

4263

It couldn't be, I thought, as I punched in Reese's number on my phone. It went to voicemail.

"Elf me!" I said loudly, making a valet give me a curious look. I'd gotten so used to Buster and Mack's alternative curses, I'd forgotten how to swear properly. I left a message explaining my theory and clicked off.

I still needed to find Brianna and our missing ornaments, plus I had no idea of knowing if my wild hunch was right. Hurrying to the left of the hotel, toward Twenty-ninth Street and the nearest street parking, a noise drew my attention to the Four Seasons courtyard tucked back between two buildings.

"Don't move, Kris." The voice wasn't loud, but it was forceful, and I knew I'd heard it before.

I followed the sound--walking quietly on my toes--until I'd reached the paved area scattered with outdoor seating and a round raised flower bed that now held only greenery. Since the temperature had dropped, no one was outside. No one but a Santa and a cop with his gun drawn.

A cop that I could see in the landscape uplighting had the badge number 4263. I'd been right about the number being a policeman's badge. The cop mentioning Leatrice wanting to take his badge number had made me realize the connection, but I hadn't been sure who the badge would belong to. Until now.

I didn't make a sound as I watched Officer Rogers, and the Santa I was sure was Brianna, facing away from him and holding a cardboard box in her arms.

It all made sense. Officer Rogers had been the one to suggest that Stanley had killed Kris, which sent us off on a tangent. He'd also been at Fern's break-in, so he probably suspected that Kris wasn't dead, and when the blood results came back, he knew Kris was alive. If he had a reason to want the singing Santa dead, he'd probably been trying to track him down—and Stanley, as well—for days. It explained why Stanley was so nervous and why he didn't trust us when Kate mentioned that I was engaged to a cop. He had no way of knowing if my cop was the bad one or not.

I swallowed hard as I watched the officer steady his aim at Brianna. As much as I despised her, I couldn't let her get shot.

"That's not Kris." A second voice came from beneath one of the trees in the corner, and I had to stop myself from gasping as a second Santa emerged from the shadows of the branches. It was Kris Kringle Jingle and, from what I could tell in the eerie uplighting, he looked completely unscathed.

Rogers swung his gun to Kris. "I knew you weren't dead. Just like I knew Stanley planted your suit with the fake blood. Where is he, by the way?"

"Safe and out of your reach," Kris said. "Just like Jeannie and the others."

"How did you know?" Rogers asked.

Kris shrugged. "I didn't at first, then I realized why you seemed so familiar when you'd taken the Georgetown beat. You used to be in tight with the guys running drugs and stolen goods through my neighborhood. I'd seen you with them before, then I saw you with them the other night when they were packing up their trucks. Only you didn't stop them."

Brianna hadn't taken a step, but I saw her twist her head around.

"I thought I saw you running off that night," Rogers said, raising his gun higher. "I was just curious."

My heart pounded. Was he going to shoot Kris right here outside the Four Seasons? I opened my mouth to yell for help when the pop of a gun made my knees buckle. Brianna screamed and dropped the box, taking off through the courtyard toward the canal.

My eyes didn't leave Kris, who still stood, but I saw Rogers fly forward, the momentum causing him to spin and land on his back. Daniel rushed forward, his gun still drawn, and kicked Roger's gun out of the way.

"You shot him?" I managed to say, my voice barely a croak.

"In the shoulder, so he wouldn't shoot Santa here," Daniel said, glancing at me. "You okay?"

I nodded, even though I felt dizzy. Staggering to the raised flower bed, I sat on the brick border. Kris sat next to me while Daniel cuffed Rogers, who screamed as his arms were wrenched behind his back.

"So have you been behind all the criminals being nabbed and dressed up in Santa paraphernalia?" I asked him.

"Not just me." He tugged his white beard down so I could see his mouth. "All of my friends. When you live on the streets, you see everything that goes on. We didn't like that crime was on the rise, so we decided to take care of it our way."

"We saw Stanley last night. I assume he's been part of it?"

Kris rubbed a hand over his red belly. "Aside from helping me stage my own death, he's been helping me take out the bad guys. Stanley was special forces, so he's been a big help."

My stomach tightened. Another homeless vet. "Who tipped us off about the flowers in the dumpster? Was that you or Stanley?"

He shook his head, but grinned. "Jeannie, but it was me who took care of the guys who went into your building looking for your friend."

"I should have known when those goons were able to track Leatrice down so fast. She even said it. Only law enforcement or hackers have such fast access to license plate information. And those guys didn't look like hackers." My phone buzzed in my pocket, and I answered it when I saw Kate's name on the screen.

"Where are you, Annabelle?"

"In the courtyard with Kris Kringle Jingle." I patted the singing Santa on the leg. "It's all over."

"For you maybe," Kate said. "Buster and Mack just had to pull two brawling Santas apart down here. Leatrice had Brianna pinned down and was snapping her beard over and over."

"I'm sorry I missed that."

"No sign of the ornaments, though."

"I've got the box up here." I eyed the cardboard container Brianna had dropped and said a little prayer that they weren't all shattered. "And she definitely took it. I saw her with it in her hands before she ran off."

"Good. I, for one, look forward to pressing charges. I already called your man, so the cops should be here soon."

"I left him a message telling him what the clue meant." My heart leapt at the thought of seeing Reese. Even though I knew he wouldn't be thrilled to find me in the middle of another crime scene, there was no one I'd rather be comforted by. "And yours is up here cuffing Officer Rogers."

"Come again?"

"I'll tell you everything later," I told her, clicking off as I spotted Reese's car screech to a stop in the valet line, the portable police light flashing on top.

Kris stiffened next to me. "I guess I have some explaining to do."

"Don't worry," I said. "It's my fiancé. He's one of the good guys, like you." I stood up then turned back to him. "How would you and your Santa posse like to come to a party tomorrow?"

CHAPTER 36

"I'm not sure this screams engagement party," Fern said as he stood behind me the next afternoon pulling out the ponytail he'd been horrified to find me wearing when he'd arrived. "There's no diamond ring decor or giant love balloons."

I surveyed my apartment and stifled a yawn. "It's a holiday-themed engagement party. Heavy on the holidays."

"Heavy on the last minute," Richard grumbled as he passed us with a platter of hors d'ouevres to place on the dining room table turned food station.

"Too last minute to warn me that I wouldn't recognize the place when I came home last night?" Reese asked, coming down the hall in jeans and a snug cream sweater topped with a brown herringbone jacket.

Fern drew in his breath. "Merry Christmas to me." He dropped his voice and leaned close to my ear. "He looks good enough to dip in chocolate."

"I also styled your fiancé," Richard said. "The sweater and blazer are my Christmas gifts to him."

Richard liked to give gifts that he knew people would never give themselves. For me, that meant designer handbags he knew I'd never splurge on and because, as he'd once explained to me, "It hurts my eyes to see pleather." For Reese, that clearly meant clothes a DC detective probably couldn't afford. I didn't need to touch the blazer to know it had cashmere in the blend or look at the labels to know they were European.

"I think it's a gift for all of us," Fern said, making an approving noise in the back of his throat.

With his dark wavy hair brushed back and one curl falling over his forehead, Reese did look pretty hot. My pulse fluttered as he locked his hazel eyes on me. "You look great, babe."

Fern let out a breathy sigh, and I caught myself blushing. "Thanks."

I'd found a red plaid swirl skirt in the back of my closet and paired it with an ivory sweater with a deep cowl neckline and black boots. It might not be as designer as my fiancé's new outfit, but it was pretty festive.

Richard darted his gaze over me quickly. "Not bad, darling." He tucked one side of my sweater into the top of my skirt. "A little French tuck should do the trick. There. Now it works."

"Speaking of styling," I said, "any word on when our photo shoot will be in *DC Life Magazine*?"

"Actually, they've bumped it up to the January issue, which will be fabulous for business." Richard touched a hand to my sleeve. "All those newly engaged holiday brides will just be reaching the preliminary panic stage of planning when it hits the stands."

"Sounds fun," Reese said, winking at me.

A beeping sounded from the kitchen, and Richard hurried off muttering something about his pimento cheese puffs and last-minute parties.

While the rest of us had been running the wedding at the Four Seasons--or giving statements to the police about the proliferation of Santas running around at the wedding--Richard had been tasked by Kate to get my apartment ready for today's party. Considering how little focus we'd all had to give the event, I thought he'd done an admirable job. I didn't even mind the fact that he'd repurposed items from past holiday parties.

I recognized the gold sparkly table runner from a recent house party he'd splashed all over his Instagram feed and suspected the matte gold antlers tucked into the glittering garland and ornaments filling the runner were from Friday night's rehearsal dinner (and courtesy of a coat of spray paint). White feathers tucked around the antlers were from an art deco wedding we'd had over the summer, and the gold striped paper straws on the counter between the kitchen and living room that now served as the bar were leftover from a client's baby shower. Shiny gold balls filled glass bowls and tall cylinders and were placed on nearly every available surface.

My usual piles of wedding magazines and Reese's *Sports Illustrateds* had been whisked away and replaced with decorative stacks of books covered in gold paper. I knew the book's contents were irrelevant as they were only there for visual impact, and I suspected they had been snagged from my bookshelf, as I noticed a few gaps in the rows. Even my usual throw pillows had been switched out for metallic gold versions, several with trendy phrases like "Baby It's Cold Outside" and "Let It Snow." The only element untouched was the tall Christmas tree in the corner, which had already been decorated by Richard in tip-to-trunk metallic.

"Shouldn't Kate be here by now?" Fern asked, spraying my hair with a travel-sized hairspray that he must have secreted away in his winter white suit, although I couldn't imagine how, since it fit him like a glove.

"I'm sure she's on her way. It was a long night for us. After all the drama with Brianna and Kris Kringle, we still had to run the wedding."

"You don't have to tell me." Fern unleashed a cloud of spray over my head. "I had to change out all the bridesmaids' hair after the ceremony, remember?"

I remembered Fern reluctantly pulling out the hair wreaths and giving the ladies low buns for the reception, although I could have sworn I saw a couple of the hairdos flash green and red lights later in the evening, but that could have also had something to do with the bride being from the South and that region's fondness for light-up accessories during the holidays. "At least you didn't have to stay until the very end. We were supervising the load out until after two in the morning."

"Another reason why I'm not a wedding planner. Planning Leatrice's wedding was enough for me, thank you very much."

I didn't mention that he'd only partially planned Leatrice's wedding, since I'd secretly gone behind him making sure all the details were in place.

Reese put a small portable speaker from the bedroom on the counter and tapped the screen of his phone. The sounds of holiday music immediately filled the air, and I laughed when I recognized the music from "A Charlie Brown Christmas."

He grinned at me. "It's a classic."

Richard bustled by us again, and I breathed in the savory aroma of the golden brown puffs on the platter he carried. I'd slept as late as I could after my long night, and hadn't had time to eat anything before Richard had arrived to start prepping. I knew better than to try to sneak food past him once he'd started cooking, but I planned to sample the hors d' oeuvres as soon as my hair was deemed ready.

"It's as good as I can do," Fern said, giving my hair one last blast of spray. "I'll just tell everyone we went with a tousled look on purpose."

"There's tousled and there's bed head," Richard said, passing me as he headed back to the kitchen.

Reese grinned at me. "I don't mind bed head."

"I'll bet you don't, big boy." Fern nudged me.

I tried to give him a severe look, but he ignored me, winking at Reese before going to answer the sharp knocking on the door.

"I'm here." Kate burst in as Fern stepped back, her arms filled with wrapped boxes and her bare legs covered with a red skirt so short it reminded me of an ice skating costume.

"Why so many presents?" Fern asked. "I thought we only needed one Secret Santa gift."

Kate jerked her head behind her. "I'm not carrying only mine." She gave me a pointed look, which I knew was because she'd picked up a

Secret Santa gift for me on her way in, as well. I held out little hope it wasn't the screaming goat.

Leatrice entered behind her, a deviled egg plate held outstretched in both hands, and Sidney Allen brought up the rear carrying Hermès in a red-and-green plaid blazer. Both wore a red ascot.

I walked over to greet them, glancing down at the plate. "Do those deviled eggs look like little Santas?"

Leatrice beamed at me. "I used pimentos for the hats and mouth, capers for the eyes, and piped cream cheese for the beards and trim."

Richard emerged from the kitchen, both hands on his hips. "What did I say about bringing food?"

"You said not to bring my pigs in blankets wreath," Leatrice said as she walked the plate over to the dining table and wedged it in between two of Richard's platters. "You didn't say anything about deviled egg Santas."

"She has a point," I told Richard, who gave me a murderous look.

Sidney Allen put Hermès on the floor, and the little dog immediately scampered over to Richard, spinning around so that he faced the same way as his master and giving a loud yip.

"At least someone agrees with me," Richard said before turning on his heel and disappearing into the kitchen with Hermès close behind him.

"Don't you two look dashing?" Leatrice said when she'd turned from the table and looked at me and Reese.

"Thank you," my fiancé said. "Not more festive than you, though."

Leatrice giggled and spun in her dress, the giant Santa faces flashing by as the skirt flared. "Aren't you sweet?"

I was grateful she wasn't dressed like Santa again, although I could have done without the red-and-green striped elf hat headband perched on her jet-black hair. At least Sidney Allen was dressed in his usual dark suit, the pants tucked up snug under his chin, and the red ascot his only nod to the holidays.

Kate deposited the wrapped gifts under the tree and headed for the bottles of champagne lined up on the counter between the kitchen and living room. "This calls for a drink."

"What calls for a drink, dear?" Leatrice asked.

Kate began handing out champagne flutes. "Surviving yesterday's wedding, seeing Brianna being hauled off to jail, and finding out what really happened to Kris."

"It was a big night," Leatrice said. "I'm just glad that imposter Santa didn't get away with trying to sabotage your wedding."

"Watching you fly through the air and tackle her might have been one of the greatest moments of my life," Kate said, raising an empty glass to my neighbor. "And her being arrested for stealing our escort card ornaments was a bonus."

"I'll second that," Mack said as he walked in carrying baby Merry on one hip.

Buster followed behind holding a glass vase filled with towering white amaryllis cuffed with a wreath of green holly. "It was almost a shame to pull you off her."

Leatrice blushed, her cheeks reddening beneath her heavy rouge. "That young lady was definitely on the naughty list." She rushed forward to hug Prue. "Unlike other young ladies I know."

"It's shocking to discover that one of the cops who regularly patrolled our neighborhood was actually helping out the criminals," Mack said as he shifted Merry from one hip to the other. "I can't tell you how many times Officer Rogers popped into our shop to say hello."

"I have to take some responsibility for him showing up at the hotel last night," Reese said, holding his glass still as Kate poured champagne into it. "He heard me talking to Annabelle about a Santa being at the Four Seasons, and then he heard me mention his badge number, although at the time it didn't occur to me that was what it was. I had no idea he'd been searching for Kris since his disappearance and that the crime bosses were getting irate that their men were getting nabbed and this vigilante Santa was still on the loose."

"It's not your fault," Leatrice said. "You arrived before any other cops did."

"That's because when I saw Rogers rush out, I got a feeling something was off. I went into his duty roster and saw that he showed up to every crime scene related to Santa. Then I realized that ever since he'd taken the Georgetown beat, crime had been on the rise. He was first on the scene for almost every crime, but there was never any good evidence."

"Because he probably got rid of anything that would implicate the guys paying him off," Kate said.

Leatrice shook her head. "It's sad to see such a young fellow get involved with the wrong crowd."

"He was a part of that crowd before he became a cop," a voice said from the door.

We all turned to face the tall man in the brown suit who stood in the open doorway. It took me a moment to realize it was Kris Kringle Jingle in regular clothes.

"You made it," I said, going to the door and pulling him inside by the elbow. "I invited Kris, Stanley, and Jeannie to celebrate with us."

Kris's friends shuffled in behind him, Stanley looking calmer than he had the night before—now in a blue overcoat instead of a Santa suit—and Jeannie smiling tentatively at Fern, who rushed across the room to hug her and fuss over her hair.

Faces lit up with recognition, and everyone began welcoming the new arrivals.

"Is that why you disappeared?" Fern asked Kris once he'd started working on Jeannie's hair. "You were hiding from a dirty cop?"

"That, and I thought he might have made me," Kris said.

I looked Kris up and down, thinking he cleaned up really well for someone living on the streets. "Made you?"

"I've been working undercover."

CHAPTER 37

Beatrice staggered back a few feet. "You're an undercover agent? For the CIA? The FBI? The DEA?"

Kris chuckled. "I'm actually a confidential informant. Have been for years." He glanced at my fiancé. "Sorry I couldn't let you in on it, Detective."

Reese shook his head. "No worries. I get it. You probably didn't know who to trust. Detectives keep their CIs pretty close to the vest, anyway."

"I've been working with Vice for a while. One of my old service buddies is on the squad and roped me in." Kris rocked back on his heels. "You'd be surprised how a homeless guy dressed as Santa can move around unnoticed."

"How exciting to have one of our employees also work undercover for the police," Mack said, nudging Buster who still looked gobsmacked.

"So you knew Rogers was dirty?" Reese asked.

"I'd seen him running with those same dodgy guys before he went to the academy," Kris said. "I don't think he knew I recognized him from his old life. I doubt he paid attention to a homeless guy when he was making trouble as a teenager. But I spotted him talking with his old crew while he was walking his beat one day. Then there was an uptick in shady things going at night, and the cops never seemed to be around. It didn't take long to realize it was all connected to the larger crime ring in Georgetown we'd been tracking for a while. Rogers was on the take and letting the criminals move drugs and stolen merchandise freely. Problem was, I was pretty sure he saw me when he was talking to his old pals."

"And that's when you tried to stage your own death?" I asked.

He nodded. "I didn't want to blow my cover or end up floating in the Potomac. I asked Stanley to plant the suit, but he was so nervous when Rogers showed up right as he was putting it in the dumpster that he panicked."

Stanley laughed nervously. "He knew I was lying."

"Liars are always good at spotting other liars," Reese said, handing Stanley a glass of champagne.

Kris nodded, rubbing a hand over his gray stubble. "We decided Stanley should disappear too."

"And Jeannie?"

Another nod.

"That explains the cops outside the shelter when we talked to Jeannie," I said. "Were your vice buddies watching her?"

Kris eyed me. "They were supposed to be inconspicuous."

"They were," I assured him, "but Kate's just really good at determining men's professions by their clothes."

Kate winked at him. "The boxy blazers gave them away."

"Where did you all hide?" I asked, looking between the three. "One of the shelters? Fern's storage room?"

Kris gave Fern an apologetic look. "Only a couple of times. We moved around. During the day, we didn't need to hide. We dressed as Santas and rang the bells for Salvation Army."

"Hiding in plain sight," Leatrice said. "Genius."

"And all those criminals who got nabbed?" I asked.

"Part of the larger Vice operation," Kris said, "but the Santa stuff made it seem like an amateur vigilante, so the bad guys didn't know the cops were watching them and closing in."

Reese grinned and nodded. "Not bad."

Carl walked in holding a bottle of bubbly wrapped in a gold ribbon, a black knit cap covering his close-cropped hair. As soon as I saw him, something clicked, and I pushed my way to the door. "Did you happen to dress up as Santa this week?"

The makeup artist's cheeks flushed. "So you *did* recognize me."

I remembered seeing the Santa in hipster glasses when Kate and I were outside Baked and Wired. "Not at the time, but now that I see you, I realize that's why Santa looked so familiar."

Carl handed me the bottle. "Fern roped me into being one of the Santa stand-ins."

"Of course he did," I said, wondering how many Santas had been roaming the streets of Georgetown under Fern's direction. "Well, I'm glad you're here."

"Don't worry." He gave me a conspiratorial wink and patted his jacket pocket. "I always have emergency stash of bronzer and falsh lashes on me, so we can do something to perk you up before anyone takes photos."

I tried not to take offense at that since I had been up late the night before. "Thanks, Carl."

Kate finished pouring champagne and handed both Carl and Kris a glass. "Let's raise our glasses to Kris Kringle Jingle and his amazing crime-fighting friends."

Loud throat clearing made us all look around at Richard poking his head over the counter from the kitchen and Hermès's tiny furry head right beside his. "Were you going to forget the chef?"

Kate handed him a glass, and we all clinked and drank as the dog yipped merrily.

"You know, dear," Leatrice sidled up to me as everyone began drifting around the room, "maybe we should consider adding Kris to our crime-fighting crew. We could use an experienced CI."

"We don't have a crime-fighting crew," I said, stealing a glance at Reese and seeing the corner of his mouth twitch. "And we don't need our own confidential informant."

Prue held Merry's hands while the girl attempted to toddle over to the brightly decorated Christmas tree, and I hoped not all the ornaments were as fragile as they looked. One glance at the glass coffee table and baubles at the little girl's level reminded me that my place was by no means baby-proof.

"Speaking of crime-fighting crews, Hobbes and your cop buddies are coming, right?" I asked my fiancé.

He polished off his glass and pointed it toward the door. "Here's one of them now, along with…"

I turned to see his brother, Daniel, walk in next to a tall man with sandy-brown hair. "PJ. Don't you remember? Richard's significant other."

Richard waved from the kitchen, splotches of red appearing on his cheeks. Hermès scampered out to greet the handsome man, who scooped him up, fluffed the dog's ascot, and headed for the kitchen.

"I thought you were Richard's significant other," Reese teased.

"I thought *you* were," I shot back.

He laughed, then cocked his head to one side, his brow furrowing as he looked over my head. Kate had run up to Daniel, thrown her arms around his neck, and pulled him into a long kiss.

"Did I miss something?" he asked, pulling his eyes away from his brother to look at me.

I laughed, slipping my hand into his and feeling a rush of warmth that was only partly due to his body heat. "Who knows? It's never dull at Wedding Belles."

"You can say that again."

He gave a weary sigh, and I elbowed him playfully. Before I could remind him how instrumental my crew had been in closing the case on the missing Santa, Kris Kringle Jingle and Leatrice started singing "Hark the Herald Angels Sing" along with the Charlie Brown album. We all joined in, with Merry clapping her hands off beat and Sidney Allen looking pained by the amateur attempt.

As the song wound down, I caught a whiff of perfume that was instantly familiar. I spun toward the door and stared. "Son of a nutcracker."

"I was told there was an engagement party." She smiled widely, her voice rising above the music as everyone turned.

"Is that...?" Reese stared, his voice soft in my ear as my heart hammered away.

I nodded as she dropped her overnight bag on the floor by her feet and touched a hand to her auburn bob, diamonds glittering on her fingers. Swallowing hard, I plastered a smile on my own face.

"It's my mother."

* * *

THANK you for reading CLAUS FOR CELEBRATION!

This book has been edited and proofed, but typos are like little gremlins that like to sneak in when we're not looking. If you spot a typo, please report it to:
laura@lauradurham.com
Thank you!!

ACKNOWLEDGMENTS

This book was inspired by "The Compliment Man," who walked around DC in the 90s giving out compliments to everyone he passed. He didn't ask for money, although he was homeless, he just said nice things to brighten people's days as a way to give back to people helping him. I tweaked him and made him into a Santa for this book, but the sentiment is still the same. The world needs more people like "The Compliment Man" and more Santas!

As always, an enormous thank you to all of my wonderful readers, especially my beta readers and my review team. A special shout-out to the beta readers who caught my goofs this time: Patricia Joyner, Linda Reachill, Sheila Kraemer, Linda Fore, Sandra Anderson, Cathy Jaquette, Kaitlyn Platt, Carol Spayde, Christy Kalbhin, Tony Noice, Annemarie Pasquale, Zina Loses. Thank you!!

Big kisses to everyone who leaves reviews. They really make a difference, and I am grateful for every one of them!

Wishing everyone the happiest of holidays!!

SLAY BELLS RING

AN ANNABELLE ARCHER WEDDING PLANNER MYSTERY NOVELLA #17

LAURA DURHAM

CHAPTER 1

"Are you sure you don't want to join us?" I asked my assistant, Kate, as I knelt under the Christmas tree and gathered the few wrapped presents into a large paper shopping bag.

"And crash your first Christmas as a married woman visiting your parents?" Kate grinned at me from over a large red mug as she sat on my couch with her bare feet tucked under her. "I wouldn't dream of it."

I sighed, thinking of spending the next few days with my parents and new husband, Detective Mike Reese. Even though my parents adored him—especially my mother—I'd hoped to spend our first Christmas as husband and wife at our apartment in Washington, D.C. Life had been a whirlwind since our summer wedding, and because of an ill-timed hurricane, we hadn't even taken a proper honeymoon yet.

I'd thought the few days around Christmas would be the perfect time to curl up around the Christmas tree, drink hot cocoa, and watch the snow fall. Unfortunately, my mother had managed to guilt me into driving down to Charlottesville with the reasoning that she and my father hadn't seen us since our wedding. I'd agreed only because I was afraid that if I didn't, she might show up unannounced with enough Victorian holiday decor to send my cop husband running for the hills.

"Richard is coming," I told Kate, as I stood and bumped one of the fir branches of the tree, making the red and gold glass ornaments shake. "Since his significant other is still on assignment overseas, it's just the three of us driving down. There's room for you in the car."

Kate swiped at the whipped cream on her upper lip. "Your mother and Richard are new BFFs. Me she tolerates."

"That's not true. My mother likes you."

Kate raised an eyebrow and brushed a hand through her blond bob. "She would like me more if I wore skirts that covered my knees and tops that didn't show cleavage."

That was true. My gaze went to Kate's long legs—bare even though it was freezing outside—and I smiled as I thought of the scandalized look that would have crossed my mother's face. My Southern belle mother hadn't adapted to my assistant's fondness for miniskirts and push-up bras. Then again, she also hadn't made her peace with me wearing my auburn hair up in a messy ponytail most of the time and yoga pants around the house. "You know you'd be welcome. What are you doing for Christmas, anyway?"

Kate gave me a mischievous grin. "Don't worry about me, Annabelle. I have plans."

"That's exactly what I'm worried about." I carried the paper bag to the door and set it beside the duffel bags and rolling suitcases that were already packed for our drive. "There aren't any yuletide bar crawls or Santa speed dating events, are there?"

Kate laughed. "I promise I'll behave. Besides, someone has to be on call in case our bride needs anything."

I groaned. "How did we get roped into another New Year's Eve wedding? I swore that we wouldn't take one after the last time."

As the owner of Wedding Belles, one of the city's most successful wedding planning firms, I'd done my fair share of weddings over the holidays, and every time I swore that each one would be my last. Even though weddings on New Year's Eve were festive and had a built-in theme, planning them meant we couldn't take off fully during the Christmas holidays. One week before the wedding was the time when final numbers were due to the caterer and seating assignments were sent off to the calligrapher. That meant we couldn't put up an away-from-office message and completely relax.

"I'm pretty sure it was the big, fat check," Kate said, waving a hand at the colorfully wrapped boxes remaining under the tree. "Someone has to pay for all those presents."

"You're sure it's okay to do our usual Wedding Belles holiday party after I get back? I'd hoped we could squeeze it in before today, but Reese has been working like crazy in order to get time off on Christmas Eve and Christmas Day."

Kate waved a hand at me. "It's fine. You'll be back the day after Christmas. Everyone thinks it's fun we're having a Boxing Day party, even if they don't know what it is."

"It's a British holiday that started when the aristocracy would take boxes of—"

"Yeah, yeah," Kate said. "I know it's a really old British thing, but let me imagine it's a day celebrating sweaty, muscular guys wearing nothing but shiny shorts and boxing gloves."

I rolled my eyes. Kate's fondness for any type of guys—sweaty or otherwise—was legendary. Despite working as a wedding planner with me, she was a serial dater who rarely went out with the same man for more than a few weeks. But I did have to admit she'd slowed her pace recently.

"Speaking of your hottie cop husband, isn't he supposed to be here soon? I thought he wanted to get out of the city before the snow started."

"We're only supposed to get a dusting," I said, even though Kate was right. Reese was supposed to have been home an hour ago.

"You know what a dusting of snow does to D.C. People lose their minds."

She was also right about that. D.C. residents did not know how to drive in the snow, and the city practically shut down at the first sign of flakes. "It's fine. My mother isn't expecting us until after dinner."

Kate did not look convinced, but she took another sip of her hot chocolate, closing her eyes as she swallowed. "This can't be Swiss Miss. Did you treat yourself to that Williams-Sonoma hot chocolate?"

I shook my head, heading toward my kitchen. "Nope. It's actually a mix that one of our neighbors dropped off as a holiday present."

"You exchange presents with your neighbors?" Kate twisted around to watch me through the divider between the living room and kitchen. "I didn't know you were friendly with anyone other than Leatrice and Sidney Allen."

"This is the first year any of our neighbors have given out gifts." I picked up the large Mason jar from the counter and twisted off the top that was decorated with a red-and-green-striped bow, pouring a small amount of the dark brown powder into a mug. "Don't you remember that couple I told you about? They started it with the cocoa mix, then Leatrice and Sidney Allen gave out splits of apple cider because Sidney Allen can't stand being one-upped when it comes to Southern customs."

"Is it the preppy couple?" Kate asked.

"Mindy and Kurt." I nodded. "The woman either spends a lot of time on Pinterest or went to some sort of finishing school. My mother would love her."

"Then I'm assuming we hate her?" Kate tapped a finger against her chin. "I think I remember you mentioning them."

"We don't hate her," I said. "I barely know them. They moved in to the second floor about six months ago."

A flash of recognition crossed her face. "Does the guy have tattoos and ride a motorcycle?"

I lifted the still-hot kettle off the stove and poured steaming water into my mug. "Not by a long shot. That's the guy on the third floor. He owns a bar."

Kate's eyes flared with interest. "That explains why we've only run into him when we're coming back late from weddings."

I unwrapped a candy cane and used it to stir my hot chocolate then hooked it over the side of the mug. "I think he sleeps during the day. At least that's what Leatrice says."

"Let me guess. Your resident spy wannabe has him under surveillance?"

My first-floor neighbor, Leatrice, was over eighty, recently married to a quirky entertainment director she met at one of my weddings, and was convinced that half of D.C.—including most of our neighbors in Georgetown—were spies. She preferred listening to her police scanner instead of the radio and owned a rich assortment of spy gear herself, not to mention various costumes so she could follow people undetected.

"Not anymore." I joined Kate in the living room again, taking the overstuffed chair across from her. "After a week of him doing nothing but coming home late and not emerging until the afternoon, she got bored. Luckily, she always has Mr. Kopchek."

Kate sighed. "She isn't still convinced that little old man is a Russian sleeper, is she?"

"He doesn't do himself any favors by being such a grump." I took a sip of my pepperminty hot chocolate, the rich flavor instantly soothing. "He's always complaining that people are playing their music too loudly. He even leaves notes for Mindy and Kurt about Kurt's bike, and they keep that on the first floor with Leatrice's permission."

"I guess it is a pain to haul a bike upstairs," Kate said. "But you know there's someone like that in every building. Don't you remember the lady I told you about in my apartment building? The one who uses her cane to poke people in the elevator?"

"At least you have an elevator."

Kate scooted a pile of wedding magazines over and put her mug on the crowded coffee table. "Believe me, I know firsthand what a pain it is that you live in a walk-up, but at least you're on the fourth floor. I'm on the eighth. And your neighbors may be a little nutty, but there aren't many of them."

My apartment building was located in the upscale neighborhood of Georgetown, and like most things in Georgetown, it was only a few stories high and was more charming than modern. Each of the floors of the stone-front building held two apartments, so there were fewer than fifteen residents in total.

"But does your cane lady give out written citations?" I asked.

"Citations?"

I nodded. "Somehow Mr. Kopchek has printed citations. I've

gotten them when I've parked too far from the curb or walked up the stairs too loudly."

"I'm surprised I haven't gotten one."

"Me, too," I said. Kate was a horrible driver and even worse at parking. "Although the written citations are new. Keep parking with one tire up on the curb, and you'll get one soon enough."

Kate shivered. "That reminds me of that old mother-of-the-bride who used to write down infractions in her notebook."

I took a big gulp of my warm drink. "Don't remind me of her."

"Because she was killed?" Kate whispered, even though we were the only two people in my apartment.

"That and she was an awful person. Mr. Kopchek isn't like her. He's just a little quirky."

"Then he should fit right in," Kate muttered. "Leatrice and her husband Sidney Allen left quirky in the rearview mirror a long time ago."

"I just don't get why Leatrice is convinced the old man is a spy," I said. "Wouldn't a real spy keep a lower profile? Have you ever heard of a sleeper agent who gives out neighbor citations?"

"No," Kate admitted. "But I'm not up on my spy trivia either. It would be a pretty good double feint for a spy to be a total nuisance."

"In that case, Leatrice is definitely a spy."

Kate snorted a laugh. "If she hears you say that, she'll be thrilled."

My phone buzzed in my jeans pocket, and I pulled it out, staring at the screen for a moment before looking up at Kate. "Richard is searching for parking. Why would Richard be running late? He never runs late."

Kate took out her own phone and swiped her finger across the screen. "This is what happens when we don't have a wedding a few days away, and we aren't checking the weather every hour." She held up her screen, and I could make out the weather app and the image of ice-blue snowflakes. "It started snowing two hours ago."

I jumped up and ran to the window overlooking the street, pulling back the yellow curtains and peering down. Snow was falling heavily, and the cars lining the narrow streets were already covered in white. "I can't believe it."

Kate joined me at the window. "The snow that was supposed to be a dusting is now going to be a blizzard."

"So, we're snowed in?" I squinted at a figure in the snow below us struggling with an armful of bags, my breath catching when I recognized the designer duffel. "And it looks like Richard has brought everything he owns."

"No way are you three making it out of the city now." Kate patted me on the back. "This should be cozy."

I rubbed my temples as I counted the number of bags in Richard's arms. "I think you mean crowded."

CHAPTER 2

"What do you mean we aren't going?" Richard dropped his bags on the floor and droplets of melted snow flew up. He pushed back the hood of his snow jacket to reveal miraculously unruffled dark hair.

"You did come from outside, right?" Kate asked from her perch on the couch.

Richard shot her a look as he shifted his crossbody bag, and a tiny black-and-brown mop of fur poked out of one end. His Yorkie, Hermès, scanned the room and yipped happily when he saw us. "Of course, I did, but we aren't going to let a little snow stop us, are we?"

"A little snow?" I tousled the dog's head. "You do know it's supposed to be a blizzard now, right?"

Richard set the leather bag with his dog on the couch, and Hermès spilled out, revealing that he was wearing a red plaid holiday sweater. He scampered from one end of the couch to the other and walked over Kate. "No, I do not know. Hermès and I have been on our way over here for the past hour."

"And you didn't hear the weather on the radio?" Kate asked. "Or look out the window?"

Richard narrowed his eyes at her. "I'll have you know that Hermès and I don't listen to the radio in the car. We're using drive time to learn French."

Kate rubbed the little dog's belly as he flopped over next to her. "Why am I not surprised by this?"

"Well, the storm front that was supposed to skirt by D.C. shifted suddenly, and now we're getting all the snow that was going to be heading for Pennsylvania." I took Richard's wet coat after he shrugged it off. "It won't let up for at least twenty-four hours."

"Twenty-four hours?" He gazed around him then at the bags he'd brought. "So that means we're not having Christmas in Charlottesville with your mother?"

"It would take us hours to even get out of the city at this point," I told him, hanging his coat on the rack by the door.

"You're right about that," he muttered. "Washingtonians cannot drive in the snow."

Kate picked up her mug from the coffee table and lifted it into the air. "At least we have lots of delicious hot chocolate."

Richard's eyes widened. "You don't mean we're staying *here*." He glanced around my apartment.

Although it was decorated with a Christmas tree and smelled faintly of pine and peppermint, the apartment also had tables covered with my husband's paperwork and my wedding files. Since we'd been planning to be away and not have guests over the holidays, I hadn't bothered to clean. Not that I cleaned that often, anyway.

"You want to try to drive back across town in this?" Kate asked. "I know I'll never be able to make it up Connecticut Avenue without running out of gas first."

I suspected Kate was not exaggerating since she was notorious for driving on fumes.

"We're spending Christmas *here*?" Richard asked again.

I tried not to be offended at his horrified tone. "At least tonight. Unless you and Hermès want to trek to the nearest Metro station, which isn't very close to us."

"But," Richard spluttered, "I didn't prepare for this." He waved a hand at me. "You aren't prepared for this. Tomorrow is Christmas Eve, and you probably don't have a thing to eat."

I opened my mouth and closed it again. He was absolutely right. Since we were going to my mother's for Christmas, I hadn't stocked the kitchen. There was no turkey in the freezer, no pies cooling on the counter, and no cranberry sauce bubbling on the stove.

Richard pulled out his own phone, dialing as he paced a small circle and mumbled to himself about what a disaster this was. No surprise that he considered my lack of food the most heinous part of the situation since he was the founder and owner of Richard Gerard Catering, one of Washington's most elite caterers.

"I thought I heard barking." My downstairs neighbor Leatrice walked in through the still-open door, her eyes lighting on Hermès getting a belly rub from Kate. "There's the boy I'm babysitting."

I eyed Leatrice's dress which was printed with green tree branches, lights, and ornaments. "You almost match our tree."

She beamed at me. "It's called Christmas tree camo. I'm supposed to be able to stand next to a Christmas tree and blend in."

Glancing down at her feet, I saw that she wore slippers that looked like brightly wrapped presents with bows. Not her most outrageous footwear by a long shot, and it completed the person-as-Christmas-tree look.

"Christmas tree camouflage." Kate tilted her head. "Is this part of your spy gear?"

Leatrice giggled. "Oh, no. This is just fashion."

Even though Richard was talking on the phone in low, urgent tones, he glanced up and made a derisive noise in the back of his throat. "If that's fashion, I'm Jason Momoa."

"I wish," Kate said under her breath.

If Leatrice heard Richard's comment, she ignored it. Honestly, I thought her Christmas tree camo was the least shocking thing about her. She'd dyed her hair bubblegum pink for my wedding and had decided to grow it out since then. Although I was used to seeing Leatrice with hair dyed jet-black (or occasionally platinum blond or pink), apparently her natural hair color was a snowy white. So, her

Mary Tyler Moore flip was white from her roots to her jawline, then the bottom half was pink.

"You won't need to babysit Hermès anymore," I told her as she sat down on the couch. "Richard isn't going anywhere."

Her face fell. "But I had so many fun activities planned for us."

"None of us are going anywhere," I said, picking up my mug from the coffee table, sidestepping Richard, and heading to the kitchen. "Not in this weather."

"You and the detective aren't going to your parents' house anymore?"

I hadn't talked to my husband yet, but I suspected he wouldn't want to risk our safety or sanity by attempting to drive out of D.C. in a blizzard.

"It's all settled," Richard announced as he slipped his phone in his pocket. "I talked to your mother. She's disappointed but she understands."

"*You* talked to my mother?" I put my dirty mug on the counter, suddenly wishing I had something to make the hot chocolate Irish.

Richard sniffed and touched a hand to his hair. "Gwen and I talk all the time, Annabelle. She's on speed dial."

I didn't think my mother was on *my* speed dial. "Thanks, I guess."

"You're welcome, darling." Richard walked into the kitchen. "I also put in an emergency call to my kitchens. You know we do a lot of holiday drop-offs, so the chef and his staff are still cooking. They're putting food for us on the next truck."

"You didn't have to do that."

Richard's gaze swept the kitchen. "Oh, I think I did."

"This is so exciting." Leatrice clapped her hands from the other room. "We all get to spend Christmas together."

Richard frowned as he glanced through the opening between the two rooms and saw Leatrice's white-and-pink head bobbing above the back of the couch. "I forgot about Leatrice and Sidney Allen. Of course, they're going to invite themselves. Some people just don't know when they're overstepping." He sighed and took his phone out of his pocket. "I hope you don't mind that I'm having linens sent over since you don't own a decent tablecloth. A holiday toile."

"Toile?" The French-inspired pastoral print seemed an odd choice for the holidays. "Does this have anything to do with your recent French obsession?"

He sniffed. "You know it's easier to plan with a theme."

"Is the theme for our snowbound Christmas everything French?"

He gave a me a weary look. "I prefer Christmas in the Chateau."

"Of course, you do," I mumbled. Reese was going to love this.

He pressed his phone to his ear. "If we're hosting interlopers, I'll need to add more food to our order. And lots more wine."

The door swung open, and my husband stepped inside and flipped back the gray hood of his wool coat. His eyes widened slightly as he took in Leatrice, Kate, and Hermès on the couch. His gaze went to the bags clustered around the door and then to me and Richard in the kitchen. His mouth twitched at the corners. "Anything I should know, babe?"

Before I could answer, Richard bustled out of the kitchen toward him. "Change of plans, Detective. I've called Annabelle's mother and told her that we're snowed in. But don't worry. I promise we won't starve to death. My kitchens are delivering food to feed all of us for at least two days." He swept an arm wide. "It will be a festive Christmas at the Chateau."

"Chateau?" My husband stared. "Two days?"

I followed Richard out of the kitchen and wrapped my arms around Reese. Even though his coat was still cold from being outside, just wrapping my arms around him made me feel better. "Or until the roads are passable. We can't send them out in this now."

He lowered his head to mine and kissed me softly. "We can't?"

I gave him a playful swat on the arm and laughed. I knew he was fond of my friends, even if they were a little prone to dramatics. "You really want to turn people away from the inn on Christmas?"

He frowned, although his hazel eyes danced. "I do see your point. That's not a good look for us, is it?"

"Think of it this way," I whispered. "At least I'm not doing the cooking."

"That is a plus."

I swatted him again. "You were supposed to disagree with me."

He wrapped his arms around me. "You know I would never lie to you, babe."

Richard made an impatient noise. "I hope you two aren't going to be like this the entire time."

"Give them a break." Kate grinned at us. "They're still newlyweds."

"Speaking of lovebirds," Leatrice bounded up from the couch as her own husband appeared at the door.

Sidney Allen wasn't much taller than Leatrice, who barely topped five feet. But whereas Leatrice was skin and bones, her husband was all curves. He almost always wore dark suits with his pants hitched up so high they flirted with his armpits, and when he was coordinating entertainment for an event, he wore a wireless headset so he could shriek orders into it. Luckily, he did not have a headset on at the moment.

Leaning one plump hand against the doorframe, he drew in a long breath as his gaze locked onto my husband, his face flushed. "I'm glad you're here, Mike. I need to report a crime."

Richard put a hand to his heart. "Will the catastrophes ever stop?"

CHAPTER 3

𝓜y husband's face became serious as he studied Sidney Allen's disheveled appearance. "What kind of crime?"

Sidney Allen puffed out his chest, which made it rival the girth of his stomach. "I've been threatened, and the good name of my wife has been tarnished."

Reese's shoulders relaxed a bit. "What kind of threat? Was there a weapon involved?"

"Or just a disgruntled performer?" Richard said so only I could hear him.

He had a point. Sidney Allen was known for being a diva on-site and for bossing around his performers, which he gave code names appropriate to the event. I wouldn't have been shocked if Dickens Caroler #5 had lost their temper and made idle threats.

Sidney Allen smoothed his thinning hair over his forehead and cleared his throat. "No weapon, but he did shake his finger at me."

"My poor Honeybun." Leatrice took him by the arm and pulled him inside, patting his hand as she led him to the couch.

Reese took off his coat and hung it up, then tugged off his boots and left them by the door, the melting snow creating tiny puddles. "I'm not sure if you need a Metropolitan Police Department detective for this kind of thing. It sounds more like a domestic disturbance."

Sidney Allen looked scandalized as he sank onto the couch, and both Kate and Hermès got up. "That makes it sound sordid."

"Why don't you tell the detective what happened?" Leatrice prodded, gazing upon her husband like he'd hung the moon.

"I'll grab you a beer," I said, seeing how torn Reese looked between sitting in the living room and turning around and running back out the door. I suspected he might have made a run for it if it hadn't been snowing so hard.

He gave me a quick squeeze and reluctantly made his way to the chair across from Leatrice and Sidney Allen. "I'm happy to listen, but I'm technically off duty."

I walked to the kitchen as Sidney Allen launched into his tale, which I could tell was going to be long-winded. Kate followed me, hopping up onto the counter and letting her legs swing below her as I opened the refrigerator door.

"At least it isn't a murder," she said. "I don't know if I could handle a blizzard and a murder."

"You've handled a wedding and a murder before. And a vacation and a murder." I grabbed one of my husband's favorite microbrews from the door of the fridge, making note of the sadly stocked shelves. I really should be grateful my best friend was a caterer and that he'd gotten stuck with us. Otherwise, we would have been eating leftover Thai food, yogurt, and some tired grapes for the holidays.

"True." Kate bobbled her head. "But it would be nice if we could avoid dead bodies for a while."

"It's been months since we found a dead body."

"I wouldn't go bragging about that. A lot of people never stumble across corpses."

"Now you sound like my husband. You know better than anyone that we never go looking for trouble."

"Maybe you're right." Kate shrugged then smiled at me. "It still sounds funny to hear you refer to Reese as your husband."

It had taken a while for me to get used to the tall, dark, and handsome detective being my boyfriend and then my fiancé, but calling him my husband had definitely taken the most getting used to. "It *has* been five months."

"I know." She fluttered a hand at me. "It just makes you seem so grown up."

"Speaking of maturing," I said, seeing the opening I'd been looking for, "you haven't mentioned a hot date in a while. Since before my wedding, actually. What gives? Are you really just seeing the same mystery man?"

Spots of pink appeared on her cheeks. "I don't want to jinx it."

"And telling me about him will jinx it?"

She twitched one shoulder up. "I don't know. You know the last time I was serious about someone, it didn't work out."

Kate had told me that she'd once been engaged, and her fiancé had cheated on her. It had soured her on serious relationships and been the reason she'd had the social life of a butterfly ever since.

"Not all guys are cheaters and liars," I said, my gaze going to my husband in the living room as he listened to Sidney Allen.

"I know." She craned her neck to follow my line of sight. "You got a good one."

"This secret guy of yours must be a good one if he's kept you monogamous for so long."

She laughed. "He's definitely different from my usual type." She slid off the counter. "Who knows? Maybe I'll introduce him soon."

With that, she left the kitchen. I followed behind her, my interest piqued.

"And then Mr. Kopchek accused my Honeybun of stalking him," Sidney Allen said as I crossed the living room and handed my husband a beer.

He smiled up at me then pulled me down into his lap before returning his attention to Sidney Allen. "Who's Mr. Kopchek?"

"The man who lives in 2B," Leatrice said. "The one who might be a Russian mole."

Reese took a long swig of his beer. "Were you stalking him, Leatrice?"

The pink-and-white-haired octogenarian shifted in her seat. "I don't stalk people. I only surveil them."

Sidney Allen swung his head to her. "You were following him?"

Her already rouged cheeks became even redder. "Only at a distance. I'm surprised he made me."

Richard glanced over from where he stood looking out the window and tapping his toe on the floor. "Why? Is he blind?"

Leatrice squared her shoulders. "I'll have you know I wore a trench coat and a fedora."

"Does the fedora cover all the hair?" Richard asked, looking pointedly at her pink tips.

My husband let out a quiet sigh. "So, our neighbor noticed you following him and brought this to your husband's attention?"

Sidney Allen stared at Leatrice. "I swore up and down to the man that you had no reason to do such a thing." He dropped his voice. "I thought you'd stopped."

Kate exchanged a glance with me from where she'd perched on the arm of the couch opposite Leatrice and her husband. We knew that Leatrice regularly spied on people in our building. She definitely did it less since she'd been married, but she clearly hadn't stopped.

"But I did have a reason," Leatrice insisted. "That man spends a lot of time at the park, which as anyone knows, is a prime spot for making drops or meeting contacts."

Sidney Allen put a hand over his eyes, shaking his head slowly. "I owe Mr. Kopchek an apology. I accused him of making it all up." His voice became almost a whisper. "I called him a liar and threatened to kill him if he ever insulted my wife again."

"You threatened to kill a man?" I couldn't hide the surprise in my voice. Sidney Allen had always been a bit of a diva to work with, but I'd never known him to be violent. Or even threaten violence. For one thing, I didn't think he'd be able to carry out a threat, and there were few people who would be genuinely scared by a threat from the small, pudgy man.

Sidney Allen dropped his hand. "I was upset because the snow canceled a big holiday party at the Willard hotel. I had twenty sugarplum fairies all set to flit around and pass out cocktails, but the blizzard ruined all of that. Now I have twenty angry ladies in leotards and wings stuck at the hotel. Mr. Kopchek caught me as I was coming in and getting off the phone with the sugarplum queen. I'm afraid I wasn't in the best mindset to be a good neighbor." He cut his eyes to Leatrice. "Plus, I thought he was making it all up."

"I'm so sorry, Honeybun," Leatrice said, her voice cracking.

He patted her hand. "This isn't your fault, although I would prefer it if you didn't follow our neighbors. We do have to live here."

"Don't sit where you eat," Kate added, making everyone look confused for a moment.

"I think you mean sh—" Richard started to say before I shot him a look.

Reese drained the rest of his beer. "Trust me; I know that the holidays make everyone a little crazy. We always get a big uptick in crime right around now."

Sidney Allen stood. "Still, my holiday stress is no excuse. My behavior was reprehensible." He hiked his pants up even higher. "I need to go apologize."

Leatrice popped up. "I'll go with you."

He shook his head. "No. This is something I need to do by myself —man-to-man."

Leatrice's face fell. "Are you sure?"

He pressed his lips together and gave a single nod.

"Do you want me to go with you?" my husband asked. "In case things get ugly?"

"You're too kind," Sidney Allen said, his Southern drawl thickening. "But this is something a gentleman must do alone."

He strode out of the door with only the hint of a waddle.

Leatrice sighed and flopped back onto the couch. "Isn't he the most gallant man you've ever met?"

"Mon dieu," Richard muttered.

Reese pulled me closer to him. "How long is this blizzard supposed to last again, and how much beer do I have?"

CHAPTER 4

"Forget I said anything about there not being enough booze." My husband staggered into the building as I held the front door open, the cold air whipping around us both and sending wet snow flying around the small foyer. He carried three cardboard boxes, and his eyes barely poked above the top one.

"Is that all wine?" I gaped at the boxes that were making his knuckles turn white.

"It could be cinder blocks," he said, his breath visible in the air.

"Do you want me to take one?"

He shook his head, then motioned behind him. "I've got this. There's more in the truck."

As Reese started up the stairs, I peered through the glass panes of the door into the swirling snowstorm beyond. One of Richard's catering trucks was double-parked in front of the building, its flashers blinking and glowing red through the white haze. There was a well-worn path through the snow to the truck, and I could make out two figures at the back—one of them was Richard and one was the driver.

"'Scuse me." The voice behind me made me step back. The tall skinny man wore a red knit cap and carried a matching deflated pizza carrier by his side. I recognized him as one of our building's regular pizza delivery guys.

"You're delivering pizzas?" I asked, cutting a glance outside. "In this?"

He shrugged. "People gotta eat. Besides, I get better tips in bad weather."

"Then you should make a killing tonight."

He made a face. "Not from that old guy." He jerked his head up toward the staircase. "He never does more than tell me to keep the change."

I assumed he was talking about Mr. Kopchek since no one else in the building over the first floor could be considered old. The delivery guy muttered something about cheapskates before pushing out into the cold. The door had almost closed when I saw a couple running for it and held it open.

"Thanks!" The woman I recognized as one half of "Mindy and Kurt" from the second floor bustled inside with a duffel bag bouncing on one hip.

Kurt came in after her, dragging a suitcase behind him and stomping his feet to loosen the snow on his boots. "So much for the Caribbean for Christmas."

"You were supposed to go to the Caribbean?" Now I didn't feel so bad about missing our trip to Charlottesville.

Mindy nodded. "The airports have shut down. Not that we even made it that far."

"It's a mess out there." Kurt pushed back the hood of his coat to reveal pale hair that was already starting to thin. "I hope you weren't planning on going anywhere."

I shrugged my shoulders. "Not anymore, unfortunately."

"Same." Mindy ran a hand through her chestnut brown hair and frowned as she glanced up at the staircase. "Now we're stuck here."

"At least we have your hot cocoa to keep us warm," I said. I'd already written a thank you note and slipped it under their door, but I felt like I needed to thank them in person. "It's delicious, by the way."

Mindy gave me a distracted smile. "It's definitely cocoa weather."

She motioned to Kurt with her head as she started up the stairs. "We'd better unpack these bags and crank up the heat again."

"Good luck," I called after them, knowing how temperamental the heating units in our older building could be and how they resisted a cold start.

"Look alive, Annabelle!" Richard yelled from the other side of the front door.

I pushed it open so he could enter. Richard groused a bit about my lack of focus, mumbled what was most certainly a curse word in French, and unloaded a canvas bag into my arms, leafy produce poking out from the top.

"Is that everything?" I asked, as Richard shook his feet over the vinyl floor.

"Darryl has the rest," he said, nodding toward the truck and the figure unloading at the back that I assumed was Darryl.

I hesitated about letting the door go since Darryl would need to be able to get into the building, but my fingers were also starting to freeze from standing half in and half out of the building. A gloved hand grabbed the door from the outside and pulled it open, making me stagger back a bit.

"Sorry." The man I recognized as the bar owner from the third floor came inside followed by a heavily bundled man carrying two armloads of bags—Darryl, I assumed.

Richard was already halfway up the first flight of stairs and barely glanced back as he called out directions. "It's on the top floor. Of course."

The bundled man with bags followed Richard. The bar owner stopped in the foyer with a black motorcycle helmet under one arm, pulled his black cap off, and shook it out, sending icy pellets scattering to the floor. He had brown hair and a face full of scruff with the edge of a dark tattoo curling out from underneath his collar. He was definitely what Kate would consider hot, but in a slightly bad-boy kind of way.

"You look like you're ready to ride this thing out," he said, giving me a lopsided grin.

"I guess," I said, readjusting the canvas bag Richard had given me. "We don't really have much choice."

"I hear that." He tugged off his gloves, waving one at the door. "I had to close the bar before it gets even worse. I didn't want to have a bunch of drunk guys who couldn't get home."

"That makes sense."

The door opened again, and a burly man holding a pair of stacked cardboard boxes stepped inside. "Where does Mr. Gerard want these?"

I blinked at him. Wait, if this was Darryl, who had walked upstairs with Richard?

The bar owner tucked his motorcycle helmet under the stairs and took the boxes from him. "I'll take them. I'm going up anyway."

Darryl grinned, clapping his hands together to warm them up. "Thanks, man. I want to get this truck back to the warehouse while I still can."

"Drive safe," I called after the man's retreating back as he disappeared into the snow.

When I turned, the bar owner had already started up the stairs.

"You don't have to do this," I said.

He twisted his head to look at me, smiling again. "What are neighbors for?"

I smiled back as I followed, thinking that Kate would definitely have been better at this than I was. If she was in my place, she would have been gushing over the guy and probably have set a date with him before she'd reached the top floor. At least, the old Kate would have.

"Thanks," I said. "I'm on the top floor."

"I know," he said. "You're the wedding planner, right?"

How did he know that?

Before I could ask him, he said, "The lady on the first floor talks a lot."

Leatrice. For a spy wannabe, she was extremely chatty.

"I'm Alton," he added as he reached the first landing. "I run the Salty Dog down near the water."

I already knew that—from Leatrice, no less—but I didn't tell him. "Annabelle."

"Nice to officially meet you, Annabelle." He'd stopped in front of one of the doors on the second floor to wait for me, then when I caught up, he let me lead the way. "Isn't it crazy that you can live in the same building as someone and never know them? We must have walked past each other a hundred times."

"D.C.," I said. "Everyone's too busy."

"You got that right. Not that I can complain." He adjusted his grip on the boxes as he fell in step behind me. "People being too busy and too stressed-out keeps my business afloat."

"Mine too."

He barked out a laugh. "I'll bet. Hey, didn't you just get married yourself? To a cop?"

"That's right." I was relieved that he knew I was married. Not that he'd been flirting with me exactly, but I was pretty bad at telling if a guy was being friendly or if it was something more. "He's a detective."

"Lucky us. Not every building gets to have its own built-in security."

I wanted to tell him that with Leatrice we had way more security than we needed, but that required a deeper explanation than I was willing to get into. I was just glad Leatrice wasn't bounding up the stairs with us. After a respectable amount of time, she'd gone after Sidney Allen, and I suspected they were still talking things through in their apartment. I knew the two would reappear at some point. For now, I was enjoying the break.

"So, are you here for the holidays?" I asked as we passed the door to his third-floor apartment. "I mean, I guess you are now whether you wanted to be or not."

He laughed again. "I was always here. The holidays are peak times for my bar. Not now, though. This storm looks like it's going to be a big one."

"I don't know how it snuck up on me. I'm usually on top of the weather."

"In your line of work, I'll bet. I'm guessing you don't have any weddings coming up?" He hesitated. "Or is all this stuff for a wedding?"

"No. Believe it or not, these are just supplies that my caterer friend needs to cook for the next couple of days. We were all supposed to be leaving town, but now we're not. Luckily, my next wedding isn't until New Year's Eve." My stomach tightened. "I hope all this snow has melted by then."

"Don't worry. It's Washington. When does snow ever stick around?"

He had a point. We didn't get lots of snow, and what we did usually melted quickly. Of course, it had been almost a decade since the city had seen a blizzard like this. At least, according to Richard, who had lived here longer than I had. According to my best friend, it had taken almost two weeks for everything to melt the last time there was a blizzard.

I shook my head, as if banishing those thoughts. "I'm sure you're right." We reached the fourth floor and the door to my apartment, which was slightly ajar. "Since you're stuck here over the holidays, too, you're welcome to join us." I nodded to the boxes in his arms. "I'm pretty sure we have enough."

He shook his head. "That's nice of you, but you barely know me. I don't want to butt in on your Christmas plans."

I nudged open the door with my foot. The theme song to "A Charlie Brown Christmas" was playing from someone's phone while Hermès ran in circles around the couch and Richard unloaded bags in the kitchen. My husband was unpacking bottles of wine onto the dining table while Kate was already uncorking one. The tall bundled-up figure I'd thought was Darryl stood next to the door unwinding a long scarf.

"Why does this bag have hair spray in it?" Richard called out as he held an industrial-sized can over his head. "I did not order hair spray."

"That's mine," the bundled man said, removing the scarf completely to reveal himself to be Fern. "You don't expect me to ride out a blizzard with bad hair, do you, sweetie?"

"Sacre bleu," Richard muttered, sounding just as horrified in French as he did in English. "What are you doing here?"

"I had to close my salon." Fern hooked his scarf on the coat rack and patted his pristine dark ponytail. "And I knew I'd never get across town to my own apartment, so I came here."

Kate ran up and threw her arms around him. "Did you bring any other supplies?"

He tapped on his chin and gave her a wicked smile. "I might have emptied the salon's fridge of all the Veuve Clicquot."

Richard held up a champagne bottle with the signature yellow label. "There must be half a case in here."

Kate rubbed her hands together. "Now we're ready for the snow."

I turned to Alton. "See? You don't have to worry about intruding on my quiet Christmas because I won't be having one."

His eyes were wide. "I guess not."

Fern spun around and his gaze landed on Alton. He squeezed Kate's hand as he eyed the handsome bar owner. "Looks like Santa brought us an early present."

CHAPTER 5

"I can't believe you invited a complete stranger." Richard's voice was nearly a hiss as he peeked over the space between my kitchen and living room to where Alton sat on the couch rubbing Hermès's belly.

I stood next to my best friend, unpacking bags and trying to find space for the abundance of food in my galley kitchen. The enormous turkey took up so much room in the refrigerator that we'd had to adjust the shelves. For once, it paid off not to have a fully stocked kitchen.

A small saucepan filled with mulling spices was already bubbling on the stove top, sending spicy steam into the air. Richard had explained that this way it would at least smell like Christmas until he was able to cook something.

"It's Christmas," I said. "Besides, he's not a total stranger. He's a neighbor who was going to be alone."

"A neighbor you'd never spoken to before." Richard narrowed his eyes at the back of the man's head. "Although he seems to be making fast friends with my dog."

Even though Richard had always proclaimed his disdain for children and animals, he'd taken to his significant other's Yorkie with surprising enthusiasm, renaming him something more chic than his original name, and dressing him in designer doggie outfits to match his own clothes. Hermès, for his part, had taken to the makeover with great gusto, becoming every bit as fussy as Richard.

"I'm more surprised Kate isn't all over him," I said, watching my assistant chat with Fern across from the couch. "I really think she's changed."

Richard made a noise that told me he wasn't so convinced. "She might just be worn out. She has been dating at a competitive level for years. You can't keep that up without burning out."

I frowned at him. "I'm serious. I think this mystery guy of hers has changed her." I grabbed his arm. "Do you think she might marry him?"

Richard pressed his lips together briefly. "If she gets married before I do…"

"Wait, are you and P.J. serious?" I hadn't spent much time with Richard's significant other since the man traveled frequently for his State Department job, but I did know this was the longest relationship I'd been aware of my best friend having.

Richard turned his attention back to a bag of chestnuts. "Is there any chance you have a colander, darling?"

I scanned the closed cabinets, deciding not to press the question with Richard. For now. "There's always a chance."

He sighed. "I should get hardship pay for this."

Bending over, he dug around in one of the lower cabinets until he produced a metal colander.

"It smells great." My husband poked his head around the doorframe of the kitchen. "What are you cooking?"

"Cinnamon sticks," Richard said.

Reese raised an eyebrow. "Yum?"

Richard sighed. "It's to give a festive scent to the air." He put his hands on his hips and appraised all the ingredients on the counter. "I guess I should make a stew for tonight since Annabelle's turned your apartment into a soup kitchen. If only I had the ingredients to make a bouillabaisse, it would fit with our theme."

My husband grinned, dropping his voice. "I take it this is about Alton?"

"You know Richard doesn't adapt well to new things. He barely adjusted to you."

Richard gave me a scandalized look. "Bite your tongue. I was always fond of the detective."

Now it was my turn to give him a shocked look. "What? You practically pouted for months when we started dating."

Richard twitched his shoulders. "I don't remember that."

To his credit, Richard had come around to the detective—and then some. Once he'd realized that Reese wasn't going anywhere and he'd have to learn to share me, he'd decided to co-opt him for himself. To his credit, my husband had taken to having a brand-new self-appointed best buddy with complete grace.

"My point is that new things aren't always bad," I said. "This Alton guy helped us carry up all the boxes, and he seems perfectly nice."

Richard cast another quick glance at the brown-haired man. "He's a bar owner. And he has tattoos."

"What's wrong with tattoos?" I crossed my hands over my chest. "They're pretty mainstream now. Everyone has them."

"Mmhmm." Richard dumped the bag of chestnuts into the colander and set it in the sink. He plucked a wooden spoon from a drawer and waved it at me. "Don't think I've forgotten your little dalliance with that tattooed fellow, Annabelle."

My cheeks warmed, and I narrowed my eyes at him. "It wasn't a dalliance. I went out with that guy a few times."

"I'm assuming this was before me?" my husband asked, the amusement clear in his voice.

"Don't worry, Detective," Richard said with a wave of his spoon. "There was only minimal overlap."

"Minimal?" My husband's eyebrows shot up. "Overlap?"

I stepped closer to Richard and dropped my voice to a deadly whisper. "How do you say 'I'm going to kill you' in French?"

Richard's gaze went from me to my husband and his face reddened. "I didn't mean that, Annabelle, I mean, you know she would never actually...When I said overlap, I didn't mean she was dating you both at once. She could barely date one person at a time, much less two." He looked back at me. "You weren't, were you, darling?"

"No," I said, tapping one foot on the floor. "I was not." I swiveled my face to my husband. "*You* hadn't asked me out yet."

"You did take your sweet time, Detective." Richard put a hand to his forehead. "But it's all such a blur. It was so long ago. I'm feeling hot. Is it hot in here?"

I gestured to the steam billowing up from the stove. "You're standing over the mulling spices."

"Oh." He stepped back and fanned himself with the hand not holding the spoon. "I was wondering why my sudden dizzy spell was accompanied by the scent of cloves."

My husband closed the distance between us, wrapping his arms around me from behind. He leaned down and kissed my neck. "Well, I'm glad I finally asked you out. Apparently, I had competition."

"Not really," Richard said. "I never would have let Annabelle carry on with someone who wore leather pants and..." His words drifted off when he caught sight of my face. He took his fingers and pretended to lock up his lips. "Never mind. Don't mind me. I'm going to busy myself with our dinner for tonight."

"Good idea," I said as Reese walked me back toward the doorway. "Don't forget Leatrice and Sidney Allen will probably come back up and join us."

Richard let out a tortured sigh. "I don't know where we're all going to sit."

As my husband and I made our way back out to the living room, I realized that Richard had a point. Our dining table wouldn't seat everyone, especially now that I'd invited our neighbor. Then, again, I didn't mind people sitting around with bowls on their laps. It was how Reese and I ate most of our meals, though I would never admit as much to Richard, who believed eating takeout on the couch should be classified as a misdemeanor at the very least.

"Try this, Annabelle." Kate thrust a glass in my hand.

I eyed the red contents. "What is it?"

She jerked a thumb behind her to where Fern stood at the dining table with an impressive array of liquor bottles in front of him. "We're coming up with a signature cocktail."

"For…?"

She threw her arms wide. "For the blizzard, of course. We haven't settled on a name yet, but we think this is an event that deserves a custom cocktail."

Since almost all of our weddings had a signature cocktail—and couples christened them everything from their dog's name to an odd mash-up of their own first names—it wasn't crazy for Kate to make a custom drink for the blizzard.

"I suggested the Blizzitini," Fern called. "But Kate wants the Snow Gin Fizz."

I swirled the contents of the glass. "Should I ask what's in it?"

"Not before you try it," Kate said. "But don't worry; I kept it simple and clean."

I knew that was code for a ton of alcohol and a splash of mixer. "You should probably let the expert taste it first."

"Fern already tried it," Kate said, tilting her head at me.

"Not Fern, our resident bar owner." I nodded to Alton on the couch, who was still playing with a delighted Hermès.

He looked up. "Did someone say bar?"

Fern clapped his hands together. "Why didn't I think of that? We have an in-house mixologist."

"Why not?" Kate didn't look so convinced. "Fern and I are trying to come up with a custom cocktail. Something to embody the blizzard."

"It's a wedding thing," I said, when I saw the confused look on his face.

"I'm actually not a mixologist, and the Salty Dog serves a lot of beer and whiskey, but I'm always happy to taste something."

I gladly handed him the glass, curious that Kate was watching him with a look she usually saved for bossy bridesmaids. Not only was she *not* flirting, she seemed to be going out of her way to appear uninterested in the good-looking guy.

Before he could take a swig, the door flew open and Leatrice ran in, her hands pressed to her cheeks. "Come on! You have to hurry!"

My husband stiffened behind me. "What's wrong?"

Leatrice heaved in a shaky breath, a small sob escaping from her throat. "I think he's dead!"

CHAPTER 6

"She's finally killed him," Richard said from the kitchen, his jaw hanging open.

It was no secret that Richard wasn't fond of Sidney Allen. I always suspected that it was the diva principle—you couldn't have two overly dramatic bosses in the same place for too long. And both Sidney Allen and Richard liked to be in charge. Hence, they weren't crazy about each other.

"What?" Leatrice shook her head, then beckoned us with one arm. "I didn't kill anyone, but you need to hurry."

My husband hurried after her as she disappeared from the doorway, and I followed right behind him. I paused and looked back at Kate. "Maybe you should keep everyone else entertained here." When she opened her mouth to protest, I darted my gaze to Richard then Fern. "If he really is dead, I'm guessing Reese won't want added drama at the scene."

She nodded. "You got it."

Leatrice and Reese were already a flight ahead of me, and I had to run down the stairs to catch up. When I reached the second floor, I almost smacked into my husband's broad back.

"Why did we stop?" I asked.

He was staring through the open door to apartment 2B. Small puddles of water pooled around the door where snow had obviously melted. "This is where Leatrice went."

"Why would Sidney Allen be in here? They live on the first floor."

My husband's face was grave. "I don't think Leatrice is talking about Sidney Allen."

He walked through the open door. I stood in the hallway for an extra beat before following him. I'd never been inside another apartment in my building, aside from the one Leatrice lived in with her Honeybun, but I did know that because it was an older building, each floor plan was different.

Instead of opening into one large living room like mine did, this apartment featured a short hallway that passed a galley kitchen off to one side and then spilled out into a large living-dining combination. An open pizza box lay on the counter between the kitchen and living room, the scent of pepperoni filling the room. The warm glow of a shaded floor lamp illuminated part of the large room, but the heavy, closed drapes made it feel dark. The deep autumnal colors of the furniture didn't help either.

It wasn't the burgundy-and-mustard-yellow plaid couch that drew my attention, however. It was Mr. Kopchek slumped across it that made me stop short and put a hand on the wall to steady myself. A TV tray sat to one side of the couch with a half-eaten slice of pizza and a mug with some sort of corporate insignia on it.

Leatrice stood next to the man, wringing her hands. "I checked under his nose first, and when I didn't feel any breath, I tried for a pulse."

Reese moved deliberately to the man, touching a single finger to the side of his neck and holding it for a few seconds. I didn't need him to shake his head to know that the man was dead. Although his skin wasn't pale or tinged blue like most dead bodies I'd seen, no one slept with their neck at a painfully awkward angle like that.

"You okay, babe?"

I realized that my husband was talking to me. I tore my gaze from the dead body and nodded mutely. Even though I'd seen more than my fair share of dead bodies, the sight never failed to startle me and make me feel a bit queasy. And the rich scent of pizza wasn't helping me fight the urge to puke.

"Did you touch anything?" my husband asked Leatrice when he pulled his hand back.

"Touch? What?" She hadn't wrenched her eyes away from the old man. "I don't think so. I mean, maybe. I don't remember."

Reese let out a breath, his gaze scanning the room. "Why were you in his apartment anyway?"

She glanced up at him, blinking rapidly. "I was coming back up to your place, actually. My Sugar Muffin and I had a long chat. He didn't feel like being around people yet, but I thought I'd check in and see what you kids were up to." She drew a shaky breath. "Mr. Kopchek's door was open, so I knocked."

"The door was standing open?" Reese asked.

Leatrice glanced down. "It might not have been standing open, but it wasn't closed all the way, which I thought was strange."

I saw my husband frown slightly. "So, you knocked. Then what?"

"Then I called his name a few times and told him his door was open." She chanced a look at him again, and her cheeks lost another shade of color. "When I finally walked inside, I saw him just like this. I thought maybe he was sleeping, but then I got closer."

Reese put his hands on his hips. "I don't see any obvious signs of foul play, but you did say his door was open, right?"

Leatrice nodded. "I thought maybe my Honeybun hadn't closed it well when he'd left."

Reese snapped his head to her. "Sidney Allen was here before you?"

Leatrice nodded. "He was coming down to apologize, remember?"

"And did he?" my husband asked.

"He said he did." Leatrice worked her hands together, her painted-on eyebrows pressed together in obvious distress. "You aren't suggesting that my Cupcake had anything to do with this, are you?"

"Isn't this a heart attack or something?" I asked, finally letting myself look at the body again. "It looks like he keeled over."

"Maybe." Reese walked around the room without touching

anything. "Even if that's the case, Sidney Allen might have been the last person to see Mr. Kopchek alive."

"This is awful," Leatrice murmured to herself. "First my Honeybun gets in a fight because he's defending my honor, and now the man he argued with is dead."

"What are you going to do?" I asked Reese.

"I have to call it in, but I don't know when an ME will be able to get to us." He rubbed a hand across his forehead. "For now, we need to keep the scene secured until I'm sure it was a natural death. I also need to talk to Sidney Allen."

Leatrice bobbed her head up and down. "We can lock the door. I saw a key hanging by the kitchen."

"Don't touch anything," Reese warned as Leatrice hurried toward the door.

I followed quietly as my husband pulled a pen out of his blazer pocket and used it to hook the key off the wall. We all stepped outside into the hall and let the door close behind us.

"I should go tell my Sugar Pie." Leatrice peered over the stair railing toward the first floor.

"Not yet," Reese told her. "Let's go back upstairs, so I can call this in. Then we'll go talk to Sidney Allen together."

Leatrice didn't look thrilled with this, but she didn't argue. When we reached our apartment, Reese held the door open for us. I was pleased to breathe in the comforting scent of mulling spices. Anything beat the smell of pepperoni and death.

"Well?" Kate jumped up from an overstuffed chair when we walked in. "Is he okay?"

My husband slid the key onto a shelf on the bookcase by the door. "Not exactly."

Kate looked stricken as she stared at Leatrice. "You're not saying that he's …?"

Leatrice nodded. "Dead."

Fern sucked in a breath then rushed over to Leatrice and threw his arms around her. "This is too cruel."

"Sidney Allen isn't dead," I said, watching Leatrice struggle in

Fern's smothering hug. "Mr. Kopchek is."

Alton tilted his head at me, taking a momentary break from rubbing a nearly catatonic Hermès's belly. "Mr. Kopchek?"

"Not Sidney Allen?" Fern released Leatrice, and she stumbled toward the couch, patting her disheveled hair.

"The guy we were talking about earlier?" Kate dropped her voice as she sidled closer to me. "The old man Leatrice was stalking?"

Richard came out of the kitchen wearing a Santa apron. "Wait, who's dead?"

"Mr. Kopchek," we all said at once, and Richard jumped.

"He's dead?" Sidney Allen stood in the doorway, his face ashen. "That's impossible. I just left him in his apartment."

Reese crossed to Leatrice's husband and put a hand on his shoulder. "I need to talk to you about that conversation."

"I'm telling you, my Honeybun would never kill anyone," Leatrice said. "Even for me. He might look like a tough alpha type, but he wouldn't hurt anyone."

Kate gave me a look that told me she'd never exactly considered Sidney Allen an alpha, but neither of us said anything.

Sidney Allen's eyes widened, and he swiped at his upper lip. "You can't think I had anything to do with someone's death."

"You did threaten him," Richard muttered loud enough for us all to hear.

Leatrice sank down onto the sofa and dabbed at her nose. "This is all my fault. If only I'd gotten better disguises, he never would have made me."

"Not the takeaway I was expecting," Kate said.

"I'm not accusing you of anything." Reese used his most patient tone of voice. "But I do need to establish a time line of everyone who entered Mr. Kopchek's apartment or interacted with him."

"Just because an old man died?" Alton asked. "He probably had a heart attack. He looked like he was at least seventy."

Leatrice stifled a cry, and Hermès jumped into her lap, his tail wagging.

"I don't think he had a heart attack," my husband admitted with a heavy breath. "I suspect he was murdered."

Sidney Allen slapped a hand over his mouth moments before his eyes rolled up into the back of his head, and he slumped to the floor.

"Goodness." Richard eyed the entertainment diva sprawled on the floor as Leatrice and Hermès both ran to his side. "That was a bit dramatic, n'est-ce pas?"

CHAPTER 7

"It's a good thing I'm cooking something that can hold," Richard grumbled when I joined him in the kitchen.

The stockpot on the stove was uncovered, and the savory smell of stew mixed with the sweetness of the bubbling mulling spices. My stomach growled, reminding me that it had been a while since lunch. "You do know there's been a possible murder in the building, right?"

Richard flicked his gaze to mine. "At this point, what are the chances you wouldn't stumble over a dead body? I've learned not to be shocked by murder at the most inopportune times."

I hated to admit that he had a point. Dead bodies did have a way of popping up when we least needed them.

"At least Sidney Allen isn't hurt." I peeked over the divider into the living room to where the entertainment coordinator was stretched out across the length of the yellow twill couch. Leatrice knelt next to him holding a cold compress to his forehead.

"Of course, he's not hurt. He had plenty of padding to catch his fall." He touched a hand to his flat stomach encased in a Santa apron. "Unlike some of us, who would bruise like a peach."

"Be nice." I gave Richard a stern look, or at least my best attempt at one. "He's had a big shock."

Richard shrugged. "Maybe."

"What does that mean?"

Richard leveled his wooden spoon at me and lowered his voice, casting a furtive glance toward the living room. "Has it ever occurred to you, darling, that Sidney Allen may, in fact, be a diabolical killer?"

I stared at him. "Sidney Allen? The man who gives his performers code names and falls to pieces if the vendor meals aren't up to his standards?"

"Exactly. He's so high-strung that it makes total sense he would lose his temper and kill someone in a fit of rage."

I shook my head. "There's a difference between being a drama queen and being a murderer."

Richard put one hand on his hip. "Is there?"

Hermès chose that moment to scamper into the room in his designer dog sweater, circle Richard's feet a few times, and run back out.

"For your sake, you'd better hope so," I muttered.

Richard spun back to face the stove. "I heard that, Annabelle. If you're comparing me to Sidney Allen, you can bite your tongue. I am *nothing* like him."

I opened one of the cabinets and found a glass, pressing it to the automatic water dispenser in the door of the refrigerator. "I actually came in here to get some water for him, and to ask you to hold dinner until after Reese has finished his questioning."

"At least someone is treating him like the suspect he is," Richard said, with another flourish of his spoon. "We really are lucky you nabbed a police detective considering your talent for attracting crime."

I sighed as I walked back out to the living room, handing the water to Leatrice. Sidney Allen was propped up on a pile of cushions, his face still pale but his eyes open. Kate sat in one of the chairs across from the couch, while Fern was chatting with Alton by the windows. Even from a distance, I could see that the snow fell in sheets outside.

My husband sat on the coffee table, his elbows on his knees as he leaned forward. "Why don't you tell me what happened? From the beginning."

Sidney Allen nodded, taking a small sip of the water Leatrice held to his lips. "Like I said earlier, I was just getting home from a stressful afternoon. The hotel called to cancel the event, but my performers were already on-site, which meant I still needed to pay them. Plus, with the snow coming down so hard, some of them couldn't leave, so I had an entire flock of sugarplum fairies camped out in the lobby."

Leatrice dabbed at his forehead with the cold cloth. "You poor dear."

"I didn't know a group of fairies was called a flock," Kate said. "You learn something new every day."

"So, you were upset when you came into the building," Reese prodded.

"Very." Sidney Allen shifted on the pillows. "All I wanted to do was collapse on the couch and put my feet up."

"Mission accomplished," Richard said from the kitchen, gaining him a swift glare from me.

Sidney Allen either hadn't heard Richard, or more likely, chose to pretend he hadn't heard him. "I hadn't even reached my apartment door when Mr. Kopchek came stomping down the stairs."

"So, he was inside the building?" my husband asked. "He wasn't just coming inside like you?"

Sidney Allen frowned for a moment, as if in thought. "No, he was definitely inside. He wasn't wearing a coat, and he walked down from the second floor."

Leatrice put a hand to her mouth. "He must have been waiting for you."

"What happened next?" my husband asked.

"He was pretty upset—ranting and raving about Leatrice being a menace to the building." Sidney Allen's cheeks flushed. "He said some awful things."

"That must have made you angry," Reese said.

"Naturally." Sidney Allen sat up straighter on the mound of cushions. "I tried to defend my Honeybun, but he wouldn't stop saying he was going to press charges and have her arrested."

Leatrice's face was grim, and her gaze dropped to the floor.

"Was that when you threatened him?" Reese's voice was calm and soothing, reminding me that he was practiced at getting information from suspects, and that Sidney Allen was still a suspect.

The man bobbed his head up and down. "But I didn't mean it. I was just tired and angry, and he wouldn't stop threatening my wife."

"Understandable," Reese said. "How did he react when you threatened him?"

Sidney Allen's face was mottled with patches of pink as he drew in a breath. "He said something about not being afraid of either of us."

Leatrice's head snapped up. "Why would he be afraid of me?"

"Because you stalked him?" Kate said from behind her hand as she pretended to cough.

Reese didn't turn, although I saw the corner of his mouth quiver. "Did he say anything else?"

Sidney Allen rubbed a hand across his forehead. "Not then. He stomped up to his apartment, and I came to find Leatrice after realizing she wasn't in our place."

"But when you left here, you went to apologize to Mr. Kopchek?"

"I had to," Sidney Allen said. "I'd been in the wrong."

My husband rested his chin on his entwined hands. "How did that go?"

"I knocked on his door, and he opened it. I apologized for my actions and also told him that my wife was sorry for bothering him." Sidney Allen shot a look at Leatrice. "I promised him that she would stop."

"How did he respond?" Reese asked.

"Better than I expected, but he was in the middle of eating, so maybe he was eager to be rid of me. He did seem distracted and less energetic than earlier."

My husband leaned forward. "How so?"

Sidney Allen shrugged. "He kept coughing for one. He said a bite of pizza must have gone down the wrong way, so I let him go so he could get some water."

"And that was it?" Reese leaned back, resting his hands on his knees.

"That was it. I continued down to our apartment, where I stayed until I came back up here and heard you all talking about Mr. Kopchek dying."

"Did he close the door after you?"

"I don't remember. I'm pretty sure I walked away before then, so I can't be sure if it was shut all the way or not."

Reese put a hand on Sidney Allen's shoulder as he stood. "Thanks for talking to me. This has been helpful."

I followed my husband as he walked from the living room and ducked into the kitchen. "Was it helpful?"

He nodded. "I don't think Sidney Allen killed the man if that's what you're asking."

"Don't go rushing to conclusions, Detective," Richard said, the disappointment clear on his face.

"Why not?" I asked, then held up a hand before Richard could interject. "*Not* that I think Sidney Allen is guilty."

"The way Sidney Allen described the man when he answered the door makes me think there's a solid chance he'd already ingested poison. Not to mention the fact that his skin was slightly yellow when we found the body. Of course, I'll need a tox screening to be sure."

"Poison?" Richard put a hand to his throat. "Do not say that word."

My best friend did not have a great track record with poison cases. He usually ended up being a suspect, and a caterer being suspected of poisoning was never good for business.

"It could also have been an allergic reaction, but I didn't notice a rash," Reese said. "Unless Sidney Allen is lying and had more contact with the victim than he claims, I don't see how he could have poisoned him or introduced a deadly allergen."

I grabbed my husband's arm. "The pizza! Mr. Kopchek ordered a pizza. I saw the delivery guy on his way out. He was complaining that the old man never tipped. Sidney Allen said he was eating when he knocked on his door, and we saw the open pizza box on his kitchen counter. Could the poison have been in the pizza?"

Richard inhaled sharply. "I've heard of delivery guys being upset about bad tippers, but murder seems a bit extreme, don't you think?"

"Agreed," my husband said, making Richard puff out his chest. "Unless the pizza guy had another motive, it's a stretch to think he poisoned the man. Not that the pizza wasn't poisoned, but I would guess it was done by someone who really wanted Mr. Kopchek dead."

"Who would want to kill a little old man who lives alone?" I asked.

"That's what we have to find out," my husband said, his eyes glinting with determination. "No one kills a man in my apartment building at Christmas and gets away with it."

"I like your spirit," Richard said.

I put my hands on my hips. "When I say things like that, I'm meddling and causing trouble."

Richard picked up a pot holder and fanned himself with it, smiling at my tall, dark, and handsome husband. "When your husband says it, it has a certain je ne sais quoi, darling."

I groaned. Richard's French was not helping.

CHAPTER 8

"Do you think we should be eating at a time like this?" Kate whispered to me as I handed her a bowl of stew.

I looked over the divider into the living room. Reese had gone back into my office to talk to someone at the police station, but everyone else was still gathered in the living room. Aside from Sidney Allen, who had insisted on going back down to his apartment to lie down. He'd insisted on going alone, much to Leatrice's dismay, and she sat on the couch looking distraught.

"What's the alternative?" I asked. "Everyone is starving."

She shivered. "I know, but if the man died of poisoning. . ." She glanced down at the meaty stew.

"How do you know that?" I asked. I thought only Richard and I knew what Reese suspected about the crime.

"I guessed after Richard made a point of saying that his stew was perfectly safe to eat."

I rolled my eyes. Just great. "Do you think anyone else figured it out?"

"Anyone who knows Richard."

I glanced back at the group. So almost everyone, except for the cute bar owner who was sitting on one of the armchairs with his legs crossed casually as he tapped away on his phone.

"So," I said, my gaze fixing on my assistant, "what do you think of Alton?"

Kate shrugged without looking at him. "Not my type."

"I thought breathing was your type," Richard said as he came back into the kitchen after delivering bowls.

She made a face at him. "Hilarious." She looked pointedly at her stew. "I sure hope this is safe to eat."

Richard's pupils flared. "Are you implying—"

"She's just teasing you," I said, cutting him off, "but you pretty much told everyone that the old man might have been poisoned."

Richard squared his shoulders. "I did no such thing. I merely reassured people that it was safe to eat my food."

"Why would anyone think it wasn't?" I asked.

"He *has* been accused of poisoning more than once," Kate said in a stage whisper.

"You know I was set up!" Richard's voice rose to a near shriek.

I held up my hands. "Why don't we take it down a notch? We're stuck here together until the snow lets up, and there's already been one murder."

"It's the holidays from hell," Richard murmured. "I don't know how I'm going to pull off a chateau theme with all this chaos."

There was a knock on the door, and Kate and Richard both swung their heads to me.

"Are you expecting anyone else?" Richard asked. "If you invited more random guests…"

"I didn't," I said. "I can't imagine who would be here who isn't already."

Kate stirred her stew slowly as steam billowed up. "All of our friends just walk into your apartment."

Before I could answer the door, Fern had crossed the room and flung it open. It took me a moment to place the couple standing in the doorway.

"Hey Mindy," I called as I hurried out of the kitchen. "Did you guys get your heating cranked up again?"

The couple looked a bit startled to see so many people crowded into my living room.

"We did," Kurt said finally, giving me a weak grin as I waved them inside.

Mindy followed him, but her foot caught on one of the bags still gathered near the door and she pitched forward, Kurt catching her elbow at the last minute.

I shoved a duffel bag closer to the wall. "I'm so sorry about that. We haven't taken our bags back yet."

"We haven't unpacked either," Kurt said. "Wishful thinking that we'll be able to reschedule our flight I guess."

"So, you live in the building?" Fern asked.

They both nodded, and he sagged visibly, pressing a hand to his heart.

"I thought they were one of your wedding couples, sweetie," he whispered to me. "I was very worried for you."

Mindy laughed. "I wish we could use Annabelle, but we're getting married at Kurt's family's house in Newport."

Fern's eyebrows lifted, and he appraised Mindy's hair. "Well, if you need a hairstylist, sweetie, I do travel."

She laughed as he sauntered away. "Doesn't he have a salon nearby?"

"Yes, but his passion is weddings." I decided not to mention that he often dressed to match the bridesmaids and had a penchant for doing extravagant bridal hair. "But you didn't come up here looking for a hairstylist. What can I do for you two?"

"We hate to impose," Mindy said, "but do you happen to have any cream?"

Kurt put an arm around Mindy's shoulders. "Since we're snowed in, Mindy is trying to pull together some sort of dinner."

"I've got all the ingredients for my mother's pumpkin chiffon pie except for heavy cream."

I turned to ask Richard, but he was already heading for us with a small paper carton in his hand.

"If you're anything like me," he said, with a wink, "you go through enough cream at the holidays to float a boat."

I would have been surprised by Richard's warm reception of the couple, but Mindy did have a choker of pearls around her neck and wore what appeared to be a pink cashmere sweater. The combination was kryptonite to Richard's snark.

Mindy let out a sigh and beamed at him. "This will be a pared-down Christmas, but I wanted to at least have my mother's traditional pie. Thank you so much."

Richard winked at her. "You can thank me by sharing that pie recipe."

Mindy laughed again, apparently not knowing how serious Richard was.

I nudged Richard as he stared pointedly at her then turned back to the couple. "We're having a casual dinner. Why don't you join us?"

"We couldn't," Mindy said. "We wouldn't want to impose on you and your friends."

"It isn't just friends," Richard said. "One of your other neighbors is here."

Mindy and Kurt glanced at Alton, and Kurt waved in greeting. "That's the guy who owns the bar by the water, right?"

"The Salty Dog," Richard said, his nose wrinkling, either in displeasure at the name or the bar itself.

"We've never been," Mindy said, sharing an expression similar to Richard's. "I don't even think I've noticed him in the building."

"He comes in late," I said. "Bar hours."

"We're nine-to-five people," Kurt said. "Not too many late nights anymore."

"I do know *her*." Mindy's gaze landed on Leatrice. "She used to follow me. Doesn't she have a little dog?"

"That's my dog." Richard frowned. "She only babysits."

"And she's harmless," I said. "You sure you don't want to join us?"

Kurt hesitated. "It does smell good."

Richard smiled. "Of course, it does. It's beef bourguignon, or I should say, bœuf bourguignon."

Mindy put a hand on Kurt's arm. "Why don't you start eating, and I'll run this cream down and get the pie in the oven. Then we can all have pie for dessert."

Richard clapped his hands together. "Wonderful. I can try to guess all the ingredients, and you can tell me how close I am."

"Okay," Mindy said, looking a bit confused.

"It's a game he likes to play with new dishes," I told her.

"I'll be right back," she said, slipping out of the door as Richard pulled Kurt toward the kitchen.

"What happened to there being too many people to feed?" Kate asked as she walked up to me, passing Richard and Kurt.

"The guy told him it smelled great," I said. "You know Richard is a softie with anyone who compliments his food."

Kate took a bite of her stew and moaned softly. "It is pretty delicious."

I glanced around the room, realizing that everyone was eating, and I'd left my bowl in the kitchen. I headed back but stopped in the hallway when I saw my husband emerge from my office. Even though the savory scent beckoned me, I walked past the kitchen and met him in the middle of the hall.

"Were you able to reach anyone at the police station?" I asked.

"Hobbes was still at District Two, but he doesn't know how fast the medical examiner will be able to get here." He laced his fingers with mine and walked with me toward the kitchen.

"Like you thought," I said, then I realized something that made me cringe. "You don't think the body will start smelling before they can get it out, do you?"

"In this weather and with the dodgy heaters in this building? Not a chance."

I let out a breath. It was one thing to know that there was a dead body a couple of floors down. It was quite another thing to smell it.

"Body?" Kurt asked, his spoon frozen halfway to his lips as he stepped out of the kitchen.

I'd forgotten that we hadn't mentioned the death of Mr. Kopchek to the couple. "Sorry we forgot to tell you. Your neighbor Mr. Kopchek died earlier."

"Died? The old man who lives on our floor?"

"Unfortunately. Did you know him well?"

Kurt shook his head slowly. "Not at all. We didn't even see him much."

"Didn't he complain about your bike being in the hall?" I asked.

He rolled his eyes. "I didn't take that too seriously. Besides, it's not like the bike is blocking anything since it's tucked away on the ground floor. I think he was a lonely old guy who liked to complain."

That sounded about right.

"Did you see him at all today?" my husband asked. His tone was light, but I knew he was asking because he was gathering evidence and information.

Kurt frowned as he thought. "No." He pointed his spoon at me. "You saw us running back in from our failed attempt at getting to the airport. We went straight to our apartment and then came up here to borrow the cream." He shifted his gaze to my husband. "So, what happens to the old guy now?"

"Even in a blizzard, bodies need to be processed and removed."

"Hear, hear," Richard muttered.

Reese managed a grin. "My partner is on his way, but who knows how long that will take."

"I thought Hobbes was traveling for the holidays," I said, remembering that Hobbes was supposed to visit our friend and cake designer Alexandra in Scotland. The oddly matched couple had been dating for a while and managed to make a long distance relationship work. Part of me suspected that Hobbes wasn't the only man that the exotic cake designer was dating, but that might have been my reluctance to believe someone as glamorous as she would date a slightly doughy guy with a comb-over.

My husband slipped an arm around my waist. "I don't think anyone is traveling from D.C. anymore."

"Or around it," I added.

"We made it!"

The booming voice from the front door made us both turn as our friends Buster and Mack staggered inside.

"I can't believe they're here," I said. Their floral shop was several blocks away, including a steep hill, and I knew they hadn't ridden their Harleys through the blizzard. Since traffic was at a standstill and the roads virtually impassable, that meant they'd walked.

Reese gaped at the burly men in their usual head-to-toe black as they stomped their motorcycle boots on the floor. "I can't believe they're still wearing leather."

CHAPTER 9

I helped Mack out of his cold, stiff motorcycle jacket, ignoring the melted snow dripping off him and onto my hardwood floors. "You're lucky you're not frozen."

Tiny ice crystals still dotted his dark red goatee, and he rubbed his thick arms briskly. "It wasn't so bad. No one else is out on the sidewalks."

"You're lucky you could find the sidewalks," my husband said.

Buster gave a low laugh as he adjusted the motorcycle goggles that sat on top of his bald head, and water dripped down his face. "We did lose them a time or two."

"Tell me again why you trudged through a blizzard to get here?" Richard asked, thrusting two bowls of stew at them. "For all you know, we could have already left for the holidays."

Mack lowered his nose to the bowl and inhaled deeply. "Kate texted us to say you were all stuck."

"Then Prue called us to say she was stuck at her friend's house with Merry and they were staying over there." Buster lumbered over to the couch and sat down, his leather making a painful groaning sound.

"We decided to join you all instead of staying at the flower shop,"

Mack said. "Despite all our holiday decor, it's not very cheery with just the two of us."

Kate threw her arms open wide. "The more the merrier."

"Says someone not involved in the meal planning," Richard said, pivoting on his heel and heading back to the kitchen.

"Ignore him," Kate whispered. "He's just in a mood because of the poisoning."

Reese shook his head but didn't say anything. It was impossible to unring that bell.

Both men paused with their spoons in midair. "Poisoning?"

"Not here," I told them. "Well, not *here* here. One of our neighbors died, and Reese suspects foul play."

"We're still waiting for a ME to make an official assessment," my husband said, glancing down at his phone.

Mack's spoon fell from his hand and splattered droplets of stew into his face. "Did this neighbor eat stew?"

"No, pizza," Leatrice said. "It's too bad he died, and we didn't get the chance to invite him to join us. I'll bet he would have appreciated a home-cooked meal. Especially after the run-in he had with my Cupcake."

Buster gaped at her. "It sounds like we missed a lot."

"You know a Wedding Belles event," Fern said, smoothing his hair with one hand.

"Hey!" Kate and I both said in protest.

Kurt stood as Richard reappeared with a basket of crusty bread slices. "Thanks so much for the stew, but I should probably check on Mindy. I'm sure she got caught up in baking."

"You can't rush a good piecrust," Richard said, putting the basket on the coffee table.

"I should go, too." Alton stood. "I need to make sure my tropical fish aren't too cold. Thanks for the dinner and the company."

"Tropical fish." Fern drummed his fingers across his jaw. "How fascinating."

The bar owner shrugged. "It's mostly a lot of upkeep, especially for the exotic species."

Both men thanked us again and left.

"You never do know about people, do you?" Fern asked, once the door had closed behind them. "Who would have thought a bar owner with tattoos would be into fish?"

"It's nice to get to know our neighbors more," Leatrice said, picking a piece of bread from the basket. "Naturally, I know their basic comings and goings, but I've never chatted with most of them before."

Kate caught my eye, and I knew we were both jealous of the neighbors who weren't subjected to Leatrice's often intense attentions.

"Speaking of our neighbors," my husband said, pulling over one of the dining room chairs to sit in. "What else do we know about the guy who owns the bar and the couple?"

"Not much." I eyed the quickly dwindling bread basket as Buster and Mack both popped pieces into their mouths. "Kate and I have seen Alton a few times when we're coming home late from weddings and he's rolling in from the bar."

Reese focused on Kate. "You're a good judge of character, especially with men. What do you think of the guy?"

Kate looked surprised. "Me?" She shrugged. "I guess I don't have much of an opinion. He seems nice enough."

Fern tilted his head at her. "Nice enough? Are you feeling well, sweetie?"

My assistant's cheeks flushed pink. "I don't notice everything about *all* men. The only thing I can tell you is that he isn't looking to date anyone, either."

"Since when are you not looking to date?" Richard asked.

"I'm telling you," Kate said, standing quickly. "He's not my type."

I knew for a fact that Kate had a soft spot for good-looking guys with tattoos, especially if they had a bit of a bad-boy vibe, like Alton did.

"Okay." My husband looked a bit taken aback as Kate stomped off down the hall.

"Blizzards are very stressful," Leatrice said. "I'm sure she'll feel better soon."

"Tensions do seem to be running high. We've already had a virtual brawl and a murder." Fern sighed. "I wish I'd brought my calming pheromones."

"Pheromones?" Buster asked.

Fern nodded. "They're actually cat pheromones, but I find them very soothing."

Mack choked on his bite of bread, and Buster pounded on his back.

"Why don't I go check on Kate?" I stood and followed her down the hall. As I suspected, she was sitting in the black chair in my office and spinning around in it.

"So," I said, stepping into the room and trying to avoid trampling on the favors for our upcoming New Year's Eve wedding. "What was that all about?"

Kate stopped spinning. "Sometimes I get tired of everyone assuming I'm some crazed dater."

I didn't point out that, until very recently, she had been a crazed dater. "You know they didn't mean any harm. Reese is just trying to learn more about our neighbors because they're all potential suspects."

"I know. I guess I kind of forgot that for a second." She bit the corner of her thumbnail. "Do you think your husband's mad at me?"

"Mad at you?" I laughed. "Of course not. But he does think you have unique insight into men. Usually you can tell if someone's cheating on their wife at fifty paces."

She let out a breath. "It's easier to pick apart other people's relationships than manage your own."

"No kidding." I sat down on the floor cross-legged. "Just look at me. How many weddings have I planned for other people, but my own wedding plans stressed me out?"

She grinned. "You were a mess."

"I think 'mess' might be a bit harsh, but just because we plan weddings doesn't mean we have any special skills when it comes to relationships or marriage ourselves."

"You can say that again." She leaned back in the chair. "One thing I can tell you about that engaged couple is that he's way more into her than she's into him."

I could see that. Kurt wasn't exactly heartthrob material, although he seemed nice enough.

"If you ask me," Kate said, "and your husband did, she's marrying him for his fancy house in Newport and the money I assume he has. Not that I think that nugget of insight has anything to do with the murder."

"She wouldn't be the first bride we've known to marry for money instead of love."

"It's still sad," Kate said.

"Since when did you become such a romantic?" I eyed her. "Gold diggers never used to bother you."

"I guess I'd never been in love before."

I stared at her until she looked up and met my gaze. "You're kidding me. You're in love? Like really in love?"

She gave me a thin smile. "Really, truly, miserably in love."

"Miserably?" My heart caught in my chest. "Why miserably? Is he married? Terminally ill? Does he live in Outer Mongolia?"

She choked back a laugh. "None of those."

"Then what gives?" I threw my hands into the air. "Why won't you tell me who this guy is?"

"Because it's your husband's brother," she said, her voice soft. "I'm in love with Daniel."

CHAPTER 10

I didn't speak for a few moments. For as long as I'd known Kate, she'd never even flirted with the idea of love. Lust, sure, but love she'd seemed happy to look askance at and leave for others.

"I thought you just flirted with him like you flirt with everyone."

She ran a hand through her hair. "That's what it was at first—harmless flirting. But then he took me out a few times, and we talked a lot. He actually listened to me and wanted to know what I thought. You don't know because you barely dated before you met the detective, but men in D.C. mostly talk about themselves and their careers."

That sounded like a lot of the grooms we'd worked with, so no surprise there.

"How long have you been officially dating?" I asked.

"That's just the thing. This is different from my usual relationships. For one thing, there have been no sleepovers."

This took a minute to sink in. "So, you haven't…?"

She shook her head. "Nope. He wants to take things slow."

I thought about how long it had been since Kate had talked about some new guy. "That is slow, but I guess it's good, right? Better that than wham-bam-thank-you-ma'am."

"I wouldn't mind a little wham bam at this point."

"But you are dating him, right?" I leaned back with my palms on the floor behind me. "And you're more than friends?"

She gave me a withering look. "I haven't lost my mojo entirely, Annabelle. We go out a few times a week, and he always picks me up and pays. *And* he's a really good kisser."

"I don't know why you're complaining. Most women would kill for a nice guy who takes them out, pays, and doesn't expect anything in return."

"I know, I know." She swiped at her eyes. "It's great, but I don't know if I can keep doing it."

"Why not? I thought you were in love with the guy."

"That's just it," she said. "I want more."

I studied her red-rimmed eyes. "As in...?"

She waved a hand at me. "What you have. The perfect husband who adores you."

I didn't bother to tell her that no one was perfect, and that my husband was incapable of getting his dirty T-shirts into the hamper. I was too stunned by her revelation.

"You want to get married? I thought you had sworn off the institution."

She shrugged. "I guess Daniel changed my mind."

"You should tell him," I said. "It is Christmas after all."

"No way." She pressed her lips together. "First of all, I'm not going to do it over text or the phone. And what if I freak him out or scare him off? He's almost forty, and he's never been married. What if he never wants to get married?"

"Trouble with a client?" Leatrice's pink-and-white head poked around the doorframe.

Kate straightened in the chair. "Annabelle and I were going over some details for our New Year's Eve wedding."

Leatrice tilted her head. "I though you two swore off doing holiday weddings."

"We did," I said, "but this is the second daughter in a family of four daughters."

"And they have a huge budget," Kate added. "Sometimes size does matter."

"You girls!" A flush crawled up Leatrice's wrinkled neck, and she swatted a hand through the air. "I'll leave you to your work, but I thought you'd want to know that the police are here. More police, that is."

I jumped up from the floor. "Really? I didn't think they could get here because of the storm."

Leatrice shrugged. "Maybe they prioritize dead bodies."

"Or maybe they prioritize dead bodies in buildings where cops live," Kate said.

That sounded more like it. I was sure my husband had some pull in the department, and a potential murder where he lived would definitely get bumped up the list.

Kate and I followed Leatrice back down the hall to the living room, but only Richard and Fern sat on the couch with Hermès stretched out between them and Buster and Mack jammed into the chairs across from them.

"Where's everyone else?" I asked.

Fern twisted his head toward us. "Your hot husband is with his cop friends. Unfortunately for us, he's the only tasty one in the bunch. That's why we stayed here."

"That's not the only reason," Richard said. "For once, I am not a suspect and am not needed to give a statement. Except to say I was in this apartment all afternoon."

"Aside from loading in all the food," I reminded him.

He fluttered a hand at me. "Of course, aside from that. But I couldn't exactly stop on the second floor and kill a complete stranger with an armload of bags."

He had a point. Most of us had no motive and scant opportunity.

Mack cocked one pierced eyebrow. "I'm still not clear about what happened to your neighbor."

"It's a bit of a long story," Kate said as Leatrice drew in a long breath, obviously preparing to go into every detail of said story.

"But the long and short of it is that our second-floor neighbor Mr. Kopchek," I started to say.

"Who Leatrice suspected of being a spy," Kate added.

"Dropped dead after Sidney Allen got into a heated argument with him and threatened murder." I looked between Buster and Mack. "Any questions?"

"Yes," they both said.

Leatrice huffed out a breath. "Really, dear. You left out all the important details and the part about my Honeybun being completely innocent."

"And the part about me calling in the culinary cavalry so we wouldn't starve to death," Richard said.

Fern smoothed his pristine hair. "Or about my death-defying walk from my salon carrying survival essentials."

"Hair products are not considered survival essentials," Richard told him with a tortured sigh.

"Different blokes for different folks," Kate said.

Buster frowned. "Isn't it strokes, not blokes?"

Kate grinned. "You say it your way; I'll say it mine."

Fern tapped his chin and smiled at Kate. "I like your version better, too, sweetie."

"Mon dieu," Richard muttered.

"I knew we should have come over earlier," Mack muttered to Buster. "Look at what we missed."

I headed for the door. "While you all fill in the details I forgot, I'm going to see what's going on downstairs."

Leatrice hurried over to me. "I should come with you. I did find the body."

She was right about that. "Fine, but we need to stay out of the way and let the police do their jobs."

We left Richard and Fern arguing about the merits of beauty over food, closing the door behind us. Even from two floors away, deep voices drifted up to us. I recognized the sound of my husband and his partner, Hobbes, as well as the crackling of radios. Leatrice and I walked down the stairs without talking.

When we reached the second floor, a uniformed officer was standing in front of Mr. Kopchek's door unspooling yellow police tape. He glanced up at us and frowned. "This floor is off-limits, ladies."

"We're here to see Detective Reese," I said. "I'm his wife."

He nodded, his gaze sliding to Leatrice and widening as he took in her Christmas tree camo dress and slippers that looked like wrapped presents. "And her?"

"She's a witness," I said. "She found the body."

"Mike," the officer called into the apartment, "your wife's here."

I tried not to let out an irritated sigh. The way he'd said it made me sound like a meddling nuisance.

My husband appeared in the open doorway. He wore latex gloves and the intense expression he got when he worked cases. My heart fluttered a little at the sight of him in his element.

"Hey, babe. What's up?"

For a second, the question stumped me. Why were we there? I was so used to being involved in criminal cases, I'd almost forgotten I needed a reason to insert myself into a police investigation—a detail my husband had made a point of reminding me about often in the past.

"We thought you might need Leatrice to give an official statement," I said, regaining my confidence. "Since she found the body."

He seemed about to shoot me down, then he thought better of it. "Actually, I do want her to take a look at the crime scene and make sure it's like she remembered it when she first found the deceased." He waved us forward. "But put on booties and don't touch a thing."

Leatrice and I both put plastic booties over our shoes—they barely stretched over Leatrice's oversized slippers—and followed him inside the apartment again. The pungent smell of pepperoni had faded, and my nose twitched from the telltale scent of death. I put a hand over my mouth, the bitter tang of bile tickling the back of my throat.

We walked down the short entry hall, passing the kitchen where a photographer was taking pictures of the open pizza box. In the living room, a woman wearing the same gloves as my husband was now huddled beside the body, and Detective Hobbes stood next to her in a tan blazer that strained over his belly.

Leatrice swiveled her head around the room. "Aside from all the extra people, it looks the same."

I darted a glance at Mr. Kopchek, still slumped over. The pizza on his TV tray looked cold, the cheese congealed over the lip of the plate, and a lump formed in my throat at the sad, lonely sight.

My husband nodded. "Let's go back outside, and you can give me your official statement."

As we turned to go, I stopped, my heart beating faster. "Wait. Something's different." I scanned the room again as my brain tried to replay when I'd first seen the body. I pointed to the TV tray. "There was a mug next to that plate. Where's his mug?"

CHAPTER 11

"You're sure?" Detective Hobbes asked me as we stood gathered outside Mr. Kopchek's apartment.

My husband was inside the apartment, searching fruitlessly for the mug we both knew was gone. Even the ring of condensation on the TV tray belied its absence and proved that it had been removed in a hurry.

I wrapped my arms around myself. The halls in the building weren't heated, and the gusts of icy air from the arriving police officers and medical examiner had made the stairwell cold enough for me to see the puff of my breath. "Positive. It had some sort of corporate logo on it. I didn't look close enough to notice what it said, but it was one of those basic, white mugs with a logo printed on the side in blue."

Hobbes scribbled in his notebook. "Any clue what was in it?"

"I didn't notice."

"Neither did I," Leatrice added. "Actually, I didn't notice the mug at all. I was too distracted by poor Mr. Kopchek."

Hobbes nodded without looking up. "It might have been empty by the time you saw it."

"You think that's what killed him, don't you?" Leatrice spoke in a hush. "Someone poisoned his drink?"

Hobbes glanced up at us then looked right back down without answering. My husband came out of the apartment, shaking his head.

"No luck?" I asked, although I knew the mug hadn't hidden itself, and none of the officers were foolish enough to move something at a crime scene.

"Clearly, the scene of the crime wasn't as secure as I thought it was." His forehead was furrowed in deep creases.

"But you closed the door when we left," Leatrice said. "I saw you take the key and pull the door closed."

"And all these doors lock automatically when you shut them," I said, remembering that because of this quirk, I'd locked myself out of my apartment more than once. That is until I'd had to have the locks replaced and the locksmith had installed a door that didn't automatically lock—at Kate's request since she'd gotten tired of us getting locked out and having to tramp down to get Leatrice's spare key.

Leatrice snapped her fingers, bouncing on the toes of her slippers and making the bows on them bobble. "What if someone else in the building has a key? I have a copy of your key and you two have one of mine."

Reese flicked his gaze to me. Leatrice had a key to our apartment because she'd made one using her secret agent key impression kit.

"Did *you* have a copy of Mr. Kopchek's key?" I asked her.

She gave me a look of total innocence. "Why would I have a key, dear? We barely did more than exchange greetings."

I wanted to remind her that she had been following him, but I let it go for the moment. "Mr. Kopchek didn't seem like the type to exchange keys with neighbors."

"Agreed," my husband said, looking at the floor in front of the door. "And there's no mat to hide one under." His gaze went to the only other apartment on the second floor. "I guess if he wanted anyone to have a key, it would be the people right next door."

I followed his line of sight. I wasn't so sure about that. "Kurt said they barely knew the guy. Leatrice aside, this isn't a very social building."

"I'd still like to check with them." My husband took a few long steps to the closed wooden door and rapped on it a few times.

After a beat, the door swung open. Mindy stood in the doorway, her hair pulled up into a messy ponytail. Her pink cashmere sweater had been replaced with a long-sleeved T-shirt and the sleeves were pushed up. The scent of pumpkin wafted past her and into the hall. I guessed the pie baking was going well.

She looked at my husband then past him to the commotion in the hall. "You're the cop who lives upstairs, right?"

My husband held out his hand. "Detective Mike Reese."

"Kurt told me about Mr. Kopchek." She shook her head. "So sad."

"Kurt also told us you didn't know him very well," Reese said.

"That's right." She crossed her arms over her chest. "He wasn't what you'd call chatty. He didn't mind leaving notes, but he wasn't into pleasantries."

"Did you get citations?" I asked, ignoring my husband's sharp glance.

Mindy twitched one shoulder. "I think everyone did. He didn't like the way I parked out front. He said I went over the line into the no-parking zone. As if everyone in Georgetown doesn't creep over the line. Plus, he hated that Kurt kept his bike in the downstairs hall."

"I've gotten those parking notes, too," I said. "I'm surprised my assistant, Kate, hasn't had her car papered with them. She's actually a terrible parker."

Mindy smiled. "I ignored them. It's not like they were actual tickets."

"I take it you and Mr. Kopchek didn't exchange keys then?" my husband asked, obviously trying to steer the conversation away from complaining about Mr. Kopchek's citations.

Mindy snorted out a laugh. "Exchange keys? He barely said hello when we passed in the hall."

"So that's a no?" Reese asked.

"That's a no," she said.

"You don't happen to have any copies of the citations he gave out, do you?" my husband asked. "Just for the file."

"I throw them out as soon as I get them. They never even make it up here." She twisted her head and looked behind her. "Maybe Kurt has one. Kurt, honey, do you have a copy of one of Mr. Kopchek's notes?"

Kurt appeared behind her. "About my bike? Maybe." He dug in the pockets of one of the coats hanging on the wall by the door, pulling out a crumpled piece of paper. "Here's one."

He handed it to Reese, who uncrumpled and scanned the paper. I didn't need to peer over his shoulder since I'd seen the printed citations enough times myself.

"Did these tickets create any bad blood between you and the victim?" My husband asked the couple.

Kurt looked shocked. "Bad blood? Just because he left weird notes? No way. We just laughed it off and thought he was a little nutty."

Mindy's gaze traveled to Leatrice, taking in her outfit and hair. "Georgetown is filled with eccentric types."

"I know you came in this evening after the storm started. Did you see Mr. Kopchek at any time?" Reese asked.

"Not today," Kurt answered for both of them. "We were in a rush to get out of here, then when we came home, we came straight up here. Your wife held the door open for us."

"That was when we were carrying in all the food," I said.

"Was Mr. Kopchek's door closed when you came home?" Reese asked.

Kurt paused before answering. "Definitely. Right, hon?"

"As far as I remember," she said. "It wasn't standing open."

"You must have heard me screaming when I found him," Leatrice said. "You would have been home by then."

The couple had blank looks on their faces.

"Sorry," Mindy said. "Kurt had some holiday music playing, and you know how thick these old doors are."

We hadn't heard Leatrice screaming either, but we were two floors up.

"Why all the questions?" Kurt asked.

Reese gave his own half shrug. "Trying to determine when he died and cause of death."

"It wasn't old age?" Mindy asked. "He looked pretty old."

Leatrice bristled beside me. Mr. Kopchek had looked significantly younger than she did.

"I can't say." My husband shook both their hands. "Ongoing investigation. Thanks for answering my questions."

After they'd closed the door, he turned around. "So much for them having a key."

"I'm telling you, he wasn't the kind of guy to swap keys," I said, pointing to the citation in his hand. "He gave his neighbors tickets, for heaven's sake."

"Then if there wasn't a second key, how did someone get inside the apartment I locked?" He narrowed his eyes at Mr. Kopchek's door, then angled his head. "Unless..." Hurrying to the door, he pulled the latex gloves out of his pocket and snapped them on again, kneeling down and inspecting the locking mechanism. When he stood, he blew out a breath.

"Well...?" I asked.

"My hunch was right," he said. "There are traces of some sort of sticky residue on the door's strike plate and locking mechanism."

"Residue?"

Leatrice sucked in a breath. "Someone put tape on it to keep it from locking."

"So, it didn't matter that we closed the door." Chills went through me that had nothing to do with the cold. "Whoever used the tape could go back inside anyway to remove the mug."

My husband gave me a grim smile. "And they removed the tape after they left so the door would be locked when the police arrived."

"Someone did kill Mr. Kopchek," I whispered. "And returned to remove the evidence, which means the killer was someone who had access between the time we first saw the body and when the police arrived."

"That clears me." Leatrice put the back of her hand to her forehead.

I thought back to everyone who'd been in my apartment and when they'd left. "But it doesn't clear Sidney Allen."

CHAPTER 12

"You don't think my Cupcake would murder someone, do you?" Leatrice looked at me like I'd sprouted a second head.

Even though I had seen Sidney Allen lose his temper at events before, I had a hard time imagining the man actually killing someone. Besides, poison was a premeditated method, and Sidney Allen was definitely a heat-of-the-moment type of person. Not that I wanted to think about the passionate nature of an elderly man with the physique of Humpty Dumpty.

"No," I assured Leatrice, reaching for her bony hand. "My point is that we should make a list of anyone who could have possibly gone into the apartment after we locked it—or thought we did."

"That's easy." Leatrice held up her other hand and started counting off fingers. "After we returned to your apartment, the only people who left were the cute bar owner and my Honeybun."

"But there were other people who were moving around the building," my husband said. "The couple we just talked to, for instance. And Buster and Mack."

"Buster and Mack?" My voice went up a few octaves, and the

officer stretching police tape across the staircase bannister looked over. "They didn't even know the man or that he was dead."

"I know that," Reese said, his voice irritatingly even. "But if we're really considering all possibilities, we have to add them to the mix. They did have opportunity to enter the apartment after we left it."

"But they weren't here earlier." Leatrice wagged a finger at him. "So, they couldn't have been the ones to kill him."

"That's a good point," Reese said. "That brings us back to the couple in 2A, the bar owner, and Sidney Allen. Unless there are other people in the building we haven't seen."

Leatrice shook her head, and her flipped-up hairdo swung around her face like a bell. "Both 3B and 4A left yesterday for the holidays."

There was no point in asking how she knew or if she was certain. I don't think Reese or I wanted to know the answers.

"We can't discount the possibility that Mr. Kopchek let his killer into the building, and it isn't someone who lives here," my husband said.

Leatrice shivered. "It does make more sense. Aside from being annoyed at his notes, why would anyone in the building have a reason to kill him? No one knew him."

"So, he buzzes someone in, the person kills him, leaves, and then comes back to take the mug with the poison?" I made a face. "Why not just take the mug right away? Why did the killer need to come back for it? And where would someone who didn't live here go between those two time frames? It's a blizzard outside. It's not like our stairwell has any places to hide. And people were walking up and down it, so anyone trying to hide would have been seen."

"She makes good points, Detective," Leatrice said, her head swinging back to him.

Reese gave me a smile, his hazel eyes locking on mine. "She usually does."

I returned his smile, arching an eyebrow. "What can I say? I'm married to a cop."

Hobbes cleared his throat as he walked out of the apartment and joined us. "Got some preliminary findings."

"Was I right?" my husband asked him. "Does the ME also think it's poison?"

Hobbes glanced at us quickly, but apparently gave up any thought of keeping the conversation private. "She won't know until the toxicology results come back, and that could take a while all things considered, but she agrees the victim's skin and swollen airways indicate poison."

Reese's eyes danced. "Not an allergic reaction?"

"Nope. No rash. She suspects some sort of chemical. Could be a household product or something more industrial."

My husband looked pleased that his initial assessment had been spot-on. "Because the coffee mug was missing, it's a good guess that the victim drank it. Now we just need to figure out what poison was used and who had the motive to give it to him."

Hobbes rubbed a hand across his wrinkled forehead, not looking nearly as satisfied. "We definitely have another murder on our hands."

I rubbed my arms briskly, chilled by both the cold air and the thought that someone gave an old man some sort of household or industrial poison. "I know it's poison, but it seems like a pretty violent way to kill someone."

"It wouldn't have been a fun way to go," Hobbes said. "But it would have been pretty fast. Five or ten minutes depending on how much he ingested."

"That poor man," Leatrice murmured.

"So, what next?" I asked my husband. "We don't have many suspects, and we have zero motives so far."

His partner eyed me. "We?"

I remembered too late that my husband's partner had never warmed to the idea of me and my friends getting involved with murder investigations. To be fair, Reese hadn't so much warmed to the idea as given in to the inevitable. He knew I had an uncontrollable need to fix things—which included crimes that affected my clients or friends or, in this case, neighbors—so he'd learned to work my involvement into his process.

My husband slipped his blazer off and wrapped it around my

shoulders. "What Annabelle means is that she's concerned one of our neighbors was killed and the possibility that another resident could be involved."

The navy wool blazer still held his body heat, and I stopped shivering almost as soon as he'd put it on me. "That's exactly what I meant. Not to mention, I have an apartment filled with potential witnesses. We still don't know what everyone saw as they came and went from the building."

"I'm supposed to be halfway to Scotland by now," Hobbes said under his breath, scowling at the floor.

"You were spending Christmas with Alexandra?" My husband had mentioned his partner's trip to me, but I didn't want it to sound like we'd been talking about him, so I pretended I didn't know.

"It was supposed to be a surprise," he said, finally meeting my eyes and shuffling his feet. "She didn't even know I was coming."

"How romantic." Leatrice pressed her hands over her heart. "I love it when my Sugar Muffin surprises me."

Knowing the exotic cake designer, I wasn't so sure. She didn't strike me as the type who liked having a visit sprung on her, but maybe Hobbes knew her better. Even though I didn't understand the relationship, I'd long since given up unraveling the secrets of the heart. I'd had too many couples whose match-up baffled me to harbor any misconception that love was something easily understood.

"Maybe the storm will clear, and you can get over for New Year's," I suggested.

"Maybe." He let out a tortured breath. "For now, Mike's right. We've got witnesses to question and a bunch of paperwork to file."

My husband clapped a hand on his partner's shoulder. "Let's start upstairs. Annabelle's best friend has cooked up an amazing stew. You can eat while we work." He glanced over his shoulder at the uniformed officer by the door. "You can secure the scene for us after the ME leaves, right?"

The officer jerked his head up slightly. "You got it, Mike."

"It may not be how you planned to spend the holidays," I told Hobbes, "but we do have plenty of food and booze."

He managed a smile. "Thanks. Dinner would be good. All I've eaten today has come from a vending machine."

Leatrice waved for him to follow her as she started up the stairs. "Then you're in for a treat. Richard may be a bit of a diva, but you can't beat his food."

I thought it was bold for Leatrice to call anyone a diva considering who she'd married, but I held my tongue. When we reached the fourth floor, Leatrice opened the door and waved Detective Hobbes in. The warm air hit me immediately, as did the savory scent of stew mixed with the sweet aroma of cinnamon and something else I couldn't identify.

"You're a duck!" Richard yelled as Fern pranced around the living room with his lips pursed and his rear end sticking out.

Fern straightened and put his hands on his hips with a flourish. "A duck? I'm clearly a Kardashian."

"Should I be worried that someone slipped something in our guests' drinks?" my husband whispered as he came up behind me.

I cast my gaze over my friends. "If only."

CHAPTER 13

"We're playing charades," Fern said when he noticed us staring. "What's Christmas without some games, right?"

"We're trying to take everyone's minds off the dead guy downstairs." Kate waved a hand at Hobbes. "Hi, Detective. Welcome to the party."

"I wouldn't call it a party," Richard said, his attention focused on Hermès as the little dog nosed around the bottom of the Christmas tree, sniffing at the remaining wrapped presents and bumping the low fir branches so that ornaments jingled.

"Why not?" Kate lifted a glass filled with crimson liquid into the air. "We have a signature cocktail."

Fern bobbed his head up and down, his grin wide as he picked up his glass from a side table. "The Blizzitini. But be warned, it has a bit of a kick."

"You wouldn't happen to have any more of your delicious stew, would you?" Reese asked Richard. "I promised my partner some dinner while we talked to witnesses."

Richard popped up from the couch. "You're in luck. I have beef bourguignon, and my gingerbread madeleines are almost ready to come out of the oven."

"You made cookies?" I asked. "How long were we downstairs anyway?"

He made an impatient face at me as he bustled by me to the kitchen. "The dough was premade in my catering kitchens. All I had to do was put it in the molds."

I inhaled again. Gingerbread. That was the scent I hadn't been able to place.

"You all really are set to ride out the storm," Hobbes said, his eyes still wide.

"Welcome to the chateau," Richard said with a dramatic flourish of his arm.

Hobbes looked confused, but my husband motioned for his partner to follow him, and they disappeared into the kitchen with Richard muttering in French behind them.

"Annabelle," Mack said, his rumble of a voice low. "What's this about witnesses? Did someone see the murder take place?"

I shook my head. "Doubtful, but the detectives want to talk to anyone who was up and down the stairs in the past couple of hours."

"Meaning us?" Mack glanced at Buster. "They don't think we had anything to do with it, do they?"

"Don't be silly," Kate said before I could answer. "Why would either of you kill an old man you didn't know."

Mack looked scandalized. "Or kill anyone?"

"Exodus 20:13," Buster said. "Thou shalt not kill."

Aside from being former members of a tough Harley-Davidson motorcycle club, our florist friends had become born-again Christians. They were members of the Biker Baptist Church and the Road Riders for Jesus, and they never cursed, much less committed murder.

"Why would *anyone* want to kill Mr. Kopchek?" I said, perching on the arm of my yellow twill couch. "I can't believe his citations were enough to drive someone to murder."

What I didn't say aloud was that if our neighbors hadn't killed Leatrice yet, and she had been known to follow them in disguise, then why would they kill an old man who didn't do anything but issue benign complaints?

"There must have been another reason," Leatrice said as she took the place Richard vacated on the couch. "Maybe he had some skeletons in his closet or a secret dangerous past."

"Who doesn't have a few skeletons?" Fern asked, taking another sip of his drink. "But it would have to be something pretty bad to be killed over."

"What do we know about the old man?" I directed my question at Leatrice.

After a moment, she pointed to herself. "Me? You think I know dirt on Mr. Kopchek?"

"Don't you?" Kate asked, arching one eyebrow.

Leatrice hemmed and hawed for a few seconds then finally let out a loud huff. "Fine. I may have done a little background on him when he first moved in, but I do that with everyone. It's strictly a safety precaution. You can't be too safe these days. There are so many crazies out there."

Kate glanced down at Leatrice's Christmas present slippers and gave me a knowing look. Leatrice was definitely what most people would consider one of the crazies.

"I'm assuming you got help from Boots and Dapper Dan?" I said.

She gnawed at the corner of her mouth. "Please don't mention this to my Honeybun." She stole a look over her shoulder. "Or the detective. I know they don't like me working with the boys."

"The boys" were a pair of hackers she'd met on the dark web. They were skilled at getting information no one else could and staying anonymous. Leatrice had promised she would cut off all contact with them after my husband had discovered she'd used them to hack into the D.C. police department computers and had blown a gasket. As I'd suspected, she hadn't been able to cut the cord yet.

"What did you find out?" I asked, making a point not to make any promises of secrecy. I'd learned not to keep things from my husband, although I had no problem keeping her secret from Sidney Allen.

Leatrice lifted her palms up. "Nothing. He's pretty much what you'd expect. An old man who worked for the government for his entire career, never married, no kids."

Fern frowned. "And he ended up here leaving complaints for all his neighbors? That's sad."

"No chance he was a spy hiding here under an alias?" I asked. "Maybe he was actually in the witness relocation program and his cover got blown?"

Leatrice shook her head vigorously, and her multicolored hair swung around her face. "If there was anything like that, the boys would have discovered it."

"Discovered what?" my husband asked as he and Hobbes returned from the kitchen holding bright-red plates topped with soup bowls.

"Nothing," I said. "Leatrice didn't find out anything about Mr. Kopchek that would explain why he was murdered."

"Why would she?" Hobbes asked as he and Reese took seats at the dining table.

"Our neighbor fashions herself an amateur sleuth," my husband explained with a weary look at his partner.

Hobbes scanned the room, his gaze pausing on me and then Kate. "That seems to be catching around here."

I ignored the comment while Leatrice scowled at the straight-laced detective. "The point is, we can't figure out a motive. Someone went to a decent amount of trouble to knock him off. Why?"

"I think that's for us to figure out," Hobbes said.

"You should be grateful you have all of us here." Kate drained the last drops of her drink. "We've been instrumental in solving more cases than you know."

"That's right," Fern said, flopping down on the couch between Kate and Leatrice. "If we all put our heads together, I'm sure we can get this thing wrapped up before Santa pops down the chimney tomorrow night."

Leatrice patted his leg. "Annabelle doesn't have a chimney, dear."

Fern's face fell. "That's a problem."

Kate jerked her thumb behind her. "Don't worry. He probably uses the fire escape."

"Can we get back to the case?" I asked.

"Well, if you want to know what Buster and I saw when we walked up the staircase earlier, I can tell you there was nothing out of the ordinary," Mack said.

Buster nodded. "We were the only ones on the stairs, and nothing looked any different than it usually does."

"Did you notice the door open to apartment 2B?" my husband asked.

Buster stroked his dark brown goatee. "If it was, I didn't notice, so it probably wasn't standing open."

"To be honest, we were more concerned with getting upstairs and warming our frozen hands and feet," Mack said.

"Thanks, guys," Reese said, but I could tell he was disappointed they didn't remember more and couldn't give him a clue that might break the case open.

"What now?" I asked.

"We question more witnesses," Hobbes said. "You all aren't the only people in the building."

"Reese already talked to the couple who lives on Mr. Kopchek's floor," Leatrice said. "They're another dead end."

"But we haven't talked to the guy who runs the bar," my husband said. "He left when Kurt did."

Kate stood and walked to the counter between the kitchen and living room where all the bottles of booze were lined up. "But he was here with all of us from the time we unloaded Richard's food until then."

"That's right," Fern said. "I talked to him for a while, and I can tell you that he might look like a bad boy, but he's harmless."

"He still might have seen something," Hobbes said, watching Kate as she mixed a drink in a highball glass.

There was a sharp knock on the door. Richard came out of the kitchen holding a plate of gingerbread men. "There can't possibly be any more people we know left in the city."

Leatrice bounded off the couch. "I'll bet it's my Honeybun. I knew he couldn't stay away from me forever."

She opened the door, but it was not her Honeybun. The uniformed officer from downstairs held a plastic evidence bag in one hand as he peered inside my apartment.

Hobbes and Reese stood quickly and crossed to the door.

"You found something?" my husband asked, his gaze locked on the bag.

The officer held it higher. "This was on the top of the victim's trash. The ME is going to take it back for testing, but I thought you'd want to see it first. It's the only bottle or container of liquid we found, so this might be what the old guy drank."

"Isn't that…?" I peeked around the detectives to get a better look at the half-sized wine bottle.

Leatrice let out a squeak. "One of the bottles of cider Sidney Allen and I gave as gifts to all the neighbors."

CHAPTER 14

"You don't think Sidney Allen and Leatrice could really have anything to do with this, do you?" Kate asked, following me into the kitchen and carrying a stack of dirty bowls and plates.

I set my own handful of dirty dishes on the counter as I opened the dishwasher. "Of course not. We already determined that Sidney Allen isn't the type to premeditate a murder. Besides, they gave that cider out to the neighbors days ago, and he only got into an argument with Mr. Kopchek a couple of hours ago."

"So why did your hubby and his sidekick go down to talk to Sidney Allen and take Leatrice with them?"

I loaded my dishes then stepped back for Kate to do the same. "They have to follow procedure, especially since it's someone Reese knows. How would it look if he didn't question Sidney Allen and Leatrice after they found that bottle of cider?"

"I guess you're right." Kate straightened and closed the dishwasher door. "By the way, what did you give out to your neighbors since you live in a gift-giving building now?"

"She ordered bags of Christmas cookies from me," Richard said as he walked into the kitchen.

I held up my hands. "Guilty as charged. I was too crazed getting presents wrapped and details for the New Year's Eve wedding finalized."

"And you don't have the patience for Christmas cookies," Richard added.

"Not the way you do them," I said. "I can stick a Hershey's Kiss in a peanut butter cookie, but iced cookies that look like reindeer are beyond me."

"Speaking of cookies." Kate eyed the gingerbread madeleines cooling on the metal racks on the counter.

"Don't even think about it," Richard warned.

"Actually, this is perfect." I grabbed a plate with a red bow and holly leaves painted around the rim and started stacking it with cookies as Richard gaped at me.

"What are you doing?" he cried.

"Giving us a reason to visit Alton," I said.

"Alton?" He scowled at me. "You mean tattoo boy? Why do you need to visit him, and why do you need to take half of my madeleines to do it?"

I unloaded a few of the cookies, which garnered me more scowls from Richard.

"Kate and I need to talk to him because he's one of the people who could have gone into Mr. Kopchek's apartment after Reese thought he sealed it."

Now Kate's expression matched Richard's. "Shouldn't you wait and let your husband do that?"

"If I do, he won't take you with him."

"And why do I need to be a part of this cockamamie plan?" Kate asked.

I hooked an arm though hers. "Because even though you claim to have sworn off men, you're still the best judge of them I know. I want to know why you think something's off about the guy."

"I never said something was off about him," she said, then let out a sigh when I gave her a pointed look. "I do get a vibe that he's hiding something, but I'm also a bit rusty."

"I still trust your rusty instinct." I tugged her forward. "That's why we're going to talk to him. The cookies are just our excuse."

Richard glanced at his remaining cookies. "I was going to start on the Bûche de Noël, but I suppose I'd better make more madeleines."

We left Richard fussing in the kitchen and muttering in French under his breath. As we passed through the living room, I saw that Fern was mixing up more cocktails, and Buster and Mack were FaceTiming with baby Merry while Hermès yipped into the phone.

"They won't even notice we're gone," I said to Kate as we slipped out the door.

The stairwell was surprisingly quiet after the previous bustle of the police around Mr. Kopchek's apartment, and it hadn't warmed up much since they'd left. We walked down one floor, and I rapped sharply on the door I knew belonged to Alton.

After a moment, the door opened. The man had changed into gray sweatpants and a hoodie, and his feet were bare.

"We brought you some cookies," I said, trying to make my voice as cheerful as possible as I stepped forward. "You left before my friend served them, and we didn't want you to miss them. Where should I put them?"

He looked slightly startled as he stepped back and allowed us inside. "Um, anywhere is fine. Thanks for bringing them. You really didn't have to—"

"Don't mention it," I said, talking over him as I walked down the short hallway and into the main room. Alton's apartment was a similar layout to Mr. Kopchek's, which made sense. It was directly above the old man's apartment.

Instead of thick curtains and dark, dated furniture, the bar owner had bare windows and lots of glass and black leather. No shock there. He was a single guy, after all, and single men seemed to gravitate toward black leather. A large standing aquarium stood against one wall, and a wide-screen TV took up the rest of it. Outside his windows, snow continued to fall in heavy sheets against the blackness of the night.

I put the plate of cookies on a glass coffee table then crossed to the aquarium where brightly colored fish swam around tall coral formations. "You weren't kidding about the fish."

He ran a hand through his hair. "My schedule is too crazy to have a dog, so I have fish."

It wasn't just any old fish tank. The aquarium must have been six feet long and rested on a shiny black cabinet with doors in the front. The glass was sparkling clean and the water crystal clear.

I glanced around as subtly as I could. His entire apartment was pretty spotless, aside from the pizza box on the counter separating the living room and kitchen. He might have been a single guy, but he wasn't a slob.

"So, it's just you and the fish for the holidays?" Kate asked, sinking onto one of the leather loveseats.

Alton grinned at her and nodded. "Right about now I'd rather have a dog."

"If you really want to borrow one, I'm sure we could arrange something," I said, thinking of Hermès running around like a miniature maniac in my apartment.

He laughed. "How's it going with being snowed in with all your friends?"

"It wouldn't be so bad if one of our neighbors hadn't been murdered," I said, watching his face for a reaction.

He immediately appeared chagrined. "You're right. It's awful what happened to Mr. Kopchek. They're sure it's murder?"

I decided to go out on a limb. "Pretty sure. It looks like he was poisoned."

"Really?" He looked genuinely surprised. "How?"

"Something he drank," I said.

Alton shook his head. "That's awful. I know the old guy wasn't the friendliest person in the building, but who would want to kill him?"

Kate shifted on the couch, crossing her legs. "Did you ever see him argue with anyone?"

Alton tilted his head at her, his gaze only dropping to her bare legs for a moment. "I'm not around during the day much, and I don't think the old man stays up late. I've never seen him when I've come home after closing the bar."

"And what about when you leave to open your place?" I asked. I'd run into him a couple of times in the middle of the day when he was headed out.

He shook his head. "I almost never ran into him, and if I did see him, he was always alone."

"Did you ever get citations?" Kate asked, stretching her arms wide along the couch cushions as she sat forward.

He looked confused for a moment, then he smiled. "You mean those tickets he gave out complaining about stuff? Yeah. He didn't like when I played music during the day. He thought it was too loud."

I instinctively looked down. Mr. Kopchek's living room would be right under us. I tried not to think of the body still lying on the couch. "Did you keep any of them?"

Alton cocked an eyebrow. "I think I tossed them in that bowl." He pointed to a bowl on the counter dividing the kitchen and the main living area.

"Do you mind if I look at them?" I asked, heading for the bowl that appeared to be mostly filled with change.

Another shrug. "Suit yourself. Just because he gave me tickets doesn't mean I wanted to kill him."

"I know," I said, fishing several crumpled pieces of paper from the bowl. "I got tickets, too, and I didn't kill him."

I unfolded the papers as Alton picked up one of the madeleines and took a bite.

"These are really good," he said. "A wedding planner and a baker."

Kate choked out a laugh. "Annabelle didn't bake those. If she bakes, it's only for stress relief, and it never tastes as good."

"Thanks," I said, shooting her a look then smiling at Alton. "Those were all Richard. We were lucky to get snowed in with a professional caterer."

"Were we?" Kate said under her breath.

He reached for another cookie. "My compliments to the chef then."

I took his distraction to shove the citations into my pocket. "We'd better head back. We just wanted to drop off the cookies." I motioned for Kate to follow me, and she popped off the couch.

When we reached the door, I opened it and stepped out into the hall. Alton held the door open, leaning against it with one arm stretched up against the doorframe. His hoodie rode up, and I saw a flash of a tattoo that stretched along one side of his torso.

"Thanks again for the cookies," he said.

I glanced away from his exposed skin quickly, feeling my face warming. "If you get bored hanging out with your fish, feel free to come upstairs."

"Will do," he said as he closed the door.

Kate followed me upstairs, only grabbing me by the sleeve when we reached my door. "Why did we leave so quickly? I thought the whole point was to question him about the time when he could have snuck into Mr. Kopchek's apartment."

I paused, listening for any sound in the stairwell. It was silent. "Because I found this." I pulled the citations out of my pocket.

"He told you about those." Kate looked at the formerly crumpled squares of white paper. "Mr. Kopchek didn't like him playing loud music."

I picked one citation out of the pile. "This one isn't for music. This one is for parking an SUV in the no-parking zone."

Kate stared at the paper then at me. "So? I guess he's also bad at parking."

I shook my head. "He doesn't drive an SUV."

CHAPTER 15

*K*ate snapped her fingers. "How could I forget that he rides a motorcycle?" She frowned as she stared at the citation. "So why would he have one of Mr. Kopchek's complaints about parking an SUV? Do you think he took it off someone else's car?"

I gave her a withering look as I pushed open the door to my apartment. "Why would he do that?"

Kate was in mid-shrug when I turned and came face-to-face with my husband's broad chest. His arms were crossed, and his expression was stony.

"I tried to explain about the cookies," Richard called from the kitchen, "but he didn't buy it."

"I didn't buy it because I know you too well, babe," my husband said, his gaze never leaving me. "You and Kate went to our neighbor's to question him, didn't you?"

"Busted," Kate muttered to me under her breath.

"Before you get upset that I was investigating without you—" I started to say.

"Try that you were investigating at *all*," he corrected me. "We do have two detectives working on this case, and we both happen to be stuck in the building."

I looked over his shoulder to where his partner Hobbes sat at the dining table eating a second bowl of beef bourguignon. "But you're guys."

He tilted his head at me. "Thanks for noticing. What does that have to do with anything?"

"I wanted to talk to Alton with Kate. You know, use her super powers to figure out his deal."

Fern walked up and handed us each highball glasses filled with cranberry-colored liquid and topped with an elaborate garnish of leaves and berries hugging the rims that I hoped was edible—or at least not toxic. "It's true. I've seen her spot a cheating husband at a hundred paces."

Kate beamed at him, crossing her own arms. "It's a gift."

My husband let out a tortured breath, backing up to let us walk fully into the apartment. "So, did you?"

"Kind of," I said as I closed the door behind me. "We didn't get very far in questioning him, but we did get to check out his place."

"You should see his fish tank." Kate gave a low whistle as she flopped on the couch next to Buster and Mack, holding her drink high so it wouldn't spill. "And the place is spotless."

"How does that help the case?" Reese asked.

I took a sip of the cocktail Fern had handed me then held out my open palm. "Because we found this."

My husband took the citation and read it. "Okay. It's one of those tickets the old man gave out."

"It was in a pile of them that Alton said he'd gotten. He tosses them into a bowl on the counter. All the others were for playing music too loudly during the day."

"And this one is for parking an SUV half in a no-parking zone," Reese said then his eyes widened. "But the guy who owns the bar doesn't drive an SUV. He rides a motorcycle."

I took another sip of the sweet drink, wondering how much booze was in it since I couldn't taste a thing. "See? Why would he have someone else's citation?"

"Because the person who got the citation was in his apartment and tossed it into the bowl," Kate said. "It totally explains the weird vibe I was getting off Mindy when she and her fiancé stopped by earlier. Now it makes total sense."

"What makes total sense?" Mack asked.

"Mindy and Alton are sleeping together," Kate said.

Buster and Mack both gaped at her, and Mack finally asked, "Who's Mindy?"

"Remember the bland guy who was here when you arrived?" Kate twisted to face them both. "Thinning hair, preppy."

Mack nodded. "He left with the other fellow who was…not preppy."

Kate grinned. "Exactly. Alton was the hot guy with the tattoos. Mr. Bland is engaged to Mindy, and Mr. Bad Boy is sleeping with her."

"You know this how?" Hobbes asked, walking up to join us.

"Simple," Kate told him. "They made a point not to look at each other when they were both here. If you really don't know someone, you don't avoid eye contact like that. They were hiding something. And if one of her tickets for badly parking her SUV was in Alton's apartment, and the ticket was written in the middle of the day when she's supposed to be at work, then it only makes sense that they're sneaking around behind her fiancé's back."

"Elementary, my dear," Fern said, his voice slightly slurred as he lifted his glass in salute and took a long swig.

"This is all getting to be a bit sordid." Richard came out of the kitchen with a plate of madeleines and put it on the coffee table. "Murder, affairs, spying. What kind of building do you live in, darling?"

"That's a good question," my husband said as he tapped one finger on his chin.

"Hey," I said. "This is a nice building. The murder and the affairs aren't a regular occurrence." I didn't mention the spying. With Leatrice as a longtime resident, that *was* a regular occurrence.

"We don't have evidence there is an affair," Hobbes said, clearly not convinced by Kate's expertise in body language. "And even if there is, it doesn't necessarily have anything to do with the murder."

"It does if Mr. Kopchek knew about it," I said. "You know how old people see everything that goes on. Just look at Leatrice."

"Speaking of the old girl," Richard pivoted, taking in the living room, "I thought it was unusually quiet in here."

"She and Sidney Allen decided to stay in their apartment after Hobbes and I questioned them." Reese pulled his phone out of his pants pocket. "It is pretty late. I think they were going to bed."

Kate put her hand over her mouth as she yawned. "I've lost all track of time."

"I don't know about anyone else," Richard smoothed his hands down the front of his Santa apron, "but I can't sleep knowing a murderer is galavanting around the building."

Fern put a hand to his throat. "You don't think the killer will strike again, do you?"

"I doubt we have a serial killer," Hobbes said. "From all appearances, Mr. Kopchek's murder seems targeted."

Buster shifted on the couch and his leather pants groaned. "We know that no one in here is the killer. If we stick together, we'll be safe."

"Will we?" Richard mumbled as he bustled back to the kitchen.

"Buster's right," my husband said. "Everyone should probably try to get some sleep. There isn't much more we can do tonight. I'm sure the rest of the building is sleeping already."

"I'll be heading home," Hobbes said. "There's a cruiser waiting for me outside."

"You sure?" my husband asked. "It's still snowing."

Hobbes cut his eyes to the crowded room and Fern refilling his cocktail as he hiccupped. "Positive."

Reese nodded and clapped him on the shoulder. "I'll let you know if anything develops."

Hobbes grabbed his coat from the stand. "And if I hear anything from the ME, I'll call you." He left with a cursory wave to the rest of us.

I glanced around the room. Hermès had nestled himself underneath the Christmas tree between a pair of red-and-green-striped boxes, and he was sleeping soundly. But unless anyone else fancied a spot under the tree, that meant I had to find places for Richard, Kate, Buster, Mack, and Fern to sleep. Although our one bedroom was considered roomy for Georgetown, it still wasn't huge. Just about the only place I could think to fit Buster and Mack was stretched out down the hallway. My mind went to the extra bed linens and blankets my mother had insisted on adding to our wedding registry. They'd be coming in handy tonight.

"The couch folds out," I said. "So, two people can sleep there."

Kate looked down at the cushion she was sitting on. "It does? How did I not know this? Who wants to share the foldout with me?"

Fern thrust his arm up, fluttering his hand wildly. "Me, me! Oh, this will be just like a slumber party."

My husband stepped closer to me and lowered his head to mine. "We don't have to share our bedroom, do we?"

I gave him a wicked grin. "You don't want Richard sleeping between us with Hermès at our feet?"

"Don't even joke about that," he said.

"Buster and I can sleep sitting up." Mack nodded to the oversized armchairs across from the couch.

Buster bobbed his head up and down in agreement. "We can sleep anywhere. It's a talent we acquired on long bike rides."

"You can sleep while you ride?" Kate asked.

Mack held up a finger. "Only as a passenger."

"Less impressive," Fern muttered from behind his drink.

"I'll clear space on my office floor," I said, heading down the hall. "Reese has an air mattress we can put in there for Richard."

Richard's dark mutterings about the indignities of air mattresses faded as I reached the end of the hall and opened the linen closet. I pulled out all the sheets, blankets, and pillows we had, some of them still in their packaging. One nice thing about getting married and having a mother who believed in a fully-stocked registry—we did own just about every houseware we'd ever need.

My husband came up behind me and took an armload of pillows. "Not exactly how I imagined spending our first Christmas, although I can't say I'm totally shocked it ended up in a giant sleepover with your wedding friends."

"Don't look at me," I said. "Blame the blizzard. We were supposed to be in Charlottesville with my parents right now."

He smiled at me. "Don't even try to pretend you aren't happier here with all your friends."

I attempted a scandalized look. "You know I love my parents."

He leaned over, his lips buzzing against my earlobe. "I also know you love being in the middle of an investigation and being with your friends. Christmas with your parents would have been much quieter than this. For one, there wouldn't have been a murder."

I cocked my head at him. "Snowed in with my mother for days? We can't know that."

CHAPTER 16

I sat up in bed and sniffed. Was I dreaming or did I smell coffee…and bacon?

I wasn't sure how long I'd been asleep, but it felt like my head had just hit the pillow. I twisted to look at the window where light was peeking from underneath the bottom corner of the pull-down shade. I groaned. How could it be morning already?

"What?" my husband mumbled next to me, lifting his head a millimeter off the pillow. "What's going on?"

"Nothing." I patted him on the shoulder. "I smelled something. I think Richard's already cooking."

"Cooking? I thought we saw him go to bed?"

He was right. We had watched Richard flounce off to sleep on the air mattress in my office, a drowsy Hermès tucked under his arm like a teddy bear. Since he'd been packed for a visit to my parents, he'd had pajamas to change into. Designer pajamas with a monogram. Unlike Kate and Fern, who'd both borrowed one of my oversized sleeping shirts. I was half afraid I'd find Fern with his hair in foam rollers tied up in a sleeping cap.

"I think he's starting breakfast. I smell bacon."

"Breakfast?" Reese let out a groan to match mine, opening one eye and then closing it again. "It's morning already?"

"Apparently." I slid out of bed and stepped softly to the window, peeking under the shade and being momentarily blinded by white. The snow was no longer coming down in thick sheets, but there was at least two feet of it piled up everywhere. The cars in the back alley were white lumps, and there was no trace of a road.

I pulled a pair of black leggings on underneath my oversized UVA T-shirt and headed for the kitchen, pulling my bedroom door closed quietly as my husband had fallen asleep again. The man really could sleep through anything.

The aroma of coffee grew stronger as I walked down the hall, as did the sound of bacon sizzling.

"Finally," Richard said when I joined him in the kitchen. "I was wondering when someone else would wake up."

My best friend no longer wore his crisp blue pajamas. He'd dressed in equally wrinkle-free black pants and a forest-green button-down, all covered by the Santa apron from the day before. I didn't see Hermès, and I suspected the tiny dog was still sleeping.

I glanced at the kitchen wall clock. "It's only eight o'clock—and we went to bed after midnight."

"Maybe so, but I have an entire Christmas Eve dinner to prepare, not to mention prepping everything for Christmas Day and feeding people today." Richard opened the oven door and a blast of heat billowed out. "Oh good. My French toast soufflé is ready."

I stifled a yawn. "You're really going all in on this Christmas in the Chateau theme, aren't you?"

He cut his eyes to me as he donned oven mitts. "Don't be silly, Annabelle. French toast isn't French. It just happens to be a breakfast dish that holds well, and I have a feeling people will be waking up at all different times. I have no intention of being a short-order cook today."

I glanced through the opening between the kitchen and living room and saw no movement from the two lumps asleep on the foldout couch. Both Buster and Mack sat motionless in the overstuffed armchairs with their hands folded across their broad chests and their heads tipped back, eyes closed.

"And you aren't doing all this to wake everyone up?" I asked, giving him a pointed look.

He placed the soufflé casserole on a metal rack and tossed the oven mitts down beside it. "Hardly. Once everyone wakes up, my productivity will decrease dramatically. But I also couldn't sleep the day away with so much to do." He picked up a French press and poured coffee into a mug. "Christmas does not happen by itself, darling."

I opened the refrigerator door and plucked out one of my bottled Mocha Frappuccinos. "You know I appreciate everything you're doing, but I hate to see you working yourself to the bone. We don't have to have an elaborate Christmas, you know. We *are* snowed in. We can always keep things informal."

"Bite your tongue." Richard sucked in breath. "An informal Christmas? What's next? A wedding with hot dogs and tater tots? Really, Annabelle."

"Did someone say tater tots?" Kate lifted her head, her blond hair sticking up in several different directions.

Richard arched an eyebrow at me. "I rest my case."

I popped open the top to my Frappuccino and took a long swig of the cold drink, welcoming the sweet kick of caffeine. As much as I loved the smell of regular coffee, I preferred mine with plenty of mocha, milk, and sugar—and peppermint during the holidays.

"Since you're determined to put Martha Stewart to shame, is there anything I can do to help?"

He nodded to the living room where Kate was now sitting up, and Buster and Mack were stretching their arms over their heads. "You can take them coffee." His gaze lingered on Kate's wild hair. "They're going to need it."

I poured coffee from the French press into two Christmas mugs and headed for the living room. "Caffeine, anyone?"

Buster and Mack both rumbled low as they sat up, and I handed the mugs to them.

"They aren't fancy cappuccinos like you make in your shop, but they should wake you up."

Mack put the red mug to his nose and inhaled deeply. "It's perfect."

"It's a holiday blend," Richard called from the kitchen. "It's got notes of spice cake and caramel."

"As long as it has caffeine," Buster murmured, sipping his coffee.

Fern raised his hand without sitting up. "I'll take mine Irish, please."

I shook my head. "The last thing you need is more booze."

"I beg to differ, sweetie. One shot of whiskey in my coffee, and I'll be good to go."

I eyed him lying in bed with an arm draped over his eyes. "You'll be under the table."

Kate ran a hand through her hair, smoothing down the wild locks. "You wouldn't happen to have any more of that hot chocolate, would you?"

Fern peeked one eye from under his arm. "That sounds good. I'll take my hot chocolate with a splash of Baileys."

I rolled my eyes. "No booze until afternoon. New house rule."

Fern let out a sigh. "It's afternoon in Europe. I thought this was a French-themed Christmas anyway."

I headed back to the kitchen where Richard was patting strips of bacon with a paper towel. "Your chateau theme is backfiring. Fern wants to observe European time and start drinking now."

"After last night, I don't blame him."

The murder came rushing back to me, and I shook the image of poor Mr. Kopchek out of my mind. "We've dealt with murder before. It's no reason to drink ourselves into oblivion."

"Is now the time to tell you that the French toast soufflé casserole is soaked in Grand Marnier?"

"Good," I said. "Fern can eat that instead of having a crack-of-dawn cocktail."

I scanned the counters, which were now filled with ingredients and serving dishes. "You didn't happen to see a Mason jar filled with hot chocolate mix, did you?"

Richard made a noise of surprise. "A Mason jar? I thought you had it out for Mason jars?"

"You know I have no problem with Mason jars used appropriately. It's when brides want to have Mason jars as vases for their luxury hotel weddings that it makes me crazy."

"And people say I'm persnickety," Richard said under his breath, then fluttered a hand toward the counter dividing the kitchen and living room. "I think I put it up there."

"And this Mason jar happens to be a gift." I spotted the jar and grabbed it, noticing that I only had about a third of the brown powdery contents left. "Mindy and Kurt gave them out to…"

Richard paused as he lifted a strip of bacon from the frying pan with a pair of tongs. "You really need more of your mocha, darling. You didn't even finish that sentence."

I stared down at the jar. "I just realized something. This could have been the murder weapon."

Richard dropped the bacon and it splattered on top of his shoes. He gaped at the jar in my hand then down at his feet. "My Prada loafers!"

CHAPTER 17

"Slow down, babe." My husband rubbed his eyes as I stood at the end of the bed holding the Mason jar. He was sitting up and leaning against the headboard with the sheets bunched around his waist. "I'm still waking up."

I tried not to get distracted by the fact that he was bare-chested, since he only slept in pajama bottoms. Forcing my gaze to stay on his face and not drift down to his impressive chest muscles, I did slow down. "Remember that I showed you the jar of hot chocolate mix that Mindy and Kurt gave all the neighbors?"

He nodded, his expression still sleepy. "I think so. It's the reason you had to call up Richard in a tizzy and order cookies."

"I wouldn't say tizzy."

My husband held up his palms as he swung his legs over the side of the bed. "I'm just repeating what Richard said."

"He said I was in a tizzy?" I frowned and cast a glance toward the door leading to the hall. "He's one to talk, especially after—"

"Babe?" My husband stopped me. "What about the hot chocolate mix?"

"Right." I waved the jar at him. "What if this was what was poisoned and not the cider Leatrice and Sidney Allen gave out?"

He scratched his hand over the dark stubble covering his cheeks. "It would be easier to introduce poison into a powder mix than into sealed bottles."

"Exactly. And those bottles have a screw top that's covered in foil. I know because Kate already drank ours."

My husband stood and stretched, and then I really had to work hard not to let my eyes drift. "So, your theory is that Mindy and Kurt poisoned the old guy using tainted hot cocoa?"

I cringed looking at the mix. "Pretty diabolical, right? But I don't think it was both of them. If Kate's right about Mindy messing around with Alton, then I'm sure she's the one who did the poisoning."

Reese padded over to the dresser and pulled a white T-shirt out of a drawer, tugging it over his head. "Even if Kate's right about the affair—and I'm not sure how we're going to prove that—you think Mindy killed Mr. Kopchek because he somehow knew?"

"Think about it," I said. "If Kate's also right that Kurt comes from money, maybe Mindy isn't in it for true love."

My husband dragged a hand through his hair and his one errant curl flopped back over his forehead. "They do seem like a bit of a mismatch, and I don't even have Kate's Jedi relationship skills."

"Say she got swept up by the bad-boy charm of the neighbor who owns a bar and started an illicit affair. The last thing she would want is for her rich fiancé to find out and call off the wedding."

Reese nodded. "It makes sense, but we don't have any evidence."

"Aside from the citation that was in Alton's apartment," I reminded him.

"Which might lend weight to the possibility of an affair but not a murder."

I sighed. "Mindy also had the opportunity to go into Mr. Kopchek's apartment and grab the mug. She left our apartment to go bake her pie. She could have snuck in, taken the mug and the Mason jar of mix, and gone back to her apartment without anyone noticing."

"I agree that your theory is solid, but we don't have proof."

I grinned. "You think I'm right?"

He looped an arm around my waist and tugged me so I was flush against him. "I've never said you weren't good at figuring out crimes. You did learn from an expert, after all."

I swatted at him playfully. "Are you saying you taught me everything I know?"

He leaned down and kissed me. "Something like that."

"You're impossible." I frowned at him even though his kiss made my knees wobbly. "I thought you hated me trying to solve cases."

He kissed me again. "I hate you constantly putting yourself in danger, babe."

I fought the urge to melt into him and instead peered up and drummed my fingers on his chest. "So how do we get proof?"

"The good news is we've all been snowed in since the murder. Nothing has gone out of this building aside from Mr. Kopchek's body." He opened our bedroom door. "The mug and the tainted hot chocolate have to be here somewhere."

"So, if Mindy's the killer, they're probably in her apartment." I followed him down the hall, thinking of ways I could casually search another resident's apartment without getting caught.

My husband stepped into the kitchen, and I followed him. Richard held up two oven-mitted hands to stop us.

"I'm in the middle of assembling my Bûche de Noël, and it's a very delicate process." He glanced over his shoulder at the chocolate sheet cakes on parchment paper. "Is there any way you can come back later?"

Reese cocked an eyebrow at him. "Give me some coffee, and I promise to stay out of your hair."

"Done." Richard pivoted to the French press and poured coffee into a mug then handed it to my husband.

I scanned the countertop. "Do you have any more of the soufflé? I didn't get to taste it yet."

Richard waved a hand toward the living room. "It's on the dining room table along with plates and silverware. Help yourself."

My husband took a sip of coffee as I pulled him out of the kitchen. "Soufflé?"

"Richard's been up for a while."

He took another long drink of coffee, already looking more awake. "While you try the soufflé, I'm going to hop in the shower."

I watched him head back down the hall for a moment before heading into the living room. Buster and Mack were at the table eating large squares of French toast soufflé, but there was no sign of Kate or Fern. Both the bathroom and office doors had been open, so I knew they weren't there.

"Please tell me Kate and Fern aren't making snow angels outside," I said to Buster and Mack as I stepped up to the soufflé and started to cut myself a piece.

"They're doing Richard's evil bidding," Mack said.

"I heard that," Richard called from the kitchen. "I just asked them to deliver some of my breakfast soufflé to the cute couple downstairs. I'm assuming her pie didn't cool in time for her to bring some up to us, but I'm holding out hope for that recipe. You know my best dishes are secret family recipes that I managed to sweet-talk out of people."

I dropped the knife into the casserole dish, and it clattered against the glass bottom. "Kate and Fern are downstairs with Mindy?"

"Not just her, unless her fiancé managed to tunnel his way through the snowdrifts," Buster said. "Why did you get even paler than usual, Annabelle?"

"Because if I'm right, they just took casserole to a killer."

Richard poked his head through the dividing space. "Did you say that Mindy is a killer?"

I nodded. "I don't have time to pull my husband out of the shower. Can you tell him where I went?"

I ran for the door as Richard threw down his oven mitts and followed me, yelling to Buster and Mack over his shoulder. "You heard her, boys."

CHAPTER 18

"I thought you hated this crime-solving thing," I said over my shoulder as Richard and I pounded down two flights of stairs.

"I do, but the faster it's over with, the faster I can get back to preparing Christmas Eve dinner. And I know you, Annabelle. You won't let it go until it's solved. If there's a problem, you have to fix it no matter what. It's both your best and worst quality."

"Thanks, I think."

"Not a compliment, darling, but you're welcome."

We reached Mindy and Kurt's apartment, and the door was standing open. I held out an arm to stop Richard and put a finger to my lips, miming that we should be quiet. I pushed the door open quietly and tiptoed inside.

The apartment was laid out similarly to mine, the front door opening into a single large dining and living space with a kitchen next to it divided by a pass-through counter. The room was slightly longer than mine and the kitchen seemed larger, but I noticed only two doors down the long hall toward the fire escape—presumably their bathroom and bedroom.

"Where are they?" Richard whispered as we stood inside the main room, which looked like a spread from a Restoration Hardware catalog. It was so pristine and picture-perfect it was hard to believe people actually lived there. There was no Christmas tree, but glass hurricane candles ran the length of the dividing counter with greenery wound between them. "I smell the pumpkin pie."

The apartment did have the distinctive scent of cinnamon and nutmeg, and my head swung instinctively toward the kitchen where I spotted Mindy's head as well as Fern and Kate.

"It's my mother's recipe," Mindy said. "Do you want some whipped cream on top?"

Richard clutched my arm. "Is she serving them that pie she promised to bring us?"

"I'm a purist when it comes to hot chocolate," Fern said. "Unless you have some Baileys."

My stomach dropped. Hot chocolate? Was Mindy serving them hot chocolate? Had Kate or Fern let something slip? Did she know we were on to her? Was she attempting to get rid of anyone who might suspect her of poisoning Mr. Kopchek?

I ran to the kitchen, pulling Richard with me. When I spotted Kate putting a red mug to her lips, I swatted it away from her. It crashed to the linoleum floor, bouncing instead of breaking and sending brown liquid all over the floor and Kate's legs.

"Annabelle!" she screamed, hopping around as the hot droplets hit her. "What are you doing?"

"Saving your life," I said. "That hot chocolate might be poisoned."

Fern, who'd frozen as he was lifting his mug to his lips, slowly lowered it and put it on the counter, staring at it as if it was radioactive waste. He wore a plum brocade dressing gown with a matching ascot that made him look like a British Hugh Hefner. I was impressed he looked as stylish as he did since Kate still wore a sleep shirt over yesterday's miniskirt.

"Are these granite?" Richard whispered, touching a hand to the gleaming, dark counters and gaining a sharp look from me. "I know this is off topic, but this kitchen is considerably nicer than yours, darling."

Mindy gaped at me, ignoring Richard's comments. "Poisoned? Are you crazy?"

I shook my head. "We know you had a motive to kill Mr. Kopchek, and we also know that he was most likely killed by something he ate or drank. Since the mug he was using disappeared, that had to be the way he was killed. You gave him hot chocolate mix, which would have been an easy way to administer poison."

She put her hands on her hips. "Why would I want to kill an old man I barely knew?"

"Because he knew about you and Alton," I said.

Her cheeks reddened, and she visibly flinched. "I don't know what you're talking about."

I glanced at Kate for confirmation, and she gave me a single nod. "She definitely knows."

Mindy's murderous gaze shifted to Kate. "I'm not sure what you think you know, but I don't even know this Alton guy. Is he the guy who lives upstairs? The one who was in your apartment earlier?"

"Yeah," Kate said. "The one you went out of your way to ignore."

"And he's pretty impossible to ignore," Fern added.

Kate eyed her knowingly. "If I wasn't trying really hard to be monogamous, I'd be noticing him big time."

The flush on Mindy's cheeks deepened. "Like I said, I don't know him."

"Then why was one of your parking citations in his apartment?" I asked.

That made her mouth fall open a little bit, then she folded her arms over her chest. "No idea. Maybe he took it."

"Why would a guy who parks his motorcycle behind the building have any reason to take a parking citation off your car?" I asked. "And why would your SUV get a citation in the middle of the workday when you're supposed to be at work? Unless you have a reason to come back to the building for your lunch break."

"This is all guesswork." Mindy pressed her lips together. "You don't have any real proof."

"Proof of what?" Kurt stepped into the kitchen behind me,

glancing at the spilled hot chocolate and at everyone's expressions. "Is everything okay in here?"

"They're accusing me of murder," Mindy said, her voice instantly taking on a frail, hysterical tone.

He crossed to her, putting an arm around her shoulders and glaring at us. "Murder? Of Mr. Kopchek? You came down here to accuse my fiancée of murder?"

"Actually, we came down to deliver some French toast breakfast soufflé," Fern said, waving at the plate of the golden-brown dish.

"I hope you like citrus," Richard added. "I might have gotten a tad enthusiastic with the Grand Marnier."

Kurt gave his fiancée a confused look, and she nodded her head at me. "The wedding planner is the one accusing me of murder."

"Mindy and I barely knew the man," he said. "Why would either of us kill him?"

I hesitated for a moment. Was I really sure enough to accuse her of sleeping with Alton in front of her fiancé? She was right that I didn't have hard proof, although there was circumstantial evidence and her obvious reaction when we'd mentioned him. Innocent people did not react like that.

"Because she wanted to make sure Mr. Kopchek couldn't tell you about the affair she was having with Alton," Kate said.

The room went silent for a beat, Kurt's expression freezing.

Then he turned to face Mindy. "The bar owner upstairs? Is this true?"

She shook her head vigorously, but her face was mottled red. "Of course not, hon. I was just telling them that I don't even know the guy."

From Kurt's expression, I could tell this news wasn't a total shock to him. Had he been suspecting something for a while and trying to convince himself he was imagining it?

"Our wedding is in a few months." His voice cracked. "I convinced my family that you didn't need to sign a prenup. You convinced me you didn't care about my money. Was all that a lie?"

Mindy's eyes were wild as she shook her head and grasped his hands. "Of course not. You have to believe me. All of *this* is a lie. I'm not involved with Alton. I had nothing to do with Mr. Kopchek's death, and I did not poison anyone's hot chocolate."

"I don't know about that."

Everyone spun as Reese came into the room. His dark hair was wet, with droplets of water dripping off his curls, and the white T-shirt half-tucked into his jeans was damp. "We now know the victim ingested your hot chocolate before he died."

CHAPTER 19

"How did he know the victim drank hot chocolate and not the cider?" Buster asked when we'd returned to my apartment.

"Apparently, the ME was snowed in and rushed the autopsy," Kate said, flopping down on the couch between the two leather-clad florists who were eating large servings of soufflé. "The tox report won't come back for a while, but they know Mr. Kopchek ate pizza and drank hot chocolate. Since his mouth and throat were swollen, they're positive he ingested the poison."

Mack shivered and eyed his plate. "What a horrible way to go."

"Death by cocoa," Kate said, making her voice sound dramatic and ominous.

"Don't worry," I said as Buster and Mack glanced at their mugs on the coffee table. "I'm not using the stuff Mindy gave me, although since Kate and I have been drinking it this week, I'm pretty positive it's safe."

"So where is your husband now?" Buster asked.

"Hobbes arrived right after Reese handcuffed Mindy," I said. "The streets are already being plowed, and he managed to get a cruiser through. They're searching her place now for the mug and Mason jar and the poison she could have used."

"This is all going so fast." Fern loosened the plum ascot around his throat. "I still can't believe a woman with such good hair could be a murderer. She doesn't even have frosted tips or bad roots."

"I don't think hair can indicate murderous intentions," I said.

Fern gave me a look that told me how wrong I was. "You'd be surprised, sweetie."

"Things are moving fast because a cop lives here," Richard called out from the kitchen as he poked his head through the opening. "I'm sure this case is getting preferential treatment. That makes me think. This building now has a great location *and* added security. I wonder when your old neighbor's apartment goes on the market."

Kate grinned at me. "If Mindy and Kurt break up and move out, maybe we can all move in."

I stifled a groan. As much as I adored my friends and colleagues, I did love having some breaks from them.

"I thought you hated the kitchens in this building," I reminded Richard.

"That's right. The kitchen in my place is too perfect to leave." He shrugged. "Oh, well. I suppose I'll just have to keep fighting for street parking when I visit you."

I let out a breath, more relieved than I wanted to admit. It was enough to have one nosy neighbor in Leatrice. I did not want to deal with more.

The door opened, and my husband came in followed by his partner Hobbes, who wore the same rumpled clothes he'd had on the day before.

"Any luck?" I asked.

"We found them," he said, his expression serious. "A corporate logo mug and a Mason jar of hot chocolate mix were out on their fire escape."

"Fire escape?" I naturally glanced toward the back of our apartment where the entrance to our fire escape was located. Although I'd used it before, it wasn't something I thought about often.

Hobbes nodded. "They'd been covered in snow during the night, but Mike thought we should sweep off the snow. There they were, buried under about two feet of powder."

"So, Mindy must have grabbed them from Mr. Kopchek's apartment and stashed them out there last night before her fiancé returned to their apartment," I said.

Reese nodded and frowned. "I doubt we'll get any prints off them since they were buried in snow, which started to melt once the sun hit it. They were pretty wet when I pulled them out."

"Sounds pretty open and shut to me," Kate said. "She had motive, opportunity, and you found the murder weapon on her fire escape."

"We're taking her down to the station to take a statement and book her," Hobbes said.

"Is she still claiming to be innocent?" Fern asked.

My husband ran a hand through his hair, which was still wet. "She copped to the affair, but she's keeping her mouth shut about the rest."

Kate sat forward. "She admitted to sleeping with Alton? I knew it!"

"Only because her fiancé accessed her cell phone and found text messages while we were searching." Hobbes wrinkled his nose. "It was not a pretty scene in the hallway."

"And I never got that recipe for her mother's pie," Richard said from the kitchen. "This day isn't turning out to be great for anyone."

I refrained from telling Richard that not getting a pie recipe wasn't quite the same as finding out your fiancé was both a cheater and murderer.

"What about Alton?" I asked. "Could he have been desperate to keep things going with Mindy?"

"No way." Kate shook her head. "Those two may have been doing the horizontal mambo, but I did *not* get the feeling that he was seriously emotionally attached to her."

"The horizontal mambo?" Richard said, making a face that told me exactly what he thought of that phrase.

"I'm keeping it clean." Kate glanced at Buster and Mack, who were known for their avoidance of curse words, as well as sin in general. "Would you rather I say fornicate?"

Richard shuddered. "Even worse."

"So far, it looks like Mindy was the one with the motive," my husband said. "And she did make the hot chocolate mix. Her former fiancé confirmed that she personally made and packaged all of them."

"Former fiancé?" Fern put a palm to his chest. "So much for getting to do her wedding hair in Newport."

"Poor Kurt," I said.

"Talk about a Christmas you'll never forget," Mack muttered.

"I'll question Alton since we need him to confirm the affair," my husband said, "but for now I'm going to go down and oversee the last of the search. So far we haven't found any poison that could have been used in the mix."

"No arsenic, strychnine, or cyanide?" I asked.

Reese cocked an eyebrow at me. "Should I be worried you have the names of poisons on the tip of your tongue?" Before I could answer, he went on. "Mr. Kopchek's reaction wasn't consistent with any of those poisons. And not all are powders. To mix into the hot chocolate without being noticeable, it would have been a powder."

"But since she made the mix earlier, she could have gotten rid of it," Hobbes said. "Even without finding the poison in her apartment, we have enough to book her."

My husband grabbed his coat off the hook. "I'll go into the station for a while, but I'll be back for dinner."

"You'd better." Richard waved a spoon at him from the kitchen. "You don't want to miss my Bûche de Noël."

Reese gave me a quizzical look.

"A cake that looks like a log," I whispered as I wrapped my arms around him.

"You're not selling it, babe," he whispered back, kissing me on the forehead. "But I'll be back as soon as I can."

After he and Hobbes left, Buster and Mack excused themselves to my office to FaceTime baby Merry and Fern stood, tugging the tassled tie of his brocade dressing gown. "Well, at least we solved the case before Christmas. This calls for a new signature cocktail."

I was going to say that it was still morning, but then I remembered that one of my neighbors was dead and another was being booked for his murder. "I'll drink to that."

CHAPTER 20

"Did I sleep the day away?" Leatrice asked as I opened the door to my apartment holding a martini glass in one hand. "Is it already happy hour?"

"It's past noon on Christmas Eve," Kate said. "That means it's open season on cocktails."

"Try this, sweetie." Fern rushed up and handed her a glass filled with bright-green liquid. "I call it the Murderous Mistletoe-tini."

I eyed Leatrice's red-and-white-striped jumpsuit and thought how much she looked like a candy cane. Her two-tone pink-and-white hair added to the bizarre effect. "Is Sidney Allen not joining us?"

Her wrinkled brow creased even more. "The last two days have been a lot for him. He's still recovering from the shock of being the last person to see Mr. Kopchek alive. I'm sure he'll join us later." She inhaled deeply. "It smells wonderful."

"Richard's been cooking all day." I dropped my voice. "Don't even think of going near the kitchen."

"But Christmas is tomorrow."

"But Réveillon is tonight," Richard called out from the kitchen. "The French celebrate with their main meal late on Christmas Eve and it's called Réveillon."

I shrugged when Leatrice gave me a wide-eyed look. "You know Richard and his themed Christmases. He's going to pull off a Chateau Christmas if it kills him—or us. Just be glad it's not Christmas in the Casbah again."

Kate nodded from where she perched on the arm of the couch, lifting her martini glass high. "I could live a thousand lifetimes and never need to eat sweet potato couscous again."

"Too bad." Leatrice took a sip of her drink. "I have a belly-dancing costume I haven't worn in ages."

I said another small prayer of thanks that we weren't celebrating a casbah Christmas.

"I'm with Leatrice," Fern said, hooking an arm through hers. "This holiday theme isn't great for creative outfits."

"Isn't Christmas enough of a theme?" I asked.

Fern shrugged, then glanced down at Leatrice's hair. "You know what would lift my spirits? Finally doing something with your hair."

Leatrice put a hand to her two-tone hair. "I thought it was festive."

Fern wrinkled his nose. "One doesn't want one's hair to be too festive, sweetie." He led her over to the dining room table and plopped her down in a chair, whipping out a bag of hair supplies.

Leatrice looked a little taken aback, but she didn't protest as Fern unfurled a smock over her, and Hermès ran up and leapt into her lap.

Fern stood behind Leatrice assessing her hair and tapping one finger on his chin. "What did you think about your time as a platinum blonde? Did you really have more fun?"

Leatrice thought for a moment. "When I met my Honeybun, I had black hair, so maybe I have more fun as a brunette."

Fern nodded and rummaged through his bag of hair products again. "That might go with your coloring better, although we've never tried you as a strawberry blonde."

Leatrice's face brightened. "Like Nicole Kidman? Oh, I do like her."

"What's going on in here?" Richard walked out from the kitchen with his hands covered in oven mitts.

"Fern's going to make me into Nicole Kidman," Leatrice told him with a wink.

Richard stared at the heavily wrinkled woman. "This should be interesting." He dropped his voice to a mutter. "I hope he's got a time machine in that bag of tricks."

Fern popped his head up from searching in the bag and appraised Leatrice's hair again. "Maybe we should go with something more tried and true." He held up a tube of coloring. "Havana Brown should look fabulous."

"Sounds exotic," Leatrice said. "I'm sure I have an outfit that would work with that."

Fern's eyes widened. "Holidays in Havana. I love it!"

Richard stomped his foot. "No theme changing!"

Fern held up another tube. "I also have French Roast."

"Does her hair have to match the theme?" I asked.

Fern gave me a patient smile. "One does like to stay on point. The more I think about it, French Roast is perfect."

"Now I'm craving coffee," Kate said.

"As long as the smell of hair dye doesn't overpower the smell of my food." Richard spun on his heel and returned to the kitchen. "I'd hate to have to open a window in this weather."

Leatrice twisted around while Fern busied himself mixing up the hair color. "Where's your hubby, dear?"

"He and Hobbes took Mindy down to the station."

Leatrice set her drink on the table and patted the tiny Yorkie on the head. "Mindy from the second floor? Why?"

I'd forgotten that Leatrice had missed all our discoveries about Mindy and Alton and the police finding evidence on her fire escape. "It's kind of a long story, but she's the one who killed Mr. Kopchek."

Leatrice gaped as Fern began applying hair color and folding each strand of hair in tinfoil. "I can't believe it. She seemed like such a nice girl. Why would she want to kill him? Was this about the tickets he gave her fiancé about the bike? Sidney Allen and I told Kurt it was fine by us if he left it on the first floor, and it's not bothering anyone but—"

"It's not about the bike." I cut her off. "She and Alton were having an affair, and Mindy killed Mr. Kopchek because he knew about it."

"They were?" She turned her head and Fern turned it right back. "How did I miss that?"

Kate shrugged. "You're looking for spies. They weren't spying."

"Still." Leatrice shook her head, which made Fern frown. "I should have been more attentive to what was going on in our building. I wonder how Mr. Kopchek knew and I didn't."

"He did live beneath Alton." Kate took a long swig of her drink. "My guess is that he heard more than he wanted to."

Leatrice's cheeks flushed under her heavy coral rouge. "Goodness. That must have been distressing."

Fern took a break from applying hair color and wiped his forehead with the back of his hand. "Wouldn't have bothered me."

"Or me," Kate said. "That's why I have noise canceling headphones."

The scent of hair dye wafted across the room, and my eyes watered. "He gave Mindy parking citations during the day, so maybe he put two and two together. Or maybe he spotted her going into Alton's apartment. However, he figured it out, he knew. And Mindy knew he knew."

"But why kill him?" Leatrice asked.

"Because Mindy's fiancé is rich, and she'd convinced him they didn't need a prenup," Fern said, waving his hair dye brush.

"And Kurt was way more into her than she was into him," Kate added.

"If Mr. Kopchek talked, it would ruin her chance to have a wealthy husband," I said.

Leatrice tapped a bony finger on her chin. "I wonder if she was going to use her rich husband's money to save her lover's bar?"

I nearly spluttered as I took a drink. "What do you mean?"

"That handsome fellow's bar is in serious debt," Leatrice said matter-of-factly. "He's about to go under."

Kate's eyebrows popped up. "How do you know this?"

"Please don't say your dark web hacker friends," I muttered under my breath like an incantation.

She grinned at me, her tinfoil hair making her look slightly space-age. "You're such a good guesser, Annabelle. Boots and Dapper Dan did a little digging for me after I got online last night and told them what happened."

"Was any of this digging illegal?" I immediately held up a hand. "Wait. Don't tell me. I don't want to know."

"I really didn't ask, dear." Leatrice took another sip of her drink and grimaced. "I do know that they accessed bank records and discovered just how deeply in debt he is. And he has at least one loan he personally guaranteed."

"Which means the creditors can come for his personal possessions," I muttered, more to myself than to anyone else.

Kate locked eyes with me. "Do you think this could have something to do with the murder?"

"It would explain why Mindy felt she needed to kill the old man. If she was serious about Alton and he told her about his money troubles, she might have been planning to help him out once she'd gotten married."

"So tawdry." Fern shook his head as if he disapproved, but his eyes glittered, and I knew he was loving the scandal.

"We've been assuming it was all Mindy since she had the most to lose," I said. "But this means Alton could have easily been in on the whole thing with her."

Fern's gleeful expression morphed to concern. "Just how many people in this building are killers?"

"I need to tell Reese." I pulled my phone from my jeans pocket and speed dialed him, grumbling when it went to voicemail. "He must be dealing with Mindy."

I left him a message about Alton and hung up. "Do you think we should try to question him or at least keep him busy until Reese can get back here to talk to him?"

"You can't," Leatrice said, the tinfoil swinging around her head as she shook it. "I saw him leave the building when I was on my way up."

"Leave the building?" Kate glanced at my windows which still showed a world covered in white.

"The snowplow had already been by once," Leatrice told her. "You can't hear since you're all the way on the fourth floor."

"He must have gone to his bar," I said. "He did tell me the holidays are a busy time for him."

"Or he's making a run for it," Fern said.

We all turned our heads to him, and he bobbed his shoulders up and down. "What? If my accomplice was being questioned by the police, I know I'd be making a run for it."

"Same," Kate said.

I pulled my phone out. "Should I tell Reese that he's trying to get away?"

"We don't know that for sure, dear," Leatrice said.

"You're right." I hesitated as I stared down at my phone's screen. I didn't want to call in a false alarm. The man could be innocent and just checking in on his bar.

"One way to find out," Leatrice said. "We take a peek into his apartment and see if it looks like he left it for good."

I narrowed my eyes at her. "Please tell me you didn't make a copy of everyone's key in the entire building."

She fluttered a hand at me. "Don't be silly. I mean we can peek into his place through the fire escape."

"I don't know—" I started to say but Fern had already spun on his heel and was heading toward the back of my apartment and my fire escape.

"Even if we can't see a thing, we'll have gotten out of the apartment for a while," he said over his shoulder. "And I don't know about the rest of you, but I'm going stir crazy."

"We peek in the window and come right back up," I said, following him reluctantly.

"Of course." He tossed back the rest of his drink and winked at me over his shoulder. "What else would we do, sweetie?"

CHAPTER 21

"This was a bad idea." I stamped my feet and rubbed my arms briskly.

We'd managed to slip and slide our way down the fire escape to the floor below and Leatrice, Fern, Kate, and I stood huddled outside Alton's back door.

"It was a bad idea not to wear boots," Kate said as she stood in a pile of snow that reached mid-calf.

There was a window to one side, and Leatrice had her face pressed to the glass with her hands on either side. "I can't see a thing, but all the lights are out."

The tinfoil covering her head did not make us a less conspicuous or odd-looking bunch. And the ammonia scent had me standing as far away from her on the fire escape as I could get.

"What about the aquarium?" Kate asked. "He had fancy lights in that."

I glanced at my assistant. "You noticed aquarium lighting?"

She shrugged one shoulder. "I used to date a guy who was into aquariums. I recognized the ambient lighting setup."

"No aquarium lighting that I can see," Leatrice said, straightening. "But this window is pretty fogged up."

"Well, we tried." I turned to the metal stairs. "Time to go back in."

"If only we could peek inside," Leatrice said then let out a small yelp. "Look, his window is unlocked."

I pivoted back around. Leatrice held the windowpane open, and her aluminum head was disappearing inside the apartment.

"What are you doing?" I hissed.

"Looking for clues," she said, her voice muffled from her head being inside.

"Maybe the poison is in here," Kate said. "Reese didn't find anything in Mindy's apartment."

"You know what my husband would say about this." I nibbled my bottom lip as Leatrice disappeared entirely into Alton's apartment.

"You're under arrest?" Fern said, giggling and then hiccupping and slapping a hand over his mouth.

"Pretty much." I'd done plenty of things that were quasi-legal in my pursuit of criminals, but I knew it drove my cop husband crazy, and I'd promised to stop.

"Then you stay outside, and we'll look for clues," Kate said stepping through the window. "I, for one, don't like the idea of a guy like Alton getting away with murder."

Man, she really did not like Alton.

Fern and I stood on the fire escape for another minute, shivering and looking at each other until he finally patted me on the arm. "Sorry, sweetie. I'm going in just to warm up."

I huffed out a breath and it formed a cloud of steam in front of me. "Fine. If you're all going in…" I followed him through the window, allowing my eyes a moment to adjust to the darkness.

We were inside the main room of the apartment. I could make out outlines of his dark furniture and of my friends moving around. Kate was easy to track because she was using her cell phone as a flashlight.

"Anything?" I asked.

"What exactly are we looking for again?" Fern asked.

"Some sort of powdered poison that could have been blended into the hot chocolate mix," I whispered.

"I'll check under the kitchen sink," Leatrice said, her shadowy figure groping along the walls.

Kate fumbled with something in the living room, and then her flashlight illuminated the fish tank. More specifically, the cabinet under the fish tank.

"Bingo," she said.

"What is all that?" I squinted at the plastic containers and jugs.

"Supplies for an expensive fish tank." Kate rummaged around until she found something and lifted it up. "Including some stuff to clean the tank that comes in a powder form. It's purply, but I'm sure it could be blended into dark brown cocoa."

"And is that stuff poison?" I asked, my heart racing.

"If it cleans fish tanks, I'm pretty sure it isn't good to ingest." Kate held her phone's light up to the label on the white plastic jug. "Potassium permanganate. And it's got a nice toxic warning on it."

"We should take that to Reese," Leatrice said from the kitchen. "There's nothing in here."

"Let's go." I waved at Kate even though she couldn't see me in the dark. "I do not want to be here if Alton comes back—"

My word trailed off as the front door open, and the lights came on. I glanced back at the window. Fern was already outside, but there was no way Kate and Leatrice could make it in time.

Alton walked into the apartment, stopping in mid-stride when he saw me. Then he swiveled his head to Kate and the plastic jug in her hand and his jaw tightened.

"What are you two doing here?"

At least he hadn't seen Fern leaving through the window and didn't know Leatrice was in the kitchen, although her head smelled so pungent he'd soon be able to smell her.

I decided to go with honesty. "We know that you helped Mindy poison Mr. Kopchek."

Kate opened and closed her mouth, but Alton didn't react.

"Why would I have anything to do with that man's death? I barely knew him."

"But he knew about you and Mindy, didn't he?" I pressed, making a point not to look at Leatrice's head popping over the kitchen divider.

His expression remained unconcerned. "The brunette who popped into your apartment with her fiancé? I know her about as well as I did Mr. Kopchek."

"That's not what she's telling the cops right now."

That did it. His confident smile faltered.

"They're questioning her about killing Mr. Kopchek to keep him quiet about your affair," I continued. "Her fiancé knows everything, by the way. Your girlfriend won't be marrying a rich guy and bailing out your bar, after all."

"So, it was all for nothing?" Alton glowered at me for a moment before turning and running back down the short hallway to his front door.

I was so startled, it took me a second to realize that he was trying to get away. "Stop!"

As he ran past the kitchen doorway, Leatrice launched herself at him, but he shrugged her off his back, and she landed with a hard thud on the floor. Kate and I both rushed to her as Alton dashed out the door.

"Are you okay?" I asked Leatrice, putting a hand under her elbow to lift her.

She waved me off. "I'm fine. You can't let him get away."

Kate and I ran out of the apartment, hearing footsteps on the stairs going down.

"Stop!" I yelled again and peered over the railing. He had a full flight of stairs head start on us.

Nevertheless, I hurried down, gripping the handrail to keep from slipping. Kate was right beside me, holding the other handrail. When we reached the ground floor, I almost slipped off the last step.

Alton hadn't made it outside. Daniel Reese was scuffling with him near the door. I didn't know why he was there, but he must have heard me screaming.

"He's a murderer," I yelled, as Daniel struggled to keep him from leaving.

Kate's eyes were huge as the two men fought. I looked around for something I could use to help Daniel, but there was nothing in the bare foyer. Then Alton reached around for something jammed in the waistband of his pants, and I only realized it was a gun when I heard the sharp crack.

Kate screamed, and we both ducked. The men dropped to their knees, and the gun clattered to the floor and was kicked to the side.

My skin went cold, and I squeezed my eyes shut. If my brother-in-law had been shot trying to catch a killer we'd been chasing, I'd never forgive myself. When I opened my eyes, Daniel was standing, and he had Alton in a headlock, the bar owner's face purple.

I scanned the floor for the gun and scooped it up, pointing it at Alton even though my hands were shaking. Footsteps pounded behind us, and within moments everyone from my apartment was jammed into the foyer.

Alton finally went limp, and Daniel let him sink to the floor. Buster and Mack pushed through the group and each took one of his arms, their expressions deadly. For his sake, I hoped Alton stayed unconscious until the police came for him.

I finally lowered the gun and Leatrice took it from me, patting me on the arm. "Why don't I take this, dear? You look like you might drop it."

Kate launched herself into Daniel's arms, and he staggered back in surprise, wrapping his arms around her.

When she pulled back, her face was streaked with tears. "I thought I'd lost you."

"I'm fine," he said, his voice husky. "You didn't lose me."

Kate kissed him, her hands raking through his dark hair flecked with silver at his temples.

"Well, well, well," Fern said from behind me. "This explains a lot."

"Another Reese brother," Richard said with a sigh. "And another person for dinner."

"At least he's a silver fox," Fern said, his eyebrows arching. "Merry Christmas to me."

CHAPTER 22

"You didn't know your brother was coming?" I asked my husband as I cuddled with him on the couch later that evening.

He shook his head, glancing at his older brother standing next to the Christmas tree with Kate. The two had been inseparable since he'd taken down Alton, and I wasn't sure Kate was ever going to unwrap her arms from his waist. Even though I wasn't used to seeing Kate attached to one man for so long—or for longer than an hour—I liked the look of the two of them together. And since everyone had stopped openly gaping, Daniel looked pretty content.

"I told him what happened, but he never let on he was planning to come across town to our place." Reese lowered his mouth to my ear. "Did you know they were dating?"

"Not until recently." I didn't need to drop my voice because Big Bad Voodoo Daddy's retro swing version of "Jingle Bells" was playing pretty loudly, and Hermès yipped along to the music as he scampered around the tree. I was amazed the little Yorkie could still move so quickly considering how much of Richard's Christmas Eve dinner everyone had slipped him under the table.

My husband pulled me closer. "Well, I'm glad he was here. What

I'm not happy about is you and your friends deciding it was safe to climb into a killer's window."

"We didn't know for sure he was a killer when we went in. And we never planned to go in—at least I didn't. But the window was unlocked and Leatrice went inside…"

I cast a quick glance at my neighbor who sat wedged next to Sidney Allen in one of the armchairs. Fern had rinsed and dried her now mocha-brown hair in time for dinner, and I had to admit it was a flattering color. It had been a surprise for Sidney Allen, but he seemed to take it in stride after all the shocks over the past two days, although he did look more subdued than usual. Luckily, Leatrice had talked enough for both of them, regaling everyone with a blow-by-blow account of us confronting Alton and Daniel taking him down in the foyer.

My husband tilted his head down to look at me. "Are you going to claim peer pressure as your defense? Remember, babe, I know you pretty well."

My cheeks warmed. "No, but in my defense, I did call you first. And I argued against going inside the apartment. Kate and Fern can back me up on that."

"Forgive me if I don't consider them the most reliable sources," he muttered as Fern sailed through the living room carrying a tray of martini glasses filled with both of his signature drinks—the Blizzitini and the Murderous Mistletoe-tini. He'd changed from his brocade dressing gown and wore a powder-blue velvet suit that reminded me of Jack Frost. Even the enormous blue topaz ring on his finger glittered like ice.

"I thought you'd be glad we caught the real killer," I said. "You almost booked an innocent person for murder."

"I wouldn't say innocent," Richard said as he perched on the arm of the couch next to us. He'd finally taken off his Santa apron and looked more relaxed now that dinner was over, and he'd been given a heavy helping of compliments on the impressive spread of food. "Mindy did have an affair with one of her neighbors."

"But she actually didn't have anything to do with Mr. Kopchek's murder," I reminded him. "I'm not saying she wasn't a gold digger, but she wasn't the one who put the potassium whatever in Mr. Kopchek's hot chocolate mix. We're just lucky Kate dated a guy with a fancy fish tank and knew something about the chemicals you use."

Richard mumbled something about the odds being in our favor considering Kate's dating history, but I ignored it.

"I should have questioned the evidence being on the fire escape more," my husband said, shaking his head. "It wasn't hard for Alton to climb down and put it there and then for the snow to cover his tracks."

I patted his hand. "Don't beat yourself up too much. Mindy seemed like the more obvious villain."

"Speak for yourself," Richard said. "I never trusted Alton. Like I said, too many tattoos."

"Did he really think that Mindy was going to save his bar after she was married?" I asked. "And it was worth killing over?"

My husband shrugged. "That's what he said when he finally spilled his guts at the station. The guy wasn't a criminal mastermind as much as he was desperate."

I rubbed my arms as I thought about poor Mr. Kopchek. "That makes it even scarier."

"People kill over much less," Reese said. "If the bar was his whole life, and he'd sunk every penny into it, I'm not surprised he was desperate to save the thing. He must have seen Mindy as a lifeline."

"And she was swayed by his bad-boy charm." Richard made a tsking noise in the back of his throat. "What did I tell you, Annabelle? Bad boys are never a good idea."

"You don't have to tell me," I said. "I married a cop."

"Upon my excellent advice," my best friend said, clearly remembering things a little differently than I did and forgetting how long it had taken him to warm up to Reese.

"I'm just grateful you were around, Richard," my husband deadpanned, which earned him a sharp jab in the ribs.

"You don't have to thank me." Richard waved a hand. "If you

weren't here, I might be sharing the holidays with a tattooed band leader."

I glared at Richard and tried to steer the conversation away from my past. "It's too bad Mr. Kopchek threatened to tell Kurt." I remembered what my husband told me that Mindy had finally confessed at the station. "If he hadn't, he might still be alive."

Richard frowned. "Mindy might not have killed the old man, but she withheld evidence from the police when she suspected what happened."

"She did say she was terrified that she'd be implicated," my husband said.

Richard snorted out a laugh. "More like she was scared to reveal the affair and get dumped by her rich fiancé."

I was with Richard on this one. Mindy might not have poisoned the old man, but she'd started the ball rolling by messing around and hiding it. And when he'd died and she suspected her lover might have been involved, she did nothing.

"Don't worry. She's being charged with obstructing an investigation," Reese said.

"Good." Richard smoothed his hands down the front of his shirt. "As much as I wanted her pie recipe, I'd hate for justice not to be served."

"Speaking of serving." Fern swept his tray down at our eye level. "You two look like you could use a drink."

Reese and I both took a glass from the tray, careful not to spill the bright-green and cherry-red contents. Richard glanced up at the clock on the wall and put his hands to his cheeks. "That reminds me. It's almost time for me to set out the dessert buffet."

"Dessert buffet?" I put a hand to my stomach. "Didn't we just finish dinner?"

Richard shot me a dismissive look. "Over an hour ago. Besides, we can't have a proper Christmas at the Chateau without a dessert display."

"I am looking forward to the log cake," my husband said.

"Sacre bleu!" Richard sucked in a sharp breath. "I hope you aren't referring to my Bûche de Noël as a 'log cake.'"

"It *is* a cake that looks like a log," I argued as Richard tapped one toe rapidly on the floor.

"I'm going to pretend I didn't hear that." Richard spun on his heel and flounced off to the kitchen.

"Good news." Mack appeared from the back of my apartment where he and Buster had been FaceTiming with the young woman they'd taken underwing. "The snow has been cleared enough that Prue and Merry will be able to join us for Christmas morning."

"Which is a good thing," Buster added, coming up behind Mack. "Because Santa delivered all their presents here." He gestured to the tree with a wink, and I noticed there were more wrapped boxes than there had been.

Leatrice clapped her hands. "It will be so much fun to watch Merry open her presents. Last year she was a baby, but this year she'll actually be able to rip the paper."

"She's growing up fast," Buster said, his voice more gravelly than usual.

"Too fast." Mack dabbed at his eyes. "Christmas really is more fun when you get to see it through a child's eyes."

"No crying," Fern said, pushing cocktails into Buster's and Mack's hands. "It's Christmas Eve! Even though the weather is dreadful, and everyone's plans were messed up, we're all together."

"And we solved a murder," Leatrice added.

"That's right." Fern lifted his cocktail. "Which makes it kind of a perfect Wedding Belles holiday party, if you ask me."

I stifled a groan. "Let's not make it a habit, though."

"Please," my husband murmured from behind his drink.

"A toast to the best blizzard Christmas ever!" Fern lifted his martini glass even higher.

"It's Christmas at the Chateau," Richard cried as he came out of the kitchen holding a tray of iced cookies, gingerbread madeleines, and sugary palmiers.

We all raised our glasses and drank as Richard muttered about his theme being hijacked.

"I have another toast."

We all turned to see Daniel holding his glass up. He cleared his throat. "I'd like to raise a glass to the talented, beautiful woman who figured out the pivotal clue and helped put away a killer."

Kate's cheeks flushed as she locked eyes with him.

"To Kate." He took both of her hands in his and dropped down onto one knee. "The woman I hope will agree to be my wife."

"Son of a nutcracker!" Mack said in a hushed rumble, as Kate's mouth dropped open.

The room was silent for a moment, then Kate bobbed her head up and down and threw her arms around Daniel. "Yes! Of course, yes!"

Reese quietly choked on his drink as Fern's own martini glass tipped over and the contents splattered onto my hardwood floor. Daniel had barely gotten to his feet when Fern danced over to them both, pulling them into a hug and sloshing the rest of his cocktail all over the wrapped gifts.

I managed to shake off my shock and jump up, making my way over to Kate and holding my arms out. "I can't believe it!"

"I know," she said as she untangled herself from Fern's hug, her eyes bright with tears. "We're going to be sisters."

I shook my head through my own tears. "We already are."

Then we hugged as tears streamed down both of our faces. My husband pulled his brother into a bear hug, Richard wrapped his arms around both of them, and Fern and Leatrice grabbed me and Kate from behind. Buster and Mack came up behind them, and then everyone was hugging and jumping up and down together with Hermès yipping maniacally and Richard shrieking that his designer loafers were getting trampled.

"This really is the best worst Christmas ever!" Leatrice cried from somewhere in the crush of bodies.

It was good to know that as much as things changed, some things —like the spirit of Christmas and my crazy friends and how much we meant to each other—never would.

* * *

Thank you for reading *Slay Bells Ring*!

This book has been edited and proofed, but typos are like little gremlins that like to sneak in when we're not looking. If you spot a typo, please report it to:
laura@lauradurham.com
Thank you!!

ALSO BY LAURA DURHAM

Annabelle Archer Series:

Better Off Wed

For Better Or Hearse

Dead Ringer

Review To A Kill

Death On The Aisle

Night of the Living Wed

Eat, Prey, Love

Groomed For Murder

Wed or Alive

To Love and To Perish

Marry & Bright

The Truffle with Weddings

Irish Aisles are Smiling

Godfather of Bride

Claus for Celebration

Bride or Die

Slay Bells Ring

Jewel of the Aisle

*Annabelle Archer Collection: Books 1-4

Annabelle Archer Books available as Audiobooks:

Better Off Wed

For Better Or Hearse

Dead Ringer

Review to a Kill

Annabelle Archer Collection: Books 1-4

To get notices whenever I release a new book, follow me on BookBub:

https://www.bookbub.com/profile/laura-durham

ABOUT THE AUTHOR

Laura Durham has been writing for as long as she can remember and has been plotting murders since she began planning weddings over twenty years ago in Washington, DC. Her first novel, BETTER OFF WED, won the Agatha Award for Best First Novel.

When she isn't writing or wrangling brides, Laura loves traveling with her family, standup paddling, perfecting the perfect brownie recipe, and reading obsessively.

Find her on:
www.lauradurham.com
laura@lauradurham.com

To get notices whenever she releases a new book, follow her on BookBub:

Copyright © 2021 by Broadmoor Books

Cover Design by Llewellen Designs

All rights reserved.

No part of this book may be reproduced in any form or by any electronic or mechanical means, including information storage and retrieval systems, without written permission from the author, except for the use of brief quotations in a book review.

This is a work of fiction. Names, characters, places, and incidents are the products of the author's imagination or are used fictitiously and are not to be construed as real. Any resemblance to actual events, locales, organizations, or persons, living or dead, is entirely coincidental.

Made in the USA
Middletown, DE
02 November 2023

41836952R00288